D0866471

Red Slippers

More Tales of Mithgar

By Dennis L. McKiernan

Once Upon a Winter's Night

Caverns of Socrates

THE MITHGAR SERIES

The Dragonstone

Voyage of the Fox Rider

HÉL'S CRUCIBLE:

Book 1: *Into the Forge*
Book 2: *Into the Fire*

Dragondoom

The Iron Tower

The Silver Call

Tales of Mithgar (a story collection)

Tales from the One-Eyed Crow: The Vulgmaster
(the graphic novel)

The Eye of the Hunter

Silver Wolf, Black Falcon

Red Slippers: More Tales of Mithgar (a story collection)

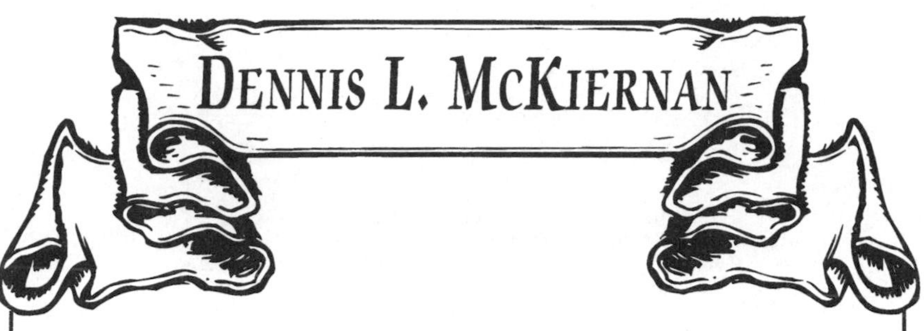

Red Slippers

More Tales of Mithgar

A ROC BOOK

ROC
Published by New American Library, a division of
Penguin Group (USA) Inc., 375 Hudson Street, New York, New York 10014, U.S.A.
Penguin Books Ltd, 80 Strand, London WC2R 0RL, England
Penguin Books Australia Ltd, 250 Camberwell Road,
Camberwell, Victoria 3124, Australia
Penguin Books Canada Ltd, 10 Alcorn Avenue,
Toronto, Ontario, Canada M4V 3B2
Penguin Books (N.Z.) Ltd, Cnr Rosedale and Airborne Roads,
Albany, Auckland 1310, New Zealand

Penguin Books Ltd, Registered Offices:
80 Strand, London WC2R 0RL, England

First published by Roc, a division of Penguin Group (USA) Inc.

First Printing, May 2004
10 9 8 7 6 5 4 3 2 1

LIBRARY OF CONGRESS CATALOGING-IN-PUBLICATION DATA:

McKiernan, Dennis L., 1932–
Red slippers: more tales of Mithgar/Dennis L. Mckiernan.
p. cm.
ISBN 0-451-45976-8 (alk. paper)
1. Mithgar (Imaginary place)—Fiction 2. Fantasy fiction, American.
I. Title.
PS3563.C376R43 2004
813'.54—dc22 2003024437

Set in Trump Mediaeval
Designed by Leonard Telesca
Printed in the United States of America

PUBLISHER'S NOTE
This is a work of fiction. Names, characters, places, and incidents either are the product of the author's imagination or are used fictitiously, and any resemblance to actual persons, living or dead, business establishments, events, or locales is entirely coincidental.

Again to Martha Lee McKiernan

So it began and still is

Acknowledgment

Throughout all the tellings of the various Mithgar stories, I have been blessed with loyal readers, some who were there at the beginning, some who are recently come, and perhaps some yet to be. Among these readers are those who have kept in touch via e-mail[1] or snail mail[2], or who inhabit the Mithgarian web sites and message boards[3], or who attend book-signings or readings or panels of mine, or attend the same conventions I do. Herein I acknowledge all of these splendid folks, without whom Mithgar would be bereft.

[1]http://www.mithgar.com
[2]Dennis L. McKiernan, c/o Roc Books, Penguin Group USA, 375 Hudson Street, New York, NY 10014-3657
[3]Click on "Links" at http://www.mithgar.com

Contents

Foreword xi
Author's Notes xv

1. The Red Slipper 1
2. Gelvin's Doom 9
3. The Well 23
4. Tokens 63
5. The Drowning of Durek 93
6. Lair 119
7. The Black Throne 175
8. Broken Stones 209
9. Nexus 237
10. The Purging 265
11. Armor 293
12. Leave-Takings 367

Afterword 379

Foreword

Red Slippers: More Tales of Mithgar: what a strange title, eh? I mean, what's all this about red slippers?

Well, in the past, in several stories set in Mithgar, I have referred to a place called the Red Slipper—a bordello, an inn, a tavern in Port Arbalin, a city on the southern shores of Arbalin Isle. It is perhaps the chief trading port along the Avagon Sea, and here often a person can find the Elvenship *Eroean* docked after one of its epic voyages. And in these tales many of the stories start out in that same Red Slipper.

Yet the title says red slippers, plural, and what's that all about?

Okay, I'll tell you: a "red slipper" is a term I use to denote a loose end, and there are quite a number of loose ends left over from the Mithgarian series.

You see, way back when I wrote *The Dragonstone,* I first brought up the term "red slipper" in the foreword of that book in reference to Sherlock Holmes. Here is what I said then, and it still applies:

Although to my knowledge this never happened, still I can imagine Watson beginning a narrative as follows: "It was soon after Holmes and I had resolved the peculiar case of the singular red slipper, when there came a knock on the door of our quarters at 221B Baker Street. As I set aside the paper and prepared to answer the summons, Holmes put a finger to his lips and hissed, 'Do not under any circumstance, Watson, open our door without your pistol in hand, for the visitor can be none other than the Bengalian assassin. . . .' "

Watson would then go on to illuminate us as to the fascinating case of the circular cord.

But you know what? We never do find out about the red slipper, the one mentioned in his opening sentence.

Yet, for those of us who avidly followed Watson's narratives, we knew, *knew,* that in between, *in between,* those cases we *did* get to read about, the Great Detective was out there solving other most singular enigmas, and if we just kept our eyes open, we indeed might see him afoot, observing clues obvious to him but completely obscure to us . . . obscure, that is, until explained, at which time Lestrade might say, "Oh, how simple. Why anyone can see that." —Um, you bet.

Now, I repeat, as far as I know, Watson did not chronicle any *Case of the Red Slipper,* nor did he publish anything concerning a Bengalian assassin or a circular cord . . . but surely such things *should* have been. After all, there *was* the case of the giant rat of Sumatra, and there *was* the account of the Addleton tragedy, and the story of the red leech, and the terrible death of Crosby the banker, and many, many more cases alluded to but never published . . . each a red slipper dropped upon the Holmesian 'scape.

And there are red slippers lying all across Mithgar, and every now and again I pick up one that somehow was dropped, and in my best Sherlockian manner I examine it closely and tell you what I see.

Some Mithgarian red slippers have been: a small silver horn found in the horde of Sleeth; a logbook entry concerning a crystal spear; a mention of the long-held secret of the Châkia; a stone knife which disappeared in an iron tower; a silver sword taken from the hand of a slain Elven prince; and so on.

Some red slippers are enormous, such as a tapestry depicting a key moment in the Great War of the Ban. Some are small but have great impact, such as a stone ring given to an impossible child. These and more hold the most intriguing tales, and they are red slippers all, slippers which I may take up someday and see what they can tell you and me.

There is a problem in examining red slippers, though, for every time I take one up to tell its story, it seems more red slippers fall out.

Oh, well . . .

In any event, come with me as I pick up another one of these crimson shoes from the 'scape and let us not only see what we find but also what other red slippers might fall out.

Since I first wrote that foreword to *The Dragonstone,* I did take up some more red slippers, and still more fell out. And again I say, Oh, well. . . .

Readers, however, do not much care for the "Oh, well" response, and many have been nagging me to tell about this red slipper or that one.

So, herein are twelve chapters, ten of which speak of twelve red slippers, one of which refuses to speak of a rather large and puzzling red slipper, and two of which drop another couple of red slippers down upon the 'scape.

That's the problem with those darn things: slippers keep falling out.

Regardless, roses are red, slippers are red, and so are valentines. And this is a well-deserved valentine to those who have crossed the realms of Mithgar at my side.

Dennis L. McKiernan
May 2004

Author's Notes

Red Slippers: More Tales of Mithgar is a collection of stories that tie up several loose ends left over from the Mithgar series.

All are stories which have roots first springing up long past, and in this collection there are tales reaching back to the unnumbered years ere the First Era began, and continuing on to the early years of the Sixth Era, after the War of the Dragonstone, altogether spanning some twenty millennia.

These stories are reconstructed from several sources, not the least of which is *The Ravenbook,* as well as the addenda to Faeril's Diary, tatters of which yet exist, and more directly, notes from a fragmentary journal said to have been that of a Seer named Aylis, a journal she scribed relating tales told in the depths of night before the cold hearth in the Red Slipper.

Perhaps I have gotten many things wrong, but I also think I've gotten many things right. Regardless, I apologize to my readers for any inaccuracies, yet because my primary sources are so meager, I cannot but help in places in these tales (as in my other tellings) to fill in the gaps with assumptions; in the main, however, the stories herein are true to their root materials.

As occurs in other of my Mithgarian works, there are many instances where Humans, Mages, Elves, and others speak in their native tongues; yet to avoid burdensome translations, where necessary I have rendered their words in Pellarian, the common tongue of Mithgar. However, in several cases I have left the language unchanged, to demonstrate the fact that many tongues were found throughout Mithgar. Additionally, some words and phrases do not lend themselves to translation, and these I've either left unchanged or, in special cases, I have enclosed in angle brackets a substitute term which gives the "flavor" of the word (i.e., <see>, <fire>, and the like). Additionally, sundry words may look to be in error, but indeed are correct—e.g., *DelfLord* is but a single word though a capital *L* nestles among its letters.

The Elven language of Sylva is rather archaic and formal. To capture this flavor, I have properly used *thee* and *thou, hast, dost,* and other such; however, in the interest of readability, I have tried to do so in a minimal fashion, eliminating some of the more archaic terms.

For the curious, the *w* in Rwn takes on the sound of *uu* (w *is* after all a double *u*), which in turn can be said to sound like *oo* (as in spoon). Hence, Rwn is *not* pronounced Renn, but instead *is* pronounced Roon, or Rune.

Finally, there are highlights of various historical events excerpted in these stories, so that those who are unfamiliar with the Mithgarian sagas will not be lost. For those interested in more detail, I refer you to the works listed in the front of this book.

Down he went and down,
Down into the darkness below,
Till the glimmering gleam
Of his dwindling light
Became nought but a distant glow. . . .

Song fragment:
"Silverleaf at the Well"

Red Slippers

More Tales of Mithgar

1

The Red Slipper

Running before a westerly wind, the Elvenship *Eroean* came on and on, churning a white wake astern, with every bit of silken sail she could fly—mains and studs, jibs and spanker, staysails, topsails, gallants and royals, skysails and moonrakers and starscrapers—filled to the full. Eastward through the indigo waters of the deep blue Avagon Sea she ran, bearing some points to the north, the strong driving winds on her larboard beam aft. No other ship in the waters of Mithgar was faster, no other ship even came close.

Above the waterline her blue hull bore blackened smudges, as if she had taken damage from raiders, as of fireballs cast upon her. And indeed she had been set upon by the Rovers of Kistan in the perilous long strait north of that isle. But she had given better than she had got, for three of the crimson-sailed dhows now lay at the bottom of the sea, while two others drifted aimlessly in the waters, their masts and sails and much of their decks in ruin.

Yet that had occurred some two thousand sea miles astern, though it was but six days ago; did I not say she was swift?

At her helm stood a brown-haired female, a Human . . . or was she instead an Elf? —Nay, she was neither, but rather a Mage, that race from Vadaria who seem a mixture of both. Tall she was and slender, a sprinkle of freckles high on her cheeks. Now and again she made slight adjustments in the set of the wheel, as if an occasional minor movement in response to a twitch in the wind kept the ship running swift and true.

Standing back on the aft deck and watching the lady helmsman maintain the course of the ship was a rather corpulent Human, and though his left arm was in a sling, still his hands twitched in synchronicity with each slight shift the lady made, and he nodded vigorously in agreement at every small turn of the wheel.

Aft of them both and with one elbow against the taffrail lounged a black-haired Elven male, his tilted, sapphire-blue eyes atwinkle, a slight smile on his face as he watched.

In the late afternoon sunlight lying aglance 'cross the w'rld, up the ladder to the aft deck came an enormous Man: he was tall and sandy-haired and as broad as a great slab of beef. "M'Lady Aylis," he said as he passed the helm, but she was concentrating on the wind-ribbon above, high atop the raked-back mizzenmast, and she did not reply, but made another slight adjustment instead.

"Fat Jim," said Long Tom, nodding to the rotund Pellarian, the *Eroean*'s first steersman.

"Tom," replied Fat Jim, without looking at the big man, but instead shifting his gaze from the streaming ribbon above to watch the lady's corresponding nudge of the helm.

"Cap'n Aravan," said the huge man, nodding to the Elf.

"Long Tom," replied Aravan, shifting his attention to the first officer.

"Cap'n," said Long Tom, "th' crew has cleaned up the last o' th' damage done to th' decks, and they've replaced the two silks what was ruint by the bluidy Kistanee-flung fire. An' Brekk says that th' ballistas are as good as new, him 'n' his Dwarven warband settin' them t'rights. Th' only thing left is t'take th' soot 'n' smudge off th' sides o' th' hull and t'lay on a bit o' fresh paint, there where th' other fireballs struck. Soon as we drop anchor in Port Arbalin, I'll see the men get right to it."

Aravan shook his head. "Nay, Tom. After the injured are taken ashore and put in the care of the healers, as soon as the cargo is unladed and we moor in the harbor beyond, we'll take some time aland—a moon and a fortnight at least, mayhap more—for this voyage has been hard on us all, and we deserve a goodly rest and time for wounds to heal, both those we can see and those we cannot. Hence, apart from a watch, we'll set the crew to shore leave, rotating the ward until all have had a fine fling, and until those with the most severe injuries and who would sail on with us have had a fair chance to recover.

"And we'll have to wait for Brekk to ride to the Red Hills and recruit eight Drimma to replace those we lost, and that will take three fortnights in all for the trip there and back."

"Cap'n, Oi'd loike t'help sign on th' Men we'll need t'bring th' sailor crew up t'full complement."

"Fear not, Tom, for when it comes to recruiting more Men for the crew I would have thee at my side along with Aylis, for I would have nought but the best; hence, I'll send word to thee.

"But as for staying aboard the ship, I know thou wouldst rather hie to that redheaded wife of thine, as well as thy boy Little Tom, and I would not deny thee that."

"Cap'n, Larissa understands Oi've a duty t' th' *Eroean*."

"Mayhap, yet I think Little Tom doesn't."

A great smile of relief lit up Long Tom's face, and he said, "Oy, naow, Oi do b'leave y'r roight about that, Cap'n. Oi do b'leave y'r roight."

Aravan stepped forward and surveyed the main deck teeming with Human sailors and Dwarven warriors at the last of their chores, some of them, as did Fat Jim, yet bearing the remnants of hurt. In addition and part of the crew were two Warrows and a Pysk, those three adeck doing what they could to help with the cleanup and repairs; this trio had been especially recruited for this voyage to act as scouts, for this had not been a trading mission, but a perilous one with a long foray inland into a shadowy realm. Of the Human sailors and Dwarven warriors, normally there would be forty of each, but the crew was shorthanded now, for five of the Humans and eight of the Dwarves had been slain by a deadly apparition, there where the ship had gone. Too, under the care of the ship's chirurgeon there remained below a handful of the more severely wounded. However, the majority of the cuts and bruises and punctures the crew had suffered had healed on the voyage home.

"We'll put up at the Red Slipper," said Aravan, turning once again to Long Tom.

"Oy, th' crew'll go f'r that," came the reply. "Oi mean, we've been asea a goodly long spell, 'n' they'll welcome some toime wi' th' laidies o' th' Slipper."

"I ween the ladies themselves would welcome that as well," said Aravan, and he glanced at Aylis.

A low, throaty laugh was her response, but she took not her eye from the wind-pennant above as she made a minor adjustment to the wheel, Fat Jim behind her twitching his hands in concert, the hefty helmsman's mouth pursed in concentration.

"Besides," added Long Tom, stepping forward and looking down on the main deck, "they c'd use some gaiety to help 'em get over their grievin' for good comrades lost, 'n' t'help 'em forget our bad toime ashore."

"Land ho!" came the cry from above. "Port Arbalin dead ahead!"

As Second Officer Nikolai came up the ladder to the aft deck, Aravan said, "Stand by to hale in the studs and full reef all others; we'll take her in on nought but the stays."

"Aye, Kapitan," replied Nick, and he called orders to Noddy, former cabin boy but now the bosun of the fastest ship in the world, and Noddy piped the commands to all.

And as the crew made ready, swiftly did the *Eroean* cleave the indigo waters of the deep blue Avagon Sea.

Darting this way and that 'round the roiling brink of a great churning knot of cursing, shouting men, all of them swinging chairs or clubs or bare-knuckled fists or wrestling one another down, Dabby skirted along the verge of the mêlée in the common room of the Red Slipper and edged past the women on the stairwell, some of them shrieking insults through the banister at one or another of the combatants, while others screamed encouragement. Dabby was headed for the bar, where Burly Jack stood on the other side, calmly polishing glasses and mugs while now and then leaning this way or that to evade flying missiles of various sorts—tankards, shoes, trenchers, an occasional chair, or the like—nothing of any consequence.

As Dabby at last reached the bar, he shouted above the din, "Jack! Jack! You'll give me a pint o' th' dark for the news I have."

"Depends on what it is," grunted Burly Jack, leaning leftward as an ivory peg leg flew past.

"Oh, this'll be worth a mug, all right!" shouted Dabby.

Burly Jack inclined forward and tilted his head to listen.

"The *Eroean* is comin' into the harbor," said Dabby.

Burly Jack nodded, then drew a pint of dark ale and set it before Dabby. Dabby licked his lips and lifted up the drink. Just as he took his first gulp, a flung cudgel hit him in the back of the head.

Calmly, he drained the rest of the mug, and then fell down unconscious.

Burly took up a great padded mallet and reached overhead to a huge brass gong hanging above the bar and struck it hard thrice—*Dshzzz! . . . Dshzzz! . . . Dshzzz! . . .* —and instantly the fighting stopped.

"Th' *Eroean* is comin' in t'port," Burly Jack announced.

The women of the Red Slipper squealed in delight and clattered down the stairs and headed for the door, and the men looked at one another and nodded and followed after, for this was something to do other than fight—one of the patrons one-legged-hopping to the bar to retrieve his ivory leg, and then hopping out after the others. Soon the place was empty, but for Burly Jack polishing glasses and mugs behind the long red counter and coldcocked Dabby lying opposite on the sawdust-laden floor.

In gathering twilight, the elegant *Eroean* slid into the harbor, now running on staysails alone, and then even these were loosed to luff in the wind, and dinghies were lowered and tow ropes affixed to hale the Elvenship to dockside.

There she would deliver her wounded unto the care of healers, as well as offload the hard-won treasured cargo she held in her hold: prized, precious, translucent green stone the crew had wrested from a ghostly foe in the long-dead Lost City of Jade.

2

Gelvin's Doom

In the wee hours of the morning most of the revelers had either passed out, or had gone upstairs with a red-slippered doxy, or had disappeared to their rooms or to a friend's abode, or had gone to their own homes, as in the case of Long Tom, or to those of their kindred. Yet a double handful plus one, sipping goblets of dark Vanchan wine, sat in an arc 'round the cold hearth, which though unlit on these warm summer nights was nevertheless a gathering place. Soft words drifted through wavering candle-flame shadows, as things remembered were spoken of. But as if by some silent signal a stillness fell upon them, and Dokan—second in command to Brekk, who was now gone off to the Red Hills—cast his hood over his head, and by this sign did all know that he was thinking of the ashes of eight Dwarven pyres left behind alongside five Men in stone cairns; thirteen in all had fallen to the ghostly foe there on that distant shore.

Aravan raised his glass and solemnly said, "To absent friends."

To absent friends, came the joint reply, and most drained their goblets to the stem, though Tarly, a Fjordlander, poured a small libation into the fireplace char and added, "May Garlon keep us all," and then he drank the rest.

"Garlon?" asked Aylissa, looking up from her now-empty thimble at Tarly, an eyebrow cocked over one of her cobalt-blue eyes as she peered through her gathered shadow. "Don't you mean Elwydd?"

Tarly looked down at the cluster of darkness at his feet and, though he could not see her, he shook his head and said. "No, little one, it be not Elwydd I ask, e'en though Elwydd keeps the Free Folk. Instead, 'tis Garlon who lords over the waters o' the world, and we be a seafaring kind.'Tis His blessing I seek."

"I thought that was Rualla," said Binkton, the three-foot-six buccan, frowning, glancing from the Pysk to the Man, <wild magic> Fox Rider shadow being no bar to his Warrow vision. "—Mistress of the Sea, isn't She?"

"Oh, no, Bink," replied his cousin Pipper. "Rualla, She's the Mistress of the Winds."

"Pip's right about Rualla," said Fat Jim. "And a fickle goddess, She is: completely absent, at times; a teasing witch, at others; and you never know when She'll become a screaming harridan."

"I wouldn't say that if I were you," whispered Noddy, looking over his shoulder into the darkness, "else She might hear and then it'll be all of us who have to answer to Her rage."

Again a silence fell over all, finally to be broken by Pipper. "Hoy, now, Fat Jim, how about a tune to cheer us up?"

Fat Jim raised the arm in the sling. "Sorry, Pip, but the chirurgeon tells me the old squeeze-box'll have to wait till I get a wee bit better. —Another sevenday, he said."

"Wull then, how about someone tell us a tale," said Binkton.

They all looked at Aravan, but he had turned toward Burly Jack and was signalling for a bottle of brandy.

Clearing his throat, "I know a tale," said Noddy. "'Twas told to me by my old da, he who sailed the seas afore me. But it's a right spooky one, and—"

"Ooo, spooky," breathed Pip. "Just the thing for the still of night."

"Take care, bucco," said Binkton. "You know how these things give you a haggard horse to ride throughout the darktide."

"Aw, Bink," said Pip. "I like to hear—"

"After our experience in the City of Jade, do you think such a tale is appropriate?" asked Aylis of Aravan.

Aravan turned to Noddy. "Which tale is it?"

"Gelvin's Doom," replied the young bosun.

"Ah, that one I know," said Aravan. He looked at Aylis. "I see no harm in it. Besides, I'd like to hear Noddy's version."

Burly Jack arrived with the bottle of brandy and ten glasses on a tray. "Here y'be, Captain." The barkeep tried to suppress a yawn, but failed. "Will y'be wanting anything else?"

"No, Jack," replied Aravan. "This will do us for the eve, my friend, and thou art in need of sleep."

"Indeed, Captain, I could use some winks. But if anything else is wanted, just help yourself." He turned to go, but then swung back and said, "By the bye, Captain, that pet fox of yours is a wonder: a better ratter I've never seen. Why, I'll swear, he's kilt a hundred or more, and in just one eve alone."

A tiny giggle came from the cluster of shadow nigh Tarly's feet. Burly Jack frowned and looked for the source, but saw nought. "The fox, her name is Vex," said Aylis, "and she would appreciate bacon in the morning, have you any."

"Oy, she'll get a good meal of it, then," said Burly Jack, yawning once more. "Well, for me, I'm off to bed."

As Jack trudged away, Wooly took the tray from Aravan and began filling snifters and passing them out. From the cluster of darkness came a thimble, and Wooly dropped a dollop in that one, too.

"Now for your story, Noddy," said Pip, when all had taken up their drinks.

Noddy grew somber and looked about, as if seeking the shade of his sire to help him tell this tale. Finally, he took a deep breath and said, "Da told me that this story is true, for they found the diary of Gelvin himself and every word of it was written down therein."

As Noddy paused to take a sip of his brandy, Aravan turned to Aylis and whispered, "It's true, for Galarun was among those who discovered the journal. He told me its story long past."

Noddy set his brandy aside and went on with the tale:

"It seems that Gelvin was a master thief, and somehow he crossed over the in-between to the Demon Plane itself—"

"The Demon Plane!" burst out Pipper.

"Yar," said Noddy. "Grygar they call it, there where the Lord of the Demons, Thyrenix himself, rules."

Aravan looked at Aylis and softly sighed, shaking his head.

"A sailor's tale, my love?" she murmured.

"Aye."

Binkton turned to Pipper. "Stop interrupting, Pip, and let Noddy go on."

"Wull, I was just surprised, and all," replied the young buccan, "for they say the Demon Plane itself ain't really a Plane whatsoever, but something caught in an in-between place, and besides—"

"Pip!" Binkton said sharply.

"Oh, right," said Pipper, grinning. "Go on, Noddy. Don't let Bink here hold up the telling."

As Bink growled, and Tarly and Nikolai laughed, Noddy took another sip of brandy. "Now where was I?" he said, cupping the glass. "Oh, right. Master thief. Well, y'see, Thyrenix had this jewel, a token of power, they say, and Gelvin, being the master thief he was, thought that he would like to have it. Anyway . . ."

As Noddy went on, Aravan sank in reverie, remembering a campfire of long ago and another token of power, back when he and Galarun and a warband of Lian were returning from Black Mountain, a silver sword in hand . . . in Galarun's hand, that is, for he would let no other touch it. And the sword weighed heavily upon Galarun, for his face was drawn, and his spirit seemed spent, yet he would tell none of the cause.

But one eve as they sat about the campfire, Galarun said, "Should I fall in this mission, Aravan, then thou must see that this blade reaches the end for which it is destined, yet beware, for it is a fell weapon."

"What did they tell thee, the Mages I mean, back there at the Wizardholt?"

"I will not say, my friend. Only that this blade is fell."

They sat long moments in silence, each wrapped in his own thoughts, Galarun haggard, Aravan filled with concern.

"Look not so down in the chops," said Galarun at last.

"I am disquiet," said Aravan.

"Then let me tell thee a tale," said Galarun. "It will cheer thee."

"A tale?"

"Aye. Of Gelvin and the Three Harbingers of Doom."

"Harbingers of Doom?"

"That's what he named them in his diary," said Galarun.

"You saw this diary?"

Galarun nodded. "I was in the party that found it. It was way back nigh the beginning of what the High Kings call the First Era. I am surprised that thou hast not heard this tale ere now."

Aravan shook his head. "I've heard a ballade sung about Gelvin, but ne'er the true tale."

"Ah, feh, the ballade is entirely in error," said Galarun.

"Then say on, my friend," said Aravan, relieved that his comrade seemed somewhat less ragged, now that a tale was on his lips.

Galarun mustered a smile and said, "Well, it seems that when Gelvin was in Jûng, it was rumored that the Mogul had a great gemstone of incalculable worth, and Gelvin, even though he was nought but a petty thief, decided that he would steal it. . . ."

His heart hammering, sweat runnelling down his back, Gelvin stood still in the darkness, waiting for the guard to pass. Under his jerkin, their snouts tied by twine, three more rats struggled to be free. Yet even though he detested the feel of their greasy fur on his skin, and the scrabbling of their tiny claws, and he was certain that additional fleas now crawled along his beltline and bit into his flesh and sucked at his blood, Gelvin was not about to simply cast them aside, for he had gone to much trouble to capture them in that foul-smelling tomb of a long-dead king, and they were part of his plan. Indeed, and a clever plan it was, for the other two had gotten him this far. And he smiled to think upon how those fools of guards, scimitars in hand, had chased after the rodents, while he himself had slithered atop the wall to worm his way past them to elude the ward altogether.

Now neared the hard tread of the palace sentry on his allotted rounds, and Gelvin reached into his jerkin and took another rat in hand. If there came a need, he would loose it to draw attention away from his hiding place.

But the guard went on, not noticing ought was amiss, and Gelvin shoved the rat back into his jerkin and ran on silent feet toward the chamber where the gemstone was reputed to be. . . .

"More brandy, Captain?"

"Wha-what?" Aravan was jerked from his reverie. "Oh. Brandy. Yes."

As Wooly added a bit of brandy to all of their glasses, including another drop into Aylissa's thimble, Noddy continued his tale:

"Wull, y'see, Gelvin managed to grab the great gemstone right out from under the nose of Thyrenix and run for the in-between crossing, slipping his way through a host of Demonkind and out onto the desolate plains beyond, where he crossed back into Mithgar, or so my old da did say.

"But Thyrenix sent three terrible riders after Gelvin—Three Harbingers of Gelvin's Doom, my da named them. War, Famine, and Pestilence, Da said they were, surely in league with Demonkind, for who but Demons would suffer such wickedness to live among them. And they were mostly all bones, mostly like skellingtons, and they rode skellington horses, and they came after Gelvin, riding like the wind, their cloaks flowing out behind them like dark gloom, wisps of black shadow streaming away in the swiftness of their passing.

"Fleet, they were, but so was Gelvin's own black steed, yet the trio slowly overtook till they were upon him, and one rode up beside—War it was, him in his battered, grume-covered armor, a terrible foe like no other, all blood and rage and slaughter and screaming. With a cold iron grip he grabbed Gelvin by the arm, and then . . ."

Aravan sipped his brandy, his mind drifting once again to Galarun's tale as they sat by the small fire, a camp hastily made, one soon to be abandoned, for the mission of the silver sword was vital. And Galarun said, "His rats gone, the great jewel in his pouch, Gelvin, now no longer a petty thief, managed to escape the Mogul's palace, but the alarm had been raised, and pursuit soon followed. . . ."

Riding westward, a remount on a tether behind, Gelvin fled, and far behind he could yet hear the hue and cry of alarm, as well as the screams of the sentries as they were slaughtered for their negligence.

All that night he rode, and when the light of oncoming morningtide grew faint on the horizon, he finally slowed, for he would set camp and take rest. And he paused on a hilltop and he took a look back eastward.

What's this? Movement down by those trees? The Mogul's men? Or is it merely my eyes playing tricks in the shadows of the dawn?

Riding just beyond the crest, he dismounted and tethered his horses to scrub. Then he ran back up to just this side of the crown and, lying bellydown, crawled forward to where he could watch his backtrail. And as the morning light grew—*Yes. Someone follows. Three someones.*

He watched a moment more, but no one else emerged from the woodland. Backward he scuttled, back to the horses, and, changing mounts, once again he rode westerly.

If I can find a stream . . .

On he rode and on, his horses tiring, the three riders on his trail managing to track him still, though now and again they were lost to Gelvin's sight. Yet they were relentless in their pursuit, and always they reappeared, following Gelvin's tracks.

Days later, a sickness fell upon Gelvin, riding as he was with little or no rest, his mounts weary as well. He had a headache, and now and again dizziness claimed him, and nausea rode his gorge. And still the trio came after him. But in spite of his illness, Gelvin pressed on, until low on the horizon in the distance ahead, Gelvin could make out what appeared to be a long bank of dark clouds. He shook his head and wiped his eyes, hoping that this was no illusion born of his unwellness. And when he looked again no clouds were these, but mountains instead, a formidable range.

'Tis the Jangdis, and if I can reach the foothills, there I know I will lose the trio behind, for streams rush down through long runs of woods, and lengthy stretches of stone are on the land to hide all trace of my steeds. Then I can stop and recuperate.

On he rode, through a desolate 'scape, and as he came weaving among the many craggy tors, from the fore he heard the sounds of combat. And he rounded the shoulder of a barren hillock. . . .

Battle! Tribesmen felled. Two warlords striving to control this wasteland. Yet wait! There are loose-running steeds. If I can just catch—

Within moments, it seemed, Gelvin had caught up three of the rugged mountain ponies, and with a fresh mount under him, and two trailing after, he rode away, and if any of the combatants saw him, they were too caught up in fighting for their lives to pursue.

"Ooo!" called Pipper, his eyes wide with wonder. "He managed to escape the Demon of War, one of the three terrible skeletons Thyrenix sent after him?"

"Yar," said Noddy. "The moment War grabbed him, Gelvin, as well as being a master thief, became a mighty fighter. My da says that War sometimes does that to people caught in its iron grip."

Noddy swiftly gulped down the last of his brandy, then held out his glass for a refill.

And even as Wooly replenished the young bosun's snifter, Noddy, caught up in his own telling, continued: "War fell back, but then Famine spurred his terrible skellington horse forward, and he was the next to overtake Gelvin just as there began a dreadful storm. And gaunt Famine, his eyes hollow, his ribs all showing, his empty mouth agape, reached out through the blow with his thin, bony fingers and took hold and . . ."

Once more Aravan fell into recollection.

"So Gelvin simply rode through battle and came away unscathed?"

"Aye," replied Galarun. "There are times when one can ride through a mêlée and not be caught up in the combat, though I suspect in Gelvin's case, he rode at a distance 'round the edges."

Aravan smiled and threw a small branch on the fire. "Say on, Galarun. This has become interesting."

"All tales I tell are interesting, Aravan; didst thou not ken such?"

Aravan laughed, and Galarun thinly smiled, then continued. "Perhaps because he was ill, or in haste to get beyond the fighting, though he yet held onto the great gemstone, Gelvin forgot to take his supply of food from the horses he had abandoned, and none did he find on the steeds he had taken in their stead, as toward the Jangdi Mountains he fared. . . ."

Some days later—ailing Gelvin did not know how many—he stopped in the vale beyond another craggy tor, and he scrambled to the top and lay watching, sweat running down into his eyes. He was hot and chill by turns, for ague did grip him.

They yet follow me, and I have no weapon with which to slay them. Oh, why did I not stop to take up a bow and a quiver of arrows? Then would I lay them by the heels. But I am a fool, and now my only chance is to lose them in the Jangdi Range. Even then, I need to stop and find something to eat. Stupid! Stupid! Stupid! Why did I not take a bow? And why did I not remember my provisions?

Back down to his three rugged ponies did Gelvin stumble, and he rode away to the west.

It was nigh sundown when he came to a burnt village, corpses lying awry.

This may be why the warlords are fighting. Ah, but food no doubt there will be, and mayhap a weapon, a bow, arrows.

Gelvin dismounted and began searching, yet the buildings were burnt to the ground, and as dizziness swam through his mind, nothing in the way of provender could he find, nor a weapon of any sort.

Yet there was a plethora of roasted meat, and Gelvin wrenched an arm from a burnt child, and then remounted one of his steeds and rode away. Yet when he thought to take a second bite, he realized what he had done and cast the arm from him, and on he rode, hunger taking him to the edge of a swoon. Yet he managed to remain in the saddle, as into the Jangdis he rode, and it began to rain.

"Oh, my!" declared Bink. "So Gelvin wasn't felled by Famine. How did he manage to escape? I mean, I could see how he might get away from the iron clutch of War, but the bony grip of Famine?"

Noddy took a quick gulp from his snifter. "Da always said it was because of the rain. Y'see, Famine most often is a creature of drought, and rain surely drives him away."

"Ah, I see," said Aylissa, sipping from her thimble. "This is a morality tale, a teaching of eternal truths."

"Wull, I don't know about that, Miss Aylissa," said Noddy, speaking directly to the Pysk, for with no strangers about, she had dropped her cloaking shadow. "But anyway, Gelvin started up a steep mountain, yet the Three Harbingers of Gelvin's Doom, they just kept coming after him. And as he neared the top, it was the last member of that dreadful trio who then drew upon him. And Pestilence, with the remnants of her decaying flesh a-rot and a handful of burst pustules dripping and a coughing rattle in her chest, she reached out with a blackened, claw-fingered grip and grabbed Gelvin's flesh. And he screamed. . . ."

"He lost his ponies somewhere in the Jangdi Range," said Galarun. "And raving against the wind in his sickness, for some reason he clambered up one of the mountains, climbing across snow and ice, trying to reach the crest. . . ."

Stumbling afoot and delirious with fever, up Gelvin scrambled, the great gemstone clutched in one hand and pressed to his hammering heart. And he sang at the top of his lungs, a song of heroism, something about crowns and kings. Somewhere downslope, the last of his ponies lay dead, the other two far back trail, all of them cruelly slain by exhaustion.

Why Gelvin struggled upward, he did not know . . . or perhaps he did. *It's* my *gemstone, won fairly and squarely, and no one is going to take it from me.* And on upward he toiled to come at last to the peak. And there he sat down and died, a jewel in hand, mayhap a token of power, a gemstone forever to be known as Gelvin's Doom.

"So he died?" asked Pipper. "Pestilence got him? How awful. I mean, how can the hero of such a tale die?"

"Oh, he might be dead," said Noddy, "but that don't mean he ain't still in this world."

"What d'y' mean, Noddy?" asked Binkton.

"Wull, the way Da tells it, Gelvin now rides with the other three."

"He rides with War, Famine, and Pestilence?"

"Yar, and in his crown he wears that great jewel."

"Forget the jewel," said Pipper. "You say that Gelvin now rides with the other three?"

"Aye, only now he is known as Death."

"So thou didst find him there on a mountaintop in the Jangdis?" asked Aravan.

"We did," said Galarun. "Him and that gemstone and his journal. How he managed to write, I cannot say. Most of the latter part of it—the part during the chase—was the ramblings of a madman, but there was enough that we could deduce most of what happened."

"Did he freeze to death?"

"Nay, Aravan. He died of the plague. His tongue protruded and was black, and where his clothes were weathered, tattered, we could see many dark pustules and blotches over much of his body, some broken open, and there were great, black buboes in his armpits and groin. Aye, 'twas the dark scourge."

They fell into silence, and sat for some while, and once more it was Aravan who broke the still: "The plague, eh, Galarun? I wonder where Gelvin had come upon such."

"Who knows, my friend? Mayhap he rode through ill vapors. Or mayhap it came from the tomb rats he used when he stole the gem. Mayhap from the gem itself. Mayhap from something else altogether, for none yet know its cause. I can only say I am glad that Elvenkind falls not victim of such a curse."

Aravan stared into the fire. "Someday, Galarun, someone will find a cure for that pestilence, and that will be a boon unto Mithgar."

"Aye," said Galarun. He paused a moment, then said, "It must be dreadful to fear such a fate as to fall ill to that deadly disease. I suspect that if the Mogul's three pursuers came upon him, they fled the moment they saw his corpse. I deem that's why when we came upon his remains Gelvin yet had with him the gemstone, a huge diamond black as death."

"What happened to the gemstone?"

Galarun smiled ruefully. "We left it in Gelvin's hand, but had we known the feartoken it was, we would have destroyed it on the spot."

"Feartoken? How so?"

"Aye. Ultimately, I don't know how, it fell into Modru's hands, and he used it in the midst of battle when he invaded Duellin in Atala, back in those long past days."

Aravan sighed and said, "Atala, now gone beneath the waves."

"Aye," whispered Galarun.

They sat for long moments without speaking, thinking of that vanished realm—destroyed but some thirteen seasons past—and a somber mood fell over both.

Of a sudden Galarun shivered and looked about and said, "Someone just walked over my grave, Aravan." He stood and called to the rest of the warband, "Come, let us ride. We've a silver sword to deliver."

In the Red Slipper on a warm summer night in wavering candlelight around a cold hearth sat a double handful plus one: an Elf, Aravan; a Seeress, Aylis; a Dwarf, Dokan; two Warrows, Pipper and Binkton; five Humans, Noddy, Fat Jim, Nikolai, Wooly, and Tarly; and finally a Pysk, Aylissa, she who had been named after Aylis.

"To absent friends," said Aravan.

To absent friends, replied all.

3

The Well

"Soo," said Pipper, looking at Binkton, "you were right. Noddy's story is like to wrench me awake in the dark."

"Tol' y'," said Bink. He turned to Aravan. "How come bad things mostly chase the heroes of a story and not the other way 'round?"

Aravan smiled. "Evil oft comes hunting. Yet betimes 'tis the opposite and evil becomes the prey."

"Hunter or hunted, who can say, which be predator, which be prey," intoned Fat Jim.

"Oh, that sounds right sinister," said Pipper.

"Sinister or not," said Fat Jim, "'tis true. Many a time the one hunted turns and becomes the hunter instead."

"A cornered rat would you say?" asked Noddy.

"Yup," replied Fat Jim.

" 'Tis nearly always the case," said Aravan. Then he laughed. "I am minded of a tale told by a friend of mine, a Realmsman named Halíd, when he and Vanidar Silverleaf and Tuon went after—" Of a sudden, Aravan fell silent, and a dark look came into his eye.

"What is it, my love?" asked Aylis, taking his hand.

Aravan sighed, then glanced at Pipper and Binkton. "'Tis a tale with its roots in tragedy, for a Realmsman was slain and three other mortals were aged before their time."

"Aged before their time?" asked Bink.

"Some of their years were stolen in a dreadful instant . . . some of their life snatched away," replied Aravan.

"By an evil creature?" asked the Pysk.

"Nay, tiny one," said Aravan, "but by a friend who had no other choice."

"Then I don't want to hear that story," said Pipper, shivering. "Not now, I mean. Not after Noddy's tale."

Binkton frowned. "But you laughed, Captain, when you spoke of Silverleaf and the Realmsman and one other."

"Vanidar Silverleaf, Realmsman Halíd, and Tuon," said Aravan, faintly smiling, the darkness in his eyes retreating a bit.

Bink turning to Pipper. "Then perhaps that portion of the story isn't too dreadful."

Pip looked up at Aravan. "Is it, Captain? —Too dreadful, I mean."

"Nay, not that part of the tale," said Aravan, "though toward the end it becomes a bit grim."

Pipper frowned in doubt. "C'mon, Pip," said Noddy. "It was you who faced the wraith. How could this be more horrible? 'Sides, I would like t'hear it meself, I would."

"Yar, Kapitan," said Nikolai, "so would I."

A chorus of agreement came from the others.

"Then I would hear it, too," said Pipper, grinning, though somewhat timidly.

Aravan nodded and took a sip of his brandy, then said, "We were on the trail of Baron Stoke, a monster of another kind, and we had long searched for the Baron's bolt-hole without success, did Faeril and Gwylly and Riatha and Urus and I. We had entirely lost the track, when Faeril, a damman, insisted we find an Oracle in the desert, in the Karoo, and seek from it the answer as to the Baron's whereabouts. On our journey through that vast wasteland, we came upon a well in which dwelt a dreadful creature that benumbed us with song and came through spellcast darkness to suck the blood from us all."

"What kind of a creature was it?" asked Wooly.

"A wyrm," replied Aravan.

"Wyrm!" blurted Noddy. "D'y' mean a Drake?"

"Nay, Noddy," said Aravan, "but a long, dark thing, glistening with slime, its thick body filling the well-shaft and stretching out through its conjured darkness to where we were sleeping. Segmented it was and wormlike, its round body tapering down toward the tip, flattening, to become a loathsome, bloodsucking mouth. I saw it not myself, but Riatha described it so, as did Gwylly who saw through its myrk and managed to alert the Dara, though he could do nought else."

"Oh, my," said Pipper. "And this isn't a dreadful story?"

"That part indeed was dreadful," said Aravan, "but I'll not dwell on it.

"Instead, suffice it to say, but for our comrade Reigo, a Realmsman, whom it slew, we escaped that monster, Riatha having wounded it sorely. And after we sang Reigo into the sky, we went onward to find the Oracle.

"Find him we did, though late, and he gave the damman Faeril many visions, one of which was that of a red citadel.

"Here let me say we had a rendezvous scheduled with an Arbalina vessel—the *Bello Vento*—and that time was nigh upon us, yet the port city where we had planned to meet the ship lay leagues to the north back across the desert. Yet Riatha, Urus, and Gwylly and Faeril and I decided to travel on southward to the city of Nizari—the Red City of Assassins—where we thought might lie the citadel, a place we might find the trail of our quarry, the monster Baron Stoke.

"Even so, we also needed to send a report back to the High King. We asked Halíd to carry our account to King Garon and then to find Silverleaf and Tuon and come back and destroy the wyrm in the well. To this Halíd agreed, for he would have vengeance upon the creature who slew his boon companion Reigo.

"As we turned southward toward our goal of the Red City, Halíd took three racing camels and headed north for the port of Sabra, there on the shores of the Avagon Sea, where we hoped he would be in time to meet the rendezvous ship ere she sailed. . . ."

Just after dawn, a dirty, disheveled, exhausted Man staggered out of the Karoo and in through the city gates of Sabra. He had no water, no food, no camel, having lost all to the sands of the Erg. *Yet he had survived the* mai'ûs safra*—the desperate journey—and inward he stumbled and wearily made his way down toward the harbor, toward the quays. When he got there he asked a dockworker the whereabouts of the harbormaster, and was directed towards a portly Man overseeing the offloading of a white stallion down the ramp of a three-masted dhow and onto the quay, a group* *of admiring* shaikhîn *gathered 'round the prancing animal. The exhausted Man approached the harbormaster and spoke to him. The master drew back somewhat from this filthy wretch and pointed out to sea. There, sailing away from the anchorage against the turning tide fared the* Bello Vento.

Rage flashed over the face of the Man, and he shouted at the sky, cursing, the harbormaster backing away in alarm. The Man looked about wildly, then bulled past these desert chieftains and knocked aside the groom leading the stallion, leaping upon its bare back and thundering away northward, crying, "Yah! Yah!", *racing through the city streets and out the north gate, shouts of pursuit lost in the distance behind.*

Up along the headland he ran, galloping in full, racing for the promontory a mile or so away. In moments, it seemed, he had reached the high point, hauling the stud to a skidding halt, the horse squatting on its haunches to stop, dirt flying, dust boiling upward. The Man leapt from the blowing stallion, and wrenched his curved knife from its scabbard, turning the gleaming blade into the early-morning sun, light glancing from the glittering steel.

Long he stood on the promontory, holding the blade out horizontally before him, shifting and turning it in the bright rays. And as he heard an angry mob of people rushing up the hillside after him, he saw the Bello Vento *heel over in the wind and come about.*

Captain Legori had finally seen the Realmsman's flashing signals. . . .

As the dark-eyed Gjeenian stepped from the small, lateen-sailed tender and clambered up the ladder and onto the Arbalina craft, Legori clasped the Man's hand and welcomed him aboard. Then he glanced back at the mob on the dock. "You looked to be in some trouble, Halíd."

"I was, Captain," replied the Realmsman. "They would have killed me on the spot—slit my throat or skewered me—for the horse I took to race to the promontory was not mine, and in the Karoo, stealing horses or camels and other such is nearly as bad as stealing water, and all are deeds deserving death. Yet when I showed them my Realmsman's sigil and explained my plight, they set me free, for none in Sabra wishes a war with the High King in his great castle across the sea."

"Then that's where we're headed, to Caer Pendwyr?"

"Aye, Captain. I have a report to give to King Garon, and then a mission to fulfill beyond."

"Mission?"

"Aye. The slaughter of the foul creature that slew Reigo."

"Reigo is dead?"

Tears welled in Halíd's eyes, and he nodded.

"What of Lady Riatha, Lord Aravan, Lord Urus, Sir Gwylly, and Lady Faeril?"

"They journey on toward peril," said Halíd.

"And you go back to the King?"

"It was Lady Riatha and the others who trusted me to carry out this mission: to catch your ship before it sailed and to bear a report to King Garon, and then, with two allies she named, to rid the world of the monster that slew Reigo."

"And this monster, this creature, where is it?"

"In the heart of the Karoo," said the Realmsman.

Legori stroked his chin and nodded. "Then you'll be needing transport across the Avagon." His words were a statement, not a question.

"Aye, that I will," said Halíd.

"Then let me get underway, for though the tide is running contrariwise, the wind is fair, and once asea we'll speak of this mission you have and how we on the *Bello Vento* can aid."

Halíd nodded, and said, "In the meanwhile I'll scrub some of this grit from me."

As Halíd strode away, Legori called his first officer to him, and the bosun piped orders to all. And even as the ship tacked in the wind against the incoming tide, Captain Legori frowned in the direction the Realmsman had gone, for Halíd, a Man in his early thirties, had somehow gone grey in the temples, his locks shot through with grey as well, like one who had reached his fifties, but how could that possibly be?

With three remounts and a packhorse in tow, Halíd crossed over the pontoon bridge on the River Rissanin to come among the ruins of Caer Lindor, the island fortress that had fallen to treachery during the Great War of the Ban, a war now some five millennia agone.

And even as he came among the tumbled-down blocks of granite, he heard voices fall silent as the hooves of his animals rang upon the stone flag. There 'mid the shambles overgrown with ivy he came upon an encampment of Elvenkind. A handful of Dylvana, they were, and smaller than the Lian, the only Elves Halíd had heretofore known. The tallest looked to be no more than five foot one or two, the rest well under that height. Dressed in shades of green they were, colors that would fade into the surround of the Greatwood aft, or into the trees of Darda Erynian to the fore.

Warily did the Elves look upon this dark-skinned, turbaned Gjeenian, for he resembled foe of old—Hyrinians or Kistanians, the sometime invaders of the realms of the High King in the wars gone by. But this dark stranger raised an empty hand in greeting and said, "I am Halíd, Realmsman to High King Garon, and I seek the clever Vanidar Silverleaf with his silver-handled white-bone bow, and the warrior Tuon who bears the spear known as Black Galgor."

"I am Silverleaf," came a voice from behind, "though some would dispute whether or no I am one to be called clever."

Halíd turned to see standing high on the remains of a stone wall a Lian, bow in hand, arrow nocked, though now it was turned down and away and the draw relaxed. Even so it was not set aside, the Elf alert and ready.

Silverleaf looked to be a lean-limbed youth with golden hair cropped at the shoulder and bound with a simple leather headband 'cross his brow, his tipped ears showing through. He had a fair face with grey eyes atilt, and his hands were long and slender and deft. Clad in green with a golden belt 'round his waist holding a long-knife, he stood some five foot nine or so. Yet wary, he said, "Thou sayest thou art a Realmsman. Have thee proof?"

"Only my sigil," said Halíd, carefully and slowly pulling aside his cloak to reveal the brand 'pon the leather of his vest—a golden griffin rampant on scarlet. "You are prudent to not trust me, yet let me say I am come lately from the Karoo, from Dara Riatha and Lord Urus and Alor Aravan and the Waerlings Faeril and Gwylly. And Dara Riatha said I might find you in Darda Erynian with the Dylvana, and she bade me to say this so that you would know I speak true: 'Greetings to the Coron who gave rise to the Larkenwald.' " Halíd fell silent a moment, but then added, "Though I confess, I know not what it means."

Silverleaf smiled, then gave a low whistle, and from behind

other granite blocks stepped more Dylvana, all with bows, arrows nocked. Silverleaf laughed and said, "We didst think thou might outnumber us, Realmsman Halíd."

"Ah, yes," replied the Gjeenian, dismounting. "I have you surrounded still."

"So that's what made you smile?" said Pipper. "One Realmsman surrounding a warband of Dylvana?"

"That and other parts of the tale," replied Aravan, taking another sip of brandy.

"Stop interrupting, Pip," said Binkton. "Let the captain finish his story."

Pipper's hand flew to his mouth and he made a motion as if buttoning his lips, and Aravan smiled, then spoke on:

"Halíd told Silverleaf his tale, and in short order they crossed the River Argon at the Olorin Ferry to come to the opposite shore, and there in Darda Galion they did find Tuon.

"Setting out with fresh remounts trailing, it was not long before they were back in Caer Pendwyr, where the *Bello Vento* was anchored and waiting. They had an immediate but short audience with King Garon, who told them that he had not yet had any word from those who pursued Baron Stoke. The High King then bade them fair journey and wished them well in their mission, and then withdrew to take up other matters concerning the Realm. Leaving the Caer, the trio, under the guidance of Halíd, quickly outfitted themselves in desert garb: blue turbans with face-covering cloths to wrap 'round, light blue cloaks and shirts and pantaloons and other such. As the Realmsman explained, "Blue is the holy color, and with your eyes atilt and your ears tipped, the Sabrans will take you to be *Djinni.* However, no *Djinn* can wear holy blue, and so they might take you for *Seraphim* instead." Two days later they boarded Captain Legori's ship, and he and his crew took them across the indigo waters of the Avagon Sea to disembark in the Port of Sabra on the north rim of the Karoo. . . ."

Rumors and word ran before them as Halíd and Silverleaf and Tuon strode through the twisting streets of the city, and a general hubbub surrounded them as they passed by, for here was a Man and two who were not-Men. Surely the Man was their chattel, for who else would travel with such creatures as these not-Men, unquestionably *Djinni* or the like. And look at those weapons: a black spear in a back-sling was borne by one of the not-Men, as well as a straight-bladed long-knife in a thigh-scabbard down his right leg; the second not-Man held a silver-handled white-bone bow in his grasp, his arrows in a quiver on his right hip, a long-knife on his left thigh; and the Human chattel had a proper shamsheer, the long, slightly curved hand-and-a-half sword in a scabbard across his back, but a straight-bladed long-knife was on his thigh, though he had a suitably curved dagger at his waist. No doubt these arms were enchanted all. Ah, but once again our city is host to these terrible beings. Pah, it was just some few months ago when another pair of *Djinni* along with two *zîr Djinn* and an *Afrit* had come through, or mayhap they all were *Seraphim* instead, and they had with them Human chattel as well. Could it be that there is a gathering of demons or gods somewhere in the Karoo?

Vanidar Silverleaf laughed and, speaking Sylva, said to Tuon, ["They think we are either agents of demons or messengers of the gods."]

Halíd turned wide-eyed toward Vanidar and replied in kind. ["Alor Aravan said the exact same thing."]

["Ha!"] barked Vanidar. ["Dost thou deem all Elves think alike?"]

Halíd grinned. ["Nay, my Lord . . . even though ye all look alike to me."] Then he burst out laughing, joined by the two Alori.

Yet smiling, flaxen-haired Tuon said to Halíd, ["Thou dost speak Sylva."]

["As a Realmsman, I thought it might be useful,"] Halíd replied.

Tuon now grinned and said to Silverleaf, ["It seems we cannot talk behind his back."]

But then Vanidar rattled off a string of stark words, and Tuon replied in kind, and at Halíd's puzzled look, Tuon added in Sylva, ["But then again that wouldn't be polite."] Then all three broke out in laughter.

"What was that tongue?" asked Halíd in Common, the Realmsman yet smiling.

"Châkur, the language of the Drimma," said Vanidar.

"Ah, the Dwarves. I would like to speak it one day."

"They hold it close," said Silverleaf, "and ere I would teach thee, I deem I would need their consent."

"Like the Vanadurin and their war-tongue Valur," said Halíd.

"Aye," said Silverleaf. "Dost thou speak it?"

"Indeed, yet I would need their consent ere passing it on," said Halíd, a smile on his face.

"Tit for tat," said Tuon, grinning at Silverleaf. "Payment in kind."

The next day they went beyond the walls of Sabra to the camel market, and there did Halíd bargain for six camels—three swift *hujun* for riding and three more *jamâl* for pack animals. As he was doing so, Tuon stepped to one of the beasts to look at its teeth for signs of ageing, just as he would a horse, and as he reached for the camel's chin, Silverleaf said, "I wouldn't do that were I thee, Tuon."

Taking the animal's chin in hand, Tuon said, "Why not, Vanida—" Just then a great gob of cud-filled slaver splashed into Tuon's face, slobber running down and dripping.

"That's why," came Silverleaf's laconic reply.

"Ghah! Ghah!" exclaimed Tuon, turning aside and frantically wiping his face with both hands and flinging the drool from his fingers. "Let's get horses. They don't spit."

Halíd bent over laughing, but the camel dealer gasped in shock, for one of his *hujun* had spat upon a blue-clad *Seraph,* and surely punishment would come swiftly, punishment that might also be inflicted upon the dealer himself. Falling to his knees before Halíd, the Man babbled in Kabla; ["Tell him I will kill the beast myself. And beg him to not destroy my entire stock."]

Halíd laughed all the harder.

Finally sobering, and with a stern look upon his face, Halíd replied, ["My master will take that very beast for his own, and with a suitable riding stick he will teach the *hajîn* how to behave properly toward one of his exalted station."]

Silverleaf choked back a laugh.

The next morning, riding three *hujun* and towing three *jamâl* loaded with gear and supplies and goatskins of water, all purchased at the *suq,* and with each of the camels *hronking* in protest at being forced to bear humans and cargo, the two *Djinni*—or were they *Seraphim?*—along with their Human servant, poor chattel that he was, left the caravansary and the city of Sabra with its glistening domes and tall minarets and flat-roofed dwellings behind as they struck out across the sands of the Karoo, no doubt going to a gathering of demons—or mayhap gods—somewhere in the depths of the *Erg*.

For four days the trio fared across the endless dunes, and each of those four days, Tuon's dromedary repeatedly managed to spit upon some part of his rider, no doubt teaching this two-legged Elf a well-deserved lesson. And it happened at every stop, every time Tuon dismounted and then reapproached the beast to mount up again. In those instances when Tuon drew near, the camel would get a malignant look in its eye, as if to say, *I know you. Have you not learned?* And then it would let fly a thick glob of mucus, and agile Tuon, alert to such tactics, would leap aside, sometimes successfully, sometimes not. And as Tuon began more and more to succeed in evading the flying gobbet, the beast became craftier, began feigning unconcern, but then in the last moment . . . Thus did it happen that Tuon was spat upon several times a day.

As the fifth eve of travel drew nigh, they came to the Oasis of Falídii, with its rows of date palms and its abandoned, tumbled-down brick dwellings on one of the slopes to the south and its great stone basin deep with water. And there they did revel and bathe and swim and clean their garments.

"Why does no one live here?" asked Tuon, glancing up at the brick ruins while scrubbing his clothes to wash them of sand and grit and great stiffened swaths of dried camel slobber; "It has dates and water and once had abodes."

Halíd pointed back toward where they had entered in among the palms. "This oasis is said to be *djado*—cursed—or so the toppled stele yon says."

"The one we rode past?"

"Aye."

"Yet thou didst stay here without harm, thou and Riatha, Urus, Aravan, Reigo, Faeril, and Gwylly?"

"Aye."

"Then mayhap the curse has run its course."

"Mayhap," replied Halíd. "Yet the place feels ominous to me."

"Mayhap it feels ominous because thou dost know of the stele," said Silverleaf, floating on his back in the great pool.

"Mayhap," replied Halíd.

They set ward that night under the arc of a waning third of a moon, each taking a turn in the May eve.

Nothing untoward occurred, though Halíd on last watch jumped at every slight sound, those made by small desert rodents running through sand, slithering serpents seeking them, a scorpion or two scuttling after beetles, and other suchlike faint noises. He was greatly relieved when the onset of pale dawn shone in the sky.

That morning, with Tuon wiping camel spit from the toe of his boot, they rode away from the Oasis of Falídii and continued on southward across the *Erg*.

And six days later in fast-waning twilight they came to a vast, shallow depression, scrub growing in the wide hollow, and in the distant center stood a handful of threadbare palms, parched, the fronds yellowish and sickly, among which they could see a mortared stone ring: it was the Well of Uâjii. . . .

. . . There where the monster dwelled.

. . . There where Reigo had been slain.

. . . There where they had come to wreak vengeance dire.

It was the night of the dark of the moon.

Aravan paused in his telling. "Any more brandy?"

Wooly held up an empty bottle.

"Then, pray, fetch another," said Fat Jim to his fellow steersman. "Listening is thirsty work."

As Wooly got up and headed for the stock behind the bar, Pipper made a motion as if unbuttoning his lip and smiled and said, "That was really funny, the camel spitting all over Tuon."

"*Hmph,*" snorted Binkton, even though he smiled, too. "It wouldn't be so funny if you were on the receiving end."

"If a camel spat on me," said Aylissa, standing and stretching to her full height of eleven and three-quarters inches, "I'd probably drown."

As the Pysk sat down again, Aylis laughed and looked at the wee Fox Rider. "Smother is more likely, Liss. Camel spit is rather thick."

"Oh?" said Aravan. "And how wouldst thou know, love?"

"I spent some time in Sarain, darling. Did I never tell you so?"

Aravan shook his head, even as Wooly returned with another bottle of brandy, a small, black-footed red fox at his heels.

"Methinks Vex here be worn out from rattin'," said the West Gelender.

As if to verify Wooly's words, after receiving a stroke from Aylissa, Vex curled up next to the Pysk. And with a sigh the fox closed her eyes, her nose tucked in her tail.

As soon as glasses and thimble were replenished, Aravan took a sip of brandy, then looked about to see if the listeners were ready for him to resume the tale.

Fidgeting impatiently, Pipper said, "It was the night of the dark of the moon," and then the buccan rebuttoned his lip.

Aravan nodded. "Yes, the dark of the moon . . ."

Even as they rode down into the sandy bowl, nighttide swept o'er the land and twilight fell to blackness.

They commanded the *hujun* to kneel, the beasts complaining loudly, and as they dismounted 'neath the bedraggled palms, Tuon's camel hawked a big gob at him. As Tuon leapt aside, Halíd said, "Let us camp far away from the well, where the wyrm cannot come at us, and then survey what is to be done and make our plans in the light of day."

"But we've talked this over time and again," said Silverleaf, stringing his bow, "and I say we simply tether one of the animals nigh the well to draw the monster out, and when it comes we skewer it."

Then Silverleaf grinned. "Tuon's mount would make fine bait."

Tuon shook his head. "Nay, Vanidar, for though I repeatedly have been sneered at and spat upon by the ill-mannered beast, I have come to admire his independence of spirit, and I like it not that we would sacrifice such an unfettered creature."

In that moment *"Hronk!"* bellowed Tuon's *hajîn,* as if he somehow knew they were speaking of him.

Tuon laughed, then said, "I ween Halíd has the right of it. Let us camp afar, where we deem the wyrm cannot come upon us. But even should it do so, come out from its hole, it will be far from its sanctuary, then we may kill it more readily—I with Black Galgor, thou with thy bow, and Halíd with that great whopping blade of his."

And so it was that they set camp afar in the great basin, hobbling the camels to forage on the thorny scrub therein.

The one on watch remained especially alert, for Halíd had warned all of the deadly song of the wyrm.

And throughout the dark of the moonless night, nothing—no beast, no creature of any sort, and most of all, not the wyrm—came upon them in the black.

The next morning they stepped past the hazard stones Halíd had set months past when he and the others had been here, stones he had set after Reigo had been slain, warning any and all who could read them to leave this place ere nightfall. To the mortared rim of the shaft the trio went and peered down and within, and Halíd's mind returned to the time he and the others had done the very same:

At Halíd's nod Reigo dropped a pebble down the well, Gwylly and Faeril watching as it disappeared into the blackness below. It seemed an endless time ere they heard the plsh *of the stone striking water. "Waugh!" exclaimed Halíd. "Five heartbeats deep!"*

"How much rope?" asked Reigo.

"Two hundred sixty-six cubits," Halíd answered, "four hundred feet."

Gwylly looked up, clearly astounded. "Four hundred—? Who dug this well? Who would set mortared stones that deeply? Even beyond! I mean, if it's four hundred feet to the water, then the bottom of the well is deeper still. Who would do such?"

Halíd and Reigo both shrugged, and Aravan turned up his palms.

"That much rope will be heavy," commented Faeril, "even without a bucket of water at its end."

"How deep didst thou say?" asked Silverleaf.

"Wha-what?" Halíd was jerked from his reverie.

"How deep?" repeated Silverleaf.

"Oh. Four hundred feet or so to the water."

Tuon gave a low whistle. "Rather a chore, wouldst thou not say, drawing a drink from this well?"

"Aye," replied Halíd, remembering.

* * *

"I will draw the water," rumbled Urus, knotting together several lines.

Silverleaf glanced 'round. "Yet I see no rope, no pail."

"You but echo Dara Riatha's own words," said Halíd.

Riatha gazed about as if seeking something. "I wonder . . . if a traveller came unto this well and had no line, no way to draw up the water, would he die of thirst at well's edge? Look about: See ye winch, line, bucket? See ye a cover capping the well to keep the water from evaporating? Nay! Here is a riddle to read."

"Sayest thou that Reigo did drop a stone down the well?" asked Tuon, recalling their long conversations as they had crossed the Avagon Sea.

"Aye," replied Halíd. "A pebble."

"Then mayhap that is what wakened the creature, the noise of it striking water."

"Perhaps it was the bucket instead," said Silverleaf, "for did not ye draw up water for use?"

"Aye," replied Halíd. "That is, Urus drew the water. And as I told you, the last bucket got snagged or held, mayhap even seized by the wyrm itself."

Strong as he was, Urus was wearied, for he had hauled up bucket after bucket of liquid. "Last one," he grunted, as he started to hale up the final one. But the pail did not rise. "Caught," he growled.

"On what?" asked Gwylly, peering downward into the blackness, seeing nought but the rope dwindling out of sight.

"Mayhap on the masonry, or on a rock." Urus moved to the far side of the well, paying out slack. Then he drew upward, but it did not yield. "Garn!"

Again Urus moved, then setting one foot against the well top—"Unh!"—he wrenched up and back, the bucket coming free, the Baeran stumbling hindward, landing on his seat yet retaining his grasp on the line.

Gwylly laughed, and Aravan, smiling, said, "Here, Urus, let me," the Elf taking the rope from the Man and stepping to the wall of the well, hauling upward, his eyes widening at the weight of rope, bucket, and water, glancing at Urus in surprise. "Hai! Thou art indeed a strong one, Urus. Better had we dragooned a camel for this work." Yet hand over hand the slender Elf continued to pull up the rope, the final bucket coming to the top at last, the side holed, water running out.

"Hoy!" exclaimed Gwylly. "Good that this was the last."

Silverleaf looked about, then took up a stone the size of a melon and dropped it down within. Long moments later there came a splash. Silverleaf grinned. "Mayhap now 'tis awake."

Halíd unslung the great shamsheer from his back and drew the blade from its soft leather scabbard.

In surprise, Tuon looked at the Realmsman. "Thinkest thou that it now comes?"

"If so, I am ready," said Halíd, resting the flat of the blade on his right shoulder.

Now it was Tuon who unslung his ebon spear, but Silverleaf, casually leaning against the mortared stones, said, "I hear nought of movement below. I deem nothing therein stirs."

"Nevertheless," said Halíd.

A time passed, and at last Tuon said, "As thou didst tell us, mayhap the creature only comes out at night, when all are aslumber."

"Gwylly was on watch," said Halíd, "but it sang him to sleep, and then somehow, by some power, it cast darkness o'er all ere it emerged from the well."

"Huah, then it is the darkness we need look for," said Vanidar.

"Aye," replied Tuon, "and if cast darkness is its ally, then it will come in the depths of eve."

"It came not last night," said Halíd.

"We were bedded down afar," said Vanidar Silverleaf, turning to look at their campsite, there in the distance where a stone trough sat, a trough dragged by Urus away from the well months past when he and the others had moved their camp after the attack. "Besides, mayhap it was not then awake and sensed us not. Yet I have cast the stone, and I say this night we stake a camel nearby and see if the wyrm is drawn up to feed."

"We must not succumb to its song," said Halíd, "else we ourselves will fall unto its doom."

They rested all that day, and in the twilight they staked one of the pack camels out near the mortared ring, and Silverleaf threw several more large stones down the shaft. Then even as a thin sliver of the moon chased after the just-set sun and disappeared below the horizon, the armed trio withdrew a distance and waited.

It was nigh the mid of night when the staked-out camel bellowed in alarm and broke loose from its tether and fled.

"Mayhap we need capture it and return it to the stake," said Tuon.

"I deem it would be too wild with fear," said Silverleaf. "Instead, let us wait and see if the wyrm comes up regardless."

"If it does, again I say, 'ware its song," said Halíd.

They waited . . . waited . . . waited . . . yet no song came forth and the darkness did not deepen at the rim of the well.

At dawn, Halíd mounted his *hajîn* and rode away, and ere the sun had risen the width of two fists into the sky, he came riding back leading behind the animal that had bolted in the night.

As they broke fast, "Methinks we should try it again, with a different camel staked more securely," said Silverleaf.

"Methinks we should have brought with us a goat or sheep for the bait," said Tuon. "Camels are quite strong, and I fear any we tether will break away."

Silverleaf laughed. "Mayhap we ought stake one of us."

Tears of rage instantly flared in Halíd's eye, and he spat, "You would not say that had you seen Reigo," then stood and stalked away, remembering.

Halíd had levered himself into a sitting position, and he was rocking and moaning and staring toward what remained of Reigo . . . the Realmsman's body no longer resembling that of a Man, but rather that of a flaccid, emptied skin, covered with slime and blood and drained.

Riatha slumped down in the sand beside Halíd. "Halíd. Don't look. Reigo would not wish thee to look at him the way he is."

But Halíd could not look away. "I heard you shout a war cry. I saw the blue light pressing back the murk.

"I saw the . . . the thing. *I could not move. . . . I could* not *move! . . . I could* not *move! And now Reigo is dead!"*

Silverleaf watched Halíd walk away. A hundred paces the Realmsman took, and he stopped under another of the sickly palms. After a moment Silverleaf got to his feet and followed to come unto the Man's side.

"I am sorry for my thoughtless remark, my friend. I did not think ere speaking in jest."

Halíd turned, unshed tears yet clinging to his lashes. "Ah, Silverleaf, 'tis not your fault, the jape. 'Twas my own memory o'erwhelmed me, for I yet feel that had I done something, anything, Reigo would still be alive."

"I think thou couldst do nought," said Vanidar. " 'Twas only by the power of Riatha's Truenamed blade that any of ye survived; without Dúnamis ye all would have perished."

"I know," said Halíd, brushing the grey of his sideburns. "I know. Yet still guilt lingers." He touched the sigil on his breast and looked at Vanidar. "I am a Realmsman, you see."

Vanidar threw an arm across Halíd's shoulders and said, "Come then, my friend, let us finish breaking our fast and tonight we shall stake out a different camel, this time more thoroughly, and see if we cannot draw forth and slay this creature of the dark."

That nighttide the staked camel did not bolt, nor did the wyrm emerge from the well.

The following eve again they tried, still with no success.

"Mayhap the wyrm is dead," said Silverleaf.

"But the first staked camel bolted," said Halíd.

"Aye, but we know not why," said Silverleaf.

"Dost thou deem such beasts e'en think?" asked Tuon, gazing out to where the hobbled animals placidly grazed on the thorny scrub.

"Your beast does," said Halíd, grinning. "And he's a sly one at that."

"Malignant, I would say," said Tuon, frowning down at his clothes, streaked again with dried spittle.

Silverleaf laughed but said, "Though I admit that thy noble

beast seems to have a mind of its own, I ween a butterfly might have more wit."

"I deem a butterfly to be more brilliant," said Tuon, "and certainly more pleasant withal. As to why the one bolted that first night, mayhap it were nought more than a scorpion sting or a strange odor on the wind."

Silverleaf pondered a moment, then turned to Halíd. "Say again what Riatha told of its size and how sorely she did wound it."

"Why dost thou ask this?" said Tuon.

"I have the glimmerings of an idea," said Vanidar.

Halíd bowed his head a moment, then looked at Silverleaf. "She saw not the creature's full length, for though it extended from the well, it had not fully emerged. . . ."

Rolling forward to her feet, Riatha saw the thing, *the wyrm, recoiling up and away from Faeril's body, its oval maw oozing slime and blood, the hideous, segmented, black monstrosity shrinking back from the sword's blue radiance, trying to withdraw, to escape down the well. Yet more than thirty feet of it extended from the circular opening, and it was bloated, engorged, and it struggled to force itself back in.*

Dread hammering through her entire being, "Yaaahhhh!" *shrieked Riatha in a wordless yell, running forward, blue flaming sword raised high in a two-handed grip.* Shkk! *the blade sliced across the hideous* thing's *gut, black blood and red gushing out, spilling on the ground, the creature mewling.* Shlakk! *With a backhanded stroke Riatha drove Dúnamis again through the monster, opening another great gaping wound, blood and tissue and slime pouring forth.*

Shrilling in agony, the monstrosity whipped back into the well, disappearing downward, the blackness collapsing, the stars shining down.

Pursuing, Riatha ran to the lip of the well and peered inward, the azure glow of Dúnamis shining into the depths of the black hole, revealing only massive streaks of slime and blood down the dark stone throat.

The thing *was gone.*

Halíd fell silent a moment, but then added, "If Dara Riatha had not Truenamed her sword, then we all would have perished."

As Silverleaf nodded, Tuon cleared his throat. "Thou didst say thou dost have a glimmer of an idea, Vanidar?"

Silverleaf looked at his own *hajîn,* munching placidly with the others on thorny scrub. Then he turned to Halíd and Tuon. "Think ye on this: what *if* the wyrm is dead?"

"Dead?" said Tuon.

Silverleaf gestured at Halíd. "Riatha said she wounded it sorely. It may have gone to ground and died."

"But the first camel fled," said Halíd, pointing to where the beasts grazed.

"Aye, but as Tuon has said, mayhap it was the sting of a scorpion or a strange odor on the breeze. It could have been aught other than the wyrm. And see, nought has happened since. So, mayhap the wyrm is dead."

"If so, what wouldst thou have us do?" asked Tuon.

"Someone need descend into the well and see," said Vanidar, "and I propose that be me."

"No, no," said Halíd. "You must not do that, Silverleaf. If the wyrm lives, then it would be suicide to venture into its lair."

"Not so," declared Vanidar. "Should the creature still be alive, then we can swiftswarm me to safety, and—"

"Swiftswarm?" asked Halíd. "And just what is that?"

"I climb hand over hand while at the same time thou and Tuon hale the rope upward. It is—"

"Nay!" declared Halíd. "Swiftswarm or no, it is too perilous."

"Set thy protests aside for a moment," said Tuon. "Instead, let us consider what else might be involved. Then when all is considered, in our wisdom we—"

"Wisdom, you say?" said Halíd. "Folly, say I."

"Realmsman," said Tuon, "we must hear Silverleaf out. Didst thou not thyself say this hazard must be eliminated, for did it not slay Reigo? Didst thou not say that by other bone fragments ye found, ye all didst deem others had fallen victim to this creature as well?"

Halíd took a deep breath and then nodded.

Tuon turned to Vanidar. "Then say on, Silverleaf."

"There is this," said Silverleaf, "if the wyrm is as large as Riatha has described it, then surely there must be a hollow or cavern or some such down in the well for the creature to dwell within. If so, and if it is dead, then that's where we will find its corpse. If it is not dead, then that's where we might make a stand to slay it."

Tuon nodded, then said, "Mayhap thou art right about a place where it dwells—basin or bowl, cavern or hole—but then again, mayhap thou art wrong. Still, we will never know unless one of us goes down."

"Know that I am against such a plan," said Halíd, "but I will join in on the discussions, if for nought but to dissuade you from this mad course."

"Well and good, Halíd," said Silverleaf. Then he glanced at the mortared ring. "It may be that, whatever hollow in which the creature dwells, that hollow lies in the wall of the well rather than at the bottom, and if so, then mayhap I will not need to descend all the way, but only part."

"If thou dost go," said Tuon, glancing at the sun, "then let it be in the day, for mayhap the creature is averse to Adon's light." The Elf looked at Halíd for confirmation.

Halíd shrugged. "I only know that the wyrm came up in the night. Yet that may only be because it waited until all were asleep."

"The one on watch was not," said Silverleaf. "Even so, I deem Tuon is right: going in the day seems best."

"The light of day does not penetrate deeply into the shaft," said Halíd.

"If the creature be averse to light," said Tuon, "we can lower a lantern on the end of the rope and mayhap provide a margin of safety."

"Well, then," said Silverleaf, "if need be, we can . . ."

They debated for much of the day, looking for advantage, looking at risk, and in the end, they decided to stake out camels for three more nights. If the wyrm did not emerge, then Silverleaf would make the descent. If he found that the wyrm were dead, then they would ride away the next day in that sure knowledge. However, if the wyrm were not dead . . .

And so for three nights running they used a camel as bait, and on the second of these the beast fled, just as had the one eves past. This time though, as planned beforehand, the trio ran to the well and peered in by lantern light; they could discern nought.

The next night passed uneventfully.

In spite of another *jamâl* having bolted, Silverleaf insisted that he had to go down the well and see what might be there.

Halíd argued otherwise, but Tuon sided with Vanidar.

Halíd then pointed out that they had been short of sleep for nigh a sevenday in all, and he insisted they needed to be well restored ere attempting Silverleaf's mad plan.

And so they rested throughout the next day, doing nought but eating and dozing and taking care of other needs, as well as sharpening blades and plaiting together five lengths of rope so that Silverleaf could make the rappel down without any knots to hinder him. Too, from an empty goatskin water sack, they made a leather pad to drape over the rim of the well to prevent the rope from chafing on the stone lip.

That day as well Halíd said, "Instead of swiftswarm, we will use a camel to hale you up. It will be faster."

"Aye, faster," said Tuon. "Yet I can see Silverleaf being dragged through thorn and rock and across hardpack behind a fleeing camel."

"To say nought of what would happen to me as he rips me o'er the rim," said Silverleaf.

"But I would ride the beast," protested Halíd. "Have it under my complete control."

"Indeed," said Tuon.

"Without a doubt," said Silverleaf.

"Aargh!" growled Halíd.

Silverleaf turned to Tuon. "Swiftswarm it is."

That night again they camped far from the mortared stone ring, out where they deemed the creature would not come, and Halíd and Tuon sat guard, but not Silverleaf, for his companions insisted that he needed his sleep to be fully alert in his venture. Of course, oft did Silverleaf wake and engage the ward in converse.

The next morn dawned bright, but they waited until the sun neared the zenith ere Silverleaf made ready to go, for descent into the depths at the onset of the noontide seemed somehow more prudent to them, even though the light of day would be hard-pressed to reach the full four hundred feet to the bottom.

Tying a short length of rope 'round a nearby palm tree, and threading the main line through a brake made of three pairs of snap-rings, they affixed a lit lantern some ten feet from the end and lowered it down and within.

Down it went and down, and they paused now and again when one or the other or the third thought he saw something out of the ordinary—false alarms all—and then they would lower farther still.

At last when nigh four hundred feet had been payed out: "I ween I see a glimmer of water," said Silverleaf.

As Vanidar strapped on his climbing harness and slung his bow across his back, Tuon jam-locked the snap-ring brake at the palm tree. Gauging the surplus of the main-line coil, he said, "We have more length shouldst thou need such, Silverleaf, mayhap twenty-five ells in all."

Silverleaf nodded and slipped the line through the snap-ring rappel-brake clipped to his harness, then stood on the rim of the mortared stones. He made certain his arrows were secure in the quiver on his hip, as well as the long-knife in its scabbard strapped to the opposite thigh, and as he did so he said, "Remember swiftswarm, should the need arise."

Then with a rakish grin he stepped backward over the brim and down.

Down he went and down, while Tuon and Halíd leaned against the lip of the well and watched, Halíd's fists clenched, his knuckles white, his breath coming in rapid gasps.

Tuon's breathing and stance seemed unaffected, though the look in his eyes was grim.

Down and down descended Silverleaf, the Elf silhouetted by the lantern below, his feet touching now and again against the stones, the rope *zzzing* through the snap-ring brake as he rappeled deeper and deeper into the shaft.

Zzzz . . .

Down . . .

Zzzz . . .

Deeper . . .

Zzzz . . .

But at last he stopped.

"More line," came the faint call. "Another twenty feet."

Tuon stepped to the tree, and taking two turns of the line about his waist, he released the brake and payed out twenty feet more.

"He asks for another five," said Halíd, yet peering into the depths of the well.

"Enough," said Halíd when that had been done. Then, "Set it, he's at the bottom."

Again Tuon jam-locked the snap-ring brake.

"What dost thou see?" said Tuon as he came back to the brim.

"I think he's swinging," said Halíd as the light repeatedly bobbed in and out of sight. Then he turned pale. "Oh, Rualla, what if it's the wyrm that's got him and is wrenching him about."

Even as he grabbed up his own climbing harness and strapped it on, Tuon called, "Art thou well, Silverleaf?"

"*Vio,*" came the faint answer from below, even though the light continued to pass in and out of sight.

Halíd let out a great sigh of relief. "Ah . . ."

Tuon then took up Black Galgor and strapped it across his back. "What passes?"

"It looks as if Silverleaf has taken the lantern from the rope," said Halíd. "I see the glow moving about, though I cannot see the lantern itself. —Oh, wait, the rope is twitching again."

As Tuon took station at the well, Halíd slipped into his own climbing harness, and fixed his shamsheer across his back.

Time passed, and as both watched down the length of the shaft they could occasionally see the faint glow of the lantern gleam in the darkness below, as if Silverleaf were bearing it about.

Finally, the glow returned, and some moments later Silverleaf's silhouette swung into view. . . .

. . . He was making an ascent.

"No sign of the wyrm," said Vanidar, somewhat winded as he clambered over the rim. "However, 'tis a labyrinth down there, a flowing stream at bottom, deep and shallow by turns, and caverns running out beyond seeing, splits and joins water-carved. Dead or alive, the creature could be anywhere in that maze."

Tuon looked at Halíd. "Let us hale up the rope and coil it right here, then all retire unto the camp and decide what be our course. —We need another plan."

Long did they talk and explore options, but in the end it was Halíd who said, "There is an old saying in the Karoo concerning the prophet Shat'weh."

Tuon looked at Halíd and raised an eyebrow, and Halíd said, "If

Shat'weh goes not to the mountains, then the mountains must come unto him."

Again Tuon raised an eyebrow.

Halíd sighed and said, "In this case it is we who are the mountains and the wyrm Shat'weh, and if the wyrm comes not to us, then we must go unto it."

Hence it was decided: they would all descend into the well and, if the wyrm were alive, they would slay the creature in its lair.

Or so they hoped.

At midmorn of the next day, they belted on their climbing harnesses and weaponry: each had a long-knife strapped to one thigh and a dagger at his belt; Silverleaf had his strung bow across his back and a quiver of arrows along his other thigh, the shafts secured within by a slipknotted cord; Tuon had Black Galgor harnessed behind; Halíd had his shamsheer across his own back.

Down the shaft they lowered the line with three lanterns affixed, as before, ten feet from the end, one of them lit. And when they had payed out all, Tuon said, "I will go first."

"Why so?" asked Silverleaf.

Tuon reached back over his shoulder and tapped Black Galgor. "At shaft-bottom my spear is the better weapon to take on the wyrm, superior to thy bow."

"My shamsheer is better than either," said Halíd.

"My spear has a longer reach than thy sword, Halíd."

"Nevertheless, my blade will cleave the creature in twain, and it is the weapon of choice to take on the wyrm."

"My spear," Tuon said.

"Nay," said Silverleaf. "Ye are both in error, for with my bow I can safely pierce the wyrm at range."

They argued over the merits of each, and finally Silverleaf took up three dried blades of grass and broke them to three lengths. "Long goes first; short, last."

Moments later, Silverleaf clipped onto the rope. "I'll see ye below." He stepped to the brim and then down and in.

Halíd clipped on next; Tuon last.

As they waited for Silverleaf to reach bottom, Tuon called, "How didst thou cheat, Vanidar?"

An echoing laugh was his answer.

* * *

The shaft itself came to an end some twenty feet above the pool. The mortared stone, however, belled outward to form a heavy arch spanning the width of the water, the base of the arch curving down to come to rest upon stone ledges on either side, one on the more or less northerly verge, the other on the south.

As Silverleaf came to the end of the shaft, he paused, his eyes seeking a stir in the water, or movement in the shadows beyond. None. Down he continued until he reached the lanterns; there he unclipped from the rope and, hand over hand, went past them to the bottom of the line. He then used the rope as a swing to reach the northern ledge. While keeping hold of the end of the line, he unslung his bow and set it aside, and freed the arrows in his quiver. Then he untied the lanterns. Finally, as he took up his bow he let the rope swing loose, the signal for Halíd to come next. Down came the Realmsman and then Tuon to join Vanidar. As Tuon unslung Black Galgor he said, "Who built this curious place?"

Tying the end of the rope 'round a jagged projection of stone, Silverleaf shrugged and said, "I know not whose hands sunk the shaft to reach this reservoir, nor who laid and mortared the stone, though mayhap a Drim would know, for they are skilled in the ways of such work."

Halíd took up a lantern and lit it and looked through the glow at the stream running into the pool and out the opposite side. "I wonder how they even knew the water was here?"

"Mayhap they had a skilled dowser," said Tuon.

"Well," said Silverleaf with a sigh, "no matter who found it, no matter who dug it, no matter who laid the stones, I ween they did not know of the creature who laired within this maze."

At mention of a maze, both Halíd and Tuon held lit lanterns on high and looked up and down the stream, and they could see branchings in the dimness beyond.

"Speaking of the Drimma," said Tuon, turning to Silverleaf, "I would that we had several with us, for they cannot lose their feet."

"I've heard that about Dwarves," said Halíd. "It is said to be their gift. Though as you say, would that we had some with us."

"We'll simply blaze our trail as we go," said Silverleaf, touching the dagger at his belt.

"Upstream or down?" asked Halíd, looking first one way, then the other.

Tuon looked both ways as well. "I say we go upstream."

"Any particular reason?" asked Silverleaf.

"I rather like going against the grain," replied Tuon.

"So be it," said Silverleaf.

With Tuon and Halíd bearing lit lanthorns, and with an unlit one at Silverleaf's waist, and with Black Galgor in Tuon's free hand, and the shamsheer in Halíd's, and Silverleaf wielding his bow, arrow nocked, the trio edged their way 'round the pool, then clambered down into the flow. Wading against the current, they quickly came to a branching, a trickle of water coming from the left-hand way, the bulk of the stream from the right-.

"Given the size of the creature," said Vanidar, "and that water seems to be its home, let us bear to the right."

As they passed the juncture, with his dagger Vanidar scratched an arrow in the stone, the blaze pointing back the way they had come.

On they went, twisting 'round a bend and then another and then one more, and from the fore they could hear the fall of water, and pressing on they came to the base of a fifteen-foot slant, down which the water plunged into a pool at the bottom.

"Dost thou think the creature lives beyond?" asked Tuon.

"Mayhap," replied Silverleaf, and so up the channel they struggled, to find two branches before them at the top, both bearing water to the fall.

"Again, let us take the right-hand way," suggested Halíd, and Silverleaf paused long enough to scratch another arrow.

On they went and on, past branchings and splits leading off into the dark, some of them dry, others with but a trickle, some of them with water flowing freely. Through twisting and curling passages they fared to come into water-carved chambers, their walls shaped into strange, flowing forms of stone. In places water fell adrip from the ceilings, and stalactites hung overhead like icicles of stone, and stalagmites like Dragon's teeth jutted up from the floor. In one chamber, the walls were covered with large rounded nodules, a thin layer of water flowing down over all. In another, there was a handful of great, standing stones, like megalithic sentries silently warding the way.

Through pools they waded, and some they swam, and always did they come again into a myriad of passages, splitting and joining, depending on which way one looked. 'Twas a labyrinth by anyone's measure, and within this warren did the trio fare, searching for a monster, dead or alive.

At junctures they chose the right-most way when it seemed the best, taking one of those to the left when it proved better, and Silverleaf blazed their trail.

At times they had to double back on themselves when the way became impassable or came to a dead end, such as at the place where the passage had tapered down to a wide, horizontal crack, water flowing out, the cleft too narrow for them to pass through, or at the place where the water welled outward through a myriad of tiny cracks, none of which could they enter.

"Once when I was in Drimmen-deeve," said Silverleaf as they sloshed back from another of these turnarounds, "we came to a stream under, and it was Ursor, a Baeran of enormous size and strength, who found a passage beyond. Ah, me, but I wish he were with us now."

"When was that?" asked Halíd.

"Two centuries and some after the Winter War," said Vanidar, "during the time of the Battle of Kraggen-cor."

Halíd's eyes widened. "Why, that was—what?—six, seven hundred years ago?"

"Aye, some such," said Silverleaf.

Halíd shook his head in wonder, for the Elf before him seemed no more than a lean-limbed youth, and yet this "youth" had strode the world long past. Even so, had Halíd known that Silverleaf had been on Mithgar for some twenty millennia, the Realmsman would have been stunned.

"I deem we need start back for the well-shaft," said Tuon, "for the sun is but four hands from setting, and though the light of day reaches not unto these passages, still would I rather we not hunt this creature in the night."

"As would I," said Halíd, accepting Tuon's word, for well was he aware that one of the Elven gifts was to know at all times where stands the sun and moon and stars, e'en when they could see them not, and if an Elf said that the sun was but four hands from setting, then that's where it stood.

By lantern light they swashed back along the emblazoned trail, Silverleaf's dagger-scratched arrows pointing the way. Passage after passage they followed, slogging through chambers, wading through pools, swimming now and again. They had just emerged from another pool when of a sudden Silverleaf said, "List!"

They paused. . . .

Listening . . .

Above the gurge and swirl of the running stream there came a soft purl, as of a faint singing, just on the edge of perception.

Halíd sucked in air through clenched teeth and said, "The wyrm."

"'Tis its song?" asked Tuon.

"It must be," said Halíd.

"Thou dost not remember?"

"I was enspelled," said Halíd, "and only Gwylly of all who were entranced gave ear to the singing. Yet this that we hear is akin to his description."

"Mayhap we are not actually 'hearing' the song," said Silverleaf, "but perceiving it instead. —Yet wait! It echoes, so we must be hearing."

"Perceiving, hearing, it matters not," said Halíd, "however it comes to us, we must not fall under its spell, else we are fordone."

"Let us not stand here debating whether 'tis heard or perceived," said Tuon. " 'Tis a song, and if it comes from the wyrm, then the monster yet lives, and we are here to slay it."

With that, Tuon strode forward along the way, Halíd following, Silverleaf coming last.

They came to a split, and after listening down each passage, they took the left-hand way. Silverleaf did not emblazon an arrow, for this passage was one that they had trod in the opposite direction, and it was already marked.

The song got louder.

Halíd paused and pressed a hand to his brow.

"Art thou well, Realmsman?" asked Silverleaf.

"I am somewhat affected," said Halíd.

"I, too, feel its effect," said Tuon.

"Then let us sing in counterpoint," said Silverleaf, and he broke out in a bawdy song, that of Snorri, Borri's son, and the Mystical Maid of the Maelstrom.

And so, singing to stay awake, to fend off the wyrm's spell, the trio sloshed forward along the way, pausing only when they came to a junction, only long enough to find the way toward the wyrm. It was always along the path they had already traversed in the opposite direction.

"It's as if the wyrm lies along our own route, mayhap tracking us, it is," said Tuon.

"Aye," replied Silverleaf, "likely hunting us."

On they went, and the farther they advanced down the way, the less they knew what they were doing, for the wyrm's song upon them did grow. Down passage after passage they stumbled, now nearly entranced, barely fending off the spell of the wyrm by hoarsely singing of the sexual appetites of the Mystical Maid of the Maelstrom, and of Snorri Longhaft doing his best to satisfy her wanton lusts, the verses now ajumble, none singing what the others did.

Staggering ahead, they crossed the chamber where large nodules clung to walls, with water sheeting down over all. Just ere they reached the tunnel leading out the far side, Silverleaf blearily peered ahead. "Unh," was all he managed to call out.

Even so, sluggishly Tuon and Halíd held their lanterns on high, and hurtling down the passage toward them came a great wall of blackness and, still mumbling about Snorri and his three-legged dog, they stared dumbly as it came on.

Ssss . . .—an arrow flew—*ssthock!*—it struck . . . something.

A shrill mewling split the air, and suddenly Tuon and Halíd were free of the insidious spell, Silverleaf, too, but the darkness rushed on.

"Waugh!" cried Halíd, and he dropped his lantern asplash and brought his great shamsheer up in two hands.

Tuon cast his own lantern aside, and braced the butt of Black Galgor against a water-carved hollow in the stone floor.

Ssss . . . —another arrow flew past—*ssthock!*—to strike again.

Another mewl split the air, but still the shadow hurtled on.

And then as another arrow hissed past the lantern lights went out, drowned in the water. Utter darkness fell.

And a great massive *thing* smashed into and onto and over the trio, slamming them back into the pool, burying them under its bulk, its great weight threatening to crush them, to smother them, for they could not breathe. Yet even had they been able to draw a breath, they would have drowned, trapped underwater as they were, a great, heavy, slimy thing lying atop, mashing down.

Yet even as they were dying, the creature writhed, and Tuon, hacking and coughing, got free.

He gagged once or twice at the dank malodor filling the air. Gasping and wheezing past broken ribs, he staggered to his feet and stumbled through the pitch-darkness, feeling along the side of a slimy bulk. He found someone's foot jutting out—Halíd's—and in spite of Tuon's hurts he managed to drag the Realmsman free. Together, they located Vanidar's arm extended out from beneath the monster, and they prized him from under. But his chest was still and he moved not, and in the blackness, Tuon breathed air into Silverleaf, until that Elf began breathing on his own.

Halíd, nursing a forearm, one of the bones cracked, fumbled in the darkness for the lanterns. He found but one, and that one smashed, its oil gone. Neither could he find his great shamsheer, nor Tuon's black-hafted spear.

Gripping long-knives, they sat in ebon dark, waiting for Silverleaf to regain consciousness, a monster at hand, unmoving—stunned or dead, they knew not, but if it stirred, they would do their best to slay it, broken ribs, cracked arm or no.

At last, Vanidar moaned, and hacked a cough, and managed to croak, "Wh-where . . . ?"

"I am here, as is Halíd," said Tuon.

"Is it dead?"

"We know not," said Tuon.

"What is that awful smell, the *thing?*"

"Aye," replied Tuon.

"Why are we in the dark?"

"The lanterns are smashed," said Halíd. "That is, one is smashed. I can't find the other."

Vanidar sat up, and Tuon and Halíd could hear him fumbling about. There came the momentary flare of a striker, then light filled the chamber.

"I had this one at my waist," said Vanidar, holding the lantern on high.

Before them they saw a hideous, segmented, black monstrosity stretching across the chamber. Like a great slime-laden worm it looked, its girth a yard or more through. They stepped toward what they thought was its fore, and it tapered down to a blunt, wedge-shaped end, though the wedge itself was split in twain for fully a yard or more, and there they found Silverleaf's three arrows embedded to the fletching. And just behind the split and protruding up and through what mayhap could be called the wyrm's head was the point of Black Galgor.

As they struggled to pull the black-hafted spear from the creature, they rolled the forefront of the wyrm a bit over, and they found Silverleaf's bow in the water beneath, as well as Halíd's shamsheer, the blade yet wedged in the great split. They also found two large gashes, partially healed, there where Riatha's blade had cut.

Too, they could see the cloven remains of what was left of the creature's mouth, and after examining it, Silverleaf said, "A three-toothed maw with a sucker 'round. This might be a monstrous leech."

"That's what Gwylly called it," said Halíd.

"A leech it may be—a bloodsucker—yet this one could cast a spell," said Tuon.

"Aye, by size alone 'tis no ordinary leech," said Silverleaf, looking at its grotesque length.

"Let us leave this foul place," said Tuon, Black Galgor now in hand.

"Not yet," said Halíd.

Vanidar and Tuon looked at the Realmsman. "Not yet?" asked Silverleaf.

"They say that worms cut in two can grow again," said Halíd. "Leech or worm, I would not have that be."

"What wouldst thou have us do?" asked Silverleaf.

"Worms cut into fine pieces grow not again," said Halíd, and he held up his great shamsheer. "Here is the tool, but my arm is broken."

Vanidar looked at Tuon. "My ribs," said that Elf.

Vanidar sighed and handed his bow to Halíd and took the shamsheer in exchange.

Fully twenty paces in extent was the wyrm, and it took long for Silverleaf to cut the creature into segments, all the while with

Tuon and Halíd commenting loudly on Silverleaf's technique, Vanidar swearing vengeance as he went about the grim task. When he at last came to the end, slathered with ichor and gore and grume as he was, there, too, he found a sucker, this one much larger than the one 'round the mouth. "Aye, though monstrous and able to cast darkness and sleep, at base 'tis a leech," called Silverleaf. "With suckers at each end, 'tis like all other leeches; that's how he climbed up and down the well-shaft—holding with one while moving the other, alternating between the two, rather like an inchworm, though leeches expand and contract rather than hump in the middle."

"If thou art finished with thy butchery," said Tuon, "thou canst expound all about leeches later, for I would leave this foul place."

"Oh, Tuon," said Halíd in exaggerated disappointment, "can we not stay and learn all there is to—"

"Aargh!" shouted Silverleaf. "Let us be gone ere I take this great whopping blade unto thine own rounded bodies."

As they readied to go, Silverleaf first cleaned the shamsheer and then slipped it into its scabbard across Halíd's back. "A fine weapon, Realmsman," said the Elf, as he secured the blade in place.

"Aye," replied the Realmsman. "After all, it slew the wyrm, clove it right down to its gullet."

"What?" said Tuon. "Nay, 'twas Black Galgor did it in, pierced it through and through."

Silverleaf said, "Did ye two not see where my arrows went? Straight into the brain, I ween. My bow and arrows felled the creature, and 'twas but its own impetus that carried it forward to run o'er us."

"My blade," said Halíd.

"My spear," declared Tuon.

"Faugh, ye are but pretenders," said Silverleaf.

And arguing, down the tunnels they went, each claiming the victory, following emblazoned arrows back to the well.

Aravan fell silent.

"Is that it?" said Pipper.

Aravan nodded. "Aye. The wyrm was slain, and Reigo avenged. They accomplished the task."

"Yar," said Binkton, "but tell me, how did they all get out of the well? I mean, Tuon had broken ribs, and Halíd's arm was cracked, so just how did they get out?"

"I believe they used climbing stirrups in conjunction with ring brakes to act as ascenders," replied Aravan.

"Oh, right," said Binkton, a bit embarrassed, for he was well trained in climbing. With a *harrumph,* he cleared his throat. "That's what I would have done myself."

"Did you ever go back by the well, Aravan?" asked the Pysk. "—I mean after you and Riatha and Urus and the others were there?"

Aravan nodded. "Thrice altogether: twice did I pass it going and coming when I went again to Nizari to settle an old score, and once more when Bair and I went to see Dodona, during the Dragonstone War."

"The well was safe then, right?" asked Fat Jim.

"In spite of the slaying of the wyrm," said Aravan, "still there was for me an air of evil at that place. Mayhap just a whim based on the time it slew Reigo; yet again, mayhap not."

"Did your amulet grow cold?" asked Aylis, referring to the small blue stone 'round Aravan's neck, a stone that sensed peril when certain creatures were about.

Aravan shook his head. "Nay, it did not grow chill. Yet heed, it did not grow chill the first time we were there, until the wyrm came nigh the surface. It happened when Gwylly held it, when he was on watch, and though he fell under the spell of the monster, still the stone grew cold in his hand, and that plus Riatha's True-named sword saved us all. . . ."

Holding the stone, Gwylly took a seat on a boulder, his senses alert to the surround, warding his companions. How long he sat thus, he knew not, yet ever did his eyes sweep across the starlit sand. But he saw only the vague silhouettes of the camels grazing, the animals eating the thorny brush and wisps of grass. And so, amulet in hand, he sat on the rock, watching the desert, guarding his comrades, listening to the rustling of the faint breeze among the sparse palm fronds, the susurration whispering above, a soft sibilancy murmuring in his ear, almost as a faint, faint song dimly in the distance, a purling aspiration, a wafting ripple, singing, singing, insistently, inviting him to listen to its soft echo, a gentle breeze shushing, bidding him to rest, singing, singing, darkness falling, sleep, sweet sleep overcoming, blackness flowing, stars winking out, dreaming wonder drawing closer, closer, ebon darkness growing, flowing up and out and over the stone rim, followed by a thing of beauty, leaning down, gently kissing companions, joyfully receiving, lips smacking, liquid dripping, maw masticating, hand burning, fierce with cold, silent screaming, eyes open, never closed, seeing, seeing, seeing—

Struggling against the irresistible, Gwylly squeezed his hand tightly upon the burning cold amulet, his mind shrieking for him to move, yet he could not, for he was frozen in place. Still he fought with desperation, striving to focus his mind on what he was seeing, praying for the fiery pain of the frigidly cold blue stone to aid him. Slowly, he began to apprehend, and dimly through the ebon darkness, he could see the motionless bodies of his companions lying as still as death. But at the well . . . at the well . . . he could see a black thing, *extending up and out from the well, a thick, segmented, wormlike body, laden with glistening slime, filling the round well-shaft . . . filling the shaft. Gripping the freezing amulet, drawing strength from it, forcing himself to* see, *Gwylly followed the arc of its shape up and over and down through the murk, the roundness tapering down, flattening, coming to a blunt end, a mouth fastened to Reigo's still form, and it was* feeding. *Slime dripped from its bloody maw, horrid sucking sounds filled the air, Reigo's body like a bag of blood being drained. The sight burned into Gwylly's mind, and he shouted in terror, but all that came out was a feeble moan. Straining, in small wrenching movements, he managed to turn his head slightly, and saw that next in line for the hideous creature to* feed *upon was* Faeril!

And even at that moment, the creature raised up from Reigo, blood and slime dripping from its red maw. And with sucking, slurking sounds, its glistening orifice opened and closed, and the eyeless head of the creature—nothing more than a hideous, flat, blunt tip—slowly moved back and forth, as if seeking the whereabouts of new prey. And when its ghastly, drooling, sucking mouth pointed toward Faeril, the dreadful questing stopped.

Shrieking in silent horror, with all of his might, Gwylly tried to leap up, and slowly, ever so slowly, he toppled from the stone, slamming into the ground, the crash jolting him, driving back his enthrallment but barely. Straight in front of him lay Riatha and Urus, unmoving.

Driven by desperation, grimly he inched himself forward until he came to the Elfess. Agonizingly, he forced his arm ahead, placing his hand in hers, pressing the frigid amulet into her palm, against her skin. Reaching down deep inside for his last dregs of strength, Gwylly managed to utter words, his voice whispering, croaking, "Riatha. Riatha. Help. It will kill Faeril."

And then he knew no more.

Words, like dark stones falling into a black pool . . .

Help . . . help . . . elp. It will kill Faeril . . . it will kill . . . Faeril . . . Faeril . . .

. . . fell into Riatha's empty dreams of dread.

Urgent words:

Riatha . . . help . . .

Desperate words:

It will kill . . .

Whispered words:

Help . . . Riatha, help . . .

She struggled . . .

Something cold, frigid . . .

. . . and came awake, remnants echoing in her mind . . .

Help . . . help . . . elp. It will kill Faeril . . . it will kill . . . Faeril . . . Faeril . . .

Who called?

She did not know.

But something icy burned her hand . . .

. . . and this she did know.

Amulet!

Danger!

She could not move.

She forced her eyes open. She could not see. All was blackness. Impenetrable. In the distance she could hear the bellowing of terrified camels, yet at hand was a hideous sucking *and* slurking *and* bubbling, *and she could smell the iron tang of free-running blood, overpowering all. Yet there was another odor on the air, close and dank, sickening to the senses.*

She closed her hand upon the amulet, gripping it tightly, driving back the thralldom slightly.

Willing her arm to move, with tiny jerking motions she inched her empty hand downward, fingers extended, straining to reach the sword lying at her side. Sweat beaded on her brow, and she ground her teeth with the effort, all the time sweet blackness sucking at her mind. At last she touched the jade grip and managed to close her fingers 'round, and her very soul wept at what she was about to do, her mother's voice echoing in her mind—"It has a Truename . . . it draws strength and energy and *life* . . . a terrible price . . . mortals may lose . . . years from their span . . . years . . ."*—yet had she any choice?*

"Dúnami," *her voice whispered, Truenaming the sword, and suddenly she was filled with a burst of strength, of energy, of* life, *and could* move! *And a pale blue light streamed outward from the blade, piercing through the unnatural blackness, and she could* see!

And something shrilled thinly.

"This sword of hers," said Noddy, "it seems like a terrible fine weapon t'me."

"Terrible, indeed," said Aravan, "for it stole years from all mortals within its range. Riatha yet bears appalling guilt for having had to use it, though she had no choice."

As they pondered these words, Binkton asked, "What about Halíd? Where is he now?"

"Dead," replied Aravan.

"Dead? Oh, my," said Pipper.

"We gauged Dúnamis took some twenty years of life from the mortals nearby, and though the Realmsman was in his early thirties when we arrived at the well, he was as a man in his fifties when he left it." Aravan paused a moment in concentration. "It was some thirty years ago when he and Tuon and Silverleaf slew the creature, and he died some seventeen years after."

"Oh, my," said Pipper again, "that sword is indeed terrible."

"Indeed," said Aravan. "Terrible."

"Yes," said Aylis, "but had those years not been taken when you and your party were first at the well, then all of you would be dead."

"Even so, my love, Halíd died well before his time."

A momentary silence fell over them all, but then Aylis turned to Aravan, tears springing to her eyes. "Oh, love, I just realized, Lady Faeril had years taken from her, and that means she too will—" Aylis leaned against Aravan and said no more.

"Indeed, *chieran,* indeed," whispered the Elf as he stroked her hair.

Again silence fell over them all, and then Pipper whispered to Binkton, "Well, at least the wyrm is dead, and the well safe once more."

Even as the last of the trio emerged from the shaft, far below and unheard by them, one of the large, bulbous shapes on the wall cracked and split, and out from it something unfolded, its sucker-like mouth blindly questing in hunger. There came a soft splash as it fell into the water, and, following the trail of the taint swirling 'round, the creature fastened upon the remains of its hermaphroditic parent and began to sing and feed. And weeks from that moment, when it had finished consuming all the pieces of the hacked-up corpse, it would one by one break open the other nodules along the wall and feed upon its siblings.

4

Tokens

"Tuon and Vanidar were right," declared Dokan.

"Right about what?" asked Tarly, cocking an eye at the Dwarf.

"They should have thought to bring along some Châkka to aid in the hunt for the wyrm," said Dokan. "Then Silverleaf would not have had to blaze a trail. Besides, had Châkka been on that venture, there would have been no question as to whether arrow, spear, or sword slew the thing."

"No question?" asked Nikolai.

"No question," replied Dokan.

"Then which of those three would have been the one to do the wyrm in?" asked Noddy.

"None of those three," said Dokan. "Instead it would have been a Châk axe that slew it."

Fat Jim roared in laughter, joined by the others. And when Dokan huffed in offense, Fat Jim managed to choke out, "Ah, me, Dokan, but the Dwarves' tall-standing pride in their prowess towers well above their own Dwarven height." Then he began laughing again, and Dokan's beard quivered in indignation, which brought on more laughter from all.

At this uproar of noise, Vex raised her head and looked about, seeking signs of danger. Tiny Aylissa stood and stroked the fox and soothed her, and Vex went adoze again. Then the Pysk took a stance before them all and, fists on hips, said, "We have all seen

Drimma in action, and I for one believe Dokan is right." She turned to Dokan, and her features shifted into an exaggerated pout and, in a voice to match she said, *"Châkka shok, Châkka cor."* Then she broke into giggles, and once again all the others roared. And even Dokan began to smile . . . then laugh . . . then howl.

When the laughter finally died down, Binkton said, "Dokan has a point, though. Dwarves would have come in handy, what with that maze and all." He turned to Pipper. "But y'know, Pip, Warrows would have been quite handy, too. I mean, after all, we seem able to see fairly well through spellcast darkness."

"We can?" said Pipper.

"Well, sure. I mean, see here, Aylissa's shadow is spellcast, and—"

"No it isn't," said Aylissa. "It's a natural thing with us Pysks."

"Mages would call it <wild magic>," said Aylis, looking down at the tiny Fox Rider.

"Yes, yes, of course," said Binkton, waving a hand of dismissal. "What I mean is that Warrows can see through 'magical darkness,' and I'll just bet that we could have seen through the wyrm's spellcast darkness, too."

"Weren't you listening to the story, Bink?" said Pipper. "It was Gwylly who *did* look through the wyrmcast blackness and catch sight of that terrible creature in just barely enough time to warn Riatha."

"Oh, right," said Binkton, frowning. Then he brightened. "W'll anyway, Warrows would have been right good for Halíd and the others to have had on their mission to see through that gloom. I mean, after all, during the Winter War we were the ones who saw best through the Dimmendark."

"Yar," said Noddy. "And a Warrow took care of Modru, too"—he glanced at Bink—"or so it is I hear."

"On two occasions, Noddy, it was a Warrow who proved to be Modru's undoing," said Aravan. "Once in the Great War of the Ban, and then again in the Winter War."

"That's us Warrows, all right," said Pipper, a look of satisfaction on his face. "Took care of Modru twice, when others couldn't even beat him once."

Aravan shook his head. "You overreach, wee one, for others have defeated Modru as well."

"Oh, yeah?" said Binkton. "Who?"

"Dalavar Wolfmage, for one," said Aravan. "Thrice altogether he faced Modru and thrice he bested him."

"Oh, well, that was a Mage fight," said Binkton, dismissively, "whereas we Warrows are just common folk."

"Hah!" said Aylis. "About as common as fleas on a dog, would you say? Fleas you are, perhaps, but common, nay. Rather you are a quite unique folk, linchpins in many a strife."

"W'll, I'll admit we seem to— No, wait! What I meant to say all along is that no one else ever defeated Modru in war," declared Binkton.

"Nay, my friend, thou art mistaken," said Aravan. "Not only did Dalavar best Modru on two of the three occasions he faced him during the Great War of the Ban, but the Elves defeated Modru in war as well, though all was decided in a single battle there in the streets of Duellin."

"Duellin?" asked Pipper.

"A city on Atala," said Aravan, "now gone beneath the sea."

"Ah, Kapitan," said Nikolai, "you must tell. Elves and Modru: they fight in no-longer city on no-longer isle, eh? You were there in fight?"

"Nay," said Aravan. "I was not. Yet some years after, when I was planning to build the *Eroean,* I went to the smitheries of Duellin seeking a recipe for a hull paint to ward away barnacles. It was the best of the smiths I had gone to see, and not only did he give me the formula, he spoke of that struggle when I asked, for he was there."

" 'Oo wos 'e?" asked Noddy.

"Dwynfor," said Aravan.

"Dwynfor?" said Dokan. "The weapons-maker? The famous Elven smith? He who forges weapons of power?"

"Aye," replied Aravan. "The same."

"And you talked with him?"

"I did."

"Would that some of the Châkka smiths could do the same."

"They can," said Aravan.

"But I thought that he had gone down with Atala when it sank beneath the sea," said Dokan. "You mean he survived?"

"He did. When Karak exploded and Atala went down into the

depths, Dwynfor was upon Adonar, and the Sundering kept him there until just ten years agone, when the ways between the Planes were restored."

"Ah," said Dokan. "Then we Châkka must arrange to see Dwynfor, for we would learn from him how to forge weapons of power."

Aravan shook his head. "Nay, my friend, he cannot teach thee, for Dwynfor himself knows not the manner 'tis done."

"What?" said Dokan. "Then how—?"

Aravan gestured at the Pysk and said, "Just as the Mages name Fox Rider shadow-gathering as <wild magic>, so, too, into that realm falls that which Dwynfor does."

"How so?" asked Aylissa, frowning.

"Dwynfor told me this: he seems entranced when he creates a special weapon, and he has little memory of doing so. He knows not why it happens, but occasionally, when he is at the forge, he loses all track of time and place. And when the forging is done and he sees what he has made, sometimes he knows the properties of such, at other times not."

"Magic swords? Does he make magic swords?" asked Pipper. "Like in the legends?"

"I would not name them 'magic,' Pip. Instead, they are 'special.' "

"Magic or special," said Pipper, "did he ever make swords like those named in the legends?"

Aravan nodded. "Three, if not more."

"Three?"

"Aye. He was entranced when he forged Bane and Bale—a sword and a long-knife with gemstones embedded in the blades, gemstones which glow when Foul Folk and other fell beasts are near. These weapons were given to Gildor Goldbranch, and they served him well. Yet during the Winter War, Gildor gave over the long-knife to—"

"To Tuckerby Underbank, a Warrow," blurted out Binkton. "It was the one called Bane!"

"Just so, Bink," said Aravan. "Just so."

"You named three, um, special swords: what was the other one?"

"'Twas Dúnamis, the blade given over to Reín but now borne by her *irrin* Riatha."

"*Irrin?*" asked Wooly.

"Daughter," replied Aravan. "Riatha is Reín's daughter, and Reín gifted the blade to Riatha when she came unto Mithgar."

"This is th' sword what cut th' wyrm at th' well?" asked Noddy.

"Aye. 'Twas the very same."

"What else did he make?" said Pipper. "—Other magic weapons, I mean."

Aravan sighed. "I say again, Pip, I would not name them magic. Special, yes; magic, no."

"But didn't you say <wild magic> is involved?"

Aravan nodded and looked at Aylis and smiled. "That's what the Mages say. Tell them, *chier,* what is this so-named <wild magic>."

" 'Tis a form of"—Aylis paused, searching for a way to explain it—"manipulating <fire>."

"<Fire>?" asked Pip. "What is <fire>?"

Aylis sighed. "Mayhap you would call it aethyr, but by any name it is the energy that permeates all. We of Magekind use some of our own meager store of aethyr to influence the greater, and the greater in turn cascades to become the feats you name magic, rather like casting a pebble just so, to shape and control a landslide."

Pip looked at Bink and shrugged, and Bink turned up his hands and shook his head.

Fat Jim took a swig of his brandy and said, "Lady Aylis, let's just say we don't quite catch your drift, but go on and tell us more about this here <wild magic> and such."

Again Aylis sighed, then pressed on: "<Wild magic>: we of Magekind understand it not. At times it is a power that comes and goes unpredictably, such as the redes spoken by Rael Crystalseer or the visions of Arin Flameseer. At other times it is an expected talent, mayhap a gift, such as the shadow-gathering of the Fox Riders. Yet <wild magic> always seems a power brought to bear by those not of Magekind, but every other Race instead, be they Hidden Ones, Elves, Dwarves, Baeron, Utruni, Dragons, Warrows, even Humans."

At the mention of Utruni, Aylissa fingered a small glittering stone on a silver chain about her neck, and it seemed as if she would speak, but Dokan said, "Dragons? Dragons use <wild magic>?"

"Mayhap," replied Aylis, "for they have the power to see the hidden, the invisible, the unseen, and it seems they can sense things afar. We of Magekind understand it not, and so we name it <wild magic>."

Dokan nodded in accord, but Pipper, his eyes wide in wonder, said, "What about Warrows? You included us in your accounting, but what <wild magic> do we have?"

Aylis sighed. "Oh, Pip, you know it yourself. 'Tis the ability to see through spellcast or <wild magic> darkness."

"Oh," said Pipper, disappointed. "Is that all? I didn't think of that being anything special. I was hoping for something, um, extraordinary." He sighed, then turned to Aravan and said, "Well, magic or special or whatever, what else did Dwynfor make along those, um, <wild magic> lines?"

Aravan shrugged and grinned. "I know not his catalogue, Pip, yet these I do know he spoke of: Black Galgor the spear; the axe *Eborane,* Sylva for Dark Reaver, though the Drimma now name it—"

"—*Drakkalan:* Dark Shedder," said Dokan. "Used by Brega at the Iron Tower. It clove right through the haul chain."

"Indeed," said Aravan, taking a sip of brandy.

"Go on," said Pipper. "What other weapons of power were made there in Duellin?"

Aravan smiled. "There was the blade *Talarn,* Sylva for Steelheart, though it is told that the smith Gilian made that blade, used by Galen at the Iron Tower as well—"

"If we're talking about the Iron Tower," said Binkton, "what about the Red Quarrel that Tuck used against the Myrkenstone? Yar, that and the Atalar Blade. It is told that both the long-knife and the quarrel were found in the tomb of Othran the Seer."

Aravan shook his head. "As to the long-knife, I cannot say, but the quarrel mayhap 'twas Gilian who fashioned it, for 'tis said she favored archers; Silverleaf claims his bow was her work."

"Th' same bow Silverleaf used against th' wyrm?" asked Noddy.

"Aye," said Aravan.

"Coo," breathed Noddy.

"What of the Rage Hammer?" said Dokan. "Did Dwynfor or Gilian fashion it?"

"Nay," said Aravan. "Dwynfor believes that the Kammerling—which the Drimma name Rage Hammer—was forged by one of thy folk: the First Durek. Dwynfor also believes Durek as well crafted the Horn of Narok—though for both hammer and horn, 'tis said Durek himself knew not how he did it nor did he know their purpose."

Dokan furrowed his brow. "We Châkka always thought that Durek the First made them both, yet that history is lost in the ages. We also believe that it was Durek who gave over the Rage Hammer unto the Utruni for safekeeping."

"What about the horn?" asked Pipper.

"Oh, Pip, you know all about that trump," said Binkton. "It's the Horn of the Reach, a clarion given to Patrel by Vidron, during the Winter War."

"Oh, I know *that,*" said Pipper. "But what I don't know is what did Durek *do* with it?" He looked to Dokan for an answer.

Dokan shrugged and said, "Durek hid away the Horn of Narok in the depths of Drimmen-deeve, though later it was borne unto the holt of Blackstone." Dokan paused a moment, then growled. "Where it was safe until Sleeth came, and then Foul Elgo."

"Thou dost name him Foul Elgo," said Aravan, "yet others name him a hero and call him Sleeth's Doom."

"Pah!" spat Dokan. "Elgo the Thief, Elgo the Japer, Elgo the Treasure Stealer we name him."

Aylis said, "Yet, Dokan, because Elgo did go unto Blackstone, the horn made its way back unto Drimmen-deeve where it found its final use."

"Bah!" said Dokan. "Tokens of power have a way of fulfilling their own destiny, and Thief Elgo or no, the horn was fated to come unto Kraggen-cor when needed."

"Let us not pick at this old wound, Dokan," said Aravan. "Instead let me say that in the forging of these fated tokens, Dwynfor weens that some higher power directs such smiths as himself and Durek in their crafting, and then the higher power withdraws, leaving the smith with little or no memory of doing it and no knowledge of how 'twas done, and only now and again knowing what the weapon might do or who should bear it."

Dokan nodded. "I can believe Adon guided Durek in the fashioning of the Rage Hammer and the Horn of Narok, for both were used here on Mitheor in Adon's struggle against Gyphon."

"Adon? Adon directed Durek?" asked Pipper. "But I thought Elwydd was the patron of the Dwarves. Why wouldn't Elwydd guide Durek's hand in the forging?"

Dokan made a gesture of negation. "We believe that Elwydd is a bringer of peace, and so I deem she would not use Durek so."

"But both of those did indeed bring peace, for both were used to end a war," said Binkton.

The Pysk shook her head. "I side with Dokan here. Elwydd is gentle, and both the horn and the Kammerling are—or were—things of violence."

They fell silent for a moment, and then Tarly looked at Aylis and said, "Mayhap that's what *all* <wild magic> is: the power of gods working through lesser beings."

"That is one possibility," said Aylis, "especially for those sporadic and unpredictable manifestations. However, that does not explain such things as the Fox Rider ability to gather shadow, for that is done at the will of the wielder."

"Oh, that," said the Pysk. "You said it before, Aylis: it's merely a gift Elwydd gave to us."

Tarly smiled. "Even so, even though it is manifested at the will of the wielder, still I stand by my guess concerning the nature of <wild magic>: it is something that comes from the gods."

"I t'ink all t'ings come from gods," said Nikolai.

Again they lapsed into silence, but then Pipper said, "Well, this all started when we were talking about the defeat of Modru in the city of Duellin at the hands of the Elves." He turned to the Dwarf. "I mean, smiths and such are all well and good, Dokan, but me, I'd like to hear of the battle."

Aravan smiled at the Warrow. "Ah, but Pipper, 'twas smiths and such at the heart of things."

"Really?"

"Indeed."

"Then go on, Captain. Tell us."

"First," said Wooly, standing and unstoppering the decanter of brandy, "time for a refill."

He replenished the glasses all 'round, including the Pysk's tiny thimble, and when the steersman resumed his seat, then did Aravan turn to the others and say, "Would someone care to make a toast?"

Fat Jim cleared his throat. "I think you put it right the first time, Captain." He raised his glass and said, "To absent friends."

To absent friends.

Tarly poured a small libation once more into the cold hearth and whispered a prayer to Garlon, and when all were well settled, then did Aravan begin:

"It was back in the early years of the First Era, when Modru came in a great black galley unto the harbor of Duellin. In those days, though none knew him for the monster he truly was, still he was shunned; even so, he walked into the city unimpeded. . . ."

"Adon," exclaimed Tall James down on the docks, jumping from his seat on one of the pilings and gazing out to sea, "look at wot comes into th' harbor."

Ruddy turned and looked to where Tall James pointed. "Huah. Wot d'y' think she be?"

Like a monstrous black spider creeping toward a paralyzed prey, a great ebon galley, her banks of oars dipping and pulling and rising to swing back to dip and pull again and again, came bearing westward out from the ocean and into the bay and across the waters toward the docks of Duellin.

"I dunno," said Tall James, "but wote're she be, I don't like th' looks o' her."

"Me, too, I don't like 'er looks, but there is this: if she's got cargo aboard, we gon' t'elp offlade 'er? Might be a pretty penny involved."

"Might not, too," replied Tall James.

"Wull, I says we waits and sees," said Ruddy.

"Right. But if there be somethin' smells wrong, I says we amble off."

Ruddy nodded at Tall James' words, and they continued to watch the great dark ship, her black sails hanging lank on the breathless day, row toward the quays, the banks of oars dipping, pulling, rising, and swinging back to dip and pull again.

On she came and on, until finally a sigil could be seen centered on her dark foresail: a ring of fire on black.

"Oh, lor'," said Ruddy, "she be from Gron."

"Gron?" said Tall James. "How d'y' know?"

"Th' circle o' fire on black," said Ruddy. "I've 'eard tell o' it. They say nought good'll come o' any who'd 'ave dealings wi' them as is from Gron."

"Wull then, if she be that bad, should we be considerin' offladin' her, assumin' there's offladin' t'be done?" said Tall James.

"I don' want no part o' 'er," said Ruddy. "I says we hie out o' 'ere."

Tall James frowned, then shook his head. "Nar. Not yet, Ruddy. 'Stead let's wait and see wot's wot. Then if need be we'll run."

Onward came the ebon ship, and now they could hear the beat of a drum, marking the stroke of the oars. And she angled toward an empty slip, but kept her forward way. And shortly ere reaching the slot, with the rattle of the drum and then a single beat, the banks of oars backed water . . . and another single beat and again the oars backed water . . . and backed water again and again, and the galley slowed and slowed to finally slide into the space between the piers even as the oars were haled in through the ports.

A handful of swarthy Men stood adeck—Kistanians, Hyrinians, Jûngarians, or the like they seemed, yet as to which, neither Tall James nor Ruddy could say. Two of the crew leapt onto the portside dock as the craft eased in, and bow and stern hawsers were cast to them. The aft line was whipped 'round a piling to bring the ship to a halt, the craft to ponderously swing and thump against the great jute bolsters. The fore line was then wrapped to snug the ship to the pier, leaving just enough slack to account for the rising and falling of tides.

The crew set a footway between ship and wharf, and then drew back as a single being appeared on the deck, and both Ruddy and Tall Jim sucked air in between clenched teeth.

Man-height, he was, yet no Man was this, but a Mage instead. He was clad all in black and a black cloak hung from his shoulders. Black gauntlets covered his hands and forearms, spikes jutting out from his fists and along the outside edge of his wrists, and he walked in iron-shod boots. Yet most disconcerting of all, he was masked with an iron-beaked helm, like the snouted face of a gargoyle of legend, and only his eyes could be seen, and they did imperiously glare. He stepped from the great black galley and onto the docks, and up from the harbor he strode and through the unlading area with its warehouses, and toward the high ramparts of the walled city beyond, its massive gate standing open. And more than one eye followed him, and more than one person shrank away as he passed, while others fled down the streets ahead, as into the city he trod.

He stopped not at all to ask directions, for it seemed he knew where he was headed, though as far as anyone could recall, such a person as he, masked as he was, had not been in Duellin before.

Along the cobbles and past establishments he strode: past those of boatwrights and shipwrights and sail-makers and other such shipfitting crafts; past inns with names such as the Safe Harbor, the

Fouled Anchor, the Fair Wind, and the like, every one of which catered to merchantmen and sailors and captains all; past gaudy bordellos, where painted ladies leaning on balconies drew back as he stalked by below; past the shops of jewelers and leather-workers and weavers and other skilled craftsmen of all manner did he stride, as well as beyond dwellings, some palatial, some modest, some mean. And he ignored all until he came into the district where he was headed—the famed armories of Duellin at the far western edge of the city. Here were forged swords and axes and other such weaponry, as well as shields and helms and plate and chain and the many other accoutrements of war, all without parallel. Yet it was to but one of these foundries that the being in black was bound: the forges of Dwynfor the Elf, a smith beyond compare.

Into the establishment the Mage strode, the walls weapon-hung, the shelved counters laden with more, and arms and armor on standing racks were here and there displayed.

Behind one counter sat a young Dara, an Elven child not yet in her maturity, but rather in her midteens. Dressed in a pale blue jerkin with a skirt to match, with her flaxen hair falling 'round her narrow face as she studied a tome before her, she was completely absorbed in the flowing script.

The Magus stepped opposite her and set a large pouch down unto the countertop. With sapphire-blue eyes the Dara looked up at the visage at hand and could not suppress a gasp.

"Sir?" she managed, glancing away so as not to peer into the enshadowed harsh gaze behind the dreadful iron mask.

"I would see your master Dwynfor," the Magus whispered, his tone chill to the bone.

The Dara shivered as these words icily fell into the now cold air between them. Even so she plucked up her courage and said, "I can help thee if it is a sword or such thou dost require, for I—"

"Your master, I said," hissed the Mage, and she knew behind the mask he glared.

"Sir, I am fully cognizant of my sire's—"

The Magus smashed his black-gauntleted fist to the counter, the Elven maid to start.

"Did you not hear me? I would have Dwynfor!"

"I am Dwynfor," came a soft voice from behind, and the Magus turned to see a silver-haired Elf, though in spite of his argent mane by no means did he look aged. He was slender and tall and wore grey leather leggings and black boots with a silver-buckled black belt to match, as well as a grey silken shirt. His eyes were a sapphire blue, just like those of his *irrin.*

"I have come to purchase blades from you, Dwynfor—axes, swords, lances, pikes and the like—enough to equip an army." And the Magus opened the pouch and poured out a sparkling cascade of diamonds, cut and polished all.

The young Dara's eyes widened at this treasured spill, yet she glanced at the set of her sire and knew him to ill favor any dealings with this being, no matter the offered fee.

"Thou art Modru, art thou not?" said Dwynfor.

"Yes," replied the Magus. "I am Modru of Gron."

"Take thy business elsewhere, Mage, for I will sell thee nought."

Modru pulled himself up to his full height. "Sell me nought?"

"Aye, nought, Modru of Gron, for thy character precedes thee, and I will not further thine aims, no matter what they be."

Modru's gauntleted left hand twisted into a clawlike shape, and he raised it toward Dwynfor.

"I would not, were I thee," said Dwynfor softly, and he gestured up and 'round.

Modru looked, and on catwalks above stood some half-dozen Elven archers, arrows nocked, bows drawn.

"Bah!" spat Modru. "With one gesture I could slay all."

"Mayhap 'tis true, mayhap not," said Dwynfor, "for e'en an aimed arrow loosed from a dead hand yet will find the mark, and there are six now aimed at thee. Regardless, whether 'tis we who live or die, or thee, thou wouldst not gain the weapons thou dost seek."

Trembling with fury, Modru stood long moments, his enraged stare locked with Dwynfor's calm gaze.

"Pah!" Modru said, and turned and scooped the diamonds back into his pouch, and spun on his heel and stalked out.

When the Magus was gone, Dwynfor signalled the archers to stand down even as sudden tears flooded his eyes. Brushing the wetness from his cheeks, he stepped 'round the counter and took his *irrin* in his embrace, and she could feel him tremble.

"*Athir,* art thou well?" she asked.

"I am now, Elinda. I am now."

"*Athir,*" said the Dara, "is it true that he could have slain all with but a single gesture?"

"Mayhap, Elinda. Mayhap. Yet I ween he would have been feathered to the fletchings e'en as he brought death unto all those of us standing here."

"Oh, my," said Elinda, shivering.

Dwynfor clasped his child even tighter and said, " 'Twas a terrible risk I took, for I did not care to hazard thy life, *Irrin,* yet I gambled that he would not gamble with his."

"How didst thou know to have the archers at hand, *Athir?*"

"Word came running before him, Elinda," said Dwynfor. "And I did suspect what he had come for."

"But, *Athir,* didst thou not see the treasure offered? Will not someone sell him what he wants?"

"I think not, *Irrin,* not here in Duellin at any rate, for I did send runners to all other armorers and smiths in the city, especially did I send Fanir unto Gilian, for like me, she occasionally makes a weapon of power."

Elinda shivered. "Oh, but I do hope my *jarin* runs not into Modru, for the Magus is a dreadful thing; he makes my very essence cower."

Dwynfor kissed her on the forehead. "Modru is an evil creature, *Irrin;* 'tis meet thou dost see him so."

To weapons-maker after weapons-maker and armorer after armorer did Modru go, and none would yield up to him ought, and enraged and cursing and vowing vengeance, back unto his black galley did he storm, a bagful of gemstones in hand.

And Tall James and Ruddy watched as he stalked aboard and lashed out at a nearby deckhand, felling the Man with one backhanded blow.

The crew cast off and used oars to thrust away from the slip, and with the sail yet hanging lank in the breathless day, away did the craft bear, the beat of a drum marking the stroke, with oars dipping, pulling, rising, swinging back to dip and pull again.

Aravan paused in his telling to take a sip of brandy, and none said ought as he did so, though Pipper made a motion as if to unbutton his lip, but Binkton glared him down.

Setting his glass aside, Aravan continued: "Some centuries later, when nearly all in the city had forgotten the visit of the Black Mage, a great, crimson-sailed Rover fleet and one black galley rode the tide into the harbor on a cloud-covered, moonless night, and they offladed in the dark. By morning the citizenry of Duellin could see a horde of invaders set to fall upon them: a throng of Foul Folk as well as a multitude of Men from Jûng, and with them they had brought a dreadful siege engine: the great ram Whelm to batter for entrance, its mighty iron head shaped like a monstrous, clenched left fist mounted on an enormous wooden beam, all covered by a brass- and iron-clad canopy to protect those within. And driven by huge Trolls, toward the massive gates of the city trundled that dreadful feartoken. . . ."

Boom! . . . thundered the ram. *Boom!* . . . 'gainst the gate. *Boom!* . . . hammered the mighty iron fist, knocking for entry. *Boom!* and *Boom!* and *Boom!* The gates of Duellin juddering with every blow. Arrows and fire rained down upon the siege-engine canopy, yet the cladding warded all away.

Among the Men and Elves on the ramparts above stood Vanidar, his silver-handled white-bone bow in hand, yet he withheld his shafts, for no target was presented. Only the Troll-driven ram was present, the bulk of the invaders standing well back, for it seemed they had not with them any other siege machines—no towers, no scaling ladders, no catapults. The ram was all.

Boom! . . .

Boom! . . .

Boom! . . .

"Oil!" called Railan, commander of the city watch. "We need oil under the gate, to burn them from below."

Boom! . . .

Swiftly a team was dispatched, a vat of oil fetched and overturned to flow beneath the gate, a torch planted, a whoosh of fire gushing under . . .

Boom! . . .

Boom! . . .

. . . but iron plates set in mud spread upon the cobbles by Rûcks fended the running fire aside. . . .

And—

Boom! . . .

—driven by the awesome power of the Trolls—

Boom! . . .

—the gate began to splinter—

Boom! . . .

Boom! . . .

—as the monstrous Ogrus drove the great iron fist into the portal again and again.

Boom! . . .

Boom! . . .

Boom! . . .

"Caltrops!" called Vanidar above the cracking and splitting. "We'll need caltrops to ward away the Trolls."

"That and fire," said Railan, "else we are fordone."

"Shall I take a party to fire the ships?" asked Vanidar.

"Nay," replied Railan. "Nay, 'tis best we meet them here at our very gates and send them running than to lay waste to their ships, for I would rather drive these invaders back across the sea than strand them on our isle to roam and rape and pillage."

Now the sound of the ram began to change, for the gate was giving way, the ram hammering through.

"We'll need set traps for them, the Ogrus," said Fallor, "for they will soon be in the city."

"Go!" said Railan. "Take as many defenders as thou dost need."

With a massive *whoom!* the gates fell inward, torn from their hinges by Whelmram, and with a blatting of brazen horns and yawling howls, the invading army charged—Rûcks, Hlôks, Jûngarians, Rovers, and a gang of Men from Hyree.

A sleet of arrows flew from the walls, and Men and Spawn died screaming, but black-shafted arrows hissed in return, and Elves and Men fell victim as well.

And with horns blaring and the horde howling, the multitude poured forward, the invaders racing toward the sundered gate. And the Trolls from Whelmram stepped through, only to be met by a rain of burning oil from above. Screaming and slapping at the flames clinging to their scales and throwing off their blazing garments, the Trolls fled away from the portal to escape the conflagration blazing in the gap, the bulk of them running toward the black galley, though some Ogrus had charged into the city and were now loose in the streets.

And still, horns blowing, the howling invaders rushed forward and toward the breach, swart Rûcks and Hlôks and Men of Jûng and Hyree and Rovers of Kistan to run through the flames and through the gap, swinging cudgels and scimitars, war hammers and sickles. And they were met by shouting Men and Elves with long pikes and gleaming swords, poleaxes and brutal maces. Battle cries and oaths and death screams rent the air. Rûcks were slain and Hlôks, along with Hyrinians and Kistanians and Jûngarians, as well as Men and Elves of Duellin.

And back into the mêlée came the Ogrus, twelve feet tall, swinging great warbars, killing invaders and defenders alike, and neither blade nor arrow harmed their stonelike hides.

"Fall back!" cried Railan, and he signalled to Imondar, third in command, to sound a silver horn, the clarion call piercing the air, and the gate and walls above were abandoned.

"Now we fight from the rooftops above and the streets below," he said to Vanidar as they retreated, "where they will pay dearly for every step gained."

"As will we, my friend," said Vanidar. "As will we."

And together they faded into the byways of Duellin, where the battle would be won or lost.

While back at the torn-down gate, the teeming invaders poured through.

And behind them all and unseen by the retreating defenders came a black-clad Magus masked with an iron-beaked helm, its likeness the snouted face of a gargoyle. 'Twas Modru, come for his revenge, and only his eyes could be seen, and they did blaze with triumph.

"Coo, now," said Noddy, "you say it was centuries after, yet this here Modru still held a grudge?"

"Indeed," said Aravan. "I ween he never forgot even an insignificant slight or a sign of disrespect nor any affront, whether small or middling or ought greater . . . especially a defeat."

"Yar," said Pipper. "I mean we Warrows defeated him in the Great War of the Ban and—"

"You Warrows?" growled Dokan. "Defeated him single-handedly, I suppose."

"Well, we *did* have a bit of help," mumbled Pipper.

"Ha!" barked Fat Jim. "Dokan, I apologize. Here I said that your Dwarven pride towered far over your stature, but it seems you have been greatly out-towered by this pip-squeak here." Fat Jim broke into roaring laughter, and others smiled or laughed with him, though Aylissa the Pysk joined them not.

"I don't like that name 'pip-squeak,' " she said, standing, her fists on her hips. "It's quite demeaning."

Fat Jim immediately stopped laughing. "Ooo, now, Liss, don't be getting out those tiny arrows of yours. I didn't send that name your way."

"Well, I'd rather you use something other than 'pip-squeak,' " she replied. "Nor do I think"—she glanced at Vex—" 'runt of the litter' is very nice either. Instead, were I to describe Pipper"—the corners of her mouth twitched—"I think I would call him a 'trifle.' "

The Pysk broke into giggles, and Pipper, feigning outrage, said, "Is this a tiny pot calling a bigger kettle black?"

Now all roared.

When calm reigned, Binkton said, "No matter the claim of my cousin, I know that Modru did hold a long grudge against the Warrows. I mean, after the Great War of the Ban, he held onto his rancor against us for some four thousand years in all, and during the Winter War he diverted an entire Horde—ten thousand Foul Folk—to destroy the Boskydells."

"Wull, if he held a grudge against you Warrows for four thousand years," said Noddy, "then a few centuries to gain revenge against th' folk o' Duellin don't seem all that long, now, does it?"

"Not at all," said Pipper, cocking an eye of superiority toward Fat Jim. "Not bloody long at all."

"Talk fine," said Nikolai, "but I want to hear Kapitan's story."

"It's not my story, Nikolai," said Aravan, "but Dwynfor's instead."

"Your story, his story, it no matter, Kapitan, edge of my chair not comfortable, an' I would hear rest so I can sit back once more."

Aravan chuckled and held up a hand. "All right, Nikolai, I would not have thee the least bit distressed."

Aravan took a sip from his snifter, and then said, "Hard-fought was the battle, every street, every building, every stride yielded in nought but furious struggle. Even so, the *Spaunen* and Kistanians and men of Jûng and Hyree slowly gained sway, for even though they had been slaughtered by the hundreds, still it seems they far outnumbered the defenders of Duellin. . . ."

* * *

"The more we kill, the more it seems there are," said Vanidar.

"Aye," replied Railan. "It is a thing that seems unright."

At that moment Fallor came panting up to the roof of the building where Vanidar and Railan sped arrows into the masses below.

"We've eliminated the last of the Trolls," Fallor reported. "Took three out with fire and the last with iron caltrops. Who would think the soles of their feet so tender? How goes the battle?"

"We are losing," gritted Railan. "They are too many."

"Too many? But I've seen hundreds fall."

"Aye, yet it seems they keep coming."

Vanidar and Railan flew more arrows into the mob below, and then Railan said, "Something arcane is at work here. Vanidar, Fallor, I would that ye find the cause."

Vanidar frowned. "Arcane? Dost thou deem they are aided by a Mage?"

"I know not," said Railan. "Yet I would have ye twain see whence these multitudes arise."

A runner came bearing a fresh box of arrows. "My Lord Railan, make each and every one of these count, for the supply runs low." With that he rushed away.

As Vanidar replenished his quiver, he looked at Fallor and said, "If aught of Magekind is with them, he will be hindward of their advance."

Fallor nodded and took up arrows for himself, then said, "Let us see."

Making their way back in the direction of the sundered gate, together they crossed roof after roof, leaping over alleyways, climbing down to cross streets, and then gaining the rooftops once more. They had not gone more than a handful of thoroughfares when they saw surrounded by a warding gang of Hyrinians a black-clad, iron-masked figure. And he stood amid slain invaders and held a hand on high, something darkly glittering gripped within, while arcane words spewed forth from his mouth, and corpses rose up from among the dead and took up their weapons and marched into the battle once more.

Vanidar gasped and whispered to Fallor, "Aie! *This* is why we make no headway."

"What is it he has in his hand?" asked Fallor.

Vanidar, ever keen of sight, looked long and finally said, "It is a gemstone of a sort, I ween a great black diamond."

"Hoy, now," blurted Noddy. "You mean a gem loike Gelvin's Doom?"

"Noddy," said Aravan, "it *was* Gelvin's Doom."

"Bu-but," protested Noddy, "just how did they get it out o' Death's crown?"

"Noddy, my lad, it never was in Death's crown. The tale thou wert told wasn't exactly the truth. Oh, Gelvin did steal a gem, all right—a great black diamond—but he did so here on Mithgar, and not on the Demon Plane. And he died with it atop a mountain. Somehow, years later, Modru came into possession of it, and with it he raised the dead."

"Ooo," said Pipper, awed, but Noddy exclaimed, "I *knew* it had somethin' t'do with death. That part o' my story was roight."

"Aye," said Aravan. "That part of thy tale indeed was correct, for through it Modru did cast his spells, and the dead did rise up and walk. . . ."

Vanidar set an arrow to string and took aim at the Black Mage. *Thunn* . . . he loosed, *shsss* . . . sped the arrow, but lo! it veered to strike harmlessly unto the cobbles below.

And Modru looked up and laughed, while a hail of black-shafted arrows flew up in response, as Vanidar and Fallor threw themselves flat, the missiles to *zizzz* . . . overhead like hornets in flight.

Vanidar nocked another shaft, and rose to one knee and let fly again . . . only to see his arrow jink away in midflight to strike the street below.

Once more he threw himself flat as the return arrows hissed past.

"We'd better report to Railan and get some help," said Fallor.

Bellydown, Vanidar and Fallor slithered hindward, then, crouching, made their way across the roof until they could safely stand and run. Back toward Railan's position they fled, leaping alleys, climbing down and darting across streets and climbing up again, only to discover that another great swath of the city had been lost to the invaders.

They found Railan a handful of streets farther west than where they last left him, for the defense had been battered that far hindward, and some two-thirds of the city lost.

" 'Tis Modru, I deem," reported Silverleaf. "Though I have never seen him ere now, assuming it is him—iron-masked and black-garbed as he is. A company of Hyrinians protect him, and I deem he is warded by a spell, for my arrows cannot strike him at all, but are somehow deflected away. He bears a great black gemstone, through which I ween he casts his spells. He raises the dead, Railan, and they come again into the fight. That is why their numbers diminish not. How can we defeat an army whose slain remain not dead?"

"Is there no Mage in Duellin to counter him?" asked Fallor.

"Nay," replied Railan. "None are here."

"What be his goal, thinkest thou?" asked Imondar. "Mayhap if we knew it, we could see a way to thwart him and his army of the slain."

"Vengeance is what he seeks," said Railan. "Vengeance for a refusal centuries past. That be what he seeks. Yet what he drives for are the armories of Duellin, to gain the weaponry there and to make slaves of the smiths and have them do his bidding."

"Then we must send them away," said Imondar.

" 'Tis already done," replied Railan. "They are the very reason Duellin exists and therefore to be protected above all. And so, along with those who are too young or too old to fight or those who are untrained, I commanded the smiths and armorers to ride for Darda Immer e're Modru's Horde came ashore. They will be safe in the Brightwood."

"Thinkest thou?" asked Vanidar. "Not I, for Modru will not be satisfied unless he has Dwynfor and Gilian and all the others in his grasp. And with that black gemstone of his, powered by the <fire> of our own slain, and an army of risen dead that we must kill over and again, he is all but unbeatable. Once more I ask, who can defeat an army none can permanently kill? With it he will not only conquer the city, but go on to capture the smiths as well."

"Nay, Silverleaf," said Railan. "Hast thou forgotten? There is an in-between in Darda Immer, and they can escape unto Adonar. And Modru would not dare follow them unto the High Plane, unto Adon's very own realm."

"He might if he has an ally therein," said Vanidar. "Recall, 'tis said that Gyphon Himself favors the Black Mages, and can we find no way to defeat Modru, I would not put ought past Dark Gyphon, even unto abetting an invasion of Adonar itself."

Railan sighed, and then said, "Mayhap thou art right, Silverleaf, but then again mayhap not. Regardless, we have a war to wage against the foe, though it seems even as we slay them, they are raised to fight again. Come, let us make a last stand at the armories, and then, if it comes to a time when all is lost, I will command a retreat out through the western posterns, and all will hie unto Darda Immer."

"I like not this plan, Railan," said Fallor, "yet I can think of no other."

"Why not kill the Mage?" said Vanidar.

"Didst thou not see thine own arrows fly astray?" said Fallor.

"Aye, but mayhap if enough of us loose shafts at him, he cannot deflect all. And if he does manage, then let a sufficient number rush him and slay him out of hand."

"Many will fall in such an attempt," said Railan.

"Have we any choice?" asked Vanidar.

"I think not," replied Railan. "Let us fall back unto the armories and gather those who will make the attempt."

Even as Vanidar and Railan and Fallor and Imondar retreated, onward came Modru's forces—Hlôks, Rûcks, Kistanians, Hyrinians, Jûngarians—the living and the risen dead, and they hammered their way toward the armories of Dwynfor and Gilian and other bladesmiths of renown. And behind strode Modru, a black gemstone in hand, and he took the <fire> of the dying defenders and used it to raise from the dead his own slain. And though some were beyond resurrection, still his forces numbered nigh that with which he had started, though of Trolls he had none, for they would not come into clinging fire, nor step where iron caltrops were strewn. Even so, even though he was without these mighty engines of destruction, Modru cared not, for he knew he would triumph without them, for they had done the task he had set for them: the destruction of the massive gates of Duellin to let his conquering army within.

And the fighting was bitter—each alley, each street, each byway contested, each building a trap, each house a covert whence deadly missiles and savage forays issued.

Still, Modru's army advanced, a havoc of destruction in its wake, of corpses and fire and wrack.

And back fell the defenders and back, and still the battle raged on, though fully three-quarters of the city was lost as Modru pressed toward his goal.

And before the armories on the western fringe, Vanidar crouched on the cobbles, a circle of Men and Elves about him. "When we are certain as to Modru's approach, we twenty archers will take to the rooftops on either side of that street, while you fifty hand-to-hand fighters make ready to secrete yourselves away in flanking alleys and dwellings and shops. When the front of the battle passes us, then we set the ambuscade and wait for Modru. For those of ye on the roofs, when I loose my first shaft, ye will all then loose thy shafts as well. Again and again will we fly arrows at the Black Mage—at Modru—and mayhap one will win through. Mayhap with—"

"Silverleaf!" came a call, and Vanidar frowned.

"Silverleaf!" Again the call, this time closer, and Vanidar stood and peered in the direction whence it came even as the circle opened and Imondar passed within. Somewhat out of breath he said, "Dwynfor calls for thee."

"Dwynfor? But I thought he rode for Darda Immer."

"He did, yet he found himself at his forge, and he has made a weapon, an arrow, and he calls for thee."

"Mayhap something to kill Modru," said Fallor.

"Where is he?" asked Vanidar. "—Dwynfor, I mean."

"Yet at his forge," said Imondar.

Vanidar turned to Railan. "If I come not again . . ."

"I will see thy plan is carried out," said Railan.

Vanidar looked at the surrounding Men and Elves. "I wish ye well, and may Adon guide ye."

"You, too," said Bran, leader of the Men gathered.

Turning on his heel, bow in hand, Vanidar trotted away, heading for the forge of Dwynfor.

"I know not what it is for, what it will do, Silverleaf, only that it is meant for thee," said Dwynfor, his silver hair matted 'round his face from the sweat of metalworking, the look in his sapphire-blue eyes yet somewhat dazed.

Vanidar took up his bow and nocked the shaft and drew it full to his anchor point; the span from the raven-feather fletching to the iron head was exactly right. "Blunt though it is, I believe I know its purpose: 'tis to slay a Mage."

"Mayhap thou art right," said Dwynfor. "Yet if this arrow is a token of power, and I believe it is, know this: tokens of power have ways of fulfilling their own destinies, and if this one is meant to slay a Mage, then it will do so . . . unless it is wielded wrongly, in which case even a token of power can be thwarted, at least for a while."

"My bow was crafted by Gilian," said Vanidar. "This arrow by thee. Together they may fulfil that which they were meant to do."

"My hands did craft the arrow, Silverleaf, yet I was not present when 'twas done."

"As thou hast said ere now, my friend, when we were in our cups." Vanidar glanced in the direction of the fires, there where mayhem ruled. "Yet heed, now is no time to discuss the mysteries, for Duellin is falling, and we both have that which must be done: thou to leave the city ere Modru can come upon thee; I to see if I can stop him ere he has that chance."

Dwynfor nodded and gestured toward his smithery. "Out back in the alley my horse awaits."

Vanidar grinned. "As do the rooftops wait for me. Fare well, my friend. When this is over, *then* we shall discuss the enigmas of life."

They clasped hands and Vanidar turned and trotted across the street and clambered up and over the eaves above.

Watching him leave, "Adon be with thee, Silverleaf," whispered Dwynfor, then he turned and stepped back into the place where many things had been forged, perhaps none as important as that which Vanidar now bore.

Racing from rooftop to rooftop, Vanidar headed toward the clash and clangor of sword on scimitar, of axe on spear, of steel on steel, of cursing and shouting and wordless yells—all sounds of fury.

He came in sight of the bitter struggle, Men and Elves falling back, falling wounded, falling dead, yet reaving a toll even as they retreated.

Arrows flew, blades cut, and cudgels and maces and hammers smashed, spears pierced and lances stabbed, and struggles were hand to hand. Yet Vanidar passed beyond, then came unto those waiting to ambush Modru, came unto Railan and Imondar and Fallor and Bran, Vanidar pausing only long enough for Railan to point and say, "He is yon and comes, and we are ready."

On sped Vanidar alone, from roof to roof, until he saw the cluster of Hyrinians surrounding ebon-clad Modru. And Vanidar took station behind a chimney and waited and watched as the iron-masked Black Mage came on, raising the dead as he did so.

Vanidar nocked the iron-headed arrow, and stood with the bow down at his side, the shaft not yet drawn or aimed. And he waited, while Modru slowly neared, while a handful of streets hence death and slaughter reigned.

And Vanidar waited. . . .

. . . waited . . .

. . . waited . . .

. . . until at last Modru stood well within range just ahead.

Vanidar now lifted his silver-handled white-bone bow, made for him by Gilian, and drew the shaft crafted by Dwynfor full to its iron head. And he aimed at Modru's heart.

But then . . .

But then . . .

He hesitated.

Then shifted his aim and let fly.

Ssss . . . hissed the arrow, all but silent in its flight.

And in a cast that mayhap no other could have done, the arrow struck true, the blunt, iron head smashing into the black diamond, into Gelvin's Doom, and the gemstone shattered into pieces beyond number, tiny, pulverized fragments, like glittering powder, flying wide, and Modru screamed in pain and grabbed his gauntleted wrist with his other hand and doubled over in agony.

And at that very same moment, fully half of the invaders fell lifeless to the cobbles; the dead were dead again.

And Vanidar set another arrow to string and loosed it at the Black Mage, yet the shaft veered to harmlessly strike street stone.

Black-shafted arrows flew in response, to miss as Vanidar took shelter behind the fire vent.

And then Modru roared in rage, and straightened up and reached a hand in the direction of the chimney, and it exploded!—bricks hurtling, some broken, others yet held together by mortar, and they would slay anyone caught in the blast.

But Vanidar was not there; instead he was in full flight back the way he had come, for he had no weapon with which to assail Modru; yet the reverse was not the case with the Black Mage, and he swore vengeance against the one who had destroyed the gem, though he knew not who that was. Even with the source of his necromantic power now destroyed, still he pressed the war forward.

And though fully half the invaders had fallen slain, the battle was yet in doubt, for the ranks of the defenders had taken great hurt and they were yet sorely outnumbered.

But even as Vanidar fled across the rooftops, he heard the call of silver clarions, and in the distance on the plains to the west there came thundering horses beyond immediate count, riders astride, horns blowing.

The Lian of Darda Immer had come.

And down in an alley nigh the western wall, the moment he heard the ring of trumpets, Dwynfor, strapping on the last of his armor, snatched up his sword and leapt to his horse and rode to the posterns and threw them wide. Through the gates came horses in full career, the Elves of Darda Immer astride, the smiths of Duellin among them, Gilian in the fore, with Dara Elinda, no longer a child, at her side, a gleaming saber in hand. For when Elves in Duellin had died in the battle, and their Elven death redes had stricken the hearts of loved ones afar in the Brightwood, and when the smiths and armorers and other refugees brought word of Modru's invasion, it had taken the morning for swift heralds to crisscross the forest and sound the alarm, and time for the Lian to assemble. And they had raced the ten leagues—the thirty miles—to come unto the city, and now they were here on charging horses, swords riving, lances impaling, sharp hooves trampling under.

They drove the invaders back and back, and Modru, depleted of power, fled to his ship, cursing and swearing vengeance. Trolls bearing Whelmram scrambled aboard the black galley just after, and they stroked away defeated, and they took the mighty fist with them.

Leaderless, the foe broke and ran, and some managed to board the crimson-sailed dhows of the Rovers, and they fled across the sea and away. Yet more than three-quarters of the invaders were left behind, dead or dying.

The defenders of Duellin had won in the end, but at a terrible cost, and many years were to vanish into the past ere they recovered from the war.

"Oh, my," said wee Aylissa, her mouth agape. "But that was close, wasn't it? I mean if Modru had succeeded in taking the armories and the smiths of Duellin as well, huah, he would have had all of those weapons at his disposal, and who knows what that might have led to?"

"Exactly so, tiny one," said Aravan. "Yet it was Silverleaf's incredible cast and the arrival of the force from Darda Immer that saved the day."

Noddy shook his head. "I don't understand why Silverleaf just didn't shoot Modru instead."

Aravan said, "Silverleaf knew that should he loose at Modru, in spite of it being a special arrow, his shot might go astray. Besides, the iron-headed shaft was quite blunt, and did not seem to be meant to take a life. And so he aimed at the black diamond instead. It was a token of power versus a token of fear, and the token of power prevailed."

"Wull, even though it weren't aimed at Modru, still it hurt his hand," said Noddy.

"Indeed," said Aravan. "And because of what happened in Duellin, from that time forward Modru worked his schemes through surrogates, and only once thereafter did he appear in battle, and that was at Hèl's Crucible, where with his overwhelming forces and a Dragon ally o'erhead he was certain he would win."

"Ha! But we Warrows took care of . . . of . . ." Pipper fell silent, for Dokan did once again glare at him. "Urm," amended Pipper, "with a lot of help from others, especially the Dwarves, and oh, yes, the Utruni, we Warrows made sure Modru's plans again came to nought."

"Forget not the Fjordlanders," said Tarly.

"And the Pyska," said Aylissa.

"And the Pellarians," said Fat Jim.

"And the Gelenders," said Wooly, Noddy agreeing.

"And the Elves and Mages," said Aylis.

"The Jordians," added Aravan.

"All right! All right!" said Pipper. "All the Free Folk did a bit to help us, too—a very wee, tiny bit though it was." He broke into laughter, and it infected all.

But when quiet returned, "Still," said Fat Jim, "Modru might have had his vengeance upon Duellin and the entire Atalain realm after all, for Karak blew and the isle sank down into the depths of the Weston Ocean."

"Mayhap 'twas Modru caused such," said Aravan. "Then again, mayhap not. Mayhap somehow Gyphon or one of His allies arranged it so. Or mayhap the firemountain simply exploded on its own. I deem we'll ne'er know the truth of such."

"Only Adon knows," said Aylis. Then she looked at Aravan in wonder. "*Chier,* mayhap Adon *does* know. We can ask him when next we cross over to Adonar."

"Nay, *chieran,*" said Aravan. "After Bair went and argued for the lifting of the Ban, and the cessation of all interference by the gods in the affairs of lesser beings, Adon and Elwydd and the others withdrew, and we know not where they went."

A glum silence fell over them all. But then Noddy said, "Wull, at any rate, there in Duellin, Gelvin's Doom was gone, and Modru hadn't got it no more."

"Oh, my, I just had a thought," said Pipper. As all eyes turned his way, he said, "Truly, it's a good thing Modru didn't have Gelvin's Doom in the Great War of the Ban, or in the Winter War, for that matter. I mean, notwithstanding my—*ahem*—modest claims, we almost lost both of those conflicts, and had he had an army of the risen dead to help him . . . well, I just don't know what would have happened."

"Oh, Pip," said Binkton, aggravated, "he *didn't* have Gelvin's Doom in those wars, so it's no use thinking about that."

"Yes, but what if he'd had the black diamond?" said Pipper. "I mean—"

"Aargh!" growled Binkton, glancing through the windows of the Red Slipper at the glimmerings of dawn in the sky. "Me, I'm going to bed."

"Mayhap we should all go to bed," said Aravan, yawning, standing and holding a hand out to Aylis. She stood and put an arm about his waist, saying, "Mmm, bed, *chieran,*" and together they headed for the stairs.

"Captain!" called Aylissa, the Pysk gaining her feet.

Aravan stopped and turned, Aylis at his side pausing as well.

"Captain, I just had a thought: the black galley, the Trolls, would this be the same ship my sire and dam speak of? Durlok's galley? The one you and my sire and dam and Aylis and Alamar and the crew of the *Eroean* pursued across the whole of the world?"

Aravan shrugged a shoulder. "I know not, tiny one. Mayhap 'twas given over to Durlok by Modru. I think Modru was never again seen in a ship of any sort, much less the black galley." Aravan turned to Aylis. "Mayhap one of your castings would reveal whether or no this is true."

Aylis smiled and shook her head. "I think it not worth the expenditure of even a bit of my <fire>." Then she grasped him by both hands and with a throaty laugh began backing and tugging him toward the stairs. "Come, *chier,* 'tis to bed I would take you."

"I t'ink Lady Aylis be right," said Nikolai. "Time for to go to sleep."

"Har!" barked Fat Jim. "D'you really think they'll be sleeping?"

Nikolai smiled and then yawned and stood and stretched. "Maybe not Captain and Lady . . . but me, I go to bed now for to sleep."

"But I was so enjoying the stories," said Wooly, yawning as well.

"You know what? I'd like to hear about Durek," said Tarly, glancing at Dokan. "I mean, who he was, and how he forged the hammer and the horn, and—"

Dokan stood. "I am going to bed as well, but I'll tell about him morrow eve."

"Don't you mean on this upcoming eve?" said Fat Jim, casting a thumb at the growing light of the oncoming day.

"Tonight, tomorrow, whatever, I'll tell it," said Dokan.

"Come, Aylissa," said Pipper to the Pysk, "you can sleep on a pillow under my bed."

Aylissa whispered into Vex's ear, and the fox opened her eyes and looked at the Pysk and then rose and trotted for the Red Slipper's kitchen, for when the cooks came, she would have a breakfast of bacon, great ratter that she was.

5

The Drowning of Durek

The next eve, once again the small group sat in candlelight before the cold hearth, and only Nikolai was missing from those who had been there in the wee marks of the night before, for he was upstairs dallying with one of the Red Slipper ladies. But Tarly and Wooly and Noddy and Fat Jim were present, along with Aylis and Aravan and Aylissa and Vex, as well as Pipper and Binkton. And they were all looking at Dokan, Tarly again having just asked the Dwarf to tell the tale of Durek.

"I know not the full story of all of Durek's life," said Dokan, "but I can tell of his drowning."

"He drowned?" said Pipper, his face falling. "Oh, my, I'm not certain at all I want to hear this tale."

"Cousin, you can always leave," said Binkton.

"N-no," said Pipper. "Maybe it's not as bad as I imagine. —Is it that bad, Dokan?"

Dokan burst into laughter. "How should I know what you imagine, Pip?"

Pipper huffed. "Wull, what I mean is, is it a story that has him fighting for breath, struggling, and being pulled under?"

"Indeed," said Dokan.

"Oh. Oh," said Pipper. "Drowned. What a terrible way to die. — W-was he murdered?"

"I don't want to give too much away and spoil the story," said Dokan, "but this will I say:"—a hard, flinty look came into

Dokan's eyes—"here began the never-ending war between the Châkka and the Ükhs, Hrôks, Khôls, Trolls, and all other Grg . . . all other Squam."

"Foul Folk," said Noddy.

"Foul Folk, aye," said Dokan, "even back then they were known as such."

"When did this occur?" asked Fat Jim.

"That is in dispute among the Châkka," said Dokan.

"Dispute?"

"Aye. Some think it occurred in the early years of the First Era, while others think it was long before."

"What do you think?"

"I deem some Châkka have entangled two tales, one from First Durek, and one who later was named Durek as well, one of the *Khana* Dureks."

"*Khana?*" asked Noddy.

"It means 'Deathbreaker' or 'Breakdeath,' " replied Dokan.

"Deathbreaker?" said Pipper, shivering. "That sounds right ominous. —But wait. You said that he might have been one of the *Khana* Dureks. You mean there was more than one Deathbreaker?"

"There have been seven Dureks throughout Châkka history," said Dokan.

"Nothing uncommon about that," said Wooly. "I mean, many names are handed down from father to son or grandfather to grandson—"

"And from mother to daughter," piped up Aylissa. "Grandmother to granddaughter, too." The Pysk looked at Aylis and said, "Or a mother can name a daughter after a friend she considers to be her sister."

Aylis smiled at Aylissa and nodded, as Wooly said, "Aye, handing down a name is—"

"Not in this case," said Dokan. "Durek is a special name, and now and then a Châk is born so like First Durek that we name him Durek as well, for we think *Khana* Durek is reborn again."

"Reborn?" said Pipper.

"Aye," replied Dokan. "All souls are reborn, some more quickly than others. Durek, though, seems reborn more quickly than most, and that is why we name him 'Breakdeath' or 'Deathbreaker.' "

"Ah," said Pipper. "I see. And this story you are going to tell is about which one: First Durek or one of the Deathbreakers?"

"First Durek," said Dokan. "It is a tale set in the time long before the counting of Eras began, or mayhap shortly after."

"Naow, just wait a moment, Dokan," said Noddy. "'At's th' second toime y've said somethin' what don't stand t'reason. Oi mean, 'ow could it 'ave occurred before th' counting of Eras? Didn't th' First Era mark th' beginning o' Mithgar?"

"In a sense thou art right," said Aravan. "The First Era began with the crowning of the very first High King—Awain. He became the High King when he united a handful of warring nations—Pellar, Jugo, Hoven, Valon, both Riamons, and Garia."

"Yar, but there's more than those seven realms pay allegiance to the High King these days," said Wooly.

Aravan turned up a hand. "Aye, Wooly, for many more joined the Alliance in the nearly ten millennia the First Era lasted—"

"Ten millennia?" blurted Noddy. He paused a moment to count on his fingers. "Ten thousand years?"

"Nine thousand five hundred and seventy five, to be exact," said Aylis, "from the crowning of the first High King to the destruction of Rwn."

"Oh, my," said Aylissa, the Pysk sighing, "the destruction of Rwn. Scores of my Kind perished in that cataclysm, as did all the folk in the City of Bells."

"Some escaped," said Aylis, reaching over and squeezing Aravan's hand.

"Aye, some did," said Aylissa, stroking Vex. "My sire and dam and Anthera and her band, but no others among the Hidden Ones, or so my sire does say."

A pall fell upon the gathering, but finally Noddy said, "Wot does this 'ave t'do wi' th' beginning o' Mithgar, Cap'n?"

"Just this, Noddy," said Aravan. "The world and people were here long before Awain became King. Yet upon his coronation, he called his kingdom Mithgar, and when Pellarian was used as the basis for the Common Tongue, Mithgar was taken as the name for the entire globe. Up until then and even today, it was and is called many things in many tongues, all more or less meaning 'the world.' "

"Ah, Cap'n," said Noddy. "So 'at's why you say Mithgar began wi' th' First Era." Noddy turned to Dokan. "'N' you say your tale occurs before then, eh?"

"Aye. The way I was told, the tale takes place long before there was a Mithgar, back when the Common Tongue had not yet come into being."

"No Common Tongue?" asked Pipper.

Binkton huffed. "Pip, didn't you hear what the captain just said? —About Pellarian being the basis for Common?"

"Yes, but—"

"No buts about it. There simply was a time when Common hadn't yet come about."

Aylis smiled at Pipper and said, "Bink is right, Pip. It wasn't until the first High King held sway over seven realms with six different tongues that anyone thought it was necessary. Even then, even though the reasoning behind it was sound, still there were great protests, and many of those nations swore to remain pure. I understand even today, with the High King's realm greater than ever, some try to turn back time, try to make their native tongue prime over Common, try to keep their young from using a Pellarian-based word when their native tongue will do . . . the people of Goth, for example."

"We Warrows—" began Binkton, but Noddy huffed out a great breath and said, "Let's 'ear Dokan's story."

Binkton pushed out a hand of negation and glared at Noddy, then turned to Aylis. "What I was about to say is we Warrows hold onto Twyll, our tongue. Even so, we realize that Common allows all to converse together, something I believe encourages trade and helps maintain peace between nations."

"Encourages trade, aye," said Aravan, as Noddy squirmed in his chair, "and it does help maintain peace among some nations, yet the greater part of the people of the world speak it not. Far to the east nearly none in Jinga and Ryodo and Moku speak Common, nor do most of those in Bharaq and the lands 'round the north of the Sindhu Sea. Many know it not in the realms south of the Avagon—Thyra, Chabba, Khem, the Karoo, Hyree, and the lands farther south—nor in other nations too numerous to name throughout the wide, wide world."

"No surprise," said Fat Jim, "for little do they trade with the High King's realm. Yet even were they to speak Common, still they would take pride in holding to their native tongues." Fat Jim gestured about. "For example, were this isle my home, I would speak

Common, yet I would delight in knowing Arbalinian. *Com'é il mare oggi?"*

Aravan turned to Fat Jim and replied, *"Blu, con l'onda."*

Fat Jim roared, and Aravan and Aylis smiled.

"Wot did you say, 'n' wot did 'e say?" asked Noddy, pulled from his snit, looking at Fat Jim.

Fat Jim managed to stifle his laughter. "I asked 'How is the sea today?' and the captain replied, 'Blue, with waves.' " Again Fat Jim roared, and the others joined him.

Finally, Pipper said, "But Dokan says that no one spoke Common when his story about Durek begins. What I want to know is how did folks ever travel in the world, trade in the world, if they couldn't even talk to one another?"

"Here and there were some who could interpret," said Aylis, "particularly Seers—such as I—but when no interpreter was about, people simply signed to one another."

"Wull, that must've been slow and awkward," said Pipper. "I mean—"

" 'Ere naow," interrupted Noddy, " 'ow 'bout we let Dokan go on wi' 'is tale, else we'll be 'ere all noight talkin' about nothin' but talkin'."

"Well, just one other thing before you begin, Dokan," said Binkton. Noddy groaned, but Binkton went on: "How come you don't know whether this tale is set, as you said, 'in the time long before the First Era began, or mayhap shortly after'?"

Dokan sighed. "The LoreMasters say that there is an ambiguity in the records, and long have they disputed the meaning of it. Some say that in the First Era, Modru came unto First Durek and proposed an alliance, and when Durek refused, Modru took his revenge. Others say Modru proposed that alliance not to First Durek but to one of the *Khana* Dureks instead. After the Great War of the Ban, LoreMasters went to Kraggen-cor to settle the dispute, but they never came to the truth"—Dokan ground his teeth in rage—"for when the Ghath was set free in Kraggen-cor, LoreMasters were slain and records lost, and much was destroyed by Foul Folk in the aftermath."

"Ghath?" asked Pipper. "What's a Ghath?"

"A Gargon," said Aylis.

"How did a Gargon get into—?"

"Aargh!" said Noddy. "Are we never t'ear Dokan's tale?"

Pipper shot back a reply and Binkton jumped in to rail at them both, but Aylis held up a hand for quiet and said, "Pip, when Dokan's tale is done, I will tell the story how the Gargon came unto Drimmen-deeve. Until then, let us listen to Dokan."

At Aylis's words, Dokan's eyes flew wide. "You know?"

Aylis said, "I have <seen>."

"My lady, please, we Châkka ourselves know not the answer to that mystery, and—"

But Aylis said, "Go on, Dokan. Tell your tale, and then I will tell mine."

Dokan started to protest, and Noddy got up and stomped away to the bar, but Aylis simply shook her head and said, "I will recount my tale after you relate yours."

Dokan clamped his jaw shut, and for a moment it appeared he would say nought. But then he sighed and said, "I will tell the legend as I believe it to be, a tale that takes place long before the First Era began."

Dokan paused and took a sip of dark wine, then looked at the glass and swirled the drink and smiled. "Durek had journeyed long, and he had travelled through many cities in many realms and out into the countrysides beyond, for he was looking for a place where his line of Châkka could settle and forge a mighty realm. . . ."

Noddy rushed back, a jack of ale in hand, and quickly sat down.

" . . . And one day in Vancha, mayhap not far from where grapes were harvested such as those that made this excellent wine, he heard a rumor from a Gelender of four great mountains somewhere quite distant to the north and east in a chain known as the Grimwalls. And so he made ready to travel again. . . ."

He came ashore from a coaster—one of those ships that never venture out of the sight of land—disembarking at the fledgling town of River's End in Jugo, there west of the estuary where the mighty Argon flows into the Avagon Sea. Whence he had come, none knew, though one rumor said it was from one of the isles of Gelen, while another claimed it was from Jute, and still another said he came from Thol. Regardless, none like him had been seen before, at least in this part of the world, and he called himself Châk and Durek, and someone finally reasoned one of those words was the name of his Kind and the other his own name, though as to which was which, well, they didn't figure that out.

Though he stood but some four foot four, his shoulders were half again as wide as those of a Man. His hair and forked beard were black, and his eyes an arresting dark, dark grey. His vest and breeches were motley leather, the patches shading from light grey to black, as of tones of common granite. His cloak, though also mottled grey on the outer side, on the inside was mottled brown, as if it were reversible apurpose to display other tones of stone; it was clasped with a plain black brooch. 'Neath his leather jacket he wore a grey jerkin, and black boots shod his feet. A plain black belt with a black buckle was cinched about his waist, and it held a dark-scabbarded, black-handled dagger. He had a simple boiled-leather helm on his head, but in a sling across his back depended a double-bitted, oak-hafted axe. On his right hip was a strange scabbard, holding what appeared to be quarrels and a small, collapsible cross-bow. At his left hip and depending from an over-the-shoulder strap was a bindle, containing a bit of clothing, a bedroll, cooking gear, a few rations, and the like—the bare necessities of those travellers on extensive journeys throughout regions where inns and other such accommodations might be far between.

It looked as if he were prepared for a trek.

But he took quarters in the Sandpiper, one of just three inns in the town. None spoke his language, nor did he speak theirs, yet by signing he managed to inquire about mountains, great mountains. Many did not know, or didn't understand what he was asking, signing as he did, and so he sought others who might grasp his meaning. Finally, in the Grey Goose tavern, he came across some travellers who told him through gestures, [North. North. There are mountains to the north.]

[Far?] he signed, repeating it several times before one of them understood what he meant.

[Yes,] they nodded. [Far to the north.]

And so, Durek purchased supplies and two ponies—one to ride and one to bear his goods—and, more or less following the banks of the Argon, he set out to the north, riding up through the land of Jugo.

Along this way he went as days fled into the past, and he camped in the open land and stayed in crofters' lofts or in sheds or shacks or stopped in an occasional inn, and though Men looked at him askance, for they had not before seen one of his Kind, still they gave him shelter. And whenever he could he replenished his supplies from whatever store they could spare. Always he paid his hosts with good copper coin, though the images and runes thereon were quite unfamiliar to the farmers and innkeepers and woodcutters and hunters in whose dwellings he housed overnight.

Some twelve days out of River's End, he came to the beginnings of a low range of ruddy hills, and these he followed northerly, curving 'round to the west, where they rose up into craggy tors. Durek spent more than a fortnight examining the soil and locating veins of ore, and he knew these heights to be rich in iron. Here could be founded a Châkkaholt to rival the best of armories. Durek named this range the Red Hills, and from the western end of the chain, he continued on northward, for he yet sought the mountains of which he'd heard the rumor, and he would see them for himself.

He came into a land of rolling plains, and a lone crofter spoke the name of the realm: 'twas known as Ellor. The farmer also signed to him that a chain of small mountains lay to the north and west, and became greater the farther north they went. He warned Durek, though, that far to the north across the plains a barrier stood in the way. What it might be, the Man could not convey, nor did Durek understand.

And so northwestward did Durek fare, up and across the land of Ellor, the realm sparsely populated, though its plains were rich in grasses, nodding in the gentle wind. And his ponies did graze well on the ripening heads of grain, though they did not fatten, travelling every day as they were.

A nineday after leaving the crofter's place, Durek saw low mountains to the west, and he angled toward them. And he came to a gap in a low chain, some ten miles wide the slot. To the south the tors rose up into mountains; to the north they did so as well.

Durek pondered in which direction he should fare—north? south? or through the gap and then north or south?—and, in spite of the crofter's warning that some kind of barrier lay across the way, he decided that he would stay on this side of the range, the eastern side, and follow the rising chain northward.

Another nineday he fared along the range, the mountains growing taller and darker as he went, and he saw not another living soul on this land, just birds and small animals scurrying, and an occasional fox or deer. Finally he came into sight of what must be the barrier the crofter had spoken of: a sheer escarpment rising up a thousand feet or so. The next day Durek reached the foot of this great rampart, and, while his ponies grazed on rich, grain-laden grasses, Durek spent a sevenday hunting and trapping small game and fishing in a rushing brook tumbling eastward, replenishing his own food supplies. Too, he spent time reaping the now-ripened heads of the grasses for his ponies to have in the days to come.

He broke camp and westward he turned, faring up through the foothills and toward the dark, shadow-clutched mountains, following the course of the stream into the gloomy range, and although it took him a fortnight altogether, at last he discovered a twisting way up through the heights and across their slopes to reach the plateau above.

He spent another sevenday again hunting in the whin and furze of the upland and fishing in the streams flowing across this terrain, his ponies grazing on the sparse grasses growing here, their feed augmented by rations of grain from the meager store Durek yet had.

Northward Durek continued, and he fared across a rushing river, and lo! he came to where hundreds upon hundreds of widely scattered seedlings of an unfamiliar tree had been planted, some but a foot or so tall, other more mature ones head high; elsewhere, some of these trees reached a hundred feet or so.

It appeared to be a deliberate cultivation, yet what foresters had set them into the soil, Durek could not say. But he made certain to avoid stepping on any and kept his ponies clear as on northward he went.

He came to another river, and another and still more, all flowing down from the dark mountains, for this was a land of many rivers, and at times he rode upstream or down ere he found a place to ford.

On he went, northward still, along this forbidding range, and finally, on the sixth day of travel, he fared beyond the borders of the plantings, and onto a wold, where once again ripened grasses grew, and the grazing greatly improved.

Yet even as he reached this place, he noted in the distance a ruddy red peak towering above the rest.

He fared northward along the banks of a crystal-clear, south-running stream, and the crests of three more great mountains came into view—all nestled nigh the high ruddy peak—and Durek knew the rumor was true. Here were four mountains towering above the rest and mayhap they would make a suitable Châkkaholt, could a handful of halls be delved within. Surely in one of these four mountains there would be a crack or crevice or mayhap a hollow that could be enlarged as a start.

Even as he continued onward, he could see that the four mountains formed a quadrangle, the one on the southeast corner standing closest, its slopes grey. The one on the southwest corner was nearly black. The one on the northeast corner was blue-tinged. And the last one, the northwest anchor and mightiest of all, was the one ruddy red.

For five more days he followed the clear-running stream, and on the morning of the fifth day he arced 'round the flank of the grey mountain to come unto a long, open vale running westward to gradually ascend into the embrace of the four towering peaks, and though he had not yet given names to any of the mountains, he called this broad, lofty dale Baralan, which in Châkur, the tongue of the Châkka, means Rising Slope.

As Durek moved onto the cambered ground, he could see the margins of the valley became steeper where they rose up to meet the walls of the mountains on the three hemmed-in sides, and here and there they were covered with runs of birch and fir trees, as well as trembling aspen; but on the floor of the vale, heather and furze grew on the land and their scent was on the air. His gaze was drawn to the northwest end of the acclivity, where in the morning light a glittering rill cascaded in many falls down the long vee where the stone slopes of the red mountain met the ones of azure.

Durek's eyes were wide with wonder as, leading his ponies along the stream he yet followed, up the long slant he went, the grey and blue mountains to left and right, black and red yet ahead. As the sun crossed the zenith and he neared the root of the vale, he came unto a crystalline tarn, its surface like a mirror, and on its western side rose an elevated, wide stone ledge. 'Round and up to this ledge he strode, where he stood and slowly turned about and looked at the majesty of the four mountains rising, and he felt clasped in their embrace. He was o'erwhelmed by their grandeur, and tears flooded his eyes, for he knew he was home at last. Wiping his cheeks, he stepped to the edge of the ledge and looked into the pellucid waters below, and the sky and mountains were reflected all 'round, as if seen through a window an inverted world.

Then Durek raised his face to the towering slopes and declared aloud, "Here will I place a Realmstone, proclaiming these four mountains and all within their hold to be the realm of Durek and his Kind." Even unto the soaring heights did his words echo in the lofty surround, as if the vale and the mountains themselves acknowledged his decree.

That night he camped on the shore of the mere, there where a Realmstone would someday be, and he slept as would a newborn in this peaceful vale.

The next morn when he awoke he became aware of a distant gurge, as of a churn of water spinning 'round, and he frowned in puzzlement, for he could see no cause. Still, 'twas a mystery that could wait, for he would instead look for an entry—a crack, a crevice, a cave, even a crevasse—anything that would permit him admission into the living stone.

Along the slopes of the red mountain went Durek afoot, heading northerly, toward the cascading rill, for oft where there is water, there is also a shaping of stone, and mayhap the stream itself had carved a way in.

Yet even as he went this way, the sound of the gurge grew louder, a rumble from the east, from the azure-tinged mountain. And, splashing across the stream feeding the tarn, toward this grumble went Durek, his curiosity now drawing him so. And he espied a fold in the bluish stone whence the steady roar came, as of a great thunder of water.

But as he went toward the slot in this arc, he heard a howling yell, and running 'cross the slope came yawling a band of swart, bandy-legged, batwing-eared beings, brandishing cudgels and scimitars and hammers. And beyond them where he had hobbled his ponies he could see others of this kind, haling a horseling to the ground, slicing its throat, the other pony already slain, the ravagers cutting out great gobbets of meat and eating the flesh raw.

Cursing in anger, Durek ran for the fold in the stone, for he was greatly outnumbered and its entrance was the only thing close to a narrow lieu he could see, though constricted it was not. Even so, mayhap there was somewhere within they could come at him but one at a time. As he ran, he took out the crossbow from its sheath and locked the arms in place.

Into the azure-tinged fold of stone he ran, to come into a huge circular area, a hundred feet or more across, and there a secret river roared forth from the flank of the mountain itself, to rage 'round this great stone basin to disappear down into the dark again, a gaping whirlpool raving endlessly and sucking at the sky and funneling down deep into the black depths below.

On the rim of the basin, some twenty feet wide, 'round this roaring fury Durek ran, looking for a combat advantage, yet there was only stone and raving water, with no place to take shelter, though a high rocky ledge on the far brim of the basin offered him a place to stand. But in spite of it being the high ground herein, to it there was a wide, sloping approach and so it offered little to be gained. Even so, he ran up the ramp and took a stance thereon and set his axe at hand. Then he cocked his crossbow and loaded a quarrel just as the first of the howling pursuers came racing through the gap. Though he had never seen one before, he had heard of Ükhs and Hrôks and other beings from the underworld of Neddra; Foul Folk they were called, and Grg and Squam, and it seemed this one matched the description of an Ükh.

Twok, sss, thock! The quarrel took the Ükh in the throat, and the Squam fell dead even as three more raced inward, leaping over their fallen comrade.

Thok! Another quarrel took the lead one down, and Durek reloaded and shot the next Ükh even as this one charged within a pace or two. With a backhanded swipe, Durek knocked the last one from the ledge, the foe to fall screaming into the raging water and be jerked down out of sight.

Durek got off but one more crossbow shot, that one to slay one of the Ükhs in the mob that came after, and then he took up his axe and slew and slew, blood and viscera and bone and muscle flying.

Yet more came and they closed with a rush and there were too many, and he fell to a thrown cudgel. And then did the Ükhs club him unmercifully and would have slain him, but a Hrôk came bellowing among them and shoved them away from the fallen warrior.

The Hrôk sneered down at Durek, the Châk bloody and beaten and barely conscious. Even so, Durek managed to spit at the Hrôk, though the gobbet had not the strength behind it to do ought but dribble down the side of Durek's own face. The Hrôk laughed, then shouted out something in his foul tongue, and while some Ükhs danced about in a frenzy of jubilation, others howled in glee and took Durek up by the arms and legs and held him to where he could see his oncoming fate in the endless, ravening churn below. Once more the Hrôk shouted out something, and jeering in revelment, they flung Durek into the spin, and the furious maw wrenched him down and down, down into the water, down into the depths, down where he could not breathe, down into the dark below.

"Oh, my," said Aylissa, the Pysk clutching her arms to herself and glancing at Pipper. "I agree with you, Pip: what a dreadful way to die."

"Drowning, you mean?" said Fat Jim.

Aylissa nodded and said, "The only thing worse I can think of is being dragged under by a great brown trout and gobbled down whole."

Fat Jim looked down at the tiny Fox Rider and burst out laughing. "Being swallowed entire by a trout? Such a fate never occurred to me."

"I wonder why, O corpulent one?" said Tarly, puffing out his cheeks and arcing out his arms as if he himself were enormously fat and trying to encompass a great belly.

This brought on a chuckle from all but wee Aylissa, who angrily said, "Just because you can't be swallowed by a trout, Fat Jim, that doesn't mean it isn't a horror to me."

"Oi think it'd take a whale t'swallow Fat Jim," said Noddy, " 'n' it 'twouldn't 'ave an easy toime o' it neither."

At this even the Pysk laughed, though Fat Jim huffed in vexation.

As Wooly refilled glasses with dark Vanchan wine and Noddy rushed off for another jack of ale, Pipper said, "It's too bad Durek had to drown. I was hoping he would survive to get even with the Foul Folk, killing his ponies as they did, and throwing him into the whirlpool and all."

Aravan looked at Aylis and smiled and tilted his head toward the Warrow, and she smiled back in return. Noting the exchange between them, Pipper turned to Dokan and said, "Well he *did* drown, didn't he? I mean you started out this tale by saying you would tell of the drowning of Durek."

Noddy came rushing back. "Did Oi miss anythin'?"

"Just my cousin's gullibility," said Binkton.

"Eh?" said Noddy, looking puzzled.

"There are three here who are quite innocent souls," said Aravan.

"Naïve," agreed Aylis, squeezing Aravan's hand.

"Innocent? Naïve?" asked Aylissa, the Fox Rider frowning and looking about, as if trying to spot those lacking guile. "Pipper," said Aylissa, "and certainly Noddy"—again she frowned—"but who could be the third?"

Aylis broke out laughing, Aravan, too, both eyeing the tiny Pysk.

"What? Me?" protested Aylissa. "Why, I'll have you know I am just as tricky as anyone here."

"Ah, Aylissa," said Aravan, "one who is gullible among friends lacks not cunning among foe. Tricky thou art, and stealthy, and I could not ask better when it comes to deceiving those who would do harm. Yet among friends, thou art trusting to a fault, and I would have it no other way."

Mollified, Aylissa smiled, but Pipper looked at Dokan in disbelief and said, "You mean Durek didn't drown?"

Binkton groaned at Pipper, but he paid him no heed and said to Dokan, "Well?"

Dokan took a sip of wine, and when all eyes were on him, he said, "The sucking maw drew him down, and according to legend none had ever survived that fate. To the very edge of the Realm of Death and mayhap beyond was Durek taken, yet Life at last found him on a stony shore. . . ."

Nearly dead and in total blackness, Durek came to on a rocky shingle. He lay in the shallows of slowly turning water, mayhap a great eddy pool. He barely managed to crawl through the gravel and out, where he lost consciousness again.

When next he came awake, he knew not how much time had elapsed, for he was in blackness still. Groaning, he struggled to his feet, and he stood long with his hands on his knees ere he could straighten up. Nearby from the sound of it was a great run of water. *The river that brought me here? Ah, it must be.* He stumbled a step or two through the round gravel and sand toward the sound, echoing though it was, and splashed back into the pool. Moaning, stooping, he cupped his hand and lifted water to his mouth and drank. It was not bitter nor tart nor alkaline but sweet to the taste instead.

Hurting all over, he stood again and felt of his injuries: his ribs hurt, some perhaps broken, and his arms and legs were in agony as well, especially his forearms and shins. One of his eyes was swollen shut, mayhap even blinded, not that it mattered in the dark, for he could not see as it was. His leather helm was gone and his head ached and perhaps his skull was fractured, and his jaw had a great lump on one side. It was as he was probing his injuries, he discovered he yet had his dagger; even so, should he run across some of the eld creatures of the deep underearth, little good would that do.

Grunting, he turned and retraced his steps and stood on the shore once more. With one hand outstretched, he slowly moved through the dark, wary of falling into a pit or stepping into a crack, though with the water nearby, the shore was likely smooth, but for the river-rounded gravel and rocks. Finally he came to a wall of stone, where he gingerly levered himself down with his back to it, and in spite of hurting all over, he fell into a dead sleep.

When next he awoke, he was in even more pain, and he crawled back to the pool and laboriously doffed his wet clothes and eased himself into the chill turn, and he lay for a long while in the laving cool, drifting in and out of consciousness.

He awoke cold to the bone, and grunting, edged out of the pool and, struggling, he donned his garb, not that it did much in the way of warming him, wet as it was.

Movement will thaw me, yet where will I go?

Gaining his feet, back to the wall he hobbled, not concerned with caution at all, for as with all Châkka, he knew precisely any path once trod or ridden aland. It was the gift of the Châkka—<wild magic> some would say—for as the old Châkka maxim claimed, *Though I might not know where I am going, I always know exactly where I have been.*

Turning in the direction of the flow and trailing a hand along the stone, he began warily pacing forward. Long he went, the river on his left. At times he waded through shallows, at other times he had to clamber over stone outcroppings and great boulders, and always underfoot were rounded river rocks and gravel and sand along the shore. Occasionally he swam, and there was a time that the river swept him afar, though he made it to shore once again. Often he stopped to rest, for he was battered beyond what most could endure, and yet he persevered.

And so on he went and on, until from the fore in the blackness, he could hear a roar. And as he progressed, the roar grew louder still, and he came to what must be an underground waterfall, the river plunging over a linn and down. Thankful that he hadn't been swimming at the time, along the shoreline he crept, and he came to the precipice, mist swirling through the air, and down he clambered, unable to see ought, thunder all 'round.

Onward he pressed, the roar of the falls diminishing as he rounded curve after curve, and as he passed yet another turn—lo!—ahead there glowed a soft, blue-green glimmer.

Durek struggled on forward, toiling across rounded rocks and sloshing through pools, to come at last into the gentle radiance. It came from a stretch of a luminous lichen that at times and in favorable conditions grows on stone along streams underground. And here Durek stopped, tears in his eyes, for he could see at last. And, wet, disheveled, injured, and exhausted beyond his endurance, he eased himself down and slept.

How long he slumbered he did not know, and he awoke bathed in soft lichen light, and again he was thankful that he could see. He knew this lichen, for a leaching of it when mixed with the like from a luminous cave moss provided the basis of the small Châkka lanterns used in the holts of his Folk, giving light for which no fire need be kindled, nor fuel consumed, though now and then the lanterns did need to sit in the rays of the sun to refresh their power.

He groaned to his feet and stepped to an eddy, and bent over to take water, and as he did so in the soft radiance he saw a small fish. With a lunge he snatched at it, but he was too slow, and it darted away. Durek took his drink, then stood long and still. Once more there came a fish, and this one he managed to catch. Chortling, Durek stepped to the shore, and there he did gut and fillet it. As he did so, he noted it had no eyes, much like its kindred in underground streams elsewhere, living as they did all of their lives in the darker reaches of subterranean flow where light seldom if ever came.

Durek ate the fish raw. Then he ate the guts. Then he gnawed on the fragile bones, for he was hungry beyond compare.

Once again he stood in the pool, and this time he caught one larger.

And again he stood still, and once more, and snatched up a fish each time, and he consumed every one.

He rested after that.

The next he awoke, he heard a chirping, and managed to snare a white cricket. This he ate, and then another. Mayhap this was why the fish frequented the pool, even though they were blind, for mayhap whenever a cricket fell in, they would have a meal.

Durek weighed his options, meager though they were. Here was food and light, yet here he would not stay. He had to find a way out. To do so, he would need food and water and light. Water seemed to be plentiful. And for light he had the lichen. And so for the next handful of candlemarks he captured several fish and a blind eel. These he gutted, eating the viscera, and he laid the cleaned fish aside.

Then he scraped much of the lichen onto a fist-sized stone, crafting a primitive lamp. When that was ready, he stepped back to take up the fish, discovering a handful of white crickets feeding thereon. He ate the crickets and made a sack of his cloak and put the fish inside, then started downstream once more, the lichen-covered rock showing the way.

How long he followed the stream, he did not know—a day or two at the very least, for he did sleep three times. How far he had gone, he knew exactly, twenty-two twisting miles altogether, for the way was arduous and he was injured.

He was out of food, and the light from the transplanted lichen was waning, and the water was flowing down towards the roots of the earth. He had to find a way up, to come once again into the light of day.

And there on the verge of despair, he came to a cavernous branching high above, a small stream of water tumbling out.

Up he clambered, and he followed that way for a mile or two and stumbled upon a small cluster of mushrooms, growing in a smear of dung. He ate the mushrooms and eyed the dung, wondering.

His lichen light chose that moment to fade below visibility.

Tears of frustration filled Durek's eyes, and he shouted in rage. And in the answering echoes, from somewhere ahead he heard a scuttling as something fled away.

Perhaps another day elapsed, or mayhap two, for Durek did sleep twice as he fumbled his way on upward. It was after his second sleep that he came upon the luminous cave, there where it was a moss that provided the radiance. And in the loam under the soft-glowing brye he found beetles and worms and spiders, and these he ate with zest.

He cut apart his cloak and improvised a cloth basket from one of the pieces, and he partially filled it with the loose sandy soil. Then he dug up a large clump of moss including the loam it grew in, and this he placed in his basket; several other clumps he placed in there as well, covering the whole of the surface with the glowing plants. When the basket was full, he had a light that would last. In the other remnant of his cloak, he harvested moss and placed it within.

Onward he went through the caverns, and he found them wondrous, chambers beyond count, winding passages between, vast and labyrinthine and river-carved all. *Oh, what a mighty Châkkaholt this will make if I ever escape to tell of it. I name it Kraggen-cor, for it is indeed a place of Mountain might.*

For days he wandered through soaring halls and vast rooms and intricate passages, not seeing even a tenth of the whole, living on the harvested moss and an occasional mushroom or beetle, cricket or worm, and rarely a blind fish and once a small volelike animal. He would have eaten the moss from his lantern, but he needed the light.

He was in fact quite slowly starving.

And the only voice he heard was his own.

There came a day as he crossed through a great chamber he felt that he was nigh the sloping vale he had named Baralan, though he was not certain at all, for when the Foul Folk had thrown him into the whirlpool, he had lost all sense of orientation, for he had been swept underground by water and had not trod the course. Still, he felt that he was nigh the place where he would put a Realmstone if he were ever to get free. And he strode in that direction through this vast hall for nearly a mile in all, only to come to a great chasm jagging across the floor and barring the way, and he could see neither the bottom nor the other side.

Left Durek turned, to come to a wall, and the rift clove onward beyond the glow of his moss lantern.

Back he strode, opposite, only to come to another wall, and again the great fissure slashed on beyond seeing.

He needed to get to the other side, yet he knew not how far it was though echoes to his shouts told him it was nigh. Yet he had no climbing gear, and the walls were too smooth and obdurate to permit free climbing alone.

He dropped a stone into the blackness of the abyss, trying to judge its depth, yet it fell onward, now and again striking an outjut or ledge, as down and down it plunged. Durek never did hear it hit bottom, for eventually the faint sounds of its intermittent collisions simply faded away.

Durek slumped against a wall, and sat with his back to stone, resting. And after a while he fell asleep.

He awoke to a faint tapping. He was lying on the floor of the vast chamber along the verge of the rift, his ear pressed to the rock, and the tapping was as of someone working stone afar, either that or signalling as with hammers, as the Châkka were wont to do. He sat up, and the tapping vanished.

Durek placed his ear against the stone again, and once more heard the tapping. It was rhythmic, as of a code of some sort, but not one that Durek could read.

Durek took up a nearby rock and hammered it against the floor, pounding out the Châkka signal for aid.

He placed his ear once again against the stone.

The distant tapping had stopped.

Once more he hammered out the code for aid.

No answering signal came.

Over and again he hammered the stone of the cavern floor in a cry for help.

It was not answered.

Finally he gave up.

Bitter, he slumped against the wall and searched through his improvised cloth bag for a morsel of overlooked food. There was none.

Taking a deep breath, he leaned back to rest. In a moment he would get to his feet and retrace his steps to the moss cavern. In a moment . . . a moment . . .

The sound of splitting stone woke him. Once again he was lying on the floor of the cavern. He looked up to see the nearby wall fissuring, and in the soft glow of his moss light, some seventeen feet above him the rock of the wall parted, and two great diamondlike eyes looked down upon him.

Durek scrambled to his knees and scuttled away, and he snatched his dagger from its sheath and leapt up, facing this, this . . .

A great being stepped forth from the wall, and turned and, with its hands, sealed the stone shut, repairing the wall completely, as if it had never been split. It turned and faced Durek once more, and then did he realize that this was an Utrun, a Stone Giant.

The Utrun squatted, as if to make itself smaller, and it slapped a palm to its chest, and in a voice that sounded like that of sliding rock it said, "Lithon."

"Lithon?" repeated Durek. "Lithon?"

Again the Stone Giant slapped its own chest and said, "Lithon," then waited.

It was the first Stone Giant Durek had ever seen, and he was awed, for these were the creatures that moved through the fissures and faults and plates of the world, and with their power over the living stone itself they eased the quaking of the land . . . or so the LoreMasters said. Utruni, they were called, though many named them Stone Giants.

Even though the Utrun was unclothed, Durek could not tell whether it was male or female, for its groin was smooth, as if any externals of its sex had been drawn inward, mayhap as protection from the harsh, grinding rock that Stone Giants move through. Lithon's skin was a stony grey and smooth all over, with no sign of hair whatsoever. And Lithon's eyes sparkled like diamonds, and mayhap were even so.

Durek slapped his own chest. "Durek."

"Durek," repeated the Utrun.

Durek stepped forward, toward the being, and it frowned, as if having trouble focusing on the Châk. And then did Durek reason that these creatures could see through solid stone, and that to them his own form must seem ephemeral. Mayhap metal would be easier for them to see. Durek held up his dagger, and Lithon's eyes shifted that way. And Durek repeatedly jabbed the point in the direction he thought the slope of Baralan lay.

Lithon's smooth features wrinkled in a frown, and at last he looked in the direction the point was oriented. Then his eyes widened in understanding, and he looked back at Durek and smiled.

Lithon stood, and turned to the wall and reached forth, and the Utrun's fingers seemed to melt into the stone, and with a gentle, sideways pull, the stone fissured, and a gape appeared. Lithon gestured to Durek, and entered the gap, and Durek snatched up his moss lantern and followed.

Through the very living stone they went, and upward, Lithon opening the way, Durek following. Up they went and up, and then turned on a level course in the direction Durek had indicated. For mayhap three hundred of Durek's paces they went this way, and then down and down, to emerge from the stone and onto a great broad shelf, and Durek found that he was on what he knew to be the other side of the bottomless deep that had barred his way. Now Lithon turned, and they followed a natural tunnel running in the direction that Durek wished to go, Lithon stooping to pass through. Along this way they went, and it emerged into a great chamber. This they crossed, and down a short tunnel, to come at last unto a dead end, and here Lithon again fissured stone, and they stepped out into the open air, where straight ahead the light of dawn was just then breaking across the brim of the world.

A short way downslope in the glimmer of morn lay the crystalline tarn where a Realmstone would be placed one day.

Durek fell to his knees and gave thanks to Elwydd for his deliverance, then turned and gave thanks to Lithon as well.

The Utrun did not understand Durek's words, but he did know their meaning. Lithon squatted and rumbled something in that strange tongue of the Utruni, then he stood and gestured to Durek, and drew the Châk after, and stepped back to the flank of rock. With a few strokes, Lithon sealed the breach, then, opening it slightly, the Utrun showed Durek just how thin the rock was: a foot of stone and no more at this one place. Lithon gestured to Durek and then to the stone, and closed it again, then opened it once more, showing him the thickness a second time. Lithon then stepped within and with a gesture to Durek—mayhap a farewell—he sealed the wall to vanish from sight.

Durek stood puzzled a moment, but then he understood: Lithon had shown him the way in, now hidden, so that when Durek returned with his Kind and broke down this minor barrier, the Châkka could dwell within the mighty halls beyond.

The LoreMasters had always said that the Utruni appreciated the care and reverence with which the Châkka treated the living stone. And now with this invitation, it seemed as if Lithon had verified the LoreMasters' words.

Yet on the verge of starvation, Durek made his way down toward the mere, passing the splintered and weathered bones of what had once been his ponies. He knelt at the water's edge, and there not only did he drink, but he scooped up some watercress and ate it whole, roots and all.

A score of days later, a band of Elves rode into the vale, and they found Durek as he was foraging for pine nuts and tubers and roots in the woodlands on the valley slopes. And they fed him well, and from them he learned that they had slain a marauding band of Ükhs and Hrôks, and among the Foul Folk gear the Elves had recognized the axe and accoutrements of a Châk, and they had come searching for him.

Durek managed to tell them by sign that he would establish a realm within the embrace of the four mountains, and that they would be welcome guests in his holt.

The Elves seemed pleased that a strong neighbor would dwell to the north of their own lands, and they aided Durek back unto the shores of the Avagon Sea, whence he sailed for Gelen far away.

"Gelen?" blurted Noddy. "Why, 'at's where Oi was borned. 'N' you say Durek was from Gelen?"

"Aye," said Dokan. "Durek led his Folk—one of the five lines of Châkka—from the Blue Hills in Gelen, to come to mighty Kraggen-cor. And there where Lithon had shown Durek a way in—the place where the *Daûn* Gate now stands—they broke through the wall and went into the magnificence beyond.

"And though most followed Durek unto Kraggen-cor, he made Dalor a DelfLord and appointed him and others to stay in the Red Hills to found the mighty armories there.

"And so ends my tale of the drowning of Durek, and some of what happened after."

As Dokan fell quiet, "Ooo," said Aylissa, "and now the Dawn-Gate stands upon the very spot where he walked out through the mountainside and into the just-breaking light of day. How fitting."

"It's a wonder he didn't die," said Tarly, shivering. "I mean, trapped as he was in a cold stone realm, in that place we call the Black Hole. Many are the eld Fjordlander legends of folk who venture beneath the earth to never emerge again. That's why we burn our dead or bury them asea instead of consigning them to the underground realm. Aye, indeed, it's a marvel he survived at all down there in that pit. And that he got out is altogether a wonder."

"Wull, he *was* aided by the Stone Giants," said Binkton.

Dokan grunted his agreement. "As I said, Bink, Utruni admire the work the Châkkakyth do in the undermountain realm, unlike that of the Grg, who destroy the living stone rather than enhance it. That is why Durek was aided by the Stone Giants, and he went on to found the great holt of Kraggen-cor, the mightiest Châkka-holt of the five Châkkakyth and one of the few places on Mithgar where starsilver is found."

Pipper took a deep breath and let it out. "If you ask me, it's a miracle Durek survived his drowning, thrown as he was in the whirlpool. —Has it a name, Dokan?"

"The Vorvor," replied Dokan, "though some call it Durek's Wheel." The Dwarf then growled, and said, "Long have the Grg rued the day they cast Durek from that high stone ledge, for on that day the enmity with Squam began, more deadly by far than the ravening whirl of the roaring Vorvor. Even now they regret what they did, for whenever we learn of nearby Ükhs and their ilk, we run them to ground and destroy them."

"Whoa," said Noddy. "Naow wait j'st a moment, Dokan. If that took place before th' First Era began, wull then that was"—Noddy began counting on his fingers—"lemme see, th' First Era lasted some nine thousand five 'undred 'n' seventy-five years, 'n' then there's th' Second Era of, um, what? two thousand more, 'n' then . . . um . . . er . . . Lady Aylis, could you 'elp me out 'ere?"

Aylis smiled and said, "Some seventeen thousand or more years have gone by, Noddy."

Noddy's eyes widened at the vastness of time, and he turned to the Dwarf. "'N' you 'n' y'r Kind 'r' mad at them still?"

Dokan's right hand clenched into a white-knuckled fist. "He who seeks the wrath of the Châkka finds it, forever!"

"Remind me t'never rile you, then," said Noddy. He began to laugh, but chopped it short when no one joined him, and Dokan yet held a glare.

"What I want to know," said Wooly, "is what were those seedlings and trees he crossed through, and who planted them?"

Dokan took a deep breath and slowly expelled it, then shrugged. But Aravan said, "That was the beginnings of Darda Galion."

"The Larkenwald?" said Tarly. "The forest of Eld Trees? Those that are a thousand foot tall or more?"

"Aye," said Aravan, "seedlings transplanted here from Adonar by the Lian, for Elvenkind would have something of that world herein, and since Eld Trees are not native to Mithgar, the forest was brought here from there."

"The forest entire was transplanted here?" asked Tarly, as if yet disbelieving what he had just heard.

Aravan nodded. "As seedlings.'Twas Silverleaf's plan, and he made it so."

"Why, then," said Pipper, "if Vanidar Silverleaf was involved, I wouldn't be surprised if he wasn't one of the Elves among those who found Durek."

"He was," said Aylis.

All eyes turned her way, and Aravan said, "How dost thou know this, *chieran?*"

"As I said when we were speaking of the Gargon and how it had come unto Drimmen-deeve, I have <seen>."

A babble broke out, and Wooly held up his hands for quiet, and when it fell he said, "For this tale we're going to need more wine." And he stood and stepped to the bar.

6

Lair

As Wooly threaded through candlecast shadows, Aylis said, "Some of you might know parts of this story, and some might know other parts, but I think none of you know the entire tale. Scholars have made various deductions concerning the full story, some rather wild, others closer to the truth, but none has struck the mark." Aylis glanced at Dokan. "You might be surprised by some of this tale, my friend, especially the beginning"—she turned to Aravan—"and you as well, *chieran*."

"My Lady Aylis," called Wooly as he neared the bar, "please say no more till I return, for I would not miss a word."

"Very well," responded Aylis.

At this assurance, Noddy, an empty jack in hand, leapt to his feet and rushed off after Wooly.

Fat Jim said to Tarly, "Did you ever notice that the deeper Noddy gets into his cups, the more his Gelender accent comes to the fore."

"As do all of ours, I ween," said Tarly.

"All of our accents become Gelender?" said Aylissa, then added, "Roight y' are, Oi say, Oi dew, wot?" Then she broke into peals of silvery laughter, joined by all.

Wooly came back, bearing two bottles of dark Vanchan wine, Noddy trailing after, a hefty tankard in hand, the bosun licking at the foam 'round the plain tin lid.

As Wooly replenished the glasses and the thimble, Noddy sat down and said, "Wot wos that laffin' all about?"

Aylissa said, "Oi wos j'st demonstriatin' somma me tricksy wiays t'th' cap'n, 'ere."

As Woolly and the others stifled laughter, "Mmm . . ." said Noddy, as he took a swallow of his ale. He lowered the tankard with a satisfied sigh, then said, "Stealth 'n' goile, eh?" With his drink he saluted Aravan. " 'At's wot th' cap'n alwiays says, stealth 'n' goile be th' best way t'win, roight?"

"'At's roight, Cap'n," replied the Pysk, raising her thimble of wine up in salute to Noddy.

At this, the others could no longer hold their laughter, and they broke into guffaws, Noddy not the least in joining them.

Pipper, grinning widely, raised his own glass and said, "Oi say 'ere's t'Noddy."

Aravan pushed out a hand and said, "Enough, my friends. Enough. Instead, let us hear what Lady Aylis has to say regarding what she has <seen>."

"Yes," said Dokan. "I would hear of the Ghath coming unto Kraggen-cor, for long has that been a great mystery, and if Lady Aylis can shed some light through her <seeing>, then I for one would be grateful. —Oh, we Châkka have some hint of the events, for there is a story of how it came about, but I would know the truth."

Aylis said, "The story you have heard, Dokan, I'm afraid it is but fancy, for the tale of the Draedan, the Gargon, the Ghath, the Fearcaster is not one of flight, but rather one of foresight, of guile, of shaping, of revenge, of delving, of dread, of savage destruction, of heroism in a lost cause, of heroism in a cause sustained, of desperation and necessity, and, I think, nigh the root of it, it is one of <wild magic>."

"Oh, my," said Pipper, his eyes wide in wonder. "All of that in one tale."

"Nay, wee one," said Aylis. "All of that in several tales intertwined."

Binkton looked at Pipper and said, "Mayhap it's as one of our distant ancestors used to claim: it's all connected, you know." Then he turned to Aylis. "Are any Warrows involved?"

Aylis smiled. "Aye. Two."

A smug look came over Binkton, and he leaned back in his chair. "Then I think Pipper and I know at least part of your tale."

"What?" said Pipper, frowning in puzzlement. "What part do I know? —No, wait, don't tell me. I'd rather hear the story from Lady Aylis and not have any of it spoiled. I mean, that would be sort of like reading the back of the book before ever reading the front. I think it's much better to get there the way the tale-teller intended."

Noddy took a big slurp of his ale and then glared about and said, "Oi say, is this goin' t'be another one o' them tellin's where we 'ave a big long talk about som'thin' 'r' other roundabout, 'stead of getting roight t'th' tale?" He lifted his tankard. "If so, Oi'm goin' after another fill."

Aylis looked from one to another. "Any questions before I begin?"

"I have one . . ." said Tarly.

Noddy huffed and stood and started toward the bar.

" . . . Tell us how you go about <seeing>."

Noddy spun on his heel and sat down again, for he would hear this as well.

"I learned many ways to <see>," said Aylis. "But first of all I—or any Seer, for that matter—must clear the mind and calm the heart and quiet the spirit and soothe the soul, all of which are needed to achieve the proper state to focus on the issue at hand. Once that is done, I sometimes use cards on which I cast a spell while shuffling, and the order in which they then are arranged is affected, and when I turn them up, they show me that which I seek, unless there is interference or unless I have not achieved the suitable state of tranquillity. At other times I look into a black mirror and—"

"Black mirror?" said Pipper. "How can a mirror be black?"

Aylis smiled at the buccan. "I pour ebon ink into a basin of water."

"Oh, I see," said Pipper.

"As do I," replied Aylis. "—I <see>, that is."

Pipper grinned.

Aylis continued: "At times I hold something of someone long held—a locket, a pin, a brooch, a weapon—and I use it to <see> what has occurred in its past, or what might come about in the future."

"You can see the future?" said Fat Jim.

"That is quite difficult, Jim," said Aylis, "for there are branchings upon branchings beyond count, numberless choices determining what the future holds, where a decision one way leads down a different path from the same decision even slightly altered. Too, it takes much of the caster's <fire> to marshal the aethyr to <see> down those many branchings, for not only does the future depend on one person's choices, it depends on the choices many others make as well."

"It's all connected," said Binkton.

"Exactly so, Bink," replied Aylis. "One great web or tapestry. And a slight tug here makes a change there, affecting the warp and woof of all. And with our choices, all of us are constantly tugging at the fabric and the weaving of events, affecting what the future will bring."

"So as y' don't see a clear picture, Lady Aylis?" asked Noddy. "J'st a myr-myria—, um, lots o' paths, lots o' things wot moight be, dependin' on wot folks do?"

"Yes, Noddy, a myriad of ways the future might unfold, though at times some paths are more likely than others. For a Mage such as I, <seeing> the past is rather easily done, but <seeing> the future, most taxing—a trial that one does not undertake lightly."

Dokan, who had been holding his tongue and waiting for Aylis to resolve a mystery that had plagued the Châkka for millennia, said, "And now about this tale of yours—"

"Yes," said Pipper, "tell us how you came upon it."

Dokan groaned, but again held his tongue.

Aylis took a deep breath. "After the destruction of Rwn, when I was trapped on Vadaria, I came across some items of the most famous Seer of all, things that belonged to Othran. And when Aravan and I crossed the in-between and came through the nexus in Neddra and back to Mithgar, while Aravan was in Kraggen-cor to recruit a Drimm warband to sail on the *Eroean,* I made journeys of my own."

Aravan frowned. "Where? Thou didst not leave the holt."

"Nay," said Aylis. "I stayed therein, but the first journey I took was to the Gargon's Lair."

"You were in the Gargon's Lair?" blurted Pipper.

"She just said she was," said Binkton.

"Yes, I know," said Pipper. "What I meant to ask is, why?"

"That is at the heart of my tale," said Aylis. "I went there to

<see>, and found four events entwined. I will tell of the first, second, and third, and reserve the fourth event to tell last."

"Ah," said Dokan, "we come to it finally."

"Yes," replied Aylis. She looked about, and when none said aught, she continued:

"There is a tale that the Gargon was fleeing from the ruins of the Great War of the Ban when he came unto Drimmen-deeve, yet that tale is untrue, for even as the mighty ram Whelm battered for entrance at the Dawn-Gate of Kraggen-cor in that very same war, Modru saw that even this dreadful engine of fear would not succeed in breaking the gates, and so . . . —But wait, I am getting ahead of the events as they happened.

"Instead, this story begins far back before the First Era, in the time of the tale that Dokan just recounted, the tale of the drowning of First Durek. . . ."

Othran the Seer slumped back from the bowl filled with an ebon liquid. Perspiration runnelled under his raiment, and his hair was plastered to his head. Haggard he looked, worn, and he had terribly aged in this handful of candlemarks, for he had spent much <fire> in the casting, and using <fire> bears a dreadful cost: the loss of youth. And the more <fire> spent, the greater the cost. Othran had started out as a vibrant, dark-haired Mage who appeared to be no more than thirty, and he had aged some forty years. His hair was now white, his skin age-spotted, and there was a tremor in his left hand, all in the space of six candlemarks. For he had burned years of youth following thread after thread of the vision, and many of them led to the same terrible place, and he knew he had to do something to prevent that dreadful future. But what? He did not know.

Standing, slowly he straightened, and his bones creaked, his joints were stiff, and he ached all over. It would take a long <rest> on Vadaria to regain that which he had spent, as opposed to even longer on Mithgar, ten to a hundred times longer, for not only did revitalization depend on aethyric alignment, it also depended on the remaining <fire> of the caster.

But first he had to conceive and perhaps carry out a plan to thwart that which he had <seen>. Yet with those events many millennia in the future, what could he do to stop them from coming to

pass? He did not know. He did not know. But he would think on it. He had the time, though the sooner enacted, the more likely the success of whatever scheme he devised.

One of the problems with <seeing> the future was that it was most difficult <seeing> one's own actions, for that seemed a blind spot in such castings, and so he had not <seen> what he himself would do to prevent or even impede the events he knew were most likely coming.

Perhaps I should ask Thelon to look into my future and <see> what I might do. Ah, but with so many who have gone over to the dark, can I trust anyone at all? If I choose wrongly, then the whole might come to ruin. Ah, me, but I will sleep on it.

Othran hobbled over to his cot and eased himself down and fell into an exhausted sleep.

A moon went by, and then another, but at last Othran conceived his plan, and he boarded a ship and traveled to Jugo, there where the new city sat on the banks of the Avagon, there where it poured its flow into the Avagon Sea. River's End, the city was called, and there he bought four horses—one for riding, the other three to bear his supplies—for he would fare on a long journey.

A sevenday later he set out on his trek and travelled northwesterly, heading for the land of Gûnar, and a moon later he passed through Gûnarring Gap. And just beyond the Gap he came to a crofter's stead, where, for a small pittance and a stream of gossip and news, he boarded for two weeks, simply resting, for he had journeyed long and he was weary. Too, his horses needed a respite, and they grazed on rich grasses and ate the oats the farmer and his wife supplied. For the children, Othran performed small tricks of prestidigitation, augmented now and again with a trivial flick of <fire>.

But at last he felt recovered enough to press on, and so he laded his horses with new supplies, and paid the crofter in silver, then rode away to the north, saying that he would return someday.

A fortnight elapsed, as northerly he fared, across Gûnar ere coming to Gûnar Slot, a great rift in the Grimwalls, there where the mountains changed course: running away westerly on one side of the Slot, curving to the north on the other. The next day Othran rode into the vast cleft, which ranged in breadth from seven miles at its narrowest to seventeen at its widest. And the walls of the

mountains to either side rose sheer, as if cloven by a great axe. Trees lined the floor for many miles, though long stretches of barren stone along one side or the other frowned down at anyone passing below. Three days Othran rode in the Gap, for it was nearly seventy-five miles through. But at last he emerged, and on northerly he did fare.

Now he could see in the distance ahead a great ebon peak rearing up in the dark chain of the Grimwalls, and beyond that peak was one ruddy red. And that's where he was headed: to the sanguine slopes of that mighty mountain, for that's where his plan to thwart the future he had <seen> would perhaps come to fruition.

He swung a bit westerly and headed for the ford at the River Hâth, and he came to it late in the day. Crossing over, he made camp on the northerly shore, and slept that eve to the soothing burble of water running near.

The next day, following a branch of the Hâth, he swung a bit easterly to come once more to the foothills running along the shoulders of the Grimwall, where he turned north again, the range looming to his right, the rolling land of Lianion on his left.

Northerly he rode another day, and he reached the flank of the ebon mountain. For the next two days his primary sight of the Grimwalls was that of black stone, but finally he passed beyond this dark monolith to come unto the red stone of the greater mountain of the two.

Another day passed as he turned and made his way through the foothills to the place he sought, a place where a cleft in the rust-red stone opened into a passage within.

Not far from the cleft, he found a narrow but grassy box canyon, and he set camp within the canyon, not only to have a base, but to comfort the horses by its very presence while he was away and within the mountain itself. Then he strung a simple rope fence across the entry to keep his horses from straying beyond.

He slept well that night, the red coals of a small fire augmenting the light of the moon and the stars high above, and after breaking fast the next morn, he took up a heavy iron hammer and a thick iron rod nearly as tall as he, both of which he had borne all the way from the city of Kairn on the Isle of Rwn.

Bearing the burdens, from the box canyon he strode, and up the slot to the crevice leading into the flank of the red stone mountain.

He paused at the entrance and calmed his mind and spirit and heart and soul, after which he muttered a word or two, then strode on into the dark, now needing no lantern to see by.

Deep he went, far within, until he came to one of the places he had seen in his vision. Drawing on his gloves, there he set the iron rod into a crevice, and using the hammer, he drove it deeply in.

Once more he calmed himself and muttered other arcane words, and knowledge came to him of how to summon those he would have aid him.

He began hammering as hard as he could a rhythmic signal upon the embedded iron rod, pausing now and then to place his ear to the shaft and listen.

In brief spurts, long he hammered and long he listened, sweat pouring down his brow, Othran pausing now and again to simply recover from the intense labor of vigorous pounding; he was after all quite aged now. Again and again he smote the rod, and again and again he listened, trying to quell his own harsh breathing.

At last there came a response.

Once more he signalled, and once more listened to the answer.

Several times in all he hammered on the rod, changing the pattern of his message, and several times he did listen, nodding in satisfaction.

At last, he set down his hammer and turned about and went back to his camp and fell into a dead sleep.

Two more days passed while Othran waited, but on the third morning he broke fast and tended the steeds, then took up his knapsack with water and food and went again to the notch. Once more he stopped at the entrance and calmed himself and spoke arcane words, then into the rift he strode.

When he reached the rod, he took up the hammer, for to the eyes of the one coming Othran knew he himself would seem ethereal, nearly invisible, but the metal of the hammer would be seen; and then he sat down and waited.

Time passed, and he dozed, but he was awakened by the sound of stone splitting, and he looked up to see diamond eyes peering down upon him from a height of seventeen feet.

Othran smiled, and cast another spell, and said in a strange tongue, much like that of sliding rocks, "Welcome, Lithon."

* * *

"Lithon?" blurted Aylissa. "The same Stone Giant that saved Durek?"

Aylis nodded at the Pysk. "The very same Utrun, Liss."

"Wull, wot wos all that there 'ammering on th' rod about?" asked Noddy.

"It was Othran signalling for aid," said Aylis, glancing at Dokan, "much as the Drimm signal through stone to one another, so, too, did Othran hammer out signals to fetch an Utrun unto him. Through the rock of the world did Othran's signals radiate, losing strength the farther they went, yet they were just strong enough to reach the ears of Lithon."

"How did he know the code?" said Dokan.

"He cast a spell," said Binkton, then he turned to Aylis. "Right, Lady Aylis?"

"Yes, Binkton. Seers cast spells to speak other tongues, and this was but a variation of that."

"Well then he must've cast a second spell to talk to the Giant," said Pipper.

"He did, indeed," said Aylis.

"Wull, what did he want a Stone Giant for?" asked Fat Jim.

"I know," said Binkton. "It was to—"

"Hush!" cried Pipper, rounding on his cousin. "Didn't you hear what I said about reading the end of the book first? Just button that loose lip of yours and let Lady Aylis tell the story."

Bink was somewhat taken aback, and he meekly made the motions of buttoning his lip.

Satisfied, Pipper turned back to Aylis. "Please go on, my lady. I'm all at nines and elevens wanting to know what happened."

Aylis took a small sip of her dark Vanchan, then said, "Othran spoke to Lithon awhile, and then the Utrun cleft the stone, and Othran followed him up and along the corridor he made. . . ."

When Lithon had nearly reached the outer wall of the mountain, there he paused, and after a long discussion with the Seer, the Stone Giant began shaping stone, conferring with Othran as he did so. Then they went back unto where the iron rod was embedded, and from there they went deeper into the mountain, following a natural shaft. Long they went, veering left and right, ascending inclines and descending gradients, bearing ever easterly and going ever deeper under the burden of stone above. Twelve miles altogether did they go, briefly stopping now and then to let Othran catch his breath. Finally, down a long, gentle slope they came to the bank of an underground river flowing through the left-hand wall and across the passage to plunge under the wall on the right.

At this point, again the Utrun shaped the stone above, following the Seer's directions.

Then across the river they fared, the Stone Giant now bearing Othran, for the way ahead was arduous, and they would go more swiftly. At last they came to a vein of starsilver, and here did Lithon once more follow the Seer's directions, and he shaped a chamber, long and high and rectangular, with but a single door in.

And when he was finished, smooth were the walls and ceiling and floor, the chamber completely bare, but for the distant door, a silveron vein running across the floor, the argent line with many offshoots running short distances, some up the walls, one across the ceiling, each to taper off into thinner and thinner veins to disappear altogether.

Othran then looked about the completed chamber, barren of all but the starsilver veins, and he was pleased.

"It is over and done with," he said, "but for a few simple spells."

And as he calmed his mind and spirit and soul and heart and made ready to spend some <fire>, of a sudden a glazed look came over his eyes, and in a voice both like and yet unlike his own, he spoke to Lithon, and the Stone Giant set to work again.

And in the center of the chamber as Othran guided him, Lithon raised up a stone slab, a huge block with a smooth top, and he fashioned carvings along the sides. And as Othran continued to direct the Stone Giant, Lithon inset a seam of starsilver up the side of the block, and led another seam from it unto the starsilver hinges of the door. In the block at the end of the vein he fashioned a thin slot no more than an inch or so tall, but one that reached deep into the block, a silveron lining within the niche and connected to the silveron seam. And as Othran described them, Lithon shaped two faint but conjoined starsilver runes beside the crevice, a trace of silveron merging the symbols with the silveron within.

When this was done, Othran scanned the result and seemed satisfied, and touching the runes he spoke an arcane word or two, then stepped back, and the glazed look vanished from his eyes, and he staggered, as if suddenly released from an invisible grip.

Othran seemed nonplussed when he saw what had been done, and even more so when Lithon told him that all had been made at the Seer's own instruction.

"Ah, me," said Othran, sighing, "I don't remember any of it."

"Nevertheless, you so directed me," said Lithon.

Othran examined the block, and when he came to the runes he squatted and looked at them long, then cast a small spell. "It is a form of Sylva, the eld Elvish tongue, and says 'west point,' or 'west pick,' and about them is some arcane power, but one I know not."

Othran stood and turned to the Utrun. "And you say, my friend, that I seemed in a trance?"

"Aye," replied Lithon. "And spoke in a voice like and yet not like your own."

Othran sighed and shook his head. "At times I've been known to do so, or so my fellow Mages say. Never do I know why or to what end, but we shall let this stand."

They stepped to the massive door of the chamber, its starsilver hinges recessed deeply. And there Othran cast a spell. Then once again Lithon took the Seer up and they made their way back to the underground river, leaving behind the door to the chamber standing wide.

At the river, once again Lithon bore the Seer across, and there did Othran cast a spell, this on the stone Lithon had shaped above.

Now, with Othran walking, they went down the passage beyond, finally coming back to the iron rod, and this did Lithon extract.

"My friend," said Othran. "Signal your fellow Utruni, and tell them what we have done, and ask that they leave this passage and the stone herein untouched, for with it I hope to thwart Modru's plan."

And so, on the living stone itself did Lithon hammer out a signal, long and involved, and he listened for responses. And when they came he said, "The message is being passed on. Yet I hear the signal of another, and he is near, but I understand it not."

Othran handed the rod to Lithon. "Let me listen."

With a casual push, Lithon reset the rod in the stone, and Othran placed his ear against it. Long he listened, and then spoke a word, and listened some more. At last he said, "It is a call for help. It seems a Dwarf has become entrapped in the caverns beyond."

"Ah, Dwarves . . . they enhance the stone," said Lithon. "When we are finished here, I will go to his aid."

"We are finished, Lithon. You can go to him now. Me, I have but one more spell to cast, then all is set, and I can but pray to Adon that what I have seen never comes to pass. Yet if it does, then mayhap the work we've done this day will stop a dreadful end from occurring."

Lithon looked down on this ephemeral being, nearly invisible to the Utrun, but for the hammer he bore. And in that voice sounding much like rocks sliding o'er one another, Lithon replied, "As you have said." The Stone Giant plucked the rod from the wall and handed it to Othran, then turned and pulled open a rift and went within the living stone.

Othran marvelled at the ease with which the Utrun moved into the very rock, opening the way before himself, closing the way after, leaving the stone as if it had ne'er been rent.

The Seer turned and made his way back to the outer world; night now lay across the land. He paused long enough to cast a spell at the entry on the worked stone above. Then he left the rift behind and went back to his camp, where once more he fell into a deep and dreamless sleep.

In the following days, Othran made his way back in the direction whence he had come: south along the Grimwall, and south through Gûnar Gap, and south across Gûnar, and somewhere along the way he looked into a cup of inky water to <see>. And he <sent> a presentiment to an Elf named Silverleaf, there in the aborning forest of Darda Galion, as it was now called—for even then silverlarks were nesting among the more mature of the trees. The <sending> was a premonition so deeply embedded that Silverleaf had no conscious knowledge that someone had thrust this intuition upon him, and he sensed that someone was somewhere in that cambered vale some distance to the north, someone who might need aid. And Silverleaf rounded up a warband and went along the east side of the Grimwall, where he and his comrades came across a marauding group of *Rûpt*. These they slew, and within the *Spaunen* gear, they noted a Dwarven axe. . . .

Othran went on south to the city of River's End, and there he waited for a boat. And some weeks later, he set sail for Gelen, on the way to Rwn, and then to Atala beyond.

On the ship with him was a recently rescued Dwarf, going to Gelen as well.

"Hoy, naow, wos that there Dwarf this 'ere Durek wot Dokan told about?" asked Noddy, glancing owl-eyed at Dokan, that Dwarf sitting back in his chair, his eyes wide in revelation.

"Who else could it have been?" said Binkton. "It's all connected, you know."

"That's not all of the story, is it?" asked Tarly. "I mean, that chamber Othran and Lithon made, what was it for? You can't just stop here, Lady Aylis, else I'll die of the aggravation of never knowing."

"Before you continue," said Wooly, standing, "we need more wine."

Noddy arose, but then quickly sat back down. "Whoo. Oi've done gone all dizzy." He held out his tankard to Wooly. "Would y' kindly refill moi own wi' somma that good strong ale from th' 'Olt o' Vorn?"

Wooly looked askance at Noddy, but Fat Jim said, "Go on, Wooly. I mean, we only live once, and I want to see how near death Noddy says he feels on the morrow, loading up as he is on Vornholt ale."

Aravan chuckled, and when Aylis turned a curious eye on him, Aravan said, "Whene'er that ale is brought to mind, I recall a time Bair drank a great lot of it. He woke the next morn in bed with a dark-eyed woman whom he didn't remember at all. His clothes awry, he staggered downstairs, one boot in hand, the other on the wrong foot, and he didn't fare at all well that day, nor did his boot."

"His boot?" asked Aylis, just as Wooly came back from the bar.

"He was quite ill, and couldn't find a bucket," said Aravan, laughing.

"Oh, poor Bair," said Aylis, though she smiled.

"Oh, poor boot, don't you mean?" said Aylissa, grinning.

Wooly handed Noddy his tankard and then replenished the glasses all 'round. As Wooly dropped a dollop into Aylissa's thimble, the Pysk said, "Why do you suppose Othran didn't remember anything about the fashioning of the block in the chamber, or the runes set thereon?"

All eyes turned to Aylis. "I deem he was in the grip of <wild magic>, and I will have more to say about the runes."

Binkton started to speak, but Pipper said, "Button!" and Binkton clamped his lips tightly.

Aylis looked about to see if there were any more questions, and when her gaze settled on Dokan, he said, "It was Durek on that ship with Othran, wasn't it?"

"Aye," said Aylis. "Yet Othran said nought but pleasantries unto him and shared small talk as they sailed for Gelen. —Oh, Othran did win a trivial sum from Durek as they played at cards, though nought else was exchanged between them."

"He said nought of being the one who sent the Stone Giant to aid Durek?" asked Wooly. "Nor ought about sending Silverleaf, too?"

Aylis shook her head. "Nothing at all."

"And Othran sailed on to Rwn and then Atala after?" said Tarly.

"Aye."

"Then that's the end of his story, eh?" said Fat Jim, "and his attempt to foil Modru?"

"Not quite," said Aylis. "You see, to further thwart Modru and his minions, Othran sailed on to Rwn, where he conferred with Alamar—my father—a Mage whom Othran could trust. He told my sire of all that he had <seen>, and long did they ponder what might be done. And finally, even though it might give Modru some small satisfaction, Othran asked my sire to fashion an enspelled silveron nugget to give to a shapeshifter to hold in trust; it would be needed by two who were yet to come."

"Why would a silveron nugget give Modru some satisfaction?" asked Fat Jim. "And why would Othran and your sire do such a thing?"

"Had they not," said Aylis, "then an even greater calamity would have befallen all of existence."

"Wot has this t'do wi' th' Gargon?" asked Noddy.

"Nought," said Aylis. "It is another tale altogether, and one long in the telling."

"Then, *chier,*" said Aravan, "I suggest we save that one for another time."

"I agree," said Aylis, looking about. When none lodged any objection, Aylis said, "After leaving Rwn, Othran sailed on to Atala to see both Dwynfor and Gilian, one to fashion a long-knife, the other a red arrow."

"Oh, oh, I know, I know those two," said Pipper, bouncing in his chair. "They were the ones at Challerain Keep, the ones Tuck—"

"Button!" commanded Binkton. Then he grinned wickedly and added, "Tit for tat, cousin. Tit for tat."

"Right," said Pipper, sighing.

"If there is nought else . . ." said Aylis.

None had ought to say, and so Aylis continued:

"It was not for millennia upon millennia that Othran's plan had a chance to come to fruition, but in the Second Era, during the Great War of the Ban, as Whelm knocked for entrance into the vast halls of Drimmen-deeve, Modru realized that even this mighty feartoken would not be enough to sunder the Dawn-Gate and let his Horde within. Yet he would have his vengeance against the Drimm, for long past a *Khana* Durek of theirs had turned him down, a *Khana* Durek who would not yield up any starsilver in an alliance with the Foul Folk. And so he sent Thuuth Uthor—a Gargon, a Draedan, a Ghath, a Dread—to enter by a secret passage in the flanks of the stone of Drimmen-deeve and drive the Drimm out. And Modru *knew* Thuuth Uthor would succeed, for he was a terrible Vûlk, one of Demonkind, a Fearcaster against whom none could stand, or so Modru thought, yet he had not counted on events that had taken place long past.

"And so to the west side of the red mountain known as Coron to the Elves, as Rávenor to the Drimm, and as Stormhelm to others, did Modru send the Gargon. And into the secret way did Thuuth Uthor go. . . ."

Into the cleft ponderously strode the great Mandrak, a grey, stonelike creature. Eight feet tall he was and scaled like a serpent, with taloned hands and feet and glittering fangs in a lizard-snouted face. Into the ruddy stone passage he went and into the darkness beyond, daylight fading hindward until it was gone altogether. Yet Thuuth Uthor was of Demonkind, and his vision was not hampered at all. On he went and on, passing beyond splits and cracks, following the main passage.

He came to a wide flow rushing across the corridor, bursting out from the wall on the left, plunging under the wall on the right. This he waded, the run deep and chill and forceful, and though the river came to his shoulders the Draedan was moved not, for he was as massive as stone.

On he went, the way now laden with boulders and jumbles of red scree and schist, and great mounds of large round rocks. Too, there were ledges and sheer drops and climbs and overhanging buttresses looming above. Yet none of this fazed the Gargon, as onward he trod, lured by the promise of slaughter to come.

Yet—lo!—he came to a door with a chamber beyond, and the way was standing open. Forward he stalked, into a rectangular hall, a long, high room with what seemed to be an altar centered within. And as he came to that upraised slab—*Boom!*—the door hindward slammed to. And far off on the west side of the underground river—*THDD*!—a vast block of stone crashed down from the ceiling and sealed the passageway for a hundred feet or so, the echoes of its fall sounding and resounding, reverberating back and forth along the way, with no one to hear. And even farther off, at the secret entry into the flank of Stormhelm, with a great rumble an immense massif of the mountain gave way, and down it slid—*WHOOM*!—dust and debris flying into the sky, clattering stone cascading, and when all had settled, the way in was no more.

Othran's trap had sprung.

And caught inside was the Gargon.

Long did the creature rage, all to no avail, for the door seemed to have disappeared altogether, for no seams could be found, and the grain of the stone was flawless across the place where a join might have shown. And from his own excrement and fluids Thuuth Uthor smeared runes on the chamber walls and the central block, yet starsilver took the power from them and dissipated it into the aethyr.

At last the Mandrak lay down on the altar, and there it fell into a deep sleep, one that sank the creature into an enspelled dormancy.

Days passed, and then weeks, and far away in his iron tower did Modru send another to seek his demon, for though Whelmram yet battered for entry at Drimmen-deeve's Dawn-Gate, it could not break the doors down. And as of yet the Gargon had not flushed out the Drimm. Could the creature have been slain? And so the agent searched, but he did not find, for Thuuth Uthor was trapped in a starsilver cage, where Modru's deputy could not reach.

* * *

"It was really a starsilver cage?" asked Aylissa.

"The offshoots of the silveron vein enmeshed the chamber; Lithon saw to that," said Aylis. "You see, when Othran cast his vision, he saw the Gargon stride through a starsilver-rich passage on the way in. And so he and Lithon set the trap where Othran knew spellcasting would be thwarted, both that of Modru or one of his agent's doings as well as that of Thuuth Uthor himself."

"That can't be the end of the tale," said Tarly. "Surely there is more."

"There is," said Aylis, "for two more places did I visit to <see>, and in each of them the tale goes on, yet we are not done with this place known as the Lost Prison, and also as the Gargon's Lair."

"What more is there to say of this place, this Lair, this chamber where his power is nullified?" asked Wooly. "Surely the Gargon can't get out, for he is trapped in a precious cage of silveron."

"Starsilver," said Dokan, his voice bitter.

Wooly frowned. "Starsilver, silveron, it is all the same."

"You misunderstand, Wooly," said Dokan. "What I meant was, it was starsilver that led to our downfall."

"Downfall?" said Wooly. "You mean the Gargon *did* get out?"

"Aye," replied Dokan.

"But how could he? I mean he was imprisoned," said Tarly.

"Imprisoned, aye," said Aylis, "from 2E2195 to 4E780 was the Draedan trapped, nearly three thousand years in all. Yet in the end it did escape."

Binkton and Pipper looked at one another, and Pipper, glaring at Binkton, said, "We know some of this story, but not all. Lady Aylis, would you please go on?"

Blang!

"Oh!" cried Aylissa, instantly enveloped in a cluster of shadow, startled as she was, and Vex leapt to her feet, hackles raised, the fox looking about for the danger.

But it was just that Noddy's empty tankard had fallen to the floor, the bosun dead to the world, overcome by the very strong ale from the Holt of Vorn.

"Shall I pack him off to bed?" said Tarly, even as the shadow disappeared from 'round Aylissa and she spoke soothing words to Vex.

Aravan looked at Noddy and said, "Aye. In fact, let us all take a stretch and care for other needs. Drop anchor back here in a candlemark, and we'll hear the rest of the tale."

Tarly hefted Noddy over a shoulder, and up the stairs he went as the rest headed for the privies, Pipper and Binkton dragging a chair behind on which to stand, Aylis and Aylissa heading in the opposite direction, a yet troubled Vex trailing arear.

Shortly after, Aylis opened a side door of the Red Slipper, and with postures and growls and Feyan words Aylissa spoke to Vex. The fox gave a yip and darted out into an alley and Aylissa said, "She needs the run, and I've told her to be back by dawn. I wouldn't want any of these Humans hunting her."

Aylis nodded and closed and latched the door, and then she and the Pysk headed back toward the hearth. As they sat down, Aylis said, "I see that Vex's language is quite primitive, and yet she seems to understand rather well. How many words do you and she share?"

"Including different body attitudes and snarls and grumbles and barks, along with the Feyan words I say and she understands, mayhap seven or eight hundred in all."

Aylis smiled. "Could she speak your Feyan words in addition to the other signs, that's quite enough for good conversation."

"We do have a way of talking," said the Pysk. "I ask questions, using the postures and growls and barks and the Feyan she understands, and she indicates 'yes' or 'no' with her most expressive tail. At times it takes awhile to find out what she wants or what she knows or what she wants me to know, and when that happens she gets wholly impatient, no doubt thinking that I am quite slow."

The Fox Rider broke into peals of silvery laughter, Aylis joining her.

Wearing a different shirt, Tarly came back down the stairs. "Noddy threw up all over me," Tarly said by way of explanation.

"Being bounced along on someone's shoulder when you have a stomach full of ale is likely to do that," said Fat Jim, still trying to buckle his great long belt as he came back to the hearth.

"Likely to do what?" said Wooly, just then returning.

"Throw up," said Tarly. "Noddy. On my shoulder. Besotted. My shirt."

"Ah, I see."

Aravan and Dokan arrived, followed by Binkton and Pipper, the Warrows dragging their stand-upon chair behind.

When all had settled, Aylis looked at Dokan and said, "As you said ere we took respite, indeed it was starsilver that led to the downfall of your Kraggen-cor."

"Yet silveron is more precious than diamond," said Dokan. "Can you blame us for mining that vein?"

"No, I cannot," said Aylis, "for little did you know what was coming."

"Even so," said Dokan, "we did have a clue."

"You did?" blurted Pipper.

Binkton harrumphed, and said, "You don't actually mean that *you* had a clue, Dokan, for that occurred long before your time."

"He could be one of those who *were* there," said Pipper, "and since then have been reborn."

"If I was one," said Dokan, "I remember it not. Nay, when I say 'we,' I mean we Châkka."

"Ah, *that* we," said Aylis.

"Indeed," said Dokan.

"And so you had a clue about the Gargon, you say?" said Pipper.

"Aye," replied Dokan. "Ever when we were in that section of Kraggen-cor where the Ghath was trapped, we were uneasy, as if something dreadful were at hand, or once had been within those same corridors. We thought it might be our imaginations, yet it could have been one of the creatures of the deep that now and then come nigh."

"These creatures of the deep," said Aylissa, "just what are they?"

"Great burrowing wyrms and other such," said Dokan, "and the things that prey upon them, most of which are quite savage and terrible to behold—some with long sharp teeth and some with tentacles and others with rending claws, some with poisonous exhalations, some mayhap like that *thing* in the Well of Uâjii there in the heart of the Karoo. And some can move through the earth as fast as a horse or a pony can run."

"Such a creature pursued Elyn and Thork," said Tarly, "or so it is said in Fjordland."

"Thork told of it," said Dokan, "and whatever it was, it had been summoned by Andrak, or so Thork deemed."

A silence fell upon them for a moment, but then Dokan's eyes widened in revelation. "Oh, now I remember: the silveron nugget,

Lady Aylis, the one your sire made—Thork spoke of it as well." Dokan paused, then intoned, "One to hide, One to guide."

"Aye, the nugget," said Aravan. "'Twas Dalavar Wolfmage who gave it over to Elyn. Had she and Thork not had the amulet, down through the millennia the consequences would have reached, affecting all of creation far beyond the outcome of the Dragonstone War."

"That may be as may," said Fat Jim, "but I'd like to hear Lady Aylis tell the rest of her tale."

"There is just one more thing I would say," said Dokan. "Although we would have delved the starsilver on our own, it is believed among my Kind that Modru's vile gramarye led us that way, in spite of the unease we felt."

"Modru had a hand in that?" said Tarly. "I mean even though the creature was in a starsilver cage where Modru couldn't <see>?"

"Modru could <see>?" said Aylissa. "Was he a Seer like Othran and you, Aylis?"

"I think not," said Aylis. "I ween instead he used Andrak to seek out the Draedan."

"Andrak?" said the Pysk.

"One of Modru's minions who could send his astral self flying upon the aethyr. Yet even he could not penetrate a silveron cage. But even though Andrak couldn't see within the vault, still Modru believed his terrible Fearcaster was *somewhere* within Drimmendeeve, and what better place to hide his Negus of Terror than in a silveron cage? Hence Modru might have sent the Drimm delving that way, for it was within Modru's power through a surrogate to <suggest> to a Châk that silveron lay along that course, and the one so enspelled would not know it had been done, and so . . ."

Again a quiet fell upon them, but then Aravan said, "Among the Lian, we also believe that Modru's gramarye was involved, though we have no proof. Yet, heed, Dokan, ye Drimma were not the only ones who had a clue that the Draedan might have been within the Deeves."

"Eh?" grunted Dokan.

"Elven lore had long spoke of a lost prison and maintained that a great evil was entrapped therein somewhere beneath the Grimwall, and that if the evil was e'er loosed, it would be Modru's work. Yet how we might have known of such is not told."

Aylis said, "That, too, was Othran's work, for he sent a premonition unto Elmaron, future Coron of Darda Galion, indicating that such a thing might happen. Elmaron told others of his presentiment, and soon it passed into lore. Just where under the Grimwall the evil might be trapped was not within the portent, and so the entire range was suspect, and Elvenkind knew not that Drimmendeeve was the place."

"Even had we known," said Aravan, "mayhap we Lian could not have prevented the calamity, for Draedani are terrifying Fearcasters and none can withstand their gaze."

Again Pipper and Binkton looked at one another, but both managed to hold their tongues and not speak of what they knew.

"Can we get back to the story?" said Fat Jim. Then he laughed. "Hmm . . . I'm beginning to sound like Noddy demanding that the tale go on."

"Nevertheless," said Tarly.

Aylis looked about, and when none had ought to add, she said, "I stepped just outside the Lost Prison, there where the wall was shattered, and there I cast another <seeing> and this is what I <saw>:"

"DelfLord Glain," said MineMaster Relk, "Gand's hunch has proved to be right, there at the exhausted vein."

"You have struck more starsilver in the abandoned shaft?" said Glain.

"Aye," said Relk. "Long did we delve, and it looked quite unpromising, yet just as we were nigh to quitting, we came upon a new vein, and it has proved to be quite rich."

Glain slapped a palm to the arm of the throne. "Kala! I would see this treasure. Gems and gold we have, and precious, but starsilver is beyond dear."

Glain beckoned a Châk page to him, and said, "Call Orn to my side, and together we shall go see this wondrous wealth of Kraggencor."

Soon Orn came into the throne chamber. "Sire?"

"Prepare for a journey, my son," said Glain, smiling. "We go to see starsilver in its natural state."

Orn turned to Relk. "Vein or a pocket?"

"Vein," said Relk.

Orn clenched a fist in elation. "Kala!"

* * *

Some twenty miles westerly on a direct line from the throne room, but twenty-six miles away by the shortest route, a score of Châkka miners delved along the face of a precious starsilver vein, working their way through solid stone, drillers and hammerers breaking the rock, gleaners bearing the rubble away and examining it for nuggets and trace, MineMaster Gand directing all as forward they pressed.

In a hidden prison a terrible Dread muted its power and waited patiently.

Early next morn, Glain and Orn met Relk at an underground stable. There on a string of ponies they laded supplies to bear to the miners at the vein. Saddling three more, they mounted up and headed northwesterly.

Their Dwarven lanterns lighting the path, twisting through carven corridors and natural tunnels they went, down slopes here and up slopes there, Relk leading them by ways along which there were no stairs for steeds to manage, for this was the road from the mines to the forges, and the path they followed was one which was delved for ponies and horse-drawn wains to travel, and wheel tracks could be seen on the stone.

Then westerly they turned, and now and again they passed along crevasses left and right, and here they did tightly control the animals, for some of the pits were quite deep. Yet deep or no, for a steed to stumble into one would mark the end of the beast and perhaps the rider as well.

At times riding, at other times walking and leading their steeds, and still at other times stopping at way stations to rest and water the ponies and to relieve themselves, onward they went, while halls and corridors crossed and recrossed and joined and forked away from the passage they followed; millennia had gone into this labyrinthine delving, and had the three not been Châkka, they would soon have been lost within the maze.

And slowly they descended deeper under the red stone of Rávenor—Châkur for "storm hammer"—though other Folk did call it Stormhelm, after the raging tempests that oft crowned its crest.

They stopped at the noontide to feed the animals a bit of grain, and for they themselves to take a meal: bread baked that morn in Dwarven ovens, along with cheese and apples. They fed the cores to the ponies, then they took up the trek again.

Still, the general trend was downward, deeper under the mountain, and they rode and walked and rode again, hooves and voices echoing as they advanced. And the farther they went, the more restless became the steeds.

"Ever has it been in these environs," said Relk, "that an air of disquiet lies over all, and the animals sense it before we Châkka. Even so, the closer we come to the starsilver, the more we ourselves will feel the unease."

"What is it, I wonder?" said Orn. "Bad air?"

"Mayhap," replied Relk. "Some think the place too near the things of the underearth. Others think it is somehow cursed, though just how, they cannot say. Me, I think it is a peculiar shaping of the caverns down here, and though we cannot hear it, there is an undertone in the air."

"An undertone caused by what?" asked Glain.

Relk shrugged. "I am not certain. Mayhap the water, for a stream runs nigh. Mayhap the slow breathing of the air itself."

"Hnh," grunted Glain, and onward they rode.

Finally, late in the day, they came to a gathering of ponies, tended by a pair of Châkka youths. All the animals seemed restless, though none haled at their tethers. The two stable hands welcomed the diversion of visitors and asked what news of the Châkkaholt at large. Orn told them of a trading party of Elves that had come from Darda Galion to Baralan, exchanging herbs and simples and Eldwood carvings for silver to work into gem-bearing jewelry, and yes there had been rather exotic females among the Elven band.

Along with the youths, Glain and Orn and Relk began unlading the supplies: food and drink for the delvers and the two stable hands, oats for the ponies. When this was done, the DelfLord and his son and the MineMaster strode on, leaving the youths behind.

Shortly the trio came to a natural stone arch over a ravine, water tumbling in its depths. Just beyond the arch and to the left a rough passage bored off into the dark. But straight ahead the corridor slanted down and bore marks of mattocks and picks and chisels and drills: this was the shaft to the silveron, a tunnel made wider by the delvers.

Along this way did the three of them go, and from ahead they could hear the faint chank of hammers driving drill rods, and an occasional shout, all growing louder the farther the trio went.

Four miles in all did they travel, ever deeper under the mountain, and as they went downward, the uneasiness grew, as if something unseen were lurking. Shaking off these vagaries, Glain and Orn and Relk pressed onward, and at last they came to the mining crew there in a narrow shaft, and all paused as DelfLord Glain and his son Orn came in among their midst. And in the walls where they worked a soft silvery vein gleamed an argent glint, traceries splitting out in minor streaks from the central seam, for here was starsilver in its natural state.

"Kala," breathed Glain, reaching forth to touch the vein, but Orn took a deep breath and looked all 'round.

"Sire, there is something . . . something evil nigh, though I cannot—"

—At that moment DelfLord Glain's fingers touched the starsilver, and—

—WHOOM!—

The endwall of the bore blasted outward, drill rods and great shards of stone hurtling along the shaft, slaying all in the way. Delvers were killed instantly, MineMaster Gand among them. Orn and Glain and a dozen others were struck by the flying shards, yet they had survived, only to be drowned in terror, for Thuuth Uthor stepped outward, out from the Lost Prison, out from the Lair, out from Othran's trap; after three thousand years of imprisonment the Ghath was free at last, and these Dubh stood frozen in its dreadful gaze, and it would have its revenge.

With its hideous claws, it began rending, shredding, ripping, tearing Châkka apart, viscera and blood and bone and tissue flying wide in its rage.

Glain was rent asunder, as was Orn, along with the fourteen remaining Châkka, those that had not been slain outright by the flying stone as the Ghath had burst free.

Four miles away, ponies shrilled in panic, and tugged and pulled, and many broke loose and fled. The Châkka youths' hearts were pounding in terror, and yet the two took up their axes and stepped down the corridor toward where the DelfLord had gone. Over the natural arch they went and partway down the passage beyond, their dread growing with every step taken. And in spite of the chaos of the ponies arear, they could hear a horrible roaring, and hear as well shrill screams rent from raw throats.

Forward went the two young Châkka, and they held their weapons in white-knuckled grips. Of a sudden, with one final terrible roar, all ahead fell into dead silence, and the Châkka looked at one another.

And then a dreadful fear swept over them, as if something to the fore down the shaft had sensed them and was coming to slay, a wave of terror flowing ahead.

The pair turned and ran, and came once more to the ponies. They cut all the remaining ones loose, and, not bothering with saddles and tack, they leapt astride two, and galloped away.

The youngsters sounded the alarm, and warbands were assembled and sent to see what this dreadful thing was.

Many were slain, and yet some escaped, and they brought word it was a Ghath.

More warbands were assembled, and the Ghath slew and slew.

After they and others were slaughtered in one last bloody day of great butchery, the Châkka fled Kraggen-cor, out the Daûn Gate, out the Dusken Door, Châkka and the veil-swathed Châkia and children escaping to the Red Hills and the Crystal Caverns and to Mineholt North.

Yet the Châkka were not the only ones driven from this region: great numbers of Elves of the bordering Realm of Darda Galion fled as well, for a Draedan now dwelled in the north.

Too, steaders in Riamon abandoned their lands nigh the Châkkaholt, for even though Adon's Ban now reigned, they were within the Gargon's range if he decided to rampage at night.

And so things stood for some five hundred more years.

"Five hundred years?" said Binkton. "I thought the next thing would be some twelve hundred years later, in January of 4E2019."

"Be still, Bink," said Pipper. "You're not telling this tale. Besides, though I didn't know the year, she's right. The next thing isn't in 4E2019, but something earlier."

"Wull," said Bink, "what could have been earlier? I mean . . . —Oh, wait, I see."

"Right," said Pipper. "Now just shut up and listen."

Dokan sat with his hood cast over his head, for even though those events had taken place long past, still he mourned Glain and Orn and all the others slain by the Ghath.

"Lady Aylis," said Fat Jim, "you said that you went to—what? three places?—yes, three places in the Black Hole to, um, <see>. Y've told us about the Lost Prison. What were the other two?"

"The second place I went to was the Hall of the Gravenarch, and there did I find two events entwined, and the third place was at the Great Deep, and there I found one event in all."

Pipper looked at Binkton and smiled just as wickedly as Binkton had once smiled at him, as if to say, "Tol' y'."

"Say on, Lady Aylis," said Tarly, "for I would hear the end of this saga."

"No saga this, Tarly Halversson, but a short retelling instead," said Aylis. "Would you read a saga, then I suggest you see *The Ravenbook,* or the *Journal of Peregrin Fairhill.* Those are two sagas worth reading, and they tell a great part of this tale."

"You can find copies in the Bosky," said Pipper, receiving a button-your-lip signal from Binkton.

"Mayhap one day, Lady Aylis," said Tarly. "Till then, I'll be content with what you tell."

Aylis looked about. "Does anyone need a privy break? No? Well, then I'll go on:

"Some five hundred years after the Draedan broke free of the Lost Prison, Braggi collected a band of raiders, for he had a plan to slay the Gargon.

"Together they made a trip to Blackstone, and there they did recover several great spear points made of a silvery alloy, traces of a dark *smüt* within the flutes. 'Twas the deadly points from a like number of iron shafts originally meant for Sleeth the Cold-drake, but now they would be used on the Fearcaster Thuuth Uthor. And they fashioned a ballista to cast new-made iron spears bearing those tips, for during the Great War of the Ban, such a spear-throwing weapon had slain a Gargon outside the walls of Dendor.

"However, unlike the one used at Dendor, these spear points they took up from Blackstone were smeared with the deadly poison the Pysks use on their own tiny shafts—"

"What?" said Aylissa. "Where would they get Pysk poison?"

Aylis smiled. "After the destruction of Rwn, back when your

sire and dam and Aravan and the crew of the *Eroean* went after Durlok, they fashioned several great ballistas and Pysk-poisoned spears to deal with Durlok's Trolls. Not all of that poison was used, and somehow, one of the Drimm from that crew took some ashore with him after the *Eroean* was stored in the hidden grotto in Thell Cove at the end of the First Era. And that was what was on the spears meant for Sleeth."

"Wait a moment," said Wooly, "that was thousands of years later. I mean, the crew of the *Eroean* took on those Trolls right at the end of the First Era. And if Braggi and his raiders went after the Gargon around 4E1280 or so, that poison had to be some five thousand years old. Would it still be potent after all that time?"

All eyes turned to Aylissa, and she shrugged and said, "I don't think that's ever been tested. Even so, were I you and came across those spears millennia later, I think the safe thing to do is to touch them not."

Wooly nodded, then said, "Sorry I interrupted, Lady Aylis. Please go on with the telling."

Aylis nodded and said, "Braggi and his raiders then made new shafts and mounted the recovered points thereon, all with the deadly toxin. And they took the spears and the spear-caster unto Drimmendeeve, and far outside the Dawn-Gate they assembled the ballista in the light of day and cocked and loaded it, for they would not make the same fatal mistake as the Drimm who went after Sleeth.

"Cautiously, crossbows and axes in hand, into the halls of the Drimmenholt they went, rolling the ballista on the wheels of its carriage past the great doors of Dawn-Gate, torn from their hinges and flung down on the stone floor. Who had done this, the Ghath or others, they could not say, but they did not stop to ponder. Across the East Hall they went, and into the corridor beyond, the raiders all looking about with eyes of wonder, for they were in their abandoned homeland at last. Down a long hall they crept, the early-morning daylight fading with every step deeper into the holt, and they came to the Broad Shelf on the east side of the vast chasm known as the Great Deep. Onto the bridge over the mighty crevasse they pressed and across, the drop below bottomless.

"When they reached the opposite side, there did they find unlit torches and barrels of pitch, as if kept at hand for those to come who would need such to light the way. Yet they took not up these brands, but instead unhooded their Dwarven lanterns to press back the darkness.

"The raiders moved beyond the end of the bridge and into the Great War Hall, with its row upon row of Dragon Pillars reaching up to the stone high overhead. And as they rolled the ballista in among the great carven columns, then did they feel the momentary cast of the Dread, as if the Draedan searched for intruders in its dark domain. . . ."

Rokar gasped. "He knows we are here."

"Mayhap so; mayhap not," said Braggi, trying to muster courage even though his own heart pounded in the sudden fear that had passed across them and away.

"Did you not feel his gaze sweep by?" said Grath.

"Aye," said Braggi, his breath coming easier. "Yet this I ask: is he an Utrun to see through stone?"

"The LoreMasters say he does not look through stone," said Rokar, "but sends forth his senses instead."

"Aye," agreed Belkon. "Sends forth his senses like a Drake, they say, scaled and all as he is. The Humans call him a Mandrak, and I deem that means Man-Dragon."

"I deem these are but guesses," said Braggi. "Come. Let us set our weapon here in the Great War Hall, then try to entice the monster unto this place, and when it comes, then we will slay it." His words brooked no thought of failure.

They left the loaded ballista behind, concealed in the dark at the base of one of the Dragon Pillars there at the verge of the War Hall of the First Neath, and into the delved corridors of Kraggen-cor they went, seeking a monster to lure behind as they fled back to the weapon. In a long drawn-out line they went, hoping that if any at one end or the other were ensnared in the creature's gaze, the ones at the opposite end would escape and ultimately draw the monster after and slay it as it pursued, some to operate the ballista while others to the side distracted the Ghath. After all, that was the way the one at Dendor had been slain . . . or so the LoreMasters said.

Long did they stride through the mighty halls of Kraggen-cor, and now and again did a nigh-paralyzing dread slam into their hearts and threaten to overwhelm them as the cast of the Ghath swept by.

And many of Braggi's raiders wondered if any would survive this mad gamble. Even so, on they went, deliberately seeking the Fearcaster.

Twice they paused to rest and to take water as well as to eat a biscuit of crue, there in the halls and corridors of Kraggen-cor.

It was as they paused a third time that torchlight came bobbing up the passage behind.

"Hood the lanterns and take cover," hissed Braggi. "We know not who this is."

But even as they scrambled to their feet, from the other entrance into the small chamber trotted a torchbearing squad of—

"Squam!" cried Rokar, levelling his crossbow and loosing the bolt—

There were foul Squam, filthy Grg, in sacred Kraggen-cor! A thing not imagined in their plans.

—Thunn . . . ssss . . . thok! The shaft struck an Ükh in the belly, and yawling the Grg fell writhing to the stone.

More crossbow quarrels were loosed, Ükhs and Hrôks taken by the shafts. The others retreated to the safety of the corridors, but just out of sight they remained. Brazen horns blatted, answered from afar, and the raiders knew more Squam were on the way.

"We need to fight free," gritted Braggi, then gasped, as pounding fear swept over them all. The Ghath yet searched its domain.

As the dread diminished—"Back the way we came?" said Belkon.

"Aye," replied Braggi.

And so began a running battle, Braggi and his raiders fighting through the Squam in the corridor, though Dakon was slain and Krald sorely wounded. From behind they could hear more horn-blats and calls echoed in response.

Again and once more they ran into Grg, and each time they charged through, crossbows thrumming, axes hewing, yet they took on more wounds themselves from hammers and cudgels, scimitars and tulwars.

And more horns sounded.

"We might have to fight our way completely clear of Kraggen-cor altogether," panted Braggi, "and gather an army and return. Some to fight the Squam, others to slay the Ghath with the spear-caster."

With torchlight coming after and a dark passage ahead, they crossed a chamber and fled down a corridor and 'round a curve bearing south. But to the fore a large band of Grg barred the way.

Leftward a stone door stood open, and into this place they ran, slamming it behind.

They had come into a lengthy, narrow chamber with a low ceiling. One hundred paces long it was and but twelve wide. A massive arch graven with runes of power spanned the chamber midway. And a downsloping exit could be seen at the far end, an exit filled with growing torchlight coming up the passage beyond.

"Trapped," said Belkon. "Grg before and Grg after."

"Here we will make our stand," said Braggi.

Rokar shed his pack, and snatched a handful of rocknails from within. These he used to wedge shut the stone door. "Now let us fight our way through those who come up the stairs."

Toward this way they sped, but Squam poured into the chamber ere the raiders reached the passage.

All Châkka who had crossbows loosed quarrels, felling foe, but onward the Grg charged. *"Châkka shok! Châkka cor!"* shouted the raiders, and into the mêlée they leapt.

Axes hewed, cudgels smashed, tulwars and scimitars slashed. And above the war cries and screams of death a thunderous pounding came as a ram hammered at the stone door.

And nigh the door, Belkon fell amid a dozen Ükhs, but rose up again, his axe spewing blood and viscera in great, wide arcs as he hewed the foe.

Châkka rushed to his aid, and then all raiders formed a square back to back and they moved as one.

Squam fell away, some slaughtered, others fearful of coming at this formidable fighting machine.

The very bottom of the stone door aft cracked away, the remainder of the panel to swing open and dangle on broken hinges. In the corridor beyond, Grg cast aside the stone bench they had used as a ram, and they took up their weapons.

And time seemed to stop, as Squam to the fore and Squam to the rear got ready to charge the Châkka square.

Midst the many slain Grg, Braggi scooped up an extinguished fallen torch and shoved it into the sliced-open chest of a dead Hrôk and in the dark ichor of Squam he smeared his runes on the wall:

ŦΓVƎƎI

And Braggi shouted, "Come, Squam, taste death from Braggi and his raiders!"

And as one, the raiders shouted, *"Châkka shok! Châkka cor!"*

The Grg hesitated and some drew back, yet others made ready to charge. But ere the echoes of Braggi's challenge died, the surging fear of the Dread pounded through their veins, but this time it did not sweep on past but remained locked on their hammering hearts. "The Ghath," hissed Belkor, the words jerked from his throat, even as the Squam moaned in horror, and neither Châk nor Grg could move significantly, for terror nigh held them prisoner.

And down below, in the Great War Hall, the Ghath stalked toward the stairwell leading to the chamber above, his tread as of massive steps on ponderous feet of stone. And as he moved among the Dragon Pillars, with a backhanded slap the Dread sent the ballista rolling, and hindward it trundled and slowly, until it finally rolled over the nearby precipice and fell into the Great Dêop.

Now the Ghath came to the stairwell, and up he trod, Squam yielding back against the walls as he passed by, many losing control of their bowels and bladders, so close was he. Even so they could not flee, such was the terror, and some died of burst hearts.

Nor could Braggi and his raiders fly apace, for they, too, were nigh arrested, though they did try to escape. Even so, all ways out from the chamber were jammed with stationary Grg. And the raiders knew not which way to run, for they knew not by which entry the Ghath would come. Regardless, Braggi chose to head for the bridge and the Dawn-Gate beyond, and toward the distant stairs going downward at the eastern end of the room they struggled on halting steps hindered by terror.

Up the Dread came, up the steps toward the chamber—one flight, two flights, three flights, more—and the east entry at the top of the sixth flight was jammed with Squam, yet that did not stop the Ghath, for he shredded his way through, Ükhs and Hrôks dying under the rending claws.

Now the Mandrak stepped into the chamber and caught the raiders in his direct gaze, and all movement was rent from them.

And down the length of the fear-rooted Châkka column he trod on his feet of stone, shredding and rending as he went, and when he came to the last Châk, Braggi and his raiders were no more.

* * *

Dokan stood and walked away from the gathering, his hood cast over his head. Tears ran down Aylissa's face, and Pipper and Binkton stared starkly at one another, their own faces drained of blood. Aravan's features were grim, and he reached a hand out for Aylis, and she a hand for him. Wooly and Tarly and Fat Jim sat in stunned silence, their lips pressed thin, their heads down, their eyes focused as if seeing far beneath the earth.

Finally Fat Jim took a long shuddering breath and raised his glass and said, "To Braggi and his lost raiders."

To Braggi and his lost raiders, said they all.

After a moment of silence, Aylissa said, "Oh, what a terrible way to die."

"Indeed," said Aravan. "Indeed."

"What I want to know," said Tarly, "whence came the Rûcks and such?"

"They were sent there by Modru," said Dokan, standing in the distant shadows, "to hold Kraggen-cor until he could conquer all of Mithgar. Then would he have Châkka as slaves, and Châkka would mine their own starsilver for Modru's pleasure."

"Sweet revenge against a *Khana* Durek, do you think?" said Fat Jim.

"Aye," replied Dokan, returning from the shadows, his hood yet over his head in mourning for the loss of brave souls long past.

"Lady Aylis," said Fat Jim, "you said that in the hall of the Gravenarch, two events were entwined. I take it that was the hall in question, and that was the first event?"

"Aye," said Aylis.

"Then what was the second?"

"I'll speak of that when I return from the privy," said Aylis, standing.

"We can all use another break, I ween," said Aravan, and once again they made their way toward the rooms at opposite ends of the Slipper, Binkton and Pipper dragging a chair behind.

When all had relieved themselves, once again they convened before the fireplace, Wooly refilling their glasses and Aylissa's thimble with a newly opened bottle of wine. Then all settled back to hear the next chapter of Lady Aylis's tale.

"In this recounting, it begins in the hall of the Gravenarch, but ends on the bridge over the Great Deep. That's why, although this portion begins in the hall, I went to that vast chasm as well, for I would <see> the outcome for myself."

Pipper and Binkton looked at one another and grinned and nodded, then each made a buttoning motion against his own lips.

"Put in mind the Winter War when the Dimmendark spread o'er the land," said Aylis, smiling at the two. "It was 4E2018 when the war started, and many a brave soul died, and many were the heroic deeds done. But in the early weeks of 4E2019 an amazing feat occurred, one that nearly outshined all others, and at its heart is the tale of the Deevewalkers.

"Pressed by circumstance, four courageous warriors had no choice but to trod through the halls of Drimmen-deeve, all the way from the Dusk-Door on the western side to the Grimwalls to the Dawn-Gate on the eastern verge. And the Draedan yet ruled the Deeves, and Foul Folk teemed within.

"The four consisted of: First, Galen, a Man, and the High King, for his sire had been slain at the walls of Challerain Keep just weeks before. Galen was armed with an Atalar blade and a sword he had retrieved from the dead hand of Captain Jarriel, who had died heroically defending Galen's betrothed from a band of deadly Ghûls. Next was Gildor Goldbranch, an Elf, son of Rael and Talarin, twin brother of Vanidor—and I say Vanidor Silverbranch, not Vanidar Siverleaf, confuse not the two—Gildor himself, counsellor to the High King; Gildor was armed with a special sword, one forged by Dwynfor, and it had a blade-jewel that would glow red should Foul Folk be near; and its name was Bale. Third was Brega, Bekki's son, Dwarven warrior and steadfast ally, and he was armed with a Dwarven axe from his home Dwarvenholt of the Red Hills. Fourth and last, Tuckerby Underbank, Warrow, deadly archer, eyes for the High King in the spellcast Dimmendark, and he was armed with his bow and arrows—one of which was red—and the long-knife Bane, also forged by Dwynfor as mate to Bale; this blade as well had a blade-jewel, and it would glow blue if Spawn were near; it had been given to Tuck by Gildor.

"As I say, they were forced by circumstance into the western end of the Deeves, and the only way out was the far eastern end, forty-six miles away by the route they would take.

"I'll not burden you with all the details of that harrowing journey, for it is well recorded in *The Ravenbook.* Let me just say that the Draedan had become aware that there were interlopers within his realm, and he cast forth his dreadful senses to detect where the intruders were.

"The four had come forty-four miles from the Dusk-Door and were now but some two miles from their goal. They had stepped into the Hall of the Gravenarch, and there they saw signs of an ancient battle—broken weapons, shattered armor, and the skulls and bones of long-dead combatants. Too, they espied Braggi's Rune written in the blood of Squam, and at last Brega knew what had happened to Braggi and his raiders.

"On they went, heading for the eastern exit, passing among Dwarf armor and the plate of Spawn, as well as shattered axes, broken scimitars, war hammers and cudgels. And just as they passed below the rune-marked Gravenarch, the surging fear of the Dread locked onto them and arrested their steps. . . ."

He has found us!" gasped Gildor. "He comes, and is near!"

Tuck's lungs were heaving, yet he could not seem to get enough to breathe, and his limbs were nearly beyond his control, for he could but barely move.

Brega clutched his arms across his chest and air hissed in through clenched teeth; his face turned upward and his hood fell back from his head. His eyes widened. "The arch," his voice jerked out. "The keystone . . . like a linchpin . . . cut off pursuit."

Dread pulsed through them as Brega forced himself to stoop and grasp a broken war hammer. "Lift me up," he gritted. "Lift me . . . when I smite it, drop me . . . run . . . the ceiling will collapse."

"But you may be killed!" Tuck's words seemed muffled in the waves of fear.

Now Brega's rage crested above the numbing dread. "Lift, by Adon, I command it!"

Galen and Gildor hoisted the Dwarf and he stood upon their shoulders as they braced him, his left hand upon the stone of the arch, the war hammer in his right. Tuck stood behind them, and only the Warrow's eyes were upon the portal where stood the broken door. And it seemed as if he could hear massive steps stalking through the terror, ponderous feet of stone pacing toward the door. And just as something *dreadful* loomed forth through the shadows:

"Yah!" cried Brega, and swung the hammer with all the might of his powerful shoulders. *Crack!* The maul shattered through the keystone of the Gravenarch, and with a great rumble the vault above gave way. Gildor, Galen, and Brega tumbled backward, scrambling as stone fell 'round them. And Brega grabbed up Tuck and ran, for only the Warrow had glimpsed the shadow-wrapped Gargon, and the buccan could not cause his legs to move.

East they dashed for the door, just ahead of the ceiling crashing unto the floor behind them, filling the chamber with shattered stone.

And as they raced through the portal and down a flight of steps, the roof gave completely away in one great roar, blocking all pursuit.

And waves of numbing dread beat through the stone and whelmed them, and Tuck thought his heart would burst, yet now the Warrow could move again under his own power, and down a narrow hall they struggled while behind them endless horror ravened.

"Down," gasped Brega, "we've got to get down to the Mustering Chamber of the First Neath—the War Hall—for there is the drawbridge over the Great Dêop. And we must pass over it to come to the Daûn Gate. At least the lore says so.

"We are here upon the Fifth Rise," gritted Brega, his face blanched, for the power of the Dread was now locked onto their hammering hearts. "Six flights we must go down to reach the War Hall."

Passing by a tunnel on the left, east they reeled, curving south, down another flight of steps. "Fourth Rise," Brega grated, as southward the narrow passage led. They passed one more tunnel to the left and kept on straight and down another staircase. "Third Rise," said Brega, and still the fear coursed through them and they knew the Gargon pursued by a different route. The tunnel they entered bore east and west, and to the east they fled, their legs seeming nearly too cumbersome to control. Another flight of stairs; "Second Rise," came Brega's trembling voice.

Tuck and his companions were weary beyond measure and the hideous fear sapped at their will, yet onward they fled, for to stop meant certain destruction. North and south the passage now went, and rightward they turned, southward, and once more steep steps pitched downward. "First Rise," Brega counted, and beyond a footway leading west the tunnel curved east.

On they faltered in abject fear, the Dread power lashing after, and then came once more to stone steps down; "Gate Level," Brega croaked at the bottom, and still they staggered on.

Again the passage arced to the south, and, as before, they ignored another tunnel on the left, for the ways they chose bore down, south, and east, and all other paths were rejected.

One more long flight of steps they stumbled down, and *lo!* they came into a great dark hall. And they tottered outward into the chamber, and still the terror whelmed their hearts, and they could but barely carry forth.

"Ai, a Dragon Pillar," gasped Brega, pointing to a huge delved column carved to resemble a great Dragon coiling up an enormous fluted shaft. "This is the War Hall of the First Neath. To the east will be the bridge over the Great Dêop."

Leftward they reeled, their legs trembling with fear and barely under their control. Now along the lip of a deep abyss they staggered, to come to a great wooden span springing across the chasm. And *behold!* the bascule was down, the bridge unguarded!

"Great was the Gargon's pride," Galen grated, "for he ne'er thought we would reach this place, else he would have posted a Swarm here to greet us."

They passed through barrels of pitch and oil and past rope-bound bundles of torches used by the maggot-folk to light their way through the black halls of Drimmen-deeve; and they came to the bridge at the edge of the Great Deep, a huge fissure that yawned blackly at their feet, jagging out of the darkness on their left, disappearing beyond the ebon shadows to their right, as much as a hundred feet wide where Tuck could see, pinching down to fifty where stood the bridge. And sheer sides dropped into bottomless depths below.

And as they stepped upon the span: "Hold!" cried Galen. "If we fell this bridge then pursuit will be cut off."

"How?" Tuck's heart hammered, and every fiber in his being cried out, *Run, fool, run!* yet he knew Galen was right. "How do we fell the bridge?"

"Fire!" Galen's voice was hoarse. "With fire!"

No sooner were the words out of Galen's mouth than Brega,

spurred by hope, sprang to a barrel of pitch and rolled it onto the span, smashing the wooden keg open with his axe. Gildor, too, as well as Galen, rolled great casks out to Brega, and these the Dwarf smashed open as well, the pitch flowing viscidly over the wooden span.

"A torch, Tuck!" cried Galen as he pressed back for another keg.

And the buccan drew blue-flaming Bane and cut the binding on a stack of torches, and he snatched one up and ran across the span while Brega crashed open two more kegs of the oily pitch.

Standing at the eastern end of the bridge, Tuck struck steel to flint and lighted the torch. And now Gildor, Galen, and Brega came, and Tuck gave the burning brand to the Elf, saying, "You led us through, Lord Gildor; now cut off our pursuers."

The Lian Guardian hefted the torch to throw it, and Horror stepped forth out of the shadows at the far end of the span and fixed them with its unendurable gaze.

The Dread had come to slay them.

Tuck fell to his knees, engulfed in unbearable terror, and he was not at all aware that the shrill, piercing screams filling the air were rent from his own throat.

Thdd! Thdd! Onward came the grey, stone-like creature, scaled like a serpent, but walking upright upon two legs, a malevolent, evil parody of a huge reptilian Man.

Gildor stood paralyzed, transfixed in limitless horror, his eyes fastened inextricably upon a vision beyond seeing.

Thdd! Thdd! The ponderous Mandrak stalked forward, eight feet tall, taloned hands and feet, glittering rows of fangs in a lizard-snouted face.

Beads of sweat stood forth upon Galen's brow, and his entire being quivered with an effort beyond all measure. And slowly he raised up the tip of his sword until it was pointed level at the Gargon, but then he froze, unable to do more, for the Dread's gaze flicked upon him and the hideous power bereft him of his will.

Thdd! Thdd! Now the evil Gargon stalked past Tuck, the shrill-screaming Warrow beneath his contempt. And the stench of vipers reeked upon the air.

And as the Gargon passed him, the buccan was no longer under the direct gaze of Modru's Dread, and in that moment Tuck's horror-filled eyes saw Bane's blue light blazing up wildly; and shrieking in unending shock, with fear beyond comprehension racking through his very substance, Tuck desperately lashed out with all the terror-driven force of his being, spastically hewing the Elven long-knife into the sinews of the Gargon's leg, *Thkk!* Keen beyond reckoning, the elden blade of Duellin rived through reptilian scales and chopped deeply into the creature's massive shank, and a blinding blast of cobalt flame burst forth from the blade-jewel.

With a brazen roar of pain, the Gargon began to turn, reaching for Tuck, the massive talons set to rend the shrilling Warrow to shreds.

Yet the Dread's eyes now had left Galen, and the Man plunged Jarriel's sword straight and deep into the Gargon's gut, *Shkk!* the blade shattering at the hilt as the hideous creature bellowed again and glared directly into Galen's eyes, blasting him with a dread so deep that it would burst his heart. And Galen was hurled back by the horrendous power.

But at that moment came a tumbling glitter as Brega's axe flashed end over end through the air to strike the creature full in the forehead, *Chnk!* and the roaring monster staggered hindward upon the span.

And Gildor threw the torch upon the pitch-drenched wood, and with a great *Phoom!* flames exploded upward, and Brega snatched Tuck forth from the bridge as the fire blasted outward.

And they dragged stunned Galen away from the whooshing blaze, for the Man had been whelmed by the Gargon's dreadful burst of power.

And upon the bridge the Gargon bellowed brazen roars, engulfed in raging flame, an axe cloven deep in his skull, a shivered sword plunged through his gut.

In the War Hall behind there came the sounds of running feet as Rûcks and Hlôks poured forth from corridors and into the great chamber. They ran among the fourfold rows of Dragon Pillars to come to the far edge of the bottomless Great Deep. And Tuck could hear them crying, *Glâr! Glâr!*—the Slûk word for fire.

And then great waves of unbearable dread blasted outward, and *Spaunen* fell groveling upon the floor of the War Hall and shrieked in terror, while Gildor, Brega, and Tuck gasped for air and dropped to their knees, transfixed like unto stone statues.

And the dreadful crests of racking horror seemed to course through them forever.

But then the Gargon collapsed and lay in the whirling flames of the burning span, and of a sudden the harrowing dread was gone.

"Quickly," gasped Gildor, recovering first, "we must bear Galen King beyond arrow flight."

And so, weak with passing fear, they dragged the stunned Man up a flight of steps and to the outbound passage. And while Gildor worked to revive Galen, Tuck and Brega stood guard, one with an Elven long-knife, the other with Gildor's sword, the red-jeweled blade seeming awkward in the Dwarf's gnarled hand—a hand better suited to wield a war hammer or axe.

"Ai, look at the vastness of the Mustering Chamber, Tuck," said Brega, in awe, as the flames roared upward. "It must be a mile to the far end, and half that wide."

And Tuck looked past the Rûcks and Hlôks running hither and thither, and by the light of the burning bridge he saw the rows of Dragon Pillars marching off into the distance past great fissures in the floor, and he knew that Brega gauged true.

At last Galen regained consciousness, yet he was weak, shaken, his face pale and drawn, and deep within his eyes lurked a haunted look, for he had been whelmed by a Gargon's fear-blast, a blast that would have destroyed Galen; but he had been saved in the nick of time by Brega's well-thrown axe. Even so, Galen nearly had been slain, and he could not rise to his feet. And thus they waited on the stone landing above the broad steps leading down toward the shelf of the abyss while strength and will slowly ebbed back into the Dread-hammered King. And long they watched the flames until the burning span collapsed, plummeting into the Great Deep, carrying the charred corpse of the slain Gargon down into the bottomless depths.

And when the drawbridge plunged, the four Deevewalkers stood and made their way eastward, Galen on faltering feet, supported by sturdy Brega. Along a corridor they went two furlongs, up a gentle slope, up from the First Neath unto the Gate Level. Now they came to the East Hall and crossed its wide floor to pass beyond the broken portals of the Dawn-Gate and out from under the mountain, out into the open at last.

Before them in the Shadowlight of the Dimmendark stood the sloping valley called the Pitch leading down and away from the Quadran. And out upon this cambered vale the four went, heading east, soon to bear south for distant Darda Galion, to bring to the Lian word of the Horde in Drimmen-deeve, and to tell them the remarkable news of the Gargon's death.

It had taken all four to slay the Horror, and it was by mere happenstance that they had succeeded. Yet among these four heroes there was one who had struck the first spark, for as Galen King said, his voice strained, halting—for the impact of the Gargon was still upon him—"When . . . when we stood frozen . . . lost beyond all hope, Tuck, yours was the blow that released us . . . yours was the strike that told."

"Whew!" said Fat Jim. "I thought they were goners."

"So did I," said Wooly, his hand shaking with tension as he sipped his drink.

"They killed the Gargon, they did," said Pipper, "Tuckerby Underbank being the one who made it all possible, and he was a Warrow!"

Fat Jim laughed and managed to gasp out, "Tall is the pride of one so short." He glanced at Dokan, the Dwarf even then casting back his hood, as if vengeance for all the Dwarven dead had at last been achieved.

"And that's the end of the tale," said Tarly. "As Aylissa would say, 'How fitting.' "

"No I wouldn't," said the Pysk.

"You don't think it's fitting?" said Tarly, surprised.

"Oh, it's fitting all right, but it isn't the end of the tale."

"It's not?"

Aylissa shook her head. "Don't you recall, Lady Aylis said that there were four intertwined things that occurred at the Lost Prison. We only heard three: the setting of the trap by Othran and Lithon, Thuuth Uthor being ensnared, then the Dwarves delving deeply and the Gargon bursting free, and then the slaying of the Gargon. There is one more event we've yet to hear. Right?"

"Yes," said Aylis. "Just one more thing, and then the entire story of the Draedan in Drimmen-deeve will be done.

"Before I begin, does anyone need the privy? No? Well then. Put the next with his blade. The maggot-folk finally stopped coming in as enough of those in the front ranks at last turned and shoved back through the press in the notch.

A time passed, and the Seven could hear the *Spaunen* snarling and cursing, but the Slûk speech was being used, and so the comrades did not understand what was being said. For a moment it became still, and then a spate of black-shafted Rûcken arrows hissed through the cleft to strike the far chamber wall and splinter on the stone. Then there came a great shout from the maggot-folk and a rush of booted feet: they were mounting a charge. One leapt in, only to be dropped by Ursor's mace. Three more hurtled through and were slain by Anval, Borin, and Delk. More charged forward but stumbled over the dead bodies of the slain Rûcks and were themselves dispatched. Once more the Rûcks withdrew.

Just as it had been at the rope bridge over the Great Deep, the Spawn could only come at the Seven single file, and thus the *Rûpt* could not bring their great numbers to bear to their advantage. No Rûck had yet reached the third rank of the defenders. Four warders alone could hold off an entire Rûcken army, especially since the comrades flung the dead *Spaunen* one atop another to clog the entrance, forming a grisly but effective barricade.

An hour went by, and again the maggot-folk charged. Once more the defenders slew all that entered. This time the second rank killed but one Rûck; all the others were slain by Ursor and Anval. The bulwark of dead Spawn grew higher.

Borin and Delk then stepped to the first rank, relieving Ursor and Anval, who stepped back. Lord Kian and Shannon took over the second file. Perry, left out of the fight, felt useless, but he realized that in this battle the others were larger and more effective than a Warrow would be.

Suddenly, with a screeching howl a large, spear-bearing Hlôk leapt onto the dead-Rûck barricade, only to be gutted by Delk's axe. Three more Rûcks were slain by Delk and Borin. Again the attack was shorn off short, the Rûcks fleeing back up the notch.

Two more hours passed without attack, except now and again a black shaft or two would hiss into the chamber to fall with a clatter at the far wall. The guard on the cleft had been rotated, and in turn each of the Seven had walked the chamber—staying out of line of the black arrows, looking for a hidden door or passage—but

in mind the War of Kraggen-cor, some two hundred thirty-one years after the Winter War, for now that the Draedan had been slain, Seventh Durek sought to reoccupy the Drimmen-deeve. Yet he had a dilemma to resolve, for a Horde of Foul Folk now held the Deeves, and there were but two ways in: through the East-Gate and over the Great Deep, or through the Dusk-Door. But the bridge over the Deep had been destroyed, and never had an invading throng e'er won past that barrier into the teeth of a defending army. And as to the Dusk-Door, when the four Deevewalkers had been forced to trek all the way from the west entry to the east one, it was because they had fled in through the Dusk-Door when they were attacked by a hideous monster, and the doors themselves had been wrenched upon and perhaps broken by that terrible creature and then buried under tons of debris. So Durek was faced by a terrible choice: try to invade by the Dawn-Gate and over the Great Deep into the teeth of a Foul Folk Horde, or try to invade by the Dusk-Door, a door that might no longer open and perhaps yet be guarded by a monster.

"It so happened he had with him two Warrows: Peregrin Fairhill and Cotton Buckleburr, who would act as guides, for they had memorized the Brega Path, a step-by-step record that Tuckerby Underbank had precisely set down from Brega's exact description of the Deevewalkers' journey through that terrible place, for as you have learned, Dwarves cannot lose their feet.

"In the end, after listening to all the options, two plans were made: the army would go to the Dusk-Door and uncover it, for they believed that no Foul Folk would dwell in that far reach since the door was blocked; by invading through that route, they would take the Foul Folk by surprise; Cotton Buckleburr would go as a Brega-Path guide with the army. The second part of that plan involved a small force of seven people infiltrating through the Dawn-Gate and making their way through the caverns all the way to the inside of the Dusk-Door, and if it was broken, to repair it from the inside; among that party were three GateMasters, two Dwarven warriors, one Human to guide them to the Dawn-Gate, and Peregrin Fairhill as their Brega-Path guide. They called themselves the Secret Seven.

"Again, I won't burden you with the details, but ere they reached the Dawn-Gate, the Secret Seven lost two of the GateMasters: Barak, who was slain, and Tobin, who suffered a shattered femur. They were replaced by Ursor, a Baeran, and by Vanidar Silverleaf, sometimes known as Shannon—a Feyan word, meaning 'silver leaf.' Both Ursor and Vanidar had come upon the Seven during the fight in which the GateMasters had been lost.

"And so, off they went, seven strong: Vanidar Silverleaf, armed with his white-bone bow and arrows and a long-knife; Ursor, armed with a great mace; GateMaster Delk, armed with an axe; Anval and Borin, Dwarven warriors, armed with axes as well; Lord Kian, armed with a bow and arrows and a sword; and Peregrin Fairhill, armed with Bane, the very same blade that had first cut the Gargon, for after the Winter War, it had come to the Boskydells with Tuck, and two-hundred thirty-one years later, Peregrin took it to Drimmen-deeve again.

"During the day, when Adon's Ban would give the Seven a slight edge, they managed to gain entry into the Deeves, and here again I'll not burden you with details, for the entire saga can be read in the *Fairhill Journal.* Let me just say that slow was their journey along the Brega Path through the Deeves and toward the distant goal, for often were they delayed, thwarted by Foul Folk across their way.

"They managed to avoid detection for nearly half the route, but then at a place called the Grate Room, they were discovered by the Foul Folk, and were forced to flee away from the known track.

"Down they fled into the depths of the mountain, Spawn in pursuit, and little choice did they have in selecting their way. And as they fled deeper, a horrific odor grew, as of a nest of a thousand vipers. Finally they came to a tapering of the way, a narrow delved passage where a starsilver vein existed. . . ."

Perry could see the soft glimmer of silvery metal twinkling in the lantern light and running on ahead. And even though they were being pursued, the Dwarves paused long enough to reach out and touch the precious lode, for they had never before seen silveron in its native state. This was the wealth of Kraggen-cor; in only two other places in Mithgar was silveron known to exist.

Suddenly they came to what had been the last of the silveron shaft; but they could see that the end wall had been burst through from the far side: the stone was splintered as if some enormous force had blasted into the delf from beyond the wall.

They clambered over the shards of rock and came chamber. This room was the source of the foul reek, bu see nothing to cause the stench; it was as if the fetor e the very stone itself.

The chamber was long and rectangular; its far end w yond the shadows. In the center was a raised stone sla block with a smooth top and carvings on the side. Here, scrawled serpentine signs. Silverleaf held up a lantern and scanned the glyphs. They writhed across the stone and somehow evil and foul, recorded in a long-lost tongue; yet was skilled at runes and rapidly deciphered the words: " " *Uthor.'* Ai!" Silverleaf sucked in a gasp of air. "This is th Prison. The Draedan's Lair. No wonder the stone is imbued foul reek, for here trapped for ages was the Dread of Drim deeve—the Gargon—trapped till the Drimma were deceive Modru's vile gramarye and delved too deeply and set the Drae free."

"*Trapped?*" exclaimed Kian. "Trapped in this chamber? Is th no way out?"

All the lanterns were opened wide, and light sprang to the fa end and filled the room. No archways were discerned, no black tunnel mouths gaped in the walls; only smooth stone, blank and stern, could be seen. No outlet, no portal of escape stood open before them, and behind a horn blared loudly and they could hear the slap of running Rûcken feet.

"Quickly, Ursor, Anval, to the cleft!" barked Kian. "Borin, Delk, flank them. Let no Spawn through. If we are trapped, then let it cost them dear to pluck us forth."

Ursor sprang to the notch, shifting to one side, with Borin warding his flank. Anval leapt thwartwise the notch from Ursor, Delk at hand. Shannon and Kian quickly stepped to the third rank, and Perry took a place at Shannon's side. They could see torchlight wavering down the slot, and suddenly a Rûck burst forth from the breach, to be felled by Ursor's great black mace. A second Spawn came on the heels of the first, and Anval's axe clove him from helm to breastplate. A third Rûck Ursor crushed, and a fourth. The next Rûck threw down his iron bar and turned to flee but was pushed shrieking and gibbering into the chamber by those behind who did not yet know that anything was amiss, and Anval smote him and

none had been found, for this was indeed the Lost Prison, the Gargon's Lair: that terrible creature had been sealed in this chamber for nearly three thousand years in all. And as mighty as it had been, still it could not break out of this prison until a wall had been weakened by delvers. The Seven were dismayed by this knowledge, for it meant that this chamber was a dungeon of extraordinary strength: it had defied the power of a mighty Gargon for some three millennia. Hence, how could the comrades even hope to break free in a matter of mere hours in order to aid Durek—especially in the teeth of a force of Spawn?

"The Rûkha seem to have fallen quiet," said Kian, "planning some deviltry. They can afford to wait for reinforcements, for we are trapped. We must use this time to recover our own spent strength: While we are under siege, we will take turns resting. Two will hold the way while the others take ease, perhaps even sleep. Keep nearby to aid in the event of attack. Stay out of arrow flight from the cleft. Think on ways we might escape—though Adon knows how that may be."

Perry lay down off to one side. He was exhausted: the flight had taken much of his strength, for the way had been hard and he was of small stature. He rested his head against his pack, and his thoughts were awhirl. He felt something tugging and nagging at the back of his mind, but he could not bring it to the fore. He believed that something was being overlooked, yet he knew not what. He peered at the smooth-carven walls, ceiling, and floor of the chamber. The silveron vein came through the guarded broken wall and ran on across the floor to vanish into the shadows. The argent line had many offshoots, running short distances, tapering off into thinner and thinner veins, to finally disappear. One such seam zigged across the ceiling, to end in a whorl. Another seam ran to the large stone block in the center of the chamber and up the side, to come to an end among the writhing runes set thereupon by the Gargon. Yet another silver line shot up a side wall, to crash back to the floor. Perry lay there letting his gaze follow the precious seams, and even though the Rûcken enemy was but a few paces away, he gradually drifted into slumber as his eyes roamed along glittering pathways streaking across the prison.

* * *

Perry slept for five hours without moving, exhausted, exempted from guard duty by the others; but then he began to dream: he was back on the Argon, riding the raft. But the river wasn't water; instead it was flowing silveron. The argent stream rushed into a roaring gap, and the raft was borne into a tunnel. Perry looked about and saw that he was riding with the other companions, yet there was a hooded Dwarf sitting on the far end of the float whom Perry did not recognize, for he could not see the Dwarf's face.

The starsilver river rushed through dark caverns, carrying the raft along, and Rûcks sprang up to give chase. Onward the raft whirled, to come to many Dwarves delving stone and scooping up treasured water into sacks which they bore away. The float sped toward a stone wall, but just before the craft crashed into it, the wall burst outward and a dark Gargon jumped forth with four warriors in pursuit. The raft whirled into the chamber and sped across on the silveron vein and out the other side, but all the companions were tumbled off by the far stone wall, even though the float somehow went on through. The wall became transparent, and Perry could see that the raft was caught in an eddy of silveron, and the mysterious Dwarf was still aboard in spite of the invisible wall. Perry looked at the Dwarf and called, "Help us. Help us get through. You got out; how can we get out, too?"

The Dwarf turned and threw back his hood. It was Barak! The dead GateMaster! Slain by the Rûcks far away on the shores of the Argon River! *"All delved chambers have ways in,"* Barak intoned in a sepulchral voice, *"and ways out, if you can find the secret of the door and have the key. Without the key even a Wizard or an evil Vûlk cannot pass through some doors."* The raft burst into flames, and Barak lay down on the platform and uttered one more word: *"Glâr!"*

The burning raft whirled off on the swift-running silveron vein, and Perry woke up calling out, "Barak! Barak! Come back!"

When Perry opened his eyes, Silverleaf was bending over the Warrow, shaking him by the shoulder. "Wake up, friend Perry," urged the Elf, "your slumber disturbs you."

"Oh, Shannon, I had the strangest dream," declared the Warrow, rubbing his eyes and squinting at the far wall to see if it were truly transparent; but he saw only solid stone. "It was all mixed up with rivers of silveron, the Rûcks, this chamber, the Dread, and a conversation I had with Barak long ago in our last camp by the Great River Argon where he was slain."

"Though Elves do not sleep as Men, Drimma, and Waerlinga do," stated Shannon, "still I believe I can understand the way of some dreams. Though many are strange and appear to make little sense, now and again darktide visions do seem to have significance; mayhap yours is one of those."

"Maybe it is," agreed Perry. "I've got to talk to Delk. He's a GateMaster, as was Barak." The Warrow rose and went to the brown-bearded Dwarf who was standing guard at the notch with Ursor. "Delk," began Perry, "Barak and I often chatted at night. Once he told me that all delved chambers had doors, some secret; and for those what is needed is to divine each secret and to have the key it calls for. Delk, this Gargon's Lair is a delved chamber. Surely there must be a way out other than through a hole in a broken wall. Barak must be right."

"Were this chamber Châk-delved, I would agree," grunted Delk, "but it is not. The work is more like that of . . . of . . ." Delk fell silent in thought, then continued. "Old beyond measure, I deem, like the work of an ancient Folk called the Lianion-Elves—though but traces of their craft remain that I have seen."

"Lianion-Elves?" exclaimed Shannon. "The Lianion-Elves are my Folk, the Lian!" Now it was Silverleaf's turn to fall silent and study the chamber. "You are correct, Drimm Delk: this chamber *does* resemble the work of my ancestors, though it is different in some ways. I knew that my Folk had known of the Lost Prison, but that we delved it would be news to me. And if delved by the Lian, I doubt that originally it was meant to house such a guest as a Gargon—though as to its initial intent, I cannot say."

"Well, if Barak was right," said Perry, "there is a secret way out strong enough to defy even an evil Vûlk. And if we can find it, maybe we can divine the way to open it. You are a GateMaster, Delk, surely you can locate a hidden door. And you, Shannon, your Folk perhaps made this place; maybe you can find the secret way. We've got to try."

"Ah, but Friend Perry," protested Delk, "we all have searched every square inch—walls and floor alike—and we have found nought." Delk looked from the cleft to the far wall and finally at the slain Rûcks; then he growled thoughtfully, "Nay, not all; we have not searched it all. We have not searched where the Grg arrows can reach. But the dead-Ükh barricade is now high enough that if we stay low we can safely examine the stone block in the center of the chamber."

Delk awakened Borin to take his place at the cleft, and then the GateMaster, Elf, and Warrow crawled to the central platform and began the search.

Perry watched as the other two carefully inspected the stone, but his mind kept spinning back to his dream of Barak: the Dwarf had said, *"Glâr!"* yet Perry knew as a Ravenbook Scholar that *glâr* was the Slûk word for "fire." Though the raft in the dream had burst into flames, why would he dream that Barak had said a Slûk word? How did fire bear on their problem? Maybe it meant nothing. Perry watched as the search continued.

Delk had begun to examine the silveron seam running up the side of the block, and suddenly he gave a start. "This vein is not native to the stone," he muttered after long study, "it is *crafted!*—made to look like a natural branching of the starsilver offshoot. And see! Here the silveron is shaped strangely, like two runes—though I cannot fathom their message."

Shannon crawled around to join Delk, staying well below the Rûck-arrow line, and peered at the silver thread. "These are vaguely like ancient Lian runes, made to look like odd whorls of silveron in the stone. This rune, I would guess it to say 'west,' and the other rune says 'point'—or mayhap 'pick' is more accurate, I'm not sure. 'West point' or 'west pick,' that is the best I can guess these odd runes to mean."

"Hola!" exclaimed Delk, "Here is a thin slot in the stone at the end of the crafted vein, as if the silveron had run its course but the crack ran on a bit. Mayhap—"

"The Grg are up to something," rumbled Ursor at the notch, interrupting Delk. "They may be preparing another rush. They are chittering like rats, and again I can hear them calling *glâr.*"

"Glâr!" exclaimed Perry, startled. "That's what Barak— Ah yes, I see: I heard it in my sleep. Ursor, *glâr* is a Slûk word for fire." The three crawled away from the stone block and out of arrow flight, and stood beside Ursor. "What can they be up to?" asked Perry, listening to the Slûk jabber.

"I have my suspicions," growled Ursor. "We've been trapped

here many hours. Time enough for them to devise some terrible plot and secure the means to carry it out."

"Look!" cried Delk, pointing to the floor at the cleft. In through the entrance a dark liquid flowed. They could hear a wooden barrel being broken, and a surge of fluid gushed in through the notch. "It is lamp oil," growled Delk, testing it with his finger and smelling it. Then his eyes widened—"They seek to flood the chamber with oil and set it afire!"

Shannon fitted an arrow to his bow and quickly stepped across the entrance, loosing the bolt as he went. A scream came from the dark notch as the longbow-driven shaft found a victim. Delk awakened Anval and Lord Kian. The young Man joined Shannon, and they sped missiles into the cleft, and the Spawn answered with bolts of their own. In spite of the arrows, oil continued to gush forth from the notch to overspread the chamber floor.

Perry watched in desperation, for he knew that the maggot-folk were nearly ready to transform this prison into a burning tomb. *We have to get out!* thought the Warrow frantically, on the edge of panic. But then with a conscious force of will he wrenched his terrified mind toward the paths of reason. *Now settle down. Don't bolt. And above all, use your scholar's brains to think!* The buccan believed that there was a hidden door, and he felt that the secret and its solution was within his grasp if he could only get the time to think it through. What had Barak said that night long ago on the banks of the River? Something about Lian crafters. "*These doors are usually opened by Elven-made things,*" Barak had said, "*carven jewels, glamoured keys, ensorcelled rings,*" and something else, but what? What did the runes on the stone block mean, "west point"? Perry glanced up at the Elf.

"Lord Kian," urged Silverleaf, "before they put the torch to this oil, let us rush them. At least we will take some of that evil Spawn with us." Ursor grunted his agreement, Delk thumbed the blade of his axe, and Anval and Borin nodded. Shannon drew his long-knife, shaped much the same as Bane. "This edge of the Lian, forged in Lost Duellin—the Land of the West—will taste *Rûpt* blood for perhaps the last time; yet this pick, though it has not the power bound into the blade as that of the Waerling's pick, will—"

"*I've got it!*" shouted Perry. "I know the way out!" He flashed Bane from its scabbard, and its edges blazed with flaming blue light streaming from the rune-carven jewel. Perry held the sword high and laughed. "Here, as Barak would have said, is a spellbound blade. The key! Made by the Elves in the Land of the West. In your words, Shannon—and in those of the starsilver runes on yon block—it is a 'west pick'. No wonder the Gargon couldn't get out: he hadn't a key. If I am right, then this blade—or any like it—will do with a simple thrust what the Gargon in all his awesome power could not do in three thousand years."

Crouching low, the small Warrow stepped through the inflowing oil to the stone block and plunged the blade into the slot at the end of the silver line. The Elven-knife went in to the hilt, into the silveron sheath therein. There was a low rumble of massive stone grating upon stone, and a great slab ponderously swung away from the far wall; a black opening yawned before them where solid stone had been.

Shouts of astonishment burst forth from the Squad, yet GateMaster Delk had the wit to call out above their cries, "Withdraw the sword and do not plunge it in again, else the portal will close once more!"

Heeding Delk's words, Perry immediately withdrew the dazzling blade, and the door remained open; but the Warrow's thoughts were upon another GateMaster, now dead—the one who had shown him the way: "Barak, you were right," whispered the Warrow quietly. "Thank you."

A Rûcken horn blared from the notch and a stentorian voice snarled, *"Glâr!"* They were bringing a torch to fire the oil.

"Quickly!" shouted Kian, catching up his pack. "We must fly!" Each of the companions took up his own bundle and headed for the open door: Kian in the lead, Delk last. The oil made the stone floor as slippery as ice, and the footing was difficult; haste was needed yet could not be afforded. "Hurry!" Kian urged as he reached the door and stood by the open portal.

Just then there was a great *Whoosh!* as the oil was fired and flames ran into the chamber, lighting it a lurid red. The dark shadows were driven from the far recesses of the room, and through the blaze the *Spaunen* could see for the first time the opened, secret door. They snarled and howled in rage—their victims were escaping!—and their own Spawn-set fire would cut off pursuit!

As the companions tumbled across the doorsill, inches ahead of the flames, a burst of black arrows whined across the room, most to splinter against the stone wall; but one shaft took Delk through the neck, and he fell dead at the threshold. Lord Kian reached for the fallen Dwarf, but a hot blast of fire drove the Man backwards through the door as the last of the oil ignited.

The portal had opened into an undelved cavern leading away from the chamber. The companions were waiting just around a corner when Kian stumbled into their midst, singed and gasping. "Delk is dead. *Rûpt* arrow." Anval and Borin cast their hoods over their heads, and Perry bit his lower lip and tears sprang into his sapphire-jewelled eyes.

With tendrils of smoke spiralling out from the chamber and swirling 'cross the ceiling above, the raging flames aft pitched writhing shadows on the walls of the cavern, and the grotto was illuminated a dull red. Towering stark stones stared silently at the group huddled below, and the sound of weeping was lost in the roar of the blaze. Massive blocks and ramped ledges stood across the cave, barring the way for as far as the firelight shone, and the rock yielded not to the grief.

Lord Kian looked at the group standing numbly before him. "He is wreathed in flame," said Kian above the sound of the fire, "and his funeral chamber contains the weapons of the foes he slew. Thus he goes in honor on his final journey. Delk will be missed; he will be remembered. But he would urge us to mourn not, and to go on—for Durek needs us, and we are late."

For long moments no one spoke, and the only sound heard was the brawl of the fire. Then finally:

"You speak true, Lord Kian," concurred Anval, casting back his hood with effort. "There will come a time when we will mourn the loss of Delk Steelshank, but now we must go on to the Dusken Door—though how we will repair it without his aid, I cannot say. Our GateMaster has fallen, and there is little hope for our mission without his gifted hand."

"But we must try," interjected Perry, choking back his grief, "else all this has been in vain. We must get back to the Brega Path and on to the western portal—though whether there is yet time to do so, I know not."

"It is sunset of the twenty-fourth of November," announced Shannon. "There remains but one and thirty hours until Durek is to attempt the opening of the door."

"Now that Delk has fallen, I will lead," stated Borin, casting his own hood from his head, "though I cannot take his place. And I shall try to hew to his plan, turning always back toward the Brega Path when fortune allows me the choice."

"Then let us go away from this bitter place now," urged Perry. Lord Kian nodded, and Borin set forth, climbing up the ramps and across the looming stones to an exit on high. And they entered a rough-floored cavern that led them generally south and west.

The way was slow and difficult, for they had to clamber up and down steep slopes and over great obstacles. Giant Ursor often lifted Perry up to ledges just out of the Warrow's reach, or lowered him down drop-offs just a bit too far for the buccan to jump. Without the big Man's help, the journey would have been beyond Perry's abilities. Even the Dwarves were hard-pressed to negotiate this passage. Only nimble Shannon seemed at ease on the rugged way. There were no offshoots from the cavern, and so a smoother way was not a matter of choice. It took them three hours to traverse just four miles of this arduous cave; and their thirst had grown beyond measure, for their water was gone.

But then they were brought up short by both a welcome and at the same time a disheartening sight: the cavern dead-ended at an underground river. The water rushed out of the stone on the right side of the cave, and plunged under the wall on the left side. The far bank was a narrow ledge of rock, shelving out from a sheer stone wall that ran to the ceiling with no outlet. Though he was desperately thirsty, and water was within reach, Perry flung down his pack and broke into tears of frustration. "If this doesn't beat all," he vented bitterly. "Trapped again. Stone and water before us, and Rûcks and fire behind us."

And then from far off, faintly echoing down the cavern, came a discordant horn blare. "I fear the fire is no longer burning," declared Lord Kian, "and the *Spaunen* are once more in pursuit."

Aylis fell silent, and Fat Jim said, "Wull wait a moment, Lady Aylis. What happened then? Did they escape the pursuing Spawn? Did they get out? If so, how? I mean you just can't leave the story there. Aren't you going to finish the tale?"

Aylis shook her head. "Jim, I have told all that I have <seen>

concerning the delving of the Lost Prison and the events thereafter. For now you know how the Lost Prison came to be, who built it and why, how the Gargon became trapped therein, how it got free, the story of Braggi and his raiders and what happened to them, how the Dread was slain, and who did it, and lastly, the tale of what the runes on the dais meant and how the Secret Seven escaped a lair that even a Wizard or powerful Vûlk could not manage." She looked at Pipper and Binkton, then back to Fat Jim. "You will have to read the *Fairhill Journal* to know the end of that last story, or *The Ravenbook* to know the whole of the story of the Deevewalkers . . . either that or ask Pip or Bink for the full of them. For they are Warrows, and Warrows are ever steadfast, and these two know of Tuckerby Underbank and Peregrin Fairhill and a good deal of others, I ween."

Even as Fat Jim and Wooly and Tarly groaned in disappointment, Aylis glanced out at the dawning light and yawned. "I am weary, and must needs to bed, for little sleep did I get yesternight nor the early morn after." She smiled at Aravan, and inclined her head toward the stairs. *"Chieran?"*

A scratching came from the side door, and Aylis looked at Aylissa and said, "Oh, my, I almost forgot."

She sprang to her feet and stepped to the door and unlatched it, and Vex scurried in, a great brown wharf rat dead in the vixen's teeth. Vex trotted to Fat Jim and dropped the rat on his foot.

"What th—?" said Fat Jim.

"Oh, Jim, it's a sign of respect," said Aylissa, then laughed and turned to Vex and whispered loudly, "Thank you, Vex. Mayhap now he'll think twice ere he calls anyone a pip-squeak again."

Aravan broke into laughter, as did all the others, Fat Jim mayhap louder than any.

7

The Black Throne

Nigh sundown, a two-masted dhow rode the wind into the harbor, the lateen-rigged vessel gliding across the calm waters. As she tacked past the *Eroean* her foremast sail was dropped, and she rode toward the docks sailing on the main alone . . . and as she closed with the quays, the main was also dropped and, losing headway, she quietly coasted the last tens of feet into the slip to gently thump against the jute bolsters. Two huge males leapt to the dock and secured the ship to the pier. They glanced at the *Eroean* moored in the bay, then turned and looked in the direction of the Red Slipper. They nodded to one another, then stepped back aboard and, with the help of two females, stowed the sails and secured the sheets and halyards. Finally, when all was shipshape, the four strapped on weapons and took up gear bags and disembarked from the dhow and made their way toward Port Arbalin's most famous or infamous inn, depending upon one's view.

As the four stepped into the foyer, behind the counter Yellow Nell continued to frown at the lace she was tatting, trying to see just where she had gone wrong.

"We would like two rooms," rumbled a voice.

Yellow Nell looked up from her flawed handiwork and straight into a belt buckle, and she let her gaze travel up past a leather vest and then a silken collar and on up to see the smiling face of an enormous stranger; Human, he seemed, his teeth white against a dark reddish-brown beard grizzled at the tips, as was his shoulder-length hair. At his side was another enormous person—perhaps Human as well—even taller than the first by a hand or so, though this one's eyes were pale grey and his hair flaxen with an argent cast. Nell decided that both were Men. Farther back were two lithe female Elves: the golden-haired one with grey eyes so pale they looked to be silver; the other with coppery red hair and eyes a startling green.

They all four looked to be warriors, dressed in leathers as they were: the golden-haired Dara had a jade-handled sword in a scabbard across her back and a long-knife strapped to her thigh; the redheaded Dara had what appeared to be a scabbarded rapier at her belt, though she held a soft leather case in hand, one shaped as if it contained a small harp; an Elven long-knife was strapped to the thigh of the flaxen-haired Man and a Dwarven-crafted, black-iron flanged mace depended from his belt; and the other big Man's belt held a morning star.

"Rooms," repeated the Man, his amber eyes atwinkle.

"Um, yes sir," said Yellow Nell, snapping out of her astonishment over the size of these two Men. "You said, um, how many rooms?"

"Two."

Yellow Nell slid the register to the amber-eyed Man and handed him a quill, then turned about and searched among the keys hanging on the board.

The Man uncapped the inkwell and dipped the pen and signed two names. He handed the plume to the other Man, and that youth signed two names as well.

As Yellow Nell studied the board, she said over her shoulder, "Hot baths out back, two coppers each, unless you want fresh water, in which case it's four. Companionship, if you want it; the price varies according to services rendered, as well as time spent. Of course"—Yellow Nell looked over her shoulder at the two accompanying Darai—"I don't suppose you'll be needing any."

The golden-haired Dara smiled, and the red-haired one shook her head, saying, "None required."

Yellow Nell turned back to the keys. "Things might get rowdy hereabout, but you two, or rather you four, look like you can handle yourselves." She reached up and took a pair of keys from their hooks, then turned and slid them across to the Men. "You're fortunate that we have any rooms left." She raised her nose a bit in the air. "You see, the crew of the *Eroean* is in town, most staying here at the Slipper"—a look of superiority settled on her features—"includin', I might add, Captain Aravan and his lady."

The amber-eyed Man spun an auric coin onto the counter. "Indeed."

Hefting their gear, they stepped away and headed for the common room.

Yellow Nell took up the coin; with its octagonal shape, it wasn't a coin from any realm she knew, though the jasper touchstone verified that it was high-quality gold. She frowned at the depiction of a hook-nosed Man on one side and that of an eight-pointed crown on the other. Then she turned the register about to see just who these strangers were, for that might tell her whence they had come with such an odd coin. *Urus, Riatha* was inscribed on one line; *Bair; Jaith* on the next. "*Oh, lor'!*" Yellow Nell could hardly catch her breath. It was *him!* Him what had saved the world! Him who along with Captain Aravan had slain a god! Him right here in the Slipper along with his sire and dam and one other.

Yellow Nell abandoned her post to run to Burly Jim and tell him the remarkable news. But even as she slipped from behind the counter, "*Kelan!*" called someone in the common room. "*Elar!*" was the response. "Bair!" cried someone else, a female. Then "Riatha! Urus! Jaith!" A general hubbub sounded. And Yellow Nell trotted in to see those from the *Eroean* crowded about the tall youth and his sire and the two Darai, one of whom was his dam, all of them hugging the newcomers and slapping backs, gripping hands, and exchanging kisses.

Yellow Nell stepped to the bar and said to Burly Jack, "I just came to tell you that Bair himself is here, along with his mum and da, and mayhap his ladylove, though I don't know whether she's the one with the golden hair or—"

"She's the redhead," said Burly Jack. Then he wrinkled his brow. "Nell, run upstairs and tell Dark-Eyed Lara that Bair is here with Lady Jaith, and Lara's not to embarrass him in front of Jaith."

"Lara? Why would she—?"

"J'st do as I say, Nell. It's a story I'll tell you later, one concerning the time Bair was here ten years past, and him j'st sixteen at the time."

Yellow Nell grinned and, as she turned to go, said, "Lara'll tell me everything."

"Then you keep proper decorum, too," said Burly Jack. "Bair's a hero after all, and it j'st ain't right to embarrass a person of his kind, especially not in front of his ladylove, nor his sire and dam. You tell that to Lara, too, y'hear?"

"Right, Burly." Yellow Nell scurried toward the stairs, just as Lara came down, and before Nell could prevent it, Dark-Eyed Lara's voice cut through the din as she squealed, "Bair!"

Freshly bathed and shaved and clothed in fresh garments, Urus and Bair came from the baths and into the common room, Bair pausing at the entry just long enough to see if Dark-Eyed Lara were there. He didn't see her, and he strode in, smiling until his eye fell upon Riatha and Jaith and Lara off in a corner laughing. As he came toward them, Lara excused herself and made a small curtsey his way, then went to sit in the lap of one of the crewmen of the *Eroean.*

"Um, *Athir,*" said Bair, "I think I'll go sit with my *kelan* and catch up on the times."

"Very well, *Arran,*" replied Urus. "We'll be over shortly."

As Urus continued on, Bair veered toward the bar.

"Burly Jack," said the youth.

"Lord Bair," replied the barman, a great smile on his face. "Welcome again to the Red Slipper."

Bair grinned in return. "A drink if you please, Jack."

Burly Jack nodded. "How about a nice tankard of Vornholt ale?"

Bair quickly pressed out a hand of negation. "Rather would I have a goblet of the dark Vanchan."

As Jack rummaged through the bottles, he said, "It's been what, ten years?"

"Aye, Jack. Ten years since last I was here."

"Even so," said Burly Jack, pouring, "you are well remembered."

Bair glanced at Lara, and then beyond to the corner table where Riatha and Jaith were laughing, Urus roaring.

Bair sighed, then took up his drink and made his way toward the hearth, where Aravan and Aylis and Dokan and others of the crew of the *Eroean* were laughing as well, all but Noddy, that is, that young Man pale and trembling and holding his head as if it were about to burst.

As Bair slid his six foot nine into an empty chair, Aravan said, "Where have ye been, thou and thy *athir* and *ythir* and Jaith . . . and hast thou and Jaith come to an understanding?"

"Take care how thou dost answer, *chier,*" came a soft voice from behind, "for it might come back to haunt thee."

Bair looked back and up to see Jaith standing directly behind, a glorious smile on her face. He reached a hand up and she placed hers in his, and he drew her 'round to sit on his lap. Bair glanced at Aravan and replied, "You might say so, *kelan.*" He looked into Jaith's green eyes. "We are pledged."

Jaith laughed and gave Bair a quick kiss, then slid from his lap and took a seat on the floor beside the youth.

"Oh, my," said Aylis. "My heartfelt congratulations to you both."

There was a general call for toasts all 'round and, but for Noddy, each of the crew members present lofted a glass or a tankard, and a silver thimble of a tiny crew member was raised within a small cluster of shadows at the foot of Aravan's chair.

"Ah, then, *elar,* that's one thing thou hast been up to," said Aravan, "and I wish ye twain the best. Yet still would I ask, what has passed among ye four, and how came ye here?"

"As to how we got here, 'twas simple," said Bair. "Three days past, we were in our small dhow on our way to Caer Pendwyr to see High King Ryon and report on our mission. We had dropped anchor in Hovenkeep, and 'twas but happenstance I overheard a sailor on the dock saying that two days earlier he and his shipmates had seen the *Eroean* cutting through waters on an east heading. 'Like a ghost on the wind, she was,' he said. The very next day we set sail for Port Arbalin, knowing most likely you and your crew would be moored here. And where else in Port Arbalin would we find you but at the Slipper?"

"You were on a mission for the High King?" asked Pipper.

"Hush, cousin," said Binkton. "It might have been a secret mission."

"Ooo," breathed Pipper, "a secret mission was it?"

Bair smiled. "Secret it was when we left, but the cat's out of the bag after what we did."

"What did you do?" came a voice from the cluster of shadow.

Bair looked down, then said, "Pysk <fire>. I see Pysk <fire>, and something else too faint to see."

Aylis said, "'Tis my chosen niece, daughter of my pledged sister. Bair, Jaith, this is Aylissa, child of Jinnarin and Farrix."

Aylissa dropped her gathered shadow, and raised her thimble in salute.

Bair nodded, and Jaith stood and curtseyed, then settled to the floor once more. Aylissa smiled at them both and then disappeared within shadow again.

"*Kelan,*" said Bair, "you must have had a rather intriguing voyage, what with a Fox Rider along as a scout."

"Hoy, now," protested Pipper, his piercing voice causing Noddy to wince and clutch at his temples. "Bink and I were along as scouts, too."

"Cap'n, sir," said Noddy in a desperate whisper as he carefully levered himself up and out of his chair, trying to keep his head perfectly level and not let it bobble even the tiniest bit, "Oi'm goin' back t'bed. That Vorn'olt ale still has me roidin' stormy wiaves asea, up 'n' acrost 'n' daown 'underd-foot griaybeards."

"Vornholt ale, eh?" said Bair, wincing in memory. "My sympathies, Noddy, for I've been there myself. But as for getting better, I think taking in sea air is preferable to lying abed."

"Yar, sea air'll do you good," said Fat Jim, grinning, "but not down at the docks with its days-old rotten-fish smells all sniffed up y'r nose and roilin' 'round in y'r innards and bowels and makin' y' want t'puke up y'r churnin' guts. And you might consider getting something to eat, like soft-cooked eggs, all runny, and rashers of bacon swimmin' in grease, or sausages oozing globs of fat, but watch out for them thick strands of the cook's oily hair, 'cause if you get a tangle o' them long greasy strings down in your chokin' throat half swallowed, one end of them layin' across your tongue and dangling out your quiverin' lips, the other end strung down your gaggin' gullet and—"

Slapping a hand over his mouth, Noddy took off at a run for the privies, Fat Jim and Nikolai laughing in his wake.

"That wasn't very nice, Jim," said Aylis, suppressing a smile.

"Ah, Lady Aylis, but it was fun," replied Fat Jim.

"I know just how he feels," said Bair, watching the bosun run. Then he turned to Aravan. "Still, what were you after, you with a Pysk and two Warrows as scouts on your voyage?"

"We went to find the Lost City of Jade," said Aravan.

"And did you?" asked Bair.

"Aye." Aravan sighed. "Good Men and Drimm died there in those abandoned streets."

"Not completely abandoned, Captain," said Tarly, "else they wouldn't have died."

"Don't forget the ones slain on shipboard," said Wooly.

A pall fell over the assembly, but finally Bair said, "It sounds like a tale to be told one day, but not now."

Aravan nodded. "Aye, *elar,* not now."

Another moment of silence passed, and then Aylis said, "But you, Bair, you can tell us of your mission."

"Aye, and I will," said Bair, "or perhaps my sire." Then he turned to Jaith. "Or mayhap you should tell it, *chier,* you are after all a bard."

Jaith nodded. "I'll sing the song of the legend, but only after we eat, for I am famished and would have a meal not taken shipboard."

Pipper, glee in his eyes, looked at Binkton and said, "She's a real bard, and an Elven one, too."

Binkton seemed just as delighted, but he said, "What's this story, this song, this mission all about?"

Jaith bent over and looked deeply into Binkton's jewellike gaze and loudly whispered, "A black throne, Binkton, a token of fear quite insidious."

As Binkton's eyes widened in apprehension, Pipper said, "Oh, no. Not another thing to clutch at my dreams."

Jaith smiled and straightened up, and Bair stood and said, "Let us join my sire and dam and sup, *chier;* besides, 'tis a tale better told in the depths of night."

"Indeed," said Jaith, slipping her arm in his, "better told in nought but candlecast shadows"—she gestured about "and not in the glare of bright lanterns."

Candlemarks later, after all patrons had long gone from the common room of the Red Slipper but for Urus and Riatha and Bair and a handful of those from the *Eroean,* Jaith, bearing a harp, joined the arc of friends before the hearth and took a seat next to Bair.

"Oh, good," said Pipper, "now perhaps Wooly and Fat Jim and Tarly will stop pestering me and Bink."

Fat Jim said, "Well, we'd like to know the end of the story having to do with those who escaped from the Gargon's Lair—Perry and Lord Kian and Anval and Borin and Ursor and Silverleaf—only to be trapped there at the underground river."

"Yes, and the fire behind had gone out and Rûcks and such were coming down the tunnel after," said Wooly.

"And the passage ahead was blocked by the trap Othran set long ages ago," said Tarly.

"So what happened?" said Fat Jim. "At least you can tell us the end of the story?"

"They all lived happily ever after," said Binkton.

"Not so," said Pipper. "They *all* didn't live happily ever after; just four of the six did"—Pipper grinned—"and I'll not tell you which four."

As Fat Jim and Tarly and Wooly started to protest, Pipper's hand flew to his mouth, and he glanced at Dokan and said, "Oh, my, I shouldn't have made a jape where death is concerned."

"Indeed," said Binkton. "And to make up for it, mayhap we ought to tell the rest of that story."

Aravan shook his head. "Nay, wee ones. There is a copy of both *The Ravenbook* and the *Fairhill Journal* in the *Eroean*'s library. Any who so desire can read it for themselves." As Fat Jim and Tarly and Wooly groaned in frustration, Aravan added, "Still, I deem ye twain do owe this group a tale. What say ye?"

"Oh, my," said Pipper, looking in alarm at Binkton.

"Let us think on it," said Binkton. "But others should tell a story or two as well." Binkton smiled at Aylissa, the Pysk no longer in shadow, now that the common room was empty of all but her friends.

"We shall do our part," said Bair, glancing at Jaith and Urus and Riatha. "Our story concerns a black throne."

"Hadron's?" said Aravan, and upon receiving a nod from Riatha, he added, "But I thought that lost or destroyed long past."

"So did we," said Urus. "Yet word came to High King Ryon that perhaps it hadn't been. And so he sent us on a mission."

Nikolai said, "You talk chair like king sit in?"

"Aye, Nick," said Bair. "Have you not heard the song of the Black Throne?"

Nikolai turned up his hands and glanced 'round at the others, most of whom shrugged. "I t'ink not sea chantey, eh?"

Bair shook his head and turned to Jaith. "*Chier,* mayhap you should enlighten them."

"Do all of ye speak Sylva?" asked Jaith.

At the chorus of nays, Jaith said, "Then I'll try to put it in Common, though it is much more stirring in the Elven Tongue."

She took up the harp and ran a descending glissando, and then struck a discordant low chord, and said, "The Black Throne of Hadron Hall."

Tunnn . . . tunnn . . . tunnn . . .

Repeatedly, rhythmically, over and again in an ominous beat, Jaith plucked the lowest string on the harp, and, with her voice pitched deep, she began to chant to the stroke:

Away from the shores of an icy sea
Hove the ebon craft.
Full were her sails with a dark wind,
A black wake churning aft.

In the shadows a poisonous gift
Deep in her hold she bore,
Giver unknown, sinister it came,
Mayhap from a dark tower. . . .

"Radok, to me!"

"Yes, Master Nunde." Radok left the pestle in the mortar and hurried to the Necromancer's side.

"It is finished," said Nunde, his dark eyes gloating as he ran his long, bony fingers through his waist-length hair, tossing it back from his narrow face and aquiline nose.

On a low platform before the Black Mage sat an ornate ebon throne.

Radok gazed at the intricate carving and the dark velvet padding. "But, master, I see no <power> in this chair."

"Exactly so, Radok," said Nunde. "I have cast no spells whatsoever upon it, and that is its beauty, for even though it bears no touch of my <fire>, still it is a token of fear. No Mage who tests it by <sight> will think it is aught but an opulent chair of state, yet it will sow chaos and horror, and perhaps even result in the overthrow of the High Kings of Mithgar. —Damn Awain for ever uniting those realms and establishing his line."

"But, my Lord Nunde," said Radok, "Awain is long dead, and—"

"Even so, his line lives," hissed Nunde. "Could I but get my hands on Awain's corpse"—the Necromancer clenched a black-nailed fist—"ever would he regret that which he did."

"My lord?"

"Imbecile!" Nunde whirled to face Radok; the apprentice flinched away. "Pah!" spat Nunde. "Listen and learn. As long as the separate kingdoms are united, all will come to the aid of one. Hence, defeating them one at a time has ceased to be an option, which makes it that much more difficult to aid Lord Gyphon in His struggle to overthrow that simpering fool Adon."

"And how will this throne help us achieve that end, Master?"

"I intend this to go to Jute, for even now my agent prepares the death of Hadron's sire."

"I don't see just how—"

"Radok, perhaps I should never have taken you on as my apprentice, for you seem to have no mind of your own."

A guarded look came into Radok's eye, yet he said, "Yes, Master."

"Heed," said Nunde. "Jute is a formidable power at sea, and can I arrange an alliance between Jute and Kistan, then will we have control of the seas of the High King's realms—Jute the waters nigh Gelen and Rwn and Atala; Kistan the waters of the Avagon. And thereby we will hasten Gyphon's ultimate rule."

"Ah," said Radok, "I see."

"Do you? I wonder. Regardless, I want you to bear this throne to my agent in Königstadt."

"My lord, how?"

"By ship, Radok. I have arranged for one to meet you on the shores of the Boreal Sea nigh the end of the Gronfangs, well out of the suck of the Great Maelstrom.

"You will deliver it in secret. Let no one other than the agent see whence it came, and tell him it is meant for the coronation of Hadron in Heinrich's Hall, though it will be known as Hadron's Hall when the boy is king. —Now call an Ogh to bear this chair to the carpenters, and take care to have him not touch the arms; you as well, Radok. Crate it, and then journey to meet Durlok's ship."

"Ah, then Durlok has a ship."

"Didn't I just say so?"

"I didn't know," said Radok.

" 'Twas my Lord Modru's, but after that unpleasantness at Duellin, he gave it over to Durlok, along with its crew."

A sevenday later, accompanied by a well-armed escort of Drik and Ghok and Oghi, with Vulpen running scout, Radok, in a Hèlsteed-drawn waggon, rode down from the dark tower to the east of Jallor Pass, to travel by night toward the distant shores of the ice-cold Boreal Sea, the crated black throne his cargo.

A moon later, he rendezvoused with Durlok and his crew of Chûn—of Drik and Ghok and Oghi.

Across a dark sea an ebon ship
A chair of state did bring,
Regal it was, and elegant, for the crowning
Of Hadron the king.

In Hadron's Hall they placed the black throne
On a dais high,
Well in time for the coronation,
The day of which drew nigh. . . .

"Whence came this throne?" whispered one of the servants preparing the hall for the coronation.

"None knows," said another.

A third one said, "I overheard my lady saying that it came to the docks in the night, and there is a rumor it was left there by the crew of a black ship, though just whose ship it was, she didn't say. It seems it bore no flag nor sigil of any kind."

"They say the Healer who attended the king—bless Heinrich's departed soul—brought it to the attention of Prince Hadron, and the moment the prince saw it, he would have no other for his coronation."

"Gleeful, he was, or so they say."

"Hmm . . . And him with his sire not but a sevenday gone to the flames."

"A sudden illness it was, of the stomach."

"Heinrich was a good king. May Hadron do as well."

Ja, came the chorus of agreement.

Each day from that dark chair of state
Did enthroned King Hadron rule,
Yet each day did he gradually change
To grow ever more cruel.

Each day he slyly surveyed his court
And came to see in the room
Lords awhisper, ladies amurmur,
Surely they plotted his doom. . . .

Hadron gripped the arms of the throne, his knuckles white, and hoped none could see his disquiet, for they would take it as a sign of weakness and fall upon him like the ravenous pack of curs they were.

He had been king, now, for what? three years? Ah, yes, three years, though it seemed much longer. And—by the throne!—during that time he had come to realize that evil plots were afoot in the court. They were all out after his blood, each and every one, even those who were formerly fast friends of his youth. Oh, they acted innocent enough, but he knew that as soon as he was out of sight and earshot their heinous scheming began.

The only one he could trust was the court Healer, Mage Dreth. He had been the one who said all kings needed tasters, and surely the food would have been poisoned had Hadron not taken such precautions.

Dreth also suggested that there were cunning assassins following the king's every step. No doubt Dreth was right, yet even though when Hadron lay traps to ferret out even one of these skulkers he never managed to do so, for clearly they had been warned by traitors within the king's own court of the snares the king had set, and so avoiding them was but a simple matter.

The Mage also suggested to him there were foreign killers plotting foul regicide: assassins from Gelen and Rwn and Atala beyond. They wanted control of the seas, and surely they had enlisted the Dragonships of the raiding Fjordlanders in their cause. But Hadron would not yield to them. Instead, he would send his own Dragonships out to pillage and plunder. And he ordered his dukes and earls and barons to do so. And they did, and reaped the profits, though unquestionably they continued with their own nefarious plots of usurpation and rule.

And so, Hadron sat in his magnificent black throne and rubbed the ebon wood of the arms, and fondled the dark knurls alongside, and every day he knew—*knew!*—the conspirators and clandestine traitors grew ever more secretive, as well as ever more bold. After all, they were everywhere he looked.

Thus did King Hadron sink into madness,
Deeper day by day.
Insidious was the vile Black Throne
In slowly laming its prey.

Assassins and schemers were put to death,
—Lords, ladies . . . the queen!—
Till one night Hadron simply vanished,
The mad king nevermore seen. . . .

In the moonless night the weighted body sewn in canvas slid over the side of the Dragonboat to splash into the deep waters nigh Gelen, where, if the corpse ever came to light, the Gelenders would bear the blame.

As the ripples of its passage subsided under the rolling swells, "Well, Duke Richter, what now?" asked Baron Vogle.

"Though she's a bastard," said Richter, "we'll put Hadron's daughter on the throne." He paused, as if trying to dredge up a memory. "What is her name again?"

"Gudlyn, sire," answered Degroot, Richter's chief at arms. "Gudlyn the Glorious."

"Ah, yes. Gudlyn. She will assume the throne after a proper period of searching for the missing king." Duke Richter glanced over the side and broke into laughter.

Baron Vogle shook his head. "She's Hadron's get, Richter, and likely to go mad as well. She, like her sire, just might decide to have more of the court put to death."

"Should that happen, should she become a threat, there's always the sea," replied the duke, gesturing at where the body had gone.

"Sire," said Degroot. "What of the raids? Mad though he was, Hadron at least ordered us to plunder . . . to our profit, I add."

"Oh, we'll not stop our pillaging," said Richter. "It fills my coffers with gold and brings thralls to my estates and my bed."

He broke into laughter and was joined by the others, and the ship swung about and headed east for Königstadt, soon to be renamed Königinstadt, for now a queen would sit on the capital throne.

Queen after queen assumed the throne,
Where they were driven mad,
Queens bearing only stillborn sons,
Though healthy daughters they had.

The Royal Healer did consult
With others of his Kind,
Yet no direct cause was found,
It surely must be in the line.

Several Mages were brought to court
To look for a curse cast,
Yet no trace of <fire> did they find
Neither in present nor past. . . .

"How did she get in here?" asked Dreth, the Royal Healer, gazing through the candlelight down at the kneeling crone, surrounded by three men of the nightwatch.

"We know not, Lord Dreth," replied the senior of the trio of guards.

"Spare me, my lord," mumbled the crone, "I am but an humble herb woman."

"What were you doing here in the throne room?" snapped Dreth.

She flinched down, but glanced at the dais. "For centuries, now, has this realm suffered under the rule of madness, and I know whence the evil comes.'Tis the throne, Lord Dreth, it is a token of fear, and it—"

Dreth sucked air in between clenched teeth and slapped the old woman into silence. He placed a hand on her head and muttered a word, and she collapsed. He then turned to the senior guard. "Give me your knife, Korporal."

The senior officer frowned, but handed his dagger over to the Mage.

"Hold her head still," Dreth ordered the other two, and when they had done so, with three swift strokes he cut out her tongue at the root.

As blood gushed from the crone's mouth, the korporal looked at the Royal Healer in horror. Dreth handed him the severed tongue and said, "She is a witch, and I would not have her lay a curse on this hall. Now take her from here and burn her at the stake."

The korporal shoved the tongue into the pocket of the nearest unterkorporal and said, "Yes, my lord." He gestured at the other two, and they lifted up the unconscious old woman and bore her out and away.

She died of blood loss ere they bound her to the stake, but she was burned regardless.

And when asked why they were doing this, the three soldiers told of what had passed and of the Royal Healer's deed and words and orders.

And those they told in turn told others as well.

Rumors circulated throughout the court.

"The throne is cursed; 'tis a token of fear."

"They say that centuries agone it came in the night on a black ship."

"A witch did it. I saw her tongue."

"They found her in the throne room, renewing the curse."

"They say it drives the one who sits in it quite mad."

"It all started way back when Hadron was king, some five centuries agone. . . ."

The nobles demanded that the throne be destroyed, and though mad Queen Inga the Irresistible protested, they promised her an even more elaborate replacement, one of gold and ivory. By this means did their will prevail, and the ornate chair of state, the black throne of Hadron's Hall, was to be shattered and all the pieces burned, yet there was none among the nobles who would touch it.

"I shall do so," said Mage Dreth, the Royal Healer.

A collective sigh of relief swept through the assembly.

The next day, 'neath an overcast sky, many gathered in the courtyard, and a worker wheeled a barrow out among them, a barrow bearing split and splintered remains of black wood.

"If this is cursed," loudly called out Dreth as the worker dumped the fragments in a pile, "then let no one breathe the smoke and fumes."

The courtyard cleared in but an instant.

Smiling, Dreth kindled a fire in the heap, and stood back and watched it all burn, while nobles peered out through shut windows from afar and marvelled at the bravery of the Royal Healer.

Weeks later, in the depths of a moonless night, a crate was borne to the docks and laded on a black ship. And ere false dawn broke in the east, the ship was far out to sea.

Burnt to ashes on a dim day,
Smoke rising in a dark pall,
Destroyed forever by one bold,
The Black Throne of Hadron's Hall

There ends the tale of a token of fear,
Mad it drove them all.
Cursed it was by dark witchery,
The Black Throne of Hadron's Hall.

With a final descending glissando, Jaith fell silent, her chant at an end.

"Oh, my," said Aylissa, clapping her hands, "that was just wonderful."

She was joined in her applause by all the others, with Fat Jim calling, *"Bella, bella!"* and Tarly whispering, *"Vidunderlig!"*

Bair reached out and took Jaith's hand, and she threw a glorious smile his way and set her modest harp aside.

And when the clamor died, Pipper said, "Does no one know who made the throne?"

"The one who did it does," said Binkton.

"If that person is still alive," shot back Pipper. Then he turned to Jaith again. "What I meant is, who made it?"

Jaith turned up her hands, and looked at Aylis. "Mayhap a Seer could <see>."

Aylis shook her head. "I think not, for just as Durlok blocked my <sight> from Krystallopŷr, so too do I believe are all tokens of fear warded."

"Good t'ing it destroyed long past," said Nikolai. "Now no one else go mad."

"Ah, my friend," said Bair, "it was not destroyed."

"But song say it burned," said Nikolai.

"For millennia that was believed to be so," said Bair. "But that tale, that chant, that song from the First Era turned out to not be true."

"You mean more queens went mad?" said Binkton.

"Oh, more of the Jutlander queens did go mad," said Riatha. "Still do, in fact. Yet it is not a black throne driving them so, but rather there seems to be a flaw in the line."

"The latest mad queen is Eitel the Exquisite," said Tarly. "She sends her Dragonboats against my homeland as the mad queens of Jutland have always done."

"Aye," said Aravan, "and ye Fjordlanders ever raid their realm."

"Just to retaliate," said Tarly.

"They raid you; you raid them; and I suppose it has ever been so," said Aylissa. "Will it never end?"

Tarly shrugged, but Aravan said, "There was a Man named Egil, Arin's love, who, following the teachings of the Elven way, said, 'Let it begin with me.' His suasion caused many to take up the banner of harmony, and it lives on to this day."

"Harmony, yes," said Tarly, "though it is a harmony well armed. Egil did not say that fighting just wars was wrong, but simply revealed that pillage and rape and plunder were the acts of savages. Long did my people resist, for we were raiders, yet we finally came to see that honor lay in Egil's words, and we took that message to heart. Long past did the Fjordlanders stop raiding the innocent, long past did we stop rending from others that which they rightly earned. But we take vengeance against those who raid our villages and steads and homes, for it is a vengeance reaped in a just cause."

"Kala!" barked Dokan, saluting Tarly. "We Châkka have a saying: Strike me once, mayhap it was an accident. Strike me twice, mayhap it was an error. But strike me thrice, beware."

"But, Dokan, what does that have to do with what Tarly said?" asked Pipper.

"Just this, wee one," said the Dwarf, "one can ignore an offence but a limited number of times, and the Jutlanders' raids on Fjordland go well past that mark."

"Oh," said Pipper, satisfied.

"Yar," said Fat Jim, "but what does this have to do with th Black Throne of Hadron's Hall?"

"The raiding began long ere Hadron sat on the throne," said Jaith. "Yet it turned deadly under Hadron's rule. 'Take no children,' was his edict, 'for they do not make suitable thralls.' Hence, younglings were slaughtered out of hand, and oldsters as well. Only the hale and fit were taken prisoner, all else were slain."

Tarly slammed a fist to his chair arm, then stood and walked to the extent of the candlelight.

Silence fell among the group, but finally Nikolai looked at Bair and said, "You tell Black Throne not burnt?"

Bair grinned and glanced at Jaith and then back at Nikolai and said, "Aye, contrary to the words of the song, it was not burnt back in the First Era." Bair looked at Urus and barked a short laugh, then added, "Yet, mayhap this part of the tale is one my sire should tell."

"Let me refresh my tankard," said Urus, getting to his feet, "then I will."

On his way to the taps, Urus paused at Tarly's side and softly spoke with him. And then he and Tarly went on to the bar, where they each drew a tankard of the Vornholt, and came back to the arc of friends. Sitting once again next to Riatha, Urus took a long pull from the tall pewter mug and then set it aside.

"We four happened to be in Caer Pendwyr, for High King Ryon was curious to know what Riatha and Bair and I had found beyond the eastern in-between of the nexus, when—"

"Nexus?" said Fat Jim, while at the same time Aravan said, "Ye went beyond?"

"I was not with them," said Jaith. "It was some years ere Bair and I became attached."

Aravan swung his gaze to Riatha and Bair, then back to Urus. "So ye three went beyond."

"Aye," said Urus, glancing at Bair. "'Twas the in-between denied you and my son during the Dragonstone War."

As Aravan nodded, Fat Jim said, "What is this nexus?"

Bair said, " 'Tis a place on Neddra where—"

"You were on Neddra?" blurted Pipper, his eyes wide in startlement.

"Aye," said Bair. "Thrice. Some years back."

Pipper opened his mouth to say something, but Bair pushed out a staying hand and said, "The first time was during the Dragon-

stone War, when *kelan* and I crossed from Mithgar to Neddra in pursuit of the yellow-eyed stealer of the Silver Sword and the killer of Galarun. He had fled to a black fortress, and from that fortress a league and a mile away in the direction of each of the four cardinal points one can step unto four different worlds: to the north, Vadaria; to the west, Adonar; to the south, Mithgar; and to the east, a place of horror, for there lies the world of—"

"Oh, my," Aylissa gasped, and she cloaked herself in shadow.

Bair looked at the tiny cluster of darkness and frowned and said, "Um, let me save that tale for later."

Urus nodded and took another pull of the Vornholt, then cleared his throat. "As I said, we were guests of High King Ryon, when word came from a Realmsman in Hyree. It seems he had discovered the palace had a private room in which sat a black throne, a throne from which the sultan issued his most dire commands—those for assassinations, wars, raids, infanticides, tortures, dismemberments, and the like.

"The Realmsman thought it odd that there were two thrones—one for matters of pageantry and the ordinary conduct of state, the other for grim issuances—and so he obtained a sketch of the dark chair and sent it along with his message, and when Ryon showed it to us . . ." Urus turned to Jaith.

The Dara said, "It resembled the depiction I had seen of the Black Throne of Hadron's Hall, an eld painting of Hadron on his throne"—Jaith glanced at Tarly—"a portrait destroyed in one of the Fjordlanders' raids of retaliation."

Tarly shrugged noncommittally.

Urus took up the tale again. "Ryon had heard the legend, and he asked if there was any way it could be verified whether or no this was indeed the same throne. And since Jaith was the only one among us who had seen that portrait, she volunteered to go, could we find a way of her doing so.

"After much discussion, we four decided to travel through Hyree as a troupe from Sarain. Bair and I would perform astounding feats of strength and magic, while Jaith and Riatha would act as our chattel and play and sing and dance. The Darai would of course wear veils, falling from crown to shoulder, to conceal the tilt of their Elven eyes as well as their tipped ears. As for Bair and I, the fact that we were ostensibly from Sarain would explain our hair and eye color, for, though uncommon, still grey and amber eyes and fair hair are not unknown among Sarinians.

"And so, across the Avagon in a modest, two-masted dhow we sailed, landing in the Hyrinian port city of Khalísh. To establish ourselves as entertainers, we performed awhile in that city, then began making our way across Hyree toward the capital, there where we hoped to contact the Realmsman who had sent the message and then lay our plans for dealing with the throne.

"At our stops all along the way, we sang and played and danced and staged our astounding feats of strength and magic in villages and towns and caravansaries and among the bivouacs of nomads, all to the delight and dread of the patrons. And finally we reached Âsimi, the sultan's city, our destination, but not our goal. . . ."

"There," said Riatha, pointing.

Ahead, along the twisting street, a sun-faded sign bearing serpentine letters proclaimed the establishment to be the *Azrak Nijmi*—the Blue Star inn—a one-storey, mud-brick building that had seen better days.

Out of the bright sunlight and into the darkness of the interior strode Urus and Bair, Riatha and Jaith left squatting on their heels outside, tending the long string of asses bearing their common and uncommon goods as well as the entertainment gear: harp, drum, costumes, a frame, silk drapery, bars, chains, weights, and the like.

While Bair stood just inside the door, Urus crossed to the counter. Speaking Kabla, the language of the desert, "I seek Anwar," he said to the man opposite, who was carving on a piece of bone.

Barely glancing at Urus, the man jabbed a thumb over his shoulder, pointing toward a beaded curtain in an archway.

Urus looked at Bair and tilted his head toward a room to the right, where Men sat and sipped at small cups of *khawi,* a strong, dark brown drink. Receiving a nod from Bair, Urus passed 'round the counter and through the curtain, beads clacking in his wake. He came into a hallway, and strode to another opening, beyond which sat a man at a table shuffling through papyrus scrolls. The man looked up. "Yes?" he said in Hyrinian.

"I speak not that tongue," replied Urus, again in Kabla.

"Yes?" said the man, now changing to that language.

"Bright is the full moon at noon," quietly said Urus.

"And water flows up the hills," came the whispered return, the Man smiling. Then he stood and stepped to the archway and peered down the hall.

"Mandos?" said Urus.

The man nodded and kept an eye down the passage. "Best call me Anwar, instead."

"I am Urus, and Ryon sent me and three more to examine the throne."

"The throne?" said Anwar. "The black one? But why?"

"By the sketch you sent, it resembles the Black Throne of Hadron's Hall."

The Realmsman frowned.

"Do you know the old legend?" asked Urus.

Anwar's face brightened in recollection, but again his face took on a look of puzzlement. "The one in the children's song?"

"Aye," replied Urus, "though I would not call it a child's song. Regardless, if it is that throne, then it would explain much of past history."

"In what—? Ah, I see. If the legend of the curse is true, then that would make plain why the sultans of Hyree have long sent their Lakhs against the High King's realms."

"Exactly so," said Urus.

"How do you expect to gain entrance unto that chamber where the throne sits?" asked Anwar.

Urus said, "I was hoping you could tell us how. That is, you were in there to sketch the throne, weren't you?"

Anwar shook his head. "No."

"Then how did you—?"

"I have certain contacts with some rather unseemly characters, both highborn and low-. One of the sultan's own sons—Tarikh—from whom I learn much of what goes on at court, regularly comes here in disguise to purchase certain, ah, illicit powders. It was from him I learned of the black throne and the chamber in which it sits. It is Tarikh's sketch of the throne I sent by bird to Commander Rori."

"Ah, I see," said Urus. "Then perhaps it is this Tarikh who will gain us entry into the palace."

Anwar pursed his lips, then said, "Mayhap, have you something that will pique his interest, some gems to display or other such valuables. If so, perhaps he will ask you to come and exhibit your wares before Sultan Aziz himself?"

Urus grinned. "As I said, there are four of us altogether: one is Jaith—who has seen a portrait of Hadron himself sitting on the throne and who might be able to tell us if this chair of state you reported is the same one; the other three are myself, Riatha, Bair."

Anwar sucked in a deep breath and said, "Bair? Bair is here? —Oh, wait. You are Urus, his sire? And his dam is here as well?" Without conscious thought, Anwar bowed and, with his right hand, touched his breast, then lips, then forehead in a desert-honored gesture of respect.

Then Anwar said, "Nevertheless, although you have great heroes in your company, first you must gain entrance into the palace, and even then the chamber with the throne is well guarded, and—"

Urus held up a stilling hand. "We are disguised as a troupe of entertainers—magi and sylphs—and, with your permission, the Blue Star will be the place where our reputation in Âsimi begins. And since Tarikh is an habitué of your place, once he sees us perform, I am certain that he will not forgo the pleasure of our company at the palace proper. . . ."

In less than a fortnight word had spread throughout the capital that strongmen and a sorcerer and enchanting sylphs were performing at the Blue Star, and soon the small café was nigh to bursting at the seams with patrons who had come to see. And every night the onlookers were awed by the strength of two giants from Sarain, and frightened nearly out of their wits by the sorcery of the *sáhir,* though surely he was not a true Magus but a simple conjurer instead, though none could imagine how it was done. Ah, but it was the singing of the two sylphs, with voices soaring unto the very gates of paradise, and their dancing—each one graceful and tempting beyond all belief, gauzy veils concealing and then revealing, slim legs flashing, bare feet but lightly touching the floor, rounded hips swaying in circular motion, mounded breasts all but bursting free, all to the sensuous throbbing beat of a pounding drum—that fired the loins of the onlookers, especially the one who came nearly each eve, the one known as Jamal, but whose true name was Tarikh.

Within a moon, this incredible troupe was invited to perform before the sultan himself.

A league or so beyond the city proper, it was Tarikh who conducted the four about the palace, first showing them the gardens, with flowers abloom, water cascading, lovers' bowers throughout. Beyond the gardens and in the stables stood fine horses—blacks, sorrels, whites, blood bays—some saddled for couriers to ride should the sultan have dispatches to send. Tarikh was especially proud of his own fine steed, a pale gray with nimble legs and a barrel of a chest, a horse so fleet none like him had ever before been, or so Tarikh did say.

As they toured, Jaith, Riatha, Urus, and Bair noted where the well-armed guards were stationed within the walled grounds, each one at attention in his red-and-black uniform and gold turban, with a pearl-handled scimitar in a red scabbard on a gold baldric and an upright bronze lance in hand.

Like guards were posted here and there within the palace as well, and their places were noted by the four as Tarikh conducted them about, starting with the verandahs and working their way through the great throne room—where they were to perform—and the vast dining hall with its candled chandeliers and sconced lanterns, these two chambers with domes above held up by soaring wooden buttresses polished to a fine sheen, buffed to shine like the wooden floors below, with its slabs of marble inset within.

Rich woods were everywhere, in floors and ceilings and walls and banisters and chairs and desks and tables and other furniture—oak, walnut, ebony, cherry, and the like—all in a land where such trees did not grow.

"How ostentatious," murmured Riatha in Sylva.

And all the while Tarikh had shown the foursome about, he had tried to bargain with Urus, offering an unheard sum of golden dinars for just one night with either of the two sylphs—which one didn't matter.

Urus replied that he would think on it and perhaps set a suitable fee, certainly one a great deal higher than Tarikh had so far offered, for these were young virgins both.

Jaith covered up her laughter with a sudden fit of coughing.

Finally Tarikh led them up to their quarters, opulent bedchambers with pearl baths waiting, the rooms of the sylphs next to Tarikh's, the quarters of the two Men down the hall.

As soon as they could, the four met on the balcony running the length of the building.

"According to Anwar, the chamber with the Black Throne is just behind the other throne room," said Urus.

"Aye," said Riatha. "I saw the guarded door."

"Tonight, then?" asked Jaith.

"You will need to see within," said Bair.

"While thy magic scares them witless," said Riatha, smiling, "we will try to gain admittance."

"And if it is the throne?" said Urus.

"As we discussed," said Riatha, looking from Urus to Bair, "ye twain will find a way to destroy it."

"But in a silent manner or one of stealth," said Jaith, "or in a way to distract them such that we all can make our escape."

Riatha smiled. "I am of a mind to ride away on a certain pale gray horse."

"Remounts in tow, of course," said Urus.

"You three take the horses," said Bair. "I think I'll let Hunter do my running for me."

"Good, then," said Urus. "Is there aught else we can here and now plan?"

All looked at one another, but none had ought to say. As they turned to stroll along the balcony and reenter their quarters, Jaith espied Tarikh coming their way. "Should I get the chance," she said, touching the small, ornamental dagger at her slim waist, "mayhap I'll carry a certain person's manhood away with me as well."

Both Bair and Urus winced, while Riatha laughed low and long.

After the sumptuous banquet, the court entire removed to the throne room, where unusual entertainment was to be presented that eve, or so Tarikh on behalf of his father announced.

The court was awed by the size of the two huge Men, and marveled over the lithe grace of the two diaphanous-clad sylphs in attendance. Yet when the performance began with feats of strength, even though the deeds were beyond that which they had ever seen before—the breaking of chains, the bending of bars, the hefting of weights that several members of the court together could not budge, and the simultaneous lifting from the floor of many squealing and laughing volunteer guests—still they were mere feats of strength. And though all the lords of the sultan's court did lust after the houris, and the ladies of the court did lust after these giants of Men, overall they were not greatly impressed by this first act.

But then the two Men bore a tall but light framework to the center of the floor, while the sylphs came after, bearing a great swath of blue silk, mysterious symbols and runes scribed in yellow thereupon.

The sylphs retired, and the taller of the two Men stepped before the sultan and bowed, the Man touching his breast, then lips, then forehead.

"Sire," said the Man in a voice all could hear, his Kabla flawless, "I would tell thee a tale of wonderment, one of a strange curse, one wherein an ordinary Man as he slept in the desert was beset by sorcery dire."

Bair took up one end of the silk, Urus the other.

"My lord," continued Bair, as he and Urus spread the blue silk over the upright frame, and it draped to the floor all 'round, "even as the day waned, and night descended"—Bair signalled, and attendants snuffed candles and extinguished lanterns, until but a few remained in the now dim-lit hall—"and only the crescent moon and the stars looked down, the Man in the desert retired to his tent."

Urus stretched and yawned and lit a single candle in a brass candlestick holder, then stepped into the now-draped frame, while Bair closed the entry behind. "And even as the Man prepared for sleep"—Bair crouched and crept about the silk-clad framework—"there came through the night an evil *Afrit* unto the tent. . . ."

In the darkness, Jaith and Riatha slipped from the chamber and along a short corridor until they came to the warded door just aft of the throne room. Two guards stood before the closed portal, and their eyes widened at the sight of the slender females, appearing as would veiled houris from the very gardens of paradise. The guards knew, of course, that these were the sylphs of the performers who now entertained the court, but even so, their loins grew warm as they watched the two practice some of their steps, slowly moving with exquisite grace about one another, arms raised, hips gyrating.

* * *

Bair raised a trembling clawlike hand into the air and intoned, "And the dreadful *Afrit* began to cast his vile sorceries." Hunched over and dragging a foot behind, Bair crept about, touching symbol after symbol along the silk, while the spectators looked on in wide-eyed trepidation.

Inside the tent, the small candle cast Urus's silhouette against the sheer cloth. Holding the candle, Urus yawned and turned about, and his shadow did likewise, sliding 'round the silk. Then Urus set the candle to the floor.

"It was just as he prepared to lie down," said Bair, "that the sorcery struck." Bair lifted his head and emitted a prolonged howl.

Out in the hallway before the guarded door, Jaith and Riatha suddenly stopped and gasped as if in alarm. The guards, too, started at the howl. "Oh, my," called Riatha, "what monstrous thing is that?"

Within the tent the moving silhouette of the Man changed, darkness gathering 'round him, his form growing huge, gaining bulk . . .

In one collective indrawn breath, the court entire sucked in air. . . .

And then there came a terrible *Rrraaaawww* . . . !

Lunging forth from the tent came a horrible, great, monstrous creature on two legs, huge arms raised, claws swiping at the air, lips curled back, teeth bared, and it opened its mouth and another dreadful roar burst forth.

All in the court screamed in terror and scrambled back against the walls, the sultan himself leaping to his feet and cowering behind the throne.

Rrraaaawww . . . ! The first monstrous bellow echoed down the halls, followed by the screams of the Men and Women of the sultan's court.

Startled, the guards looked at one another, even as Jaith and Riatha threw their hands across their mouths and backed against the wall, and Jaith called out, "The sultan, oh, the sultan!"

And then there came a second roar.

"Save the sultan!" cried Riatha, and the guards, spears in hand, charged toward the throne room.

"Quick!" hissed Jaith, and they opened the now-unwarded door and stepped within.

It was a terrible creature that threatened the court, a huge beast covered with a reddish fur grizzled at the tips—an immense Bear from the lands across the sea, one never before seen in this part of the world—and they knew not what it was, only that a great monster was come among them, and they shrieked in terror and clustered against the walls.

Only Tarikh seemed unaffected, for he had seen this act many times. Even so, in the dimness he trembled.

His sire, crouching behind the throne, moaned in dread, for although Tarikh had warned him as to just what to expect, still Sultan Aziz was shocked beyond his wits.

Guards came rushing in, bronze lances and scimitars in hand. Yet even they were too frightened to attack this roaring monstrous thing.

The chamber was modest and bare but for a lighted single lantern ensconced above a curtained dais sitting along a back wall. Cooling air flowed through grilles to either side, drawn from subterranean chambers and exhausted through vents above.

Jaith moved forward, Riatha at her side. They drew back the curtains to reveal a dark throne on a highly polished black-walnut platform.

"Touch it not," said Jaith as she took down the lantern and held it the better to see, and together they examined the ebon chair of state, with its elaborate carvings and knurls and ridges and grooves and curls.

"Is it the one?" asked Riatha.

"Behold!" cried Bair, and the great beast stalked about and roared and feinted. "Behold what the *Afrit* hath wrought! A curse, a terrible curse, for 'tis a monster dire, a *mâsikh* to haunt the desert and from innocent travellers rend tender flesh and eat it raw!"

From those still clustered against the walls, gasps and moans and cries of terror greeted Bair's pronouncement.

But in that moment the two sylphs came whirling into the throne room, and they spun in circles around the huge fiend, and

Bair called out, "Yet down from paradise came two blessed *Seraphim*, for they had taken pity upon the poor traveller, and they guided him back from roaming the wasteland and once more into his tent."

The monster slowly dropped to all fours and, snuffling, lumbered toward the silken enclosure, the *Seraphim* holding wide the entry.

In the fiend went, and the *Seraphim* closed the way behind, and silhouetted on the tent the candlecast shadow of the monster reared up. Then a magical incantation Bair called out thrice: "Urus, Urus, Urus."

Within the tent darkness gathered, and the shadow of the monster changed, shedding bulk, growing smaller, until the silhouette of a huge Man appeared, seeming much less by comparison.

And out from the tent stepped Urus.

And the houris whipped the silk away, and nought was left inside the frame but a single lit candle in a brass holder sitting on the floor.

At first there was a collective sigh of relief, and then someone began giggling in a release of tension, followed by a smattering of applause, growing, growing, until it became thunderous, and cries of *Mâshallâh!* and *Afârim!* and *Berâwo!* punctuated the din.

The sultan had managed to regain his throne ere the lights were restored, and so he joined in the applause and cries of approval, though his heart continued to hammer with fear.

No one called for an encore.

To settle rapidly beating hearts and minds yet in turmoil, with Jaith playing the harp, both she and Riatha sang a sweet lullaby, their voices soaring in harmony, the words in the tongue of the desert.

And then to set hearts beating rapidly again, they whirled in dance, two incredible sylphs swirling to the throb of a drum.

And as Bair hammered out a deep, heady beat, sensuously did the barefoot houris gyre, their gauzy veils flying, revealing flashes of elegant thighs and mounded breasts nigh unrestrained, hips rocking, turning, swinging voluptuously, invitingly.

Thoughts of lust occupied nearly all of the Men, while most Women despaired, though some among them had carnal thoughts as well.

Urus now sat beside Tarikh, the prince garbed in embroidered finery, his fingers bedecked with four rings, of ruby and emerald and sapphire and diamond. And as the sylphs danced, Urus said, "As we put the silken tent away, I talked to the ladies concerning your offer, Prince Tarikh."

"Wha-what?" said Tarikh, not taking his eyes from the dancers, his heart pounding in synchronicity with the throb of the drum.

"You would take one of these to your bed?" asked Urus.

"Oh, indeed," said Tarikh.

"How about both?" said Urus.

Tarikh jerked about. "Both?"

Urus nodded.

"What is your price?" said Tarikh, his breath coming in rapid gasps.

"I have conditions as well as a price," said Urus.

"Name them," said Tarikh.

"The rings on your fingers," said Urus, "they are the price."

"Done," said Tarikh, stripping them.

"My conditions are—"

"No matter what they are," said Tarikh, "I'll meet them." He held out the rings to Urus.

"Hear me first," said Urus. "For the ladies to retain their reputation, there must be no witnesses."

Tarikh nodded.

"What about guards?" said Urus.

"I will send them away," said Tarikh. "There will be none in the hall tonight."

Urus nodded and said, "Then I will send both houris to your room at— Oh, wait." Urus paused, as if a new thought had just occurred. "What about warders in the gardens below? Virgins are wont to make cries of pleasure."

Tarikh moaned in anticipation. "I will dismiss them also."

"Well and good," said Urus, reaching out and taking the rings. "Send the guards away in the second candlemark after the mid of night. My houris will come to your bedchamber the moment the last one leaves."

Tarikh drew in a shuddering breath, and turned to watch the sylphs as they spun and gyred and bent over backwards while rotating their hips and shimmying their shoulders, their breasts swaying alike, all to the deep throbbing beat of a pounding drum.

* * *

Two candlemarks past the mid of night, Urus and Bair came out from the throne room and they spoke of the wonderful reception of their show by all the members of the sultan's court, while they casually strolled along the deserted hallway, deserted of all but the guards at the door of the chamber behind.

As these chatting entertainers came by the two warders, like vipers striking Bair and Urus smashed huge fists against the temples of the guards and felled them like poleaxed oxen.

They dragged them into the second throne chamber, and then Bair threw back the curtains about the dais and, with his flanged mace, he hammered the black throne into splintered wood, taking care not to touch any of the flinders. Urus then took from under his cloak a flagon of lantern oil and poured it over the remains. He then removed the lamp from the sconce above the dais and said, "Take a deep breath and inhale not, for we know not what this throne bears nor what its smoke will contain."

Each took in a lungful, and then Urus smashed the lit lantern into the pile.

Whoom! The heap blazed up, and Urus and Bair turned and stepped away.

As they passed the unconscious guards, Bair pointed at them.

Urus stooped and lifted one up and slung him over a shoulder.

Bair grabbed the other one, and they stepped out into the hall.

It was empty.

As Bair shut the door behind, he saw the dais and curtains were ablaze as well.

Lugging the sentries, up stairs they trotted to come into an empty hallway and thence to Tarikh's bedchamber. Inside they found the prince naked and gagged and trussed up like a bound pig, his eyes full of rage. Riatha and Jaith waited, both now dressed in their leathers, Riatha's jade-handled sword harnessed across her back, Jaith's rapier at her hip and her small harp in a soft leather case slung by a strap over her shoulder. Swiftly they bound and gagged the unconscious guards, and then took up their packs and moved to the windowed door and onto the balcony. As they looked at the empty gardens below, *Nâr! Nâr!* came a cry. Someone had discovered the fire.

Quickly, Riatha tied a rope to the balcony rail, and down this they slid. Men were running hither and thither, some bearing buckets, others blankets, and they paid little heed to the four as they ran to the stables. Swiftly Riatha saddled up the pale gray horse, as Urus and Jaith strung together remounts while Bair laded them with goatskins of water and saddlebags of grain. Urus and Jaith then leapt astride those steeds already saddled and meant for the couriers.

Riatha mounted and nodded toward Bair, and a darkness enveloped him and grew larger and coalesced into a great Draega, a Silver Wolf, Hunter, for just as his father was a shape-shifter, so, too, was Bair, only he was imprinted with a Draega of the High Plane and not a Bear of the Middle as was his sire. And with Hunter leading the way, out from the stables they galloped, the string of remounts behind. Toward the cadre of guards at the open palace gates they raced, and when these warders saw a monstrous argent beast, a gigantic Wolf charging, they cried in terror and fled, for surely this was an *Afrit* come to slay them.

Out into the desert the trio hammered, horses in tow, the great Silver Wolf easily loping along at their side, while behind the darkness was lighted a lurid red, as richly oiled woods of oak and walnut and ebony and cherry burned furiously against the night sky.

No longer cloaked in shadow, Aylissa clapped her hands in glee as Urus's tale came to an end, the Pysk joined by the others in applause, while Urus turned to Bair and Jaith and Riatha and raised his tankard in salute.

When the applause died down, "Didn't the palace guards chase you?" asked Binkton.

Riatha laughed. "Probably, yet we had the best horses in the kingdom. I think we left any pursuit in the dust."

"I was a bit worried that they might send a messenger bird ahead," said Urus, "but it seems they did not, for five days later when we reached the Hyrinian port city of Khalísh, we turned over the horses to the nearest stable and boarded our ship without incident and sailed away that same eve."

"Speaking of birds and messages," said Bair, "in Hovenkeep we learned that the entire palace burned to the ground, for Mandos, known as Anwar, sent a bird to King Ryon, and Commander Rori made certain that the news reached other Realmsmen by bird as well."

"What about Tarikh, him being tied up and all?" said Wooly.

"Oh, he survived, rescued naked and bound," said Bair. "I suppose he had much to explain to his sire."

They howled with laughter, but after a while a silence settled over them, and they sat long moments in thought, but finally Nikolai said, "It Black Throne of Hadron's Hall?"

"Aye," said Jaith, "it was. As we took down the silken tent and frame, I told Bair and he told Urus."

"Then Hyree be more good toward High King?" asked Nikolai. "No bad throne make evil, eh?"

"Oh, I don't know about that," said Tarly. "I mean, if the throne has tainted the sultan, then mayhap his get is tainted as well, and perhaps the whole line that follows will be just like him."

"Do you think so?" asked Pipper.

"Aye," replied Tarly. "You see, the throne was in Jute for centuries, and even when it was gone away from there, the queens that followed have ever been mad. Hence, once a line is tainted . . ." Tarly's voice trailed off, the rest of his thought left unsaid, but all knew what he meant.

Again a silence descended upon them for a while, but then Urus broke into laughter.

Riatha looked at him in puzzlement. *"Chier?"*

"Oh, I was just thinking about Tarikh, trussed up like a pig. It must have come as a great surprise for you to have done that to him."

Jaith smiled. "He was lying naked on the bed, waiting for us, his desire quite apparent."

"Yes," said Riatha, "and when we bound and gagged him, his desire, um, wilted."

This brought roaring laughter from them all. Yet when the others stopped, Urus did not; but he quelled his mirth long enough to pull a ruby, an emerald, a sapphire, and a diamond ring from his pocket and jiggle them clinking in hand and say, "I really should return these to him, you know, for services not rendered. Ah, but what a tale I told Tarikh when I gulled him." Urus burst out in laughter again and, when Riatha cocked an eyebrow his way, he managed to gasp out, "Virgins indeed."

Once more did the common room of the Red Slipper ring with howling glee.

8

Broken Stones

"Does it hurt to shift shape?" asked Binkton, eyeing both Urus and Bair. "I mean, with all of that stretching and changing of muscle and bone and other such, growing when you become a Bear or a Silver Wolf, and shrinking when you change back, surely there's some hurt involved."

Bair looked at Urus and said, "If there is, I am unaware of it."

Urus nodded in agreement, as did Aravan.

"It must be nice to be able to turn into something else," said Pipper.

"At times it comes in handy," said Urus. "Yet it has a hidden danger, too."

"A danger?" said Fat Jim. "How so?"

Urus said, "Whenever any shapeshifter changes to the creature of his imprint—he actually *becomes* that creature. For example, when I change into a Bear, I become that savage creature. I am not a Baeran in the shape of a Bear, but a Bear itself. Even so, I am a Bear where deep within frequently a wee bit of my own reason prevails, though at times not. Still, as a Bear I am driven by other urges, other needs from those of the Baeran I once had been. And so, I am a thing of the wilds, though mayhap I am a Bear cunning beyond all others, a Bear who at times has strange un-Bearlike urges and motives akin to those of the Man I was. Yet, the Bear who once was Urus only occasionally thinks along those paths; and although that Bear might again *become* Urus, there is no guarantee it will. And *that* is a danger that the Bear and I both live with: I might never again become the Bear; the Bear might never again become me. I am aware of this danger; the Bear is not.

"And so, just before I shift, I try to impress upon my mind the thought as to what it is I want the Bear to do. Sometimes the Bear remembers this; sometimes not. And if the Bear does not remember, then mayhap the thing Urus wishes the Bear to do does not get done.

"And if the Bear never thinks of that desired deed, and if the Bear never thinks of Urus again, then he will remain a Bear.

"It is said that in the Wolfwood live Bears who once were Men, and if that is so, then I think there are other creatures dwelling therein who also were Men upon a time, creatures who might never again become the Men they once were."

"Oh, my," said Pipper, "then I think I would not like to be a shapeshifter after all, getting stuck like that."

"Are there ways to keep from remaining an animal the rest of your life?" said Binkton.

"When it's time to change back," said Urus, "it helps to have someone at hand to call you by your name."

"Oh, I see," said Aylissa. "That's why the magic words Bair used in the sultan's palace were 'Urus, Urus, Urus.' "

"Aye," said Bair, grinning, "though at one of our shows in a nomad encampment the Bear smelled a honeycomb, and it wasn't until he had snuffled it out and eaten it that Jaith and *ythir* could entice him back into the silk enclosure."

After the laughter died down, Urus shrugged and said, "I told you he was a creature of the wild."

Bair nodded and said, "As is Hunter."

"And Valké," said Aravan.

"Ah," said Jaith. "I had forgotten that thou art also a shapeshifter, Aravan."

"Not a natural one, unlike Urus and Bair," said Aravan. He lifted a crystal on a chain 'round his neck out from under his jerkin. "'Tis only by this token of power that I can become a falcon."

"May I see?" asked Jaith.

Aravan slipped the crystal pendant over his head and handed it to Jaith.

Clear it was, the crystal—pellucid—six-sided down its length, each end blunt-pointed with six facets, and it glittered in the candlelight. Some three-quarters of an inch across and mayhap four inches from tip to tip was its measure. A platinum chain was anchored at one end of the crystal by an embedded platinum eyelet.

Jaith examined the chain. "The Drimm say that this metal is associated with change, somehow helping to bring it about."

As Dokan nodded in agreement, "That I cannot deny," said Aravan.

"In the college of Mages," said Aylis, "it is used in alchemy to aid in transformations."

Bair grunted, then said, "It was fashioned by *Amicula* Faeril. She told me that when she considered what metal to use for the chain of the pendant, platinum *felt* better than silver, gold, or even starsilver . . . that it somehow seemed *right*."

Jaith held the crystal closer to one of the candles. "Ah, the falcon incised within is exquisite."

Riatha smiled, remembering. " 'Twas done when Faeril's spirit was in the crystal with the Oracle Dodona. She said somehow she seemed to have fallen within. The rest of us—Urus, Gwylly, Aravan, Halíd, and I—found her lying unconscious there in the Ring of Dodona. We could not awaken her, and days passed, though Faeril said it seemed but a few candlemarks had elapsed within the crystal itself. Regardless, she said she was looking at her own reflection in one of the crystal panes, and then she gazed at Dodona's image, and . . ."

Faeril looked at her own reflection, and then at Dodona's silver flame. Suddenly she knew without knowing *how* she knew that she was seeing the true Dodona, and that the Oracle could take on any shape he desired, eld Man, young child, Elf, male, female, whatever he wished.

Dodona laughed. "I see that you have discovered one of my secrets."

Faeril's eyes widened. "You have a power somewhat like that of Urus, the power of shapechanging, that is."

"Much more, child. Much more . . ."

Faeril clapped her hands. "Oh, what a wonderful gift you have. I have always wanted to fly like a falcon—"

Faeril did not hear Dodona's cry, for the transformation was already upon her.

* * *

At Gwylly's side Halíd gave a shout of alarm, for a sudden golden light flared in the glade amid a knelling of chimes. Abruptly the glare and ringing faded and Faeril was gone, and in her place a falcon stood, blue stone on a thong about its neck, a crystal lying on the ground.

It was a thing of wildness, untamed, great amber eyes glaring, and it unfurled its wings and crouched to launch itself.

In that instant, a silver light blazed forth from the crystal, englobing the entire ring with its brightness, and neither Gwylly nor Halíd could see nor hear, for the air was filled with crystalline tintinnabulation. Rushing inward, Riatha, Urus, and Aravan were blinded and deafened as well. Yet all felt an overpowering presence step into the glade and then back out. The dazzling light faded, the ringing fell to silence, and when sight and hearing returned, Faeril lay sleeping before them, clutching blue stone and clear crystal, the falcon gone.

"Fool!" lashed out Dodona. "All shapes are possible within the crystal! You could have been entrapped forever as a falcon wild!"

Faeril shrank inward upon herself at his scathing words, then suddenly flared up in anger. "Who is it you name 'fool,' Dodona?" she spat. "Did you give any warning? I did not know, and you cautioned me not."

"Ignorance is no excuse," shot back Dodona. "Fools rush where the wise pause."

Before Faeril could reply, Dodona ground his teeth and gritted, "Don't those impatient lackwits know that time steps here to a different drum?" And he raised his face and shook his fist upward and shouted, "Wait!"

Aravan turned to the others, shaking his head. "We yet must wait."

Halíd sighed. "Nine days ere Legori sails. I must leave within three."

Aravan saw that Gwylly was weeping, and he put his arm about the Warrow. "Fear not, Gwylly. Faeril is yet in good hands. *That* I can sense."

* * *

The eld Man now looked down at the wee damman, standing on a hexagonal crystal plane, her hands on her hips, fuming. Suddenly Dodona laughed and knelt down and embraced her. "Adon! What am I to do with you, daughter? You are too bold!

"Too, you are right. I gave you no warning, and I am sorry for that.

"Yet list, all within the crystal is too dangerous for you, for you are of the Middle Plane and ill prepared. Seek not to use the crystal to *see*, for you may become entrapped forever!

"Instead, you may use the crystal as a guide, to help point the way when choices are uncertain. Use it to magnify your intuition, to aid you with vague premonition, but seek not again to fall within; for you it is nought but a door to eternal imprisonment. And you are too precious to spend that way."

Faeril returned Dodona's embrace, for she had become fond of this . . . this Hidden One, even though she had known him for only an hour or two, or for twelve days, depending on who was marking time.

Dodona took her by the hand and looked overhead. "Yes! Now! Now you may have her back!" he called up into a sky filled with hexagonal lattices interlaced, with crystal planes and windows and mirrors, with interconnected, spiralling tetrahedrons, with glowing globes of shimmering shells and clustered spheres within, those shining orbs made up of interlocking sparks spinning in a whirling glitter.

And upward they flew into this crystalline sky, hand in hand.

In the candlelight of the Red Slipper, Riatha looked about at the others. "That's when Faeril regained consciousness, and we wept in relief. It was only later that Faeril discovered that the heretofore wholly transparent crystal now had the figure of a falcon incised within."

" 'Tis good she imprinted it with that bird," said Bair, turning to Aravan, "else we would not have succeeded in our quest."

Of a sudden Bair's eyes widened in speculation. "I wonder . . . ?"

"You wonder what, *Arran?*" said Urus.

"I wonder if Dodona didn't know all along that my *amicula* would do what she did?" Bair looked about, yet none knew the answer to his question.

Dokan reached out and Jaith handed him the pendant. "*Kwarc,*" he said. "This crystal seems to be nought but common *kwarc.* Though how the bird got incised within, now that is the mystery." He passed the pendant on.

"<Wild magic>?" said Pipper, taking the crystal in hand and peering into its depths.

"Mayhap," said Aylis.

"Crystals are strange things," said Jaith, "be they common quartz or the most precious jewels, and oft have they influenced the course of events whether in hands bent on ill or good."

"Aye," said Aravan, watching as the pendant made the rounds. "Not only did Faeril's crystal provide Bair and me and Hunter and Valké a way to recover the Silver Sword, it also provided the prophecy as to who would be the Rider of the Planes, for while in Arden Vale she spoke in a trance of the birth of Bair, though at the time none knew the meaning of her words."

"And it was Rael's Rede through a crystal that first spoke of the Rider of the Planes," said Riatha. She reached out and patted Bair's hand. "Faeril's prophecy only added to that mystery."

"As all prophecies do," said Bair, "twisted in riddles and enigmas as they are."

"Faeril's crystal also showed us the way to Baron Stoke," said Urus.

"Speaking of crystals and jewels and their influence on events," said Wooly, looking at Jaith, "what about the black diamond? I mean, it was Gelvin's Doom wielded by Modru that brought great harm to Duellin."

"Durlok's crystal cavern was used for ill as well," said Aylis.

"Krystallopŷr was a crystal used for ill, then good, then ill again," said Bair.

"There were the blade-jewels in Bale and Bane," said Binkton.

"And what about the gems in Tuck's silveron armor?" said Pipper.

"They didn't do anything," said Binkton. "I mean they had no special power for good or for ill."

"Wull, Perry got arrow-struck through one of them," said Pipper, "and that was an ill thing."

"Wasn't either," said Binkton. "'Stead it was good, else he wouldn't have solved the riddle of Narok."

"See!" said Pipper. "Tol' y' the jewels had a something to do with being special."

"Aargh!" growled Binkton. "You don't know anything, do you, Pip? I mean—"

"My friends," said Aravan, "let us not argue over the merits of gems, but only speak of those that had a hand in shaping the events of the world."

Pipper smiled wickedly at Binkton as if to say *See!*

"My ring," said Bair, fishing a fine chain 'round his neck out from under his jerkin, the links threaded through a carven stone ring set with a gem of jet. "*Amicula* Faeril fashioned this chain as well; 'tis platinum like the other. The ring has a gemstone set within, but whether or no it is a jewel I cannot tell."

Dokan held out his hand and Bair passed it over.

"Hmm . . ." mused the Dwarf. "I thought at first it was obsidian, and then jet, but it is neither. Regardless, it seems semiprecious to me, though I have not seen its like before." Dokan passed the ring on.

"What about the Dragonstone?" said Pipper. "Was it a jewel?"

"It was somewhat like jade, I hear," said Jaith.

"I am told it had the look of jade," said Riatha, "but I suspect that it was more precious. But precious or semiprecious, still it was a token of evil."

"In the end, however," said Urus, "it brought about the downfall of the Dragonking."

"Your sword, Lady Riatha," said Fat Jim, "it has jade on the hilt, does it not?"

"Aye," replied Riatha.

"Then is it a token for good?"

A look of sadness filled Riatha's face, and Urus said, "Had my *chier* not called on the sword's power, several of us would not be alive today."

"Oh . . . right," said Fat Jim.

"Perhaps tokens are neither good nor evil," said Tarly, "but only the users are. And Lady Riatha certainly is a person of good."

Riatha sighed and said, "Even so, when invoked Dúnamis stole years of life from others."

A gloom settled over the company, and still Bair's ring made the rounds. As Binkton passed it onward he said, "Well, I suppose that sums up all the crystals and stones we know that have played a significant role in the world."

"Not all," said Aylissa, the Pysk with the falcon crystal lying before her.

"Not all?" said Binkton. "What did we leave out?"

"The *Eio Wa Suk,* the Groaning Stones," said Aylissa, and she fingered the small glittering stone on a silver chain about her neck.

"Are they crystal?" said Pipper.

"Pah!" snorted Binkton, shaking his head. "Cousin, how can you be so stu—?"

"Though they don't look it—covered with moss and vines and coated with earth—they are much like crystal, though not of the transparent kind, but dark and opaque instead," said Aylissa. "Yes, crystal are the *Eio Wa Suk,* and they have a life of their own."

"Crystal alive?" asked Nikolai. "I no understand."

"Jaith told us that crystals are strange things," said Pipper, "and if the Groaning Stones are crystal, then it's just another oddity." He turned to Binkton. "See, my question wasn't so stupid after all."

Urus leaned over to Aravan and murmured, "Do they quibble like that all the time?"

Aravan grinned and whispered back, "Yes, but you should see either one when the other is threatened. I deem they squabble when they have nought else to do. Otherwise they are a formidable team."

Aylis cleared her throat and said, "There are some among Magekind who think that the potential for life exists in all crystalline formations, and it seems that the *Eio Wa Suk* are evidence of that fact. Mayhap one merely needs to have a certain composition and some minimum size or heft to gain sentience."

"Sentience?" asked Fat Jim.

"Awareness," said Aylis. "Consciousness."

"What kind of consciousness does a Groaning Stone have?" asked Wooly.

"The Pysks know," said Aylis, "for they speak with the *Eio Wa Suk,* and listen to them as well."

All eyes turned to the Fox Rider.

Aylissa shrugged. "They have little sense of time, and know nearly nothing outside their own aggregate, or the aggregates of those they communicate with."

"Avast," said Fat Jim. "Heave to, tiny one. What is this thing you name 'aggregate'?"

"An aggregate of Groaning Stones," replied Aylissa.

Fat Jim looked at her blankly.

"It's like a family, Jim. Like a clan," said Aylissa. "The *Eio Wa Suk* grow in aggregates."

"They grow?" said Wooly.

"Yes. All crystals in the right surroundings grow, some in bubbling springs, others in placid pools, and still others—"

"I have seen crystals growing," said Dokan, "in hot pools that taste of mineral."

Aylissa nodded. "Regardless, the conditions need to be right to grow crystals, and the Groaning Stones are no different. They only grow in dells where water runs beneath. Even then, it's not just any dell, but one where the soil and the rock below are favorable."

"Thank'ee," said Fat Jim, glancing at Wooly, who nodded in agreement. "We didn't know. Regardless, please go on."

Aylissa took a sip from her thimble, then said, "Their so-called groaning is really the way they communicate with one another. Somehow, they can send vibrations through the ground, and that's how they talk, and we can hear that sound.

"Because they sense vibrations, if you ever pass through an aggregate, I suggest you walk softly. They do not like a heavy tread to come among them.

"They do recognize Pysks as friends, and they are willing to use their abilities to aid us to send messages afar, though I do not believe they understand the import of those messages to those of us creatures who are mobile, those of us who can roam, for they do not seem to understand what it is to be free to move: travel is a strange concept to them, and they cannot grasp its meaning."

Pipper looked at Binkton. "It rather sounds not much different from those mossback stay-at-homes in their villages in the Bosky, Bink. I mean, they move from their homes to their fields or shops and then back to the house, or to the pubs and back. Rather like aggregates they are, Warrows in their villages and hamlets, not much different at all."

"Why, Pip, I do believe that's the most intelligent thing I've ever heard you say," said Binkton.

Aravan pushed out a negating hand. "Were that completely true, my friends, then Mithgar would have fallen to Modru long past, for he twice had the chance; or mayhap the world would yet be plagued by Stoke; or Kraggen-cor might still be in the hands of the Foul Folk. Given all of that, perhaps we would not be here in the Red Slipper sharing a pleasant eve. In other words, my friends"—Aravan raised his glass in salute—"here's to Waerlinga everywhere."

"Hear, hear," said Fat Jim and Wooly and Tarly and others gathered 'round the hearth, all raising their vessels.

"It may be that your Kind do not relish travel," said Aylissa, setting her thimble back to the floor. "But they are far better off than the *Eio Wa Suk;* you see, for them motion is deadly, for they do now and again topple and fall when the land trembles, and they are slain when they are uprooted, hence movement to them means death."

"Groaning Stones die?" said Pipper.

"Indeed," replied Aylissa.

Bair said, "I recall a time when I was quite young and *athir, ythir, kelan, amicula,* and I were travelling through the Greatwood, and we came across an aggregate in that vast woodland, where all but one of the *Eio Wa Suk* had been slain."

"Thou hadst not yet seen thy tenth summer when we rode nigh," said Riatha.

"I always wondered what happened in that vale," said Bair, "with so many Groaning Stones dead."

"It was a dreadful event," said Aylissa, again fingering the tiny bit of glitter on the chain 'round her neck.

"You know what befell?" said Bair.

"No, I do not," said Aylissa, standing and heaving Aravan's Falcon Crystal over her shoulder and trudging to the captain, the platinum chain dragging behind.

As Aravan leaned down to take the crystal from her, Aylis said, "Had I something from that dell, mayhap I could shed some light."

"How so?" asked Binkton.

"Don't you remember?" said Pipper. "Lady Aylis said that there were several ways to <see>: cards, a black mirror, or something of someone long held."

Aylissa slipped the chain over her head, and held it out to Aylis, and Bair said, "Ah, that is what was too faint for me to see. A tiny bit of *Eio Wa Suk* <fire> hidden in the glare of your own."

Aylissa looked at Bair in surprise. "You are right, Bair: the piece of crystal on this chain, it is from the Stone in the very aggregate of which you spoke."

"I thought so," said Aylis, taking the chain with its tiny glitter of crystal.

"How did you know?" asked Aylissa, returning to her place.

"When Bair spoke of that aggregate, your hand went to your pendant."

"How came you by it?" asked Bair. "It seems passing strange that you would have something of that aggregate, the very same one we came across nigh seventeen years agone."

"Piffle," whispered Binkton as he leaned over to Pipper and murmured, "It's all connected, you know."

As Pipper nodded, Aylissa said, "Perhaps it is coincidence, Bair, but then again perhaps not. Regardless, let us first hear what Lady Aylis has to tell us, for I would know what befell in that dell. Then I'll speak on how I came to have the 'touchstone' in my care."

"I say, Lady Aylis," said Fat Jim, "is that tiny piece enough for you to <see>?"

Aylis stood and stepped to the candles, snuffing all but one. As she brought the last lit taper back with her, she said, "'Tis known among Seers that events leave their imprint on objects, and it is told by those of Magekind who have studied such things that when it comes to crystals, what one part has felt, so has all of it. Hence, I ween that though this bit is tiny, still it will hold the visions I seek."

Aylis placed the candle in its holder on the floor cupped midway within the arc of friends. Then she sat down on the far side, her back to the hearth and facing the flame, and beyond the flame her companions.

She closed her eyes and took several deep breaths, as if calming herself, and she held the tiny necklace with the fragment of crystal clasped within her hands. Then she opened her eyes and stared into the flame and muttered, *"Specto praeteritum tempus."*

After a moment she said, "There are many things here, of Alyssa, the *Eroean,* oh, my, the Lost City of Jade, but I would look past these and <see> those things which befell the Stone whence this grain came. . . ."

With her gaze yet focused on the candle flame, of a sudden Aylis gasped, "Oh, how wonderful. Liss, you must tell this part, for it is yours to say, since you were there. Instead I will look to <see> and speak of those events beyond your ken."

Aylis clasped her hands a bit tighter. "There is much I now see beyond"—quick tears flooded her eyes—"Oh, Bair, this is the event of which you spoke, some seventeen years ago.

"You were but nine and some, and you rode through the Greatwood along with your sire and dam and *kelan* and *amicula,* when you came upon the aggregate. . . ."

"These once were alive, but now they are dead," said Bair. "Only that tall one yet lives, and its <life> is low."

They had come across a vine-covered dell filled with huge broken Stones—shattered, cracked, toppled and burst asunder—none were whole but one, and this a tall monolith, standing at the foot of the steep valeside. . . .

" 'Tis an aggregate of *Eio Wa Suk*—Those Who Groan," said Aravan.

Riatha nodded, her eyes glistering. "So many slain. What has befallen here?"

Bair strode to the last of the monoliths standing and placed a hand against the Stone and laid his cheek alongside, as if listening. Some moments later his eyes filled with anguish and he looked at Riatha and said, "Its thoughts are slow and ponderous, not like those of ordinary rocks, which seem fixed, never to change. Yet this I can tell, *Ythir:* this tall Stone, it mourns."

Faeril's eyes flew wide in astonishment. "Rocks have thoughts . . . ?"

Riatha, too, looked on in wonder. "Thou canst list to its bereavement, Bair?"

"I don't know what it is saying, yet had it a heart, it would be broken." Bair stroked the great monolith and then stepped back, and the ground rumbled faintly.

Aravan cocked an eyebrow. "I thought that only the Pyska could converse with a Stone, yet it seems Bair can as well."

"I don't know what it said," replied Bair, trudging back up the valeside, "but it is so very sad."

With tears in her eyes, Riatha looked upon her child. "'Tis enough that it knew you cared, and it wanted you to know."

Bair sighed and turned and looked back at the vine-laden vale with its uncounted shattered Stones, and then he said, "Let us leave this place."

And they mounted up and rode on.

Yet staring into the candle flame, Aylis murmured, "Back, I go, and back, deeper into the past. Ah, here we are. It is just after the time of the Great War of the Ban, some five thousand years agone, the Baeron are— No, wait, ere that, two Pysks, Nia and Kell— No . . . there are *three* events all entwined, for Tipperton Thistledown and Rynna Fenrush are in the event before. I will tell of these in forward order, rather than the nearest one first, starting with Tipperton and Rynna; they were on a vital mission. . . ."

It was as they were riding northwesterly away from The Clearing—a vast open space in the Greatwood, on the verge of which they had met with the Baeron—that Rynna and Tip had come across a vine-covered dell filled with huge broken Stones—shattered, cracked, toppled and burst asunder—none were whole but one, and this a tall monolith, tilted askew, leaning against the steep valeside.

"This looks like an aggregate of Groaning Stones," said Tip.

Rynna nodded and peered into the vale, tears springing into her eyes. "Oh, Tip, so many *Eio Wa Suk* slain. What ever could have happened here?"

"I don't know," replied Tip, "but whatever it was, it was horribly ruinous."

Rynna sighed and tugged on the reins of her pony, the steed's head coming up from cropping grass. "Let us go away from this place, Tip. I will have one of the Fox Riders come and discover what happened here and when."

"Do only Fox Riders know how to speak with the Stones?"

"Aye, Tip. Except for other *Eio Wa Suk,* the Stones will listen to none but a Pysk."

And on toward the Blackwood rode the two, leaving the dell behind, their mission to the Baeron successful.

Aylis paused in her telling long enough to take a sip from her goblet, yet she did not take her gaze from the flame.

In the arc of friends, Tarly passed Bair's stone ring to Aylissa, but she let it lie on the floor in front of her as Aylis continued: "Tip and Rynna reported the destroyed aggregate to the Pyska of Darda Erynian, and Kell and Nia went to see if they could determine what had happened. . . ."

In late September two Pysks—Nia and Kell—came riding their foxes through the autumnal forest, the leaves now beginning to turn golden and red and russet and brown. The cool summer past, frost had come early, and chill was in the air. Into the vale they rode and among the shattered *Eio Wa Suk* in the dell. Several of the cracked Stones did they try to contact, touching bits of crystal on chains 'round their necks against the sides of the *Eio Wa Suk*, attempting to commune. Finally they went to the great monolith leaning against the valeside, where again they touched crystal to Stone.

"It is alive," gasped Nia, her face filled with relief.

"But barely," said Kell, and he closed his eyes and concentrated.

The ground but scarcely rumbled in response.

"It is ancient beyond counting, and sorely does it grieve from this eld hurt as well," he said after a moment.

Now Nia concentrated, and again the ground whispered. "Though yet alive it is damaged and no longer knows what befell the aggregate; it only remembers that once it was among others of its kind and now it is not, and only the sorrow remains. Oh, Kell, what are we to do? It has nearly been uprooted."

"Aye," said Kell. "Nearly uprooted and so very weak. It is all I can do to reach past its grief and find the Stone within. Its voice is given to soft mourning, and not to speaking afar. Mayhap, afflicted as it is, it can no longer do such."

Nia slumped down to the ground. "I think you are right, Kell. In this state it cannot speak to other Stones, cannot gain solace from other aggregates."

Kell stepped away and surveyed the great slab. "What, I wonder, did this?"

Nia's eyes filled with tears, and she looked up with blurred vision at Kell. "We must do something to restore it when this war is done. Mayhap it will grow stronger and remember, if it regains full use of its source."

"Aye," said Kell, his own gaze blurred as well. "Long has it survived less than half alive, yet it is beyond our power to upright it again, and even if we could, we might kill it in the attempt."

Nia sobbed out, "Mayhap Rynna and Tipperton will know what to do."

They wept for long moments, but finally Kell reached a hand out and pulled Nia to her feet. They bade goodbye unto the Stone, and the ground whispered in response; then they called their foxes unto them and rode away, heavy in heart.

Aylis again had tears in her eyes, yet she kept her gaze on the flame while she struggled to master her emotions.

Off among the arc of friends, Aylissa softly said, "It is told that Rynna declared, 'When this war is over, Tipperton, we will ask the Baeron and others to set it upright again. Mayhap that will restore it to its source and repair the damage done.'

"They say Tipperton sighed and nodded and gazed out on the autumn woods."

Once again in control, Aylis said, "That is the third significant event, for after the Ban War came to an end, a group of Baeron did set the Stone back upright—Pysks standing by, their hearts in their throats with the peril of such—yet the Baeron were gentle, and haled the Stone upright again. But many long years were to pass ere any of the Pysks could make contact with it, for it seemed to be in a state of shock after being shifted, and they thought that mayhap it had been destroyed by their well-meaning action. But then contact was again established; it was Phero and Picyn who did so. Afterwards, when asked, the Stone then relayed messages to other aggregates, but only to those nearby, for its own voice was too weak to reach those afar. Occasionally it received messages from those aggregates nigh."

Aylis fell silent, and frowned slightly, then pressed her hands even tighter against the fragment of crystal. She shook her head, and pressed even harder.

After a moment of silence, Tarly leaned over and whispered to Aylissa. "How does it do that," asked Tarly. "How does a Stone send and receive messages, I mean."

"Their so-called 'groaning,' " murmured Aylissa, "is really the Stones' means of communicating to one another through the living stone of the world, and it sounds much like groans and moans, though there are also pops and clicks."

"Ah, much like the *Ut!¡teri,"* said Aravan, a tick-tock clicking of the tongue in the middle of the strange word.

"U-Ut . . . um, what you said. What are they?" asked Binkton.

"*Ut!¡teri*—whales—lords of the sea. 'Tis a word in the tongue of the Children of the Sea," said Aravan. "The *Ut!¡teri* communicate through groans and moans and pops and clicks and whistles, and their speech might be akin to that of the *Eio Wa Suk."*

"Mayhap," said Aylissa, "though mayhap not. Regardless, at times the groaning is quite strong, and even if you are far away if you press your ear to the ground, you can hear their talk. If you stand nigh a Stone when it is speaking, there is a tingling in the air, a tingling much the same as sometimes happens during thunderstorms. They never speak when thunder is nigh except under great duress, for they have been struck down by lightning when doing so. That is one reason they only dwell in dells, for bolts seem to strike the higher places and only rarely come to the vales."

"Mayhap that is how this aggregate was destroyed," said Pipper. "By lightning."

"Perhaps so," said Aylissa.

"But how do you actually talk with the Stones?" said Tarly.

The Fox Rider pointed toward Aylis, who frowned and pressed her hands tighter against the Pysk's tiny pendant. The Fox Rider said, "We Pysks understand their tongue, and we speak to the Stones through small fragments, small flakes of crystal we take from their crystalline sides, like the one Aylis now holds. If we wear a piece long enough, it becomes attuned, then we can speak with the *Eio Wa Suk,* for it fills with their <fire> again."

"Ah, I see," whispered Tarly, "<wild magic>."

"Hmmm . . ." murmured Dokan. "Sending messages through the living stone: that would explain some of the mysterious shudderings we Châkka feel in our delvings."

"Perhaps," said Aylissa, shrugging.

Perspiration on her forehead, her face showing strain, Aylis, yet staring into the flame, her hands pressed tightly against the fragment, said, "I am not certain that I can <see>, for now I <look> so very far back in time—I now <peer> tens, fifties, hundreds of millennia before the onset of the First Era, I know not exactly how far back, it is so ancient." Her face slightly cleared, and she said, "Ah, but something now looms. . . .

" . . . Oh! Oh!" cried Aylis, her face gone pale. "From the sky, from the sky, the destruction, from the sky it comes. . . ."

Roaring, flame gushing, down they tumbled black on black, down from the sky, locked together talon to talon in all-consuming rage. And the air shrieked past their ineffective wings, claw to claw as they were, neither willing to release the other, even though they plummeted down and down, down toward the world below, down toward the ground, down toward upjutting monolithic rocks. They slammed into the dell, smashing Stones, crystal shards exploding upward.

They fought in a battle that had begun some three hundred leagues to the north, there at Dragons' Roost above the Great Maelstrom at the end of the Gronfangs, for it was the time of the mating. It is in this time Drakes perch on the slopes of that mountain night after night and bellow from dusk to dawn. And after many nights of this thunderous din, in the darktide and driven by the urge to mate or by lust or love—who knows?—one by one, horrendous Krakens—the mates of Dragons—come to the call, the greatest first, the least last, each burning with the green glowing daemonfire of the deeps, spinning in the vast roaring churn of the gigantic sucking maw of a whirlpool known as the Great Maelstrom.

And one by one the Drakes plunge into that fearsome spin—the most powerful Dragon first from the highest ledge, and then the next most powerful from the next ledge down, and the next Dragon and the next, and so on and so on, down the side of the roost, each plummeting from his earned place—earned by battle with those who would contest his position—Drakes plummeting down to be clutched in the grasping embrace of those hideous tentacles, each Dragon drawn under by a monstrous mate, lover and lover sucked into the whirling black abyss below to spawn beyond the light of all knowledge.

And later, somehow the Drakes return, bursting through the dark surface, struggling to wing up into the night air, and only the strongest survive.

From this dreadful mating comes a clutch of eggs, some to perish, others to hatch and spawn small serpents of the sea, some of these to perish as well. And after ages of swimming and feeding and growing, the great serpents take themselves unto the unlit depths of a vast chasm located somewhere in the waters of the wide Sindhu Sea. There, three full leagues below the surface, in a lost abyss they settle upon dark ledges lining the chasm walls, where they exude an adherent and enwrap themselves into tight spheres. The adherent hardens and they are enshelled in a crystalline glaze to begin an extraordinary metamorphosis. After a time, when the change has occurred, the crystal shell is finally shattered, and just as some caterpillars emerge from their chrysalides as butterflies whilst others emerge as moths, so too do some serpents—the males—come forth Dragons while others—the females—come forth Krakens.

It was the time of the mating that brought these two ebon Drakes to battle, for they had each vied for the same ledge. It was not one of the higher shelves, for these were yet young Drakes, and older, much larger, and as of yet more powerful Dragons ruled the ledges above.

And into the dell they crashed, dark glittering shards flying from the impact. And they grappled and rolled, smashing more Stones, and fire bellowed forth to destroy other of the tall slabs as well as huge spherical rocks.

A great thrumming roar filled the dell, and the air tingled as of a gathering storm, but the Dragons paid it no heed, for their own rage blinded them to all else—all sights, all sounds, all perils—all that is but the Dragon foe before them.

Their massive tails lashed out, slamming through dark lithic crystalline forms to smash into the enemy, as they traded blow after blow. Fire roared out from their mouths, great gouts of unbearable heat shattering Stone after Stone. Heedless of the destruction, heedless of the damage and ruin, once more the Drakes grappled and rolled, crushing all in their way, slashing at one another with mighty saberlike talons, their mouths of fangs ripping.

And the great thrumming roar from the dell diminished and diminished, as Stones were shattered and cracked by fire and uprooted and knocked down.

And still the battle went on.

Until there was but a lone rumble left, that of a single monolith nearly uprooted and leaning against the valeside. Then it, too, fell to silence, as the two black Drakes fought on.

But at last even they stopped—battered, beaten, exhausted. And they looked upon one another with hatred, yet neither had the strength left nor the fire to do ought to the other.

Long had the battle raged, and had covered league upon league: it had started at a mountain verging on the Boreal Sea and ended there in the Greatwood, though that forest was not then known by that name.

Leathery wings tattered and torn, scales ripped, blood seeping, they separately limped into the air and flew away in opposite directions, heading toward isolated lairs where they would simmer in fury even as they healed. Neither had won this day, and neither would participate in the mating at the Great Maelstrom, for they were too sorely wounded.

Thus it was that Black Kalgalath and Daagor, brothers not only out of the same clutch, but out of the very same egg, fought for the first time, and neither Drake prevailed.

Of a sudden, Aylis dropped the fragment of crystal and slumped sideways, but Aravan instantly leapt from his seat and caught her. He looked up at Wooly and snapped, "Brandy."

As the others gripped hands and glanced at one another in alarm, Wooly bolted for the bar, and in a trice he was back, snifter in hand, amber liquid swirling within.

When Aylis opened her eyes, Aravan reached out and took the glass from Wooly and lifted it her lips. "Careful, *chier,*" he said, and Aylis took but a slight sip . . . and then another . . . and finally one more.

"I-I'm all right," she said. "Just a bit overextended. I have never <seen> so far back in time, and it was a strain."

Jaith nodded and said, "This had to have happened before there was anyone living in the Greatwood—neither Baeron, nor Hidden Ones, nor Elves, nor ought other, else someone would have remembered this epic struggle."

"Someone was there, *chier,*" said Bair. "The *Eio Wa Suk.* Even so, not counting the Drakes, there was but a lone survivor, and it too damaged and filled with grief to remember."

Urus said, "There is an old Baeron legend that it was Dragonfire there in the Greatwood that burnt down the trees to make The Clearing. Mayhap 'tis true, for 'neath the topsoil, the ground is glassy, as if it had been exposed to great heat. Still, I deem there were no Baeron, Elves, or Hidden Ones therein at the time."

Aylis looked into Aravan's eyes. "My love, help me to my place."

"Art thou certain?"

"Aye."

Instead of helping Aylis up, Aravan set the brandy aside. Then, in spite of her protests, he cradled her in his arms and got to his feet and stepped to the arc of friends and eased her into her chair.

Aylis shook her head, but she smiled at him.

"My lady," said Wooly, following after, and steady as a rock he held the brandy snifter out to her. "Are you well?"

"Yes, Wooly, I'm quite all right," said Aylis. She took the proffered brandy and nodded her appreciation. Wooly bobbed his head, and returned to his own seat and took up his glass of dark Vanchan in his now-trembling hand.

"Oh, Aylis, I thank you," said Aylissa. "None could discover just how the aggregate had been shattered, for though we asked that ancient Stone, it did not know itself what had passed and, as you know, its grief was sorely heavy."

"Could it have known, even had it not been laden with sorrow?" asked Binkton. "I mean, the Groaning Stones have no eyes, and so could it have seen?"

"Maybe they have <wild magic>," said Pipper, "and need no eyes to see."

They both looked at Aylissa, and she said, "I think that even had it not been nearly uprooted, it would not have known what had passed, only that there was a great upheaval within the aggregate—shudderings, terrible heat, and the shattering of the *Eio Wa Suk*—for as you say, Bink, a Stone has no eyes."

"Even so," said Aylis, "events leave their impressions on the surround, including in this case the crystal of the Stone, and *that* is how I could <see>."

A quiet fell among them, then Aylis said, "The tale is not done"—she gestured at the tiny silver chain with its fragment of crystal lying by the low-burned candle—"for just a bit more than fifteen years past, something occurred that was most wonderful, and 'tis yours to tell, Liss."

"Oh, good," said Pipper, "something nice at last. Now mayhap this tale will not lurk in the dark, with battling Dragons to clutch at me in my sleep."

"Fifteen years past?" said Bair. "Why, that was just after the time I and my kith were there."

"It was a slim year after," said Aylis. She gestured for Aylissa to seat herself in the light. "Go on, Liss, for I would hear it from your own lips."

Thimble in hand, the Pysk stood and dragged Bair's ring by the chain to the place vacated by Aylis, where she seated herself and took up her own pendant and looped it over her head and 'round her neck once more.

She held out her thimble to Wooly and said, "A refill, if you please." Now steady again, Wooly dropped a dollop of dark Vanchan in her improvised cup and refilled other goblets all 'round, though Urus and Tarly stepped to the bar to replenish their tankards with the Vornholt. While she waited for them to return, Aylissa took a long look at Bair's ring. "Hmmm . . . But for its size, I would say this is Fox Rider work, though mayhap it is the doings of a Hidden One of greater height and heft than we Pysks."

Aylissa then stood and dragged the ring over to Bair.

Riatha said, "We deem it was delivered by Fox Riders on the night of Bair's birth, for we heard foxes barking in Arden Vale that eve."

"Mayhap," said Aylissa, noncommittally. She hefted up the links and said, "You can have it back now, Bair."

The tall Baeran leaned down and took up his ring and laughed and said, "I will always savor the image of you dragging it across the floor."

Aylissa smiled, then stepped back to her place by the candle and sat down once more.

Tankards refreshed, Urus and Tarly returned from the bar, and Pipper said, "All right, now, what about the wonderful thing that happened there in the shattered aggregate?"

Aylissa took a sip from her thimble and set it aside. "For many long years, millennia, in fact, we thought there was nought we could do to restore the Stone to full, um, health again. But then, mayhap four or so summers ere the Dragonstone War began, it occurred to us to ask the Utruni if they could help."

"The Stone Giants?" said Pipper.

"Argh," growled Binkton, glaring at Pipper. "That's what she said, cousin."

"I heard what she said, Bink," shot back Pipper. He turned to Aylissa. "What I meant was, how could they help? And how could you even contact them?"

"We went to another aggregate, the one nigh Bircehyll, the Elvenholt in Darda Erynian, for there lies the aggregate with the strongest signals of all. And we asked the Great Stone of that aggregate if sending a signal to the Utruni was even possible. . . ."

The Great Stone rumbled.

"He says that they might not answer," said Tynvyr.

"Nevertheless, we must try," said Kell.

Tynvyr turned back to the slab and pressed her fragment of crystal to its side for a long moment, her brow furrowed in communing thought . . . then she stepped away.

Now the ground rumbled loudly as the greatest *Eio Wa Suk* in Darda Erynian spoke to the living stone of the world, not directing the signal toward another aggregate—though aggregates everywhere could apprehend the message—but sending it out for any and all in the hope that the Utruni would respond. The air was filled with the tingle of pent lightning.

And lo! two days later the stone of the world rumbled again, and Kell and Tynvyr rushed to the aggregate there in the southern part of Darda Erynian. Both listened as the Great Stone relayed the message, and tears flooded their eyes, for the Utruni were on the way.

They mounted foxes, nearly all of the Pysks of Darda Erynian—the Great Greenhall, Blackwood of old—and southerly they rode, led by Nia and Kell; they left Darda Erynian as they passed across the Rissanin River through the ruins of Caer Lindor, and on the far shore they entered Darda Stor, also known as the Greatwood.

And with them went a handful of Elves—Dylvana—and in the Greatwood they were joined by a few Baeron.

They turned eastward, toward The Clearing, lying nigh two hundred miles away. Yet The Clearing was not their goal, but a lone monolith in a dell somewhat this side of that great grassy glade.

Some eleven days after setting out from Bircehyll they reached the dell, and Nia stepped to the pillar and touched her fragment of crystal to the Stone.

Moments later, the ground rumbled in response.

Nia stepped back. "The Stone says it is willing to have the Utruni try."

Three days passed, and in that time did Aylissa pick loose a tiny piece of the tall monolith, and she attached it to her silver necklace, pressing the tiny clamps down 'round the flake, clamps made for just this event.

And on the third day the ground bulged, and a great figure emerged, followed by another, and then one more.

The Utruni had arrived.

One was perhaps fifteen feet tall, the other two perhaps thirteen feet, all of them enormous towering creatures to those who had come hoping for a resurrection, especially the tiny Pysks.

Through the Stone itself did the Pysks converse with the Stone Giants—the Utruni merely by placing a hand on the side of the monolith, Nia through her fragment of crystal—and often did one or another of the Stone Giants look through the soil to the rock below.

Finally Geest, the tallest of the Giants, gestured toward the broken and shattered members of the aggregate and said, [There is no way we can restore any of those to life.] Then the Giant turned to one of the others—Brehha—and said something in that sliding-rock tongue of theirs, and that Utrun vanished into the earth.

Then the tall one turned back to Nia. [But we can set this *Eio Wa Suk* to rights.]

Nia took a deep breath and said, via the Stone, [Then please do so, but oh so carefully.]

Into the earth went the remaining two Giants—Geest and Sarsen—and for a long while nought seemed to happen, but then one of the Baeron said, "The Stone, it is moving."

And, almost imperceptibly, the great monolith was shifted toward a slightly more vertical position.

Finally the movement stopped.

Again the Utruni emerged.

And now the dell was filled with an *enormous* groaning, and the air tingled acutely.

Pysks wept for joy, and the tall Utrun grinned and said, [I believe we have restored the Stone.]

Of a sudden, the groaning rose in pitch, and the dell was filled with what all knew had to be a shout of elation.

[What is it?] asked Nia.

The tall Utrun looked into the soil and said, [Brehha is seeding crystals. There will be a new aggregate here.]

Bursting into fresh tears of joy, Nia asked, [When?] though that concept seemed difficult for the monolith to convey to the Utrun, for little do the *Eio Wa Suk* understand of time.

After much discourse with the Stone, Geest managed to convey that it would be in but two or three millennia that the little ones could begin to talk.

Laughter and tears filled the dell, along with a low, pleasant humming from the Stone, and all was well with the world. . . .

. . . or so they thought, for on that same day far to the east the Dragonstone had at last been found.

Aylissa had tears in her eyes when her tale came to an end. Yet she wasn't the only one, for others within the arc of friends wiped wetness from their cheeks as well.

"I do love a happy ending," said Fat Jim, snuffling.

"Here's to a new aggregate aborning," said Tarly, raising his tankard.

"Hear, hear!" said Wooly, raising his goblet.

And so did they all drink a toast to the *Eio Wa Suk,* known as the Groaning Stones.

Then Pipper said, "Here's to all folk as well, be they flesh and bone and blood or crystals that talk to Pysks."

Again everyone raised a glass or tankard or thimble in salute.

A satisfied silence descended upon them all, but finally Binkton said, "I wonder who are the oldest Folk on Mithgar. Not the oldest living thing, for that is likely to be trees or—"

"Pond slime," said Pipper.

"Pond slime?" said Binkton, annoyed. "How did you come up with that?"

"I dunno. It seemed like the thing to say."

Binkton took a deep breath and then let it out. "Regardless of what my cousin says, I still would like to know the oldest Folk of"—he looked at Aylis—"what did you call it, sentience?"

At a nod from Aylis, Binkton said, "Yes. The oldest living creatures or people of sentience to abide on Mithgar."

"Some say the Elves were first," said Aravan.

"Pfft!" said Aylissa. "Who says that? The Elves?"

At Aravan's nod, the Pysk broke into laughter. "The Hidden Ones were here well ahead of the Elves, or so my parents say."

"Y'know," said Tarly, "I just think it might be the Dragons. Either them or the Krakens."

"Their homeworld is Kelgor," said Bair. "So if they were the first, they had to cross an in-between to get here."

"Bears and Wolves are somewhat sentient," said Urus, "and so animals might have been the first Folk to dwell on Mithgar."

"Pah!" said Fat Jim. "I don't think most animals are sentient at all."

"I t'ink they t'ink," said Nikolai. "I t'ink Urus be right."

"Utruni," said Wooly. "They have to be the oldest, for didn't they shape the world?"

"What about the *Eio Wa Suk*?" said Pipper. "I mean, Aylis said it was tens or even hundreds of millennia before the First Era when she <saw> those Dragons fight, and the Stones were established at that time, and rocks must have been here when the world itself was made, and so . . ."

Long did the arguments last into the night, candidates proffered, some withdrawn, others put forward as well. As the light of dawn was breaking, they all finally went to bed, no wiser as to who or what was the first sentient life to grace this long-spinning world.

9

Nexus

"I had a terrible dream last night," said Pipper, raising his voice to be heard above the din, "or rather this morning."

Binkton groaned. "And now you're going to tell me about it, right?"

They sat at a table against a wall of the common room of the Red Slipper, wooden boxes on their chairs to raise the buccen up to table height. Noise and laughter and shouts filled the crowded chamber, and it smelled of pipeweed and sweat and salt and sawdust and ale, of roast beef and stew and hotcakes and bacon and other such provender, of cheap perfume and the spice of hot mulled wine, and there was an iron tang in the air, as of metal quenched. On a small stage, in spite of his injury, Fat Jim had taken his arm from the sling and was playing a song on his squeeze-box, while a besotted handful of crewmen stood behind him singing, and two other sailors just to the fore linked arms and danced a jig on the boards. Given the clamor, it was questionable as to whether anyone other than those directly about Fat Jim could hear the words of the song, though the reedy squeal of the squeeze-box rode upon the din; no doubt it was a sea chantey played and sung, and probably one quite bawdy. In the common room itself, gaudily dressed women seemed to be everywhere, some laughing and sitting on the laps of crewmembers of the *Eroean,* while others pulled their charges by the hand and led them up the spiral stairs to the bedrooms above. At a nearby table Nikolai and Wooly arm wrestled, sweat beading their brows, right hands clasped tightly, muscle and tendon standing out in stark relief as they strove and strained, neither giving an inch, while sailors ringed 'round and shouted and placed bets. Other of the seafarers played cards, and some diced for drinks. A few Men lay on the floor, dead drunk and completely oblivious to the world—Dabby the Cadger one of these, for the crew of the *Eroean* was quite generous when it came to setting up drinks for the less fortunate. Into this roar came Aravan and Aylis, and they wended their way through drunken well-wishers, and an inebriated stranger tried to bow to Lady Aylis and fell down in the effort, and Aravan laughed and hauled the Man to his feet, only to have him fall down again.

Leaving him lying on the floor behind, Aylis and Aravan joined the two Warrows just as Binkton said, "Pip, you ought not to listen to these tales being spun in the flicker of candlelight shadows, giving you bad dreams as they do."

"But I like them, Bink. Besides, I learn new things about the history of Mithgar and such."

"But if they disturb your slumber . . ." said Aylis.

"I'd rather know the history, nightmares notwithstanding," said Pipper. "To learn new things I'll put up with ill dreams like the one last night. It was quite terrible, and it did jerk me awake, but even so, hearing the stories is worth every bit of the sleep phantoms they cause."

A serving girl appeared, and they each ordered breakfast, though the sun was well beyond noontide: hotcakes and tea and rashers of bacon.

In that moment there was a great hullabaloo. Four sailors had grabbed up one of the card players, and they hauled him toward the entry, while at one and the same time they pummelled him without letup in spite of his howls. As they neared the door, one of the patrons opened it wide, and the four flung the screaming Man outward, heedless of traffic passing by—waggons, pedestrians, carriages or carts, or ought else. At the table where Nikolai and Wooly strove against one another, neither even looked up from his efforts, nor did the Men surrounding them.

As the four crewmen returned, one of them swerved over to Aravan's table and said, "Was a double-dealer, Captain. Palmed a knave off the bottom, he did. Serve him right if a wain squashed him flat. —Oh, 'n' by the bye, we kept his ill-gotten gains—won by cheating, we reck."

Aravan nodded and said, "Well done, Willam. Carry on."

"Aye, aye, sir." The Man saluted and stepped away to resume his seat at the card game.

"When it comes to gambling," said Aravan, "to seafarers the only thing worse than a card cheat is a one who rolls crooked dice, or one who takes advantage of the players' rapt attention on the game before them—a cutpurse or such."

At the word *cutpurse,* Bink looked everywhere but at the captain, though Pipper, fretting over his nightmare, seemed unfazed.

Aylis noted Binkton's discomfort and quietly smiled to herself, but then turned to Pipper and said, "What was your dream, Pip?"

"Oh, it was a dreadful great black Dragon with long teeth and big claws looking at me terriblelike. I thought he was going to eat me, but instead he said, 'Beware, my small friend, for I know your Truename.' And I managed to squeak out, 'Well, that's no secret, my name is Pipper.' And he said, 'Pipper is merely your common name. Your Truename is something else altogether, and you should keep it to yourself.'

"I asked him what he meant, but he disappeared in a swirl of darkness, and I woke up shaking."

"I think you always wake up shaking, Pip," said Binkton.

"I know. I know," said Pipper. Then he tentatively smiled at Binkton and said, "But you always tell me that everything is all right. . . . Thanks, Bink."

Binkton returned the smile and reached over and patted Pipper's arm.

The serving girl brought the rashers and hotcakes and a tin of syrup, along with a steaming teapot. They poured the bracing drink and passed the tin about, and Pipper said, "I thought only things had Truenames. Can people have them, too?"

"Mmm . . ." said Aylis, nodding, her mouth full of syrup-sweetened hotcake. She chewed and swallowed and said, "All things have Truenames, Pip. And the Dragon of your dream was right: you should be wary of ever giving your Truename to anyone."

"I don't understand," said Binkton. "What can anyone do with a Truename? Besides, how does one go about in the first place finding out what his own Truename is?"

Again Aylis had a mouthful, and she simply waved a negating hand and pointed at her lips. Finally she swallowed and said, "Let us first finish breaking our fast, and then we'll discuss Truenames."

And so they dug into the pancakes and rashers without speaking. Finally, Pipper pushed away his plate and took up the teapot and replenished his cup.

As he sipped tea and waited for the others to finish their meals, a loud argument broke out across the room, followed by shoving and name-calling and then the crunch of knuckles on flesh, and soon that side of the common room was embroiled in battle, gaudily dressed women fleeing to safety. On the stage Fat Jim simply kept on playing and his crew kept singing and jigging, all but one of those in Jim's chorus, that is, and that sailor leapt into the fray. Slowly the fighting diminished, for in the midst of all stood Bruki, one of the Dwarves of the *Eroean*'s warband, with his fists smashing oncomers while he sang a Dwarven dirge. Shortly all his opponents lay sprawled in the sawdust on the floor. As the floundering Men tried to rise but fell back, Bruki sadly looked down upon them, while he continued singing, the dirge even more mournful, for there was no one left to fight. The skirl of Fat Jim's squeeze-box discordantly rode above Bruki's song, while dancing sailors' clogging steps beat out a heavy tattoo, and louder than all were the bawdy words of Jim's chorus singing of some well-endowed lad's sexual conquest of an amorous whale.

Aylis spewed tea and nearly strangled on her own laughter.

Finally, as the common room returned to normality—though normality in the Red Slipper was an iffy thing—and as Aylis, kerchief in hand, wiped tea from her lips and chin, and then began dabbing at her garments, Binkton said, "Now what's all this about Truenames?"

Aylis looked up from her labor and said, "I repeat, all things have Truenames, and they should be well guarded."

"Why is that?" said Binkton. "I mean, why should they be guarded?"

Aylis said, "Because names have power—Truenames, that is—and should one come along who knows how to invoke that power, and should he discover your Truename, then he has power over you, for good or ill as he chooses."

"For good or ill?" asked Pipper, his eyes wide in alarm.

"Hear me, Pipper," said Aylis. "Truenames can be used to compel, but only if the one invoking the name knows the right castings to use. Hence, ordinary folks gain little by knowing a Truename unless they also have a means of taking advantage of it."

"So, if I tell my Truename to Bink, he wouldn't be able to compel me, eh?" Pipper smiled wickedly at Binkton.

"Not so," said Aylis. "There are ways he could take advantage of your Truename, even though he cannot invoke it."

"I don't understand," said Pipper. "I mean, how could Bink do such? —Not that you would, Bink."

"How could Bink do such, you ask?" said Aylis. "Heed me, for here is a true tale, one I have <seen>: Andrak's Truename was known to Black Kalgalath, yet Kalgalath himself could not invoke the name; however, he could threaten to reveal that name to someone who could take advantage of it, and *that* was the power he held over Andrak. Hence, should you tell Binkton your Truename, then he could level the same threat . . . though, as you say, Pipper, not that he would."

"Oh, I don't know about that," said Binkton, smiling wickedly at Pipper in return.

"You wouldn't tell, would you?" gasped Pipper.

"Of course not, ninny," said Binkton.

One of the Men who had been felled by Bruki got to his feet and, holding a hand to his eye, wobbled over to the table and said, "Cap'n, I just want you to know that Bruki didn't mean it."

"Didn't mean what, Trake?"

"Didn't mean t'hit me. I mean, I saw that he was in it with the crew of the *Gray Gull*, and so I jumped off the stage t'help him, and accidentally got in the way. I should have known he didn't need any help. W'll, anyway, y'have this order about no fighting among ourselves, and—"

Aravan grinned and waved a hand of dismissal. "I understand, Trake. And tell Bruki I understand, as well."

"Aye, aye, Cap'n." Trake saluted and eased about and headed for Bruki.

Binkton watched as Trake crossed the room, then the buccan turned to Aylis. "How did Black Kalgalath discover Andrak's Truename?"

"I do not know," said Aylis. "It seems that one day he simply awakened with the knowledge. How it came to him, well, it's a mystery to me. It's almost as if some Mage had slipped it into his dreams."

"Can Mages do that?" said Binkton.

"Of course they can," said Pipper. "Don't you remember that Othran the Seer slipped the knowledge of Durek's plight into Silverleaf's mind?"

"Oh, right," said Binkton. "But surely Othran didn't tell Black Kalgalath Andrak's Truename."

"If some Mage did so, then more likely it was a Black Mage," said Aylis. "Modru or Durlok or one of their ilk. That is why Mages especially guard their Truenames, for if another Mage discovers it, particularly a Black Mage of ill bent, then that Black Mage can compel the other to spend his <fire> in ill ways."

"Oh, my," said Pipper. "Speaking of black, I just realized, the black Dragon of my dreams probably was Black Kalgalath. —Or maybe Daagor."

"Nay, Pip," said Aravan. "Both are dead. So if 'twas either of those twain, then it was his ghost."

"Eep!" squeaked Pipper. "Ghost?"

Aravan pushed out a hand of negation. "I jest, my friend. I jest."

"Oh," said Pipper, visibly relieved, though a glimmer of doubt yet remained.

A great cheer went up from the small circle of Men surrounding Nikolai and Wooly, mingled with cries of dismay, and money began changing hands, for one of the two had finally won the arm-wrestling contest, but as to which one . . . ?

Pipper returned his gaze to Aylis. "Well if it had been a real Dragon, could he have known my Truename? I mean, how could he, when I don't even know it myself? Is it because Dragons have Dragonsight and can see the hidden, the invisible, and the unseen? And how does one go about discovering his own Truename, anyway? And can others discover a Truename if it isn't told to them? And—"

"Pip, Pip, slow down," said Aylis, pushing out both hands to put a stop to Pipper's questions. "Let me take those one at a time:

"First, as far as the Dragonsight is concerned, Dragons *can* see things with their 'hidden eye,' but only if the hidden, invisible, or unseen is within their range, within their domain. However, their sight cannot reveal a Truename, for it is not, as you say, something that is hidden, invisible, or unseen . . . it is merely unknown.

"Second, the way one goes about discovering their own Truename varies: some discover it in a dream; others have it told to them by a trusted elder; still others have an epiphany, a flash of realization; and it is said that some discover their Truename through divine revelation, through one of the gods. Most folk never know their Truenames—I am one of these, for none of the foregoing has ever been my fortune to experience.

"As for others discovering your Truename, I am told by my father that nought unprotected can be hidden from the dead, hence Necromancers who can summon and compel the dead might discover someone's or something's Truename, can they winnow it out from the myriad of voices of all the lost souls who crowd forward to speak at one and the same time through the mouth of the one so summoned. That is why Mages cast Truename wards 'gainst the dead."

"Oh, my, ghosts of the dead again," said Pipper, and then his eyes widened in fright. "Oh, Aravan, are you certain it wasn't the ghost of Black Kalgalath who came to my dreams? He could have known my Truename, for nought can be hidden from the dead, right?"

Shouts of giving and taking of odds and the placing and accepting of wagers came from the table where Wooly and Nikolai sat, for they had changed hands and begun arm wrestling again. Up on the stage, Fat Jim struck up another tune on his squeeze-box, and the sailors behind—one of them, Trake, with a black eye agrowing—began singing another chantey, while two others clogged, mugs sloshing in hand.

Aravan reached out to Pipper. "I deem 'twas no Dragon's ghost, Pip, for unless thou hast made an enemy of a Necromancer, I think 'twas but a bad dream."

Pipper turned to Binkton. "Have we made an enemy of a Necromancer?"

"Piffle!" said Binkton.

"What about that *thing* in the Lost City of Jade?" said Pipper.

"Oh." Binkton's eyes widened in startlement. But then he shook his head. "You killed it, Pip."

"It was no Necromancer," said Aylis, "but a thing from a lost age."

Pipper sighed in relief.

They got up from the table and moved past Wooly and Nikolai, yet striving, neither yielding. Through the milling throng of sailors they went, and to the arc of chairs sitting about the unlit fireplace, chairs that had remained empty, for all knew that they were reserved for the captain and his guests, though Aravan denied it was so.

As they took their customary seats, Binkton said, "What about the Truenames of tokens of power? How do they get their names, and what does it take to invoke them—some kind of spell?"

"As told nights past," said Aylis, "it seems the gods have a hand in creating tokens of power—tokens of fear, too. Hence, I think the gods themselves must give each token its Truename, and share that knowledge with the one who forged it.

"Some of these seem to have an innate ability to manifest their powers when their Truenames are spoken: Krystallopŷr was one, and, once named by Aravan, the Falcon Crystal another. Others require no name or word to be said, for their power seems to manifest itself at need: Bane and Bale were such, as is Bair's stone ring. And some tokens seem to always manifest their power . . . for example, Whelm, a ram that appears to be extra potent when breaking down walls and gates; Drakkalan, too, for Dokan said it hewed through a heavy haul chain, though I know not the full of that tale."

The Warrows sat a moment without speaking, their questions exhausted, and then Pipper piped up, "I say, Bink, what say we go fishing? Take Vex, too, if Aylissa will let us."

Bink grinned. "Right, Pip. Fishing it is."

In moments they were scrambling up the stairs, and moments later, scrambling down and out the door, Vex running at their side.

Aylis laughed and clasped Aravan's hand. "I can see why you enjoy their company, *chier.* Curious and naïve and innocent they are, one moment all serious, the next off on a lark. They are a joy to be around."

"Steadfast, too," said Aravan, "and formidable allies. Dost thou know the most effective warriors in the Winter War were Danner and Patrel and Tuck? Those three buccen accounted for more Foul

Folk than a full regiment of the High King's Men. And speaking of Eborane, of Dark Shedder, of Drakkalan and the haul chain, on the darkest day at the Iron Tower that trio of Waerlinga, along with three more buccen—Rollo, Harven, and Dink—and one Man, Prince Igon, one Lian, Flandrena, and one Drimm, Brega, in the teeth of the enemy set out to cross the deep and treacherous chasm beringing the tower, for on that mission depended the fate not only of Mithgar but of all creation as well. . . ."

Evening fell, night quick on its heels, and again Aravan, Aylis, Riatha, Urus, Jaith, Bair, Fat Jim, Wooly, and Tarly found themselves seated in candlelight before the Red Slipper's hearth. And as Pipper and Binkton joined the arc, Aylis said, "How was your quest for fish?"

"Bink caught six," said Pipper, holding his index fingers about three inches apart. "I didn't get any."

"Vex ate them all," said Binkton.

Aravan turned to Bair and said, "This mission of thine, at the nexus, I would hear what the three of ye found."

In that moment a cluster of shadow came down the stairs and moved in among the friends. The knot of darkness vanished, Pysk and fox emerging from gloom, Aylissa on Vex. As Aylissa dismounted, Vex looked at Binkton and Pipper as if in anticipation, and they each had to show the vixen empty hands before, disappointed, she settled down.

Bair glanced at Aylissa and said, "Aravan, mayhap this is not the time to speak of our mission beyond the nexus."

"No, no, Bair," said Aylissa. "Please do tell. Last night I was merely startled, for my dam and sire oft spoke of the days of flight, and . . . well, do go on, for I would hear of it myself."

"Are you certain?" asked Bair.

"Yes," replied Aylissa.

Fat Jim silently raised his mug toward the Pysk and smiled.

Bair took a deep breath and said, "Ever since *kelan* and I were denied the eastern crossing at the nexus, I have been curious, not only about where that in-between led, but also about the Planes.

"I went to the libraries in Arden Vale and Challerain Keep as well as those in Caer Pendwyr. It seems that there is a scholarly dispute among the learned, for some believe that all worlds are upon just three principal Planes—the Hôhgarda, the High Plane; the Mittegarda, the Middle Plane; and the Untargarda, the Low Plane—whereas other scholars believe that each world is on its own separate Plane. Thus, Vadaria and Grygar would be on their own Planes—a Mage Plane, and a Demon Plane. The Hidden Ones, too, would have their own Plane, for they came from the world of Feyer. Dragons as well would have a Plane; they are from the world of Kelgor. And who knows how many other worlds there are? Not I, nor the scholars."

"But have you formed an opinion?" asked Binkton.

"I think it is something one of your Kind said, Bink, that gave me a clue."

"My Kind?"

"Aye: my *Amicula* Faeril. She told me Dodona said she was of the Middle Plane, and yet there is a legend that the Warrows, too, once dwelt in a place other than Mithgar, a place they fled."

"But that is just a fable," said Pipper.

"Ah, but many a fable has its roots in truth," said Bair, Aravan nodding in agreement. "Hence, if that legend is based upon fact, then Dodona himself has solved the question: there are but three Planes—High, Middle, and Low—and all worlds exist on these three."

"Bair," said Aylis, "I ween you assume too much: first, that the Warrow fable is at least in part true, and, second, that Dodona would know of the origin of Warrows. However, Dodona did not say ought about Dragons or Demons or Fey and their worlds. Hence, he did not dispute the scholars who think there are more than three Planes. Further, perhaps you assume that nought exists outside the scope of Dodona's knowledge, though that is neither here nor there."

Bair shrugged. "Indeed, Aylis, I made a great leap, yet it is what I believe. Even so, the scholars do agree that there are three principal Planes, and the others, if any, are secondary."

Bair paused and took a sip of his brandy. As he set his glass aside he said, "Regardless, in the days of my eighteenth summer, two years or so after the Dragonstone War, *ythir, athir,* and I decided to see what was at the eastern in-between at the nexus, and so we travelled from Arden Vale to the narrow mouth of a stark Grimwall valley north of the village of Inge on the border between Khal and Aralan, where sits a warding garrison. . . ."

* * *

"Welcome to the end of the world," said Captain Andell, smiling, "or so it seems. 'Tis not often we get guests"—he gazed at Bair—"and certainly none of your fame, Dawn Rider."

"Captain, you give me too much credit," said Bair.

"Not I," said the captain, "but the songs."

"Bards are wont to exaggerate," said Bair, turning to his parents only to find them beaming.

"Mayhap," said Andell, "but then again mayhap not. Nevertheless, what brings you here?"

"We go to the Black Fortress," said Urus, "and then to the eastern in-between."

"Hmm . . . I think none have yet crossed the nexus to the east," said Andell, "not even the Mages. Mayhap the Neddra side is not close-matched to the other."

"Perhaps you are right," said Bair, "for without a match a crossing cannot be made."

Riatha nodded and said, "In Dhruousdarda there was a match to a point on Neddra, but we destroyed it."

Andell said, "That's one way to deal with such. Ha! Once I suggested that we should merely destroy the match at this in-between, but the Mages would hear nothing of it."

"I don't wonder why," said Bair. "The only known crossing to Vadaria lies through Neddra, north of the Black Fortress."

"Aye," said Andell, "and that's why Mages and Elves maintain that dark bastion, to ward against the Foul Folk crossing into Vadaria, or into Adonar or Mithgar, for that matter, at the other points of the nexus."

A silence fell upon them, but then Bair said, "How many *Spaunen* have crossed in the two years following the Dragonstone War?"

"None, Lord Bair," replied Andell.

"Even so, it's a needed duty," said Bair.

Andell nodded but said, "Our garrison here has a twofold purpose, for not only do we stand ward, we also coordinate shipments of supplies from Mithgar to the Black Fortress."

"Shipments?" said Bair. "But how? It isn't as if a wain can be taken through an in-between."

"No," said the captain. "Instead, everything must be ridden

across on horseback, or borne by those on foot. Most of the horseback riders—your Folk, my lady—cross over from Adonar, for on Neddra that nexus path is gentle, whereas from Mithgar to the fortress the way is rugged. Even so, once every year after the harvest in Khal and Aralan, the crofters send a good portion of it to Inge, and from there it is brought to my storehouses here. During this time the DelfLord of Kachar brings a small army of Dwarves hither, and they repeatedly cross over with what they can bear, and soon the storehouses are empty again."

"Dwarves?" said Urus.

Riatha said, "They cannot lose their feet, *chier.*"

"But how does that—? Oh, wait, I see. Once they have stepped the rite of crossing but a single time, they know it forever. Even so, there is the cant, the chant, the trance, the dream of the crossing. How do they—?"

"I believe they achieve it with a paean to Elwydd," said Andell. "Though with that harsh language of theirs, I don't see how Elwydd could consider it a song of praise."

"To each his own," said Riatha.

The captain smiled and turned up a hand in acceptance, then said, "As you can see, I and my Men are more in the line of storekeepers, of quartermasters, than guardians of Mithgar."

"I would dispute that, Captain," said Urus, "for you and your garrison stand athwart the way; ever must Free Folk be on ward against incursions, be it a single Rûck or an invading Horde."

Andell sighed and said, "Indeed, I do know that, Lord Urus, for as I tell my Men, eternal vigilance is the price of liberty, and at this place it is we who watch."

Bair paused in his telling to take another sip of brandy, then said, "We spent an eve in the garrison, and all the next day as well. *Ythir* entertained the Men with songs and tales, and *Athir* and I engaged many in practice at combat. Yet somewhat after nightfall we shouldered our packs and buckled on our weapons and, with Captain Andell and a squad of Pellarians as escort, we set out for the in-between, bearing several well-aged bottles of dark Vanchan, a gift from the Men of the garrison to the commander of the black fort. . . ."

* * *

Up the bleak vale they marched, starlight and moonlight shining down on the narrow, short valley, with the Grimwall rising up to either side, and scrub and scrawny grasses struggling for life in the infertile ground.

The full moon was nigh its zenith, mid of night drawing near—the best time for crossing to Neddra. For anyone other than Bair some candlemarks were better than others for crossing an in-between: dawn, dusk, noon, midnight—these were the best, and midnight was easiest for crossing to Neddra, whereas coming from there was less difficult at noon. But for Bair the time of day or night did not seem to matter—his crossings perhaps eased by the stone ring he wore on a platinum chain about his neck . . . or by the blood he bore in his veins—Magekind, Demonkind, *Spaunen,* Baeron, and Elvish—for he was the Rider of the Planes.

Finally, ahead in the moonlight, a flag on a short pole could be seen, marking the place of the crossing, though for Bair, with the stone ring he'd received as a birthing gift, no such mark was needed.

Andell and his Men stopped short of the in-between, and the captain looked through the moonlight at the trio and said, "Should you run into opposition, get back as quick as you might. We'll stay for a candlemark or two, just in case."

Urus grunted and nodded, though his hand went to the haft of his morning star.

The captain turned to a sergeant. "Ready weapons."

The sergeant signalled the others, and swords were drawn and arrows nocked.

"Thank you, Captain," said Bair.

"Fare you well," said Andell.

To the flag went the three, and as Bair looked at the moon Riatha said, "It is time." She stood opposite Urus and Bair: Riatha facing north, Urus and Bair facing south.

Bair began, his voice rising and falling, neither singing nor speaking, but something in between, and he was joined by Urus and Riatha. And he moved in an arcane pattern, a series of intricate steps and glides and pauses and turns, neither walking nor dancing, but something in between, and Urus and Riatha did likewise. And their minds became lost in the ritual, neither wholly conscious nor unconscious, but something in between. And they did these things on the cusp of night, neither the morrow nor yester, but something in between. And scrub and grasses lay on the land, neither flourishing nor dying, but something in between. And they stepped out the rite in a vale, neither plains nor mountains, but something in between.

And in the deep marks of mid of night in the grass lying on the vale they moved, pacing intricate steps, canting an intricate chant, Bair and Urus and Riatha slowly fading, their voices becoming soft . . . faint . . . silent.

And a short distance away in the stillness left behind, Captain Andell and his Men looked at one another and then back at the crossing and stood ready, for the ones they had escorted to the flag were now gone in-between.

Out from nothingness and into the night stepped Bair and Urus and Riatha, the trio yet pacing and chanting. And when they could see the mountains rising about them, their movement stopped and their voices fell silent in the dark. They took weapons in hand and surveyed the 'scape; nought was nigh but a flag on a short pole. Urus wrinkled his nose at a faint caustic scent on the air—rather like a tinge of brimstone—and said, "So this is Neddra."

Finding the countryside empty of foe, Bair said, "Aye, Neddra." He pointed. "See the moon."

Urus and Riatha both followed the direction of Bair's outstretched arm and peered into the sky.

"The darkness against the faint stars," said Bair.

"A black moon," said Riatha, sighing. "You had said it was so. Still, it comes as an unwelcome sight, this sneer 'gainst Elwydd."

"Gyphon's sneer," said Bair.

Urus grunted and said, "Which way, Bair?"

"North," replied the youth, pointing up the vale.

Out from the small desolate valley they trod, to enter a grim 'scape of rock and twisted trees and sliding shale and scree, the land even more stark and barren.

On they trudged and on, up and over bleak outcrops of stone, stepping up slopes and down, their eyes ever alert for sign of Spawn.

A league and a mile all told did they follow the twisting way, and finally as they topped an incline—"There," said Bair, stopping and pointing downslope.

On a high-rising hill in the basin below, castellations ringing its battlements, there stood a black fortress, its ebon walls reflecting no light, Elven sentries atop the ramparts.

A distance downslope from the bastion and circling about the base of the hill stood another battlement, a single wall running 'round. Between that outer wall and the fortress stood nought but barren ground, an uphill killing field should invaders come to call.

"It looks quite ominous," said Riatha.

"Formidable, I would say," said Urus.

"Come," said Bair, setting out downslope. "Let us go knock on the door."

"Bair, my lad, what are you doing here? And will you never stop growing?"

Bair smiled down at the green-eyed, dark-haired, young-looking Magus, who was millennia old. "Mage Alamar, let me present my *ythir* Riatha, and my *athir* Urus."

Alamar smiled and nodded at both and received like acknowledgment from them in return, and then he said, "Come, let us sit somewhere comfortable and have a drink of that splendid wine you brought, and you can tell me all about your mission, after which I'll show you to the quarters we have waiting for you."

"Thou hast quarters *waiting* for us?" asked Riatha.

"Indeed," said the Mage, standing and moving out from his office and down a hallway, the trio following. "The Seers, you see, they said you would be here this night."

"Thou hast Seers here, then?"

"Seers, Sorcerers, Alchemists, and such . . . oh, and, heh, and Elementalists like myself."

"A fortress full of Magekind—as well as my Folk, the Lian—is a formidable bulwark, indeed," said Riatha.

"Seers, eh?" said Urus. "Then that's why we had little challenge by the Elven ward on the walls."

Alamar turned up a hand. "The Seers take turns doing a casting each day to see what it will bring. This day brought you."

He stepped through an archway, leading them into a small lounge, where several cheeses and a medley of fruit lay waiting. Flasks of water sat at hand, along with one of the bottles of the dark Vanchan.

After they poured wine and took small plates of fruit and cheese, and sat down, Urus said, "With Seers it would seem difficult to attack this fort with any surprise."

"True," said Alamar, smiling, "yet casting a vision of the future is rather draining, and oft do the Seers return to Vadaria to <rest>, while others come across to take their places."

"Tell me, Mage Alamar," said Bair, "speaking of Seers, where are Aylis and Aravan? Here in the fortress or instead on Vadaria?"

"Neither. That young fool of an Elf"—Riatha sputtered in her wine at hearing Aravan called a young fool—"and my daughter eloped to Mithgar. Ran off to the sea like a couple of kids, they did, to sail the *Eroean* across the world and seek lost treasures and adventures and such."

"I wish them well," said Bair, raising his glass in salute.

Alamar grinned and raised his glass in return.

"And you, Alamar," said Bair, "what has kept you occupied?"

"Running this fort, my boy. Standing between the Free Folk and the Foul. It was a year ago that I and Magekind conquered this bastion, a year after you persuaded Adon to rescind the Ban. What ever got in your fool head, boy, to do such a thing?"

A flinty look came into Riatha's eye. "Wouldst thou rather be trapped on Vadaria? Wouldst thou have Elvenkind trapped on Adonar? Men on Mithgar? Each one of us confined to our blood Plane?"

Alamar frowned and said, "Well, no, Lady Riatha."

"Then wouldst thou yet call my *arran* a fool?"

"Ythir," said Bair, " 'tis merely Mage Alamar's way of speaking." He turned to the Mage.

Alamar spread his hands. "Indeed, Lady Riatha. I was about to compliment Bair, for I would never have thought of asking Adon to stop meddling in the affairs of the Free Folk. It was splendid."

"Oh," said Riatha, somewhat disconcerted at her flare.

Alamar looked at Urus and grinned and said, "A tigress protects her cub, eh?"

"I would not have it any other way," said Urus, returning the grin.

Alamar turned to Bair. "A splendid idea, my lad, though had I thought of it, I am not certain I would have asked Adon to stop interfering in the matters of the Foul Folk as well."

"I wanted all to be free of interference," said Bair, "Foul Folk, too. That is why I suggested you conquer this fortress and hold it against the Spawn."

Once more Alamar raised his glass in salute. "Another splendid idea, my lad, though it took a year in the making."

The Mage set aside his drink and said, "Now, what fool errand"—Alamar paused and glanced at Riatha; she smiled—"brings you three to our stronghold?"

"We plan on going to the eastern in-between in the hope of seeing what is on the other side," said Bair.

"Oh, my," said Alamar, frowning. "I would advise against such. Nothing ever comes from there, and we have not gone between, fighting off Rucha and such, as we were, and making this fortress livable."

"Nothing ever comes from there?" said Urus. "Even though the Ban is rescinded?"

"Aye."

"Have the Seers aught to say concerning that crossing?" said Riatha.

"Not a thing, other than no one from there will come this day," said Alamar. "Mayhap the match is destroyed, and nothing can cross either way."

"Regardless," said Bair, looking at his sire and dam and receiving a nod from each, "we would see."

"We plan on going on the upcoming noontide," said Riatha.

"Then if you can actually cross in between, you will be there a full half day," said Alamar, "for I think you will not be able to return until mid of night." The Mage took a sip of his wine. Then he frowned and said, "By the bye, there is always the possibility it is unfitting on the other side, and that's why nought comes."

"Mayhap I should go first," said Bair. "For if it is unfitting, then I can cross back over regardless of time's measure."

Riatha's eyes suddenly widened. "Bair, what if it is completely dreadful yon? Mayhap the air is poisonous or otherwise unbreathable. Mayhap there is no air at all. What if something horrid exists beyond, be it alive or no?"

Bair looked at Urus. "Consequences of failure, eh, Da?"

"Simple forethought," replied Urus.

Alamar said, "Give it no concern, for ere you go I will ask the Seers to see if you return unscathed."

"Well and good," said Urus. "Well and good."

They broke fast in the morn—Alamar, Riatha, Urus, Bair, Seeress Verai, and Arandor, fair-haired Elven Captain of the Guard. Verai pushed a stray dark curl away from her brow and said, "Of course there are many futures, and if you do something foolish yon"—she nodded to the east—"then you might not return at all."

"Have you looked into the past to <see> whether anyone at all has crossed through the in-between?" asked Urus.

Verai shook her head. "I came to this fortress but a sevenday past. Even so, if you will wait till the morrow, when I have recovered, I will <see> for you."

Bair shook his head. "I would go now, and hear what you have <seen> when we return."

"Ah, the impatience of youth," said Alamar.

"Lady Verai has said that we will return in the night unscathed," said Bair, "and so I would go."

"She said you will return unharmed if you do nothing foolish," said Alamar. "Yet impatience is a hallmark of youth, my boy, and often leads to quite foolish acts." Alamar quickly glanced at Riatha and said, "Not that your son is a fool, my Lady Tigress."

Riatha smiled and said, "Mitigation accepted, Mage Alamar."

Alamar laughed and managed a half bow, though seated.

"I will assemble a squad and accompany ye three to the crossing," said Arandor. "And we will return in the mid marks of night to escort ye back. E'en though Seer Verai says ye will return untouched, still 'tis better to go in numbers in this place."

"I thank thee, Arandor," said Riatha.

They spent much of the morning examining the fort, Bair showing Riatha and Urus the places where he and Aravan had gained access to the bastion, and where the breeding pit was—now an arena for games—as well as where he and Aravan had been imprisoned by Ydral. All signs of Ydral's dreadful activities in his vile sanctum had been eliminated, though an ominous atmosphere yet remained therein.

Eventually, though, the dull red sun drew nigh the zenith above the sulfur-tinged, yellow-brown haze, and the three set out for the eastern in-between, Arandor and an Elven escort accompanying them.

Soon they came to a small, dust-laden hillock, not quite on the cardinal point, but the eastern in-between nevertheless. And while Arandor and the escort stood at the base of the hill, Riatha, Bair, and Urus trod to the crest. With a farewell wave to the squad below, Bair then began the rite, Urus at his side, Riatha opposite. And under the light of the red sun at the apex—neither morning nor afternoon but something in between—stepping, turning, pausing, and gliding through the roiling dust—neither earth nor air, but something in between—singing, canting, chanting, after a long while they began to slowly fade from sight, and fade and fade and fade . . . until they were gone altogether.

And stepping, turning, pausing, gliding, singing, canting, chanting, now they appeared on the other side of the crossover. . . .

. . . They had gone in-between . . .

. . . to come to . . .

"Oh, Adon," gasped Riatha in the darkness.

Overhead, black lightning-streaked clouds churned, and reddish glows here and there lit the seething pall from below. The roiling air was filled with ominous rumblings from afar, and now and again there came vast explosions, not like thunder that boomed from above, but as of detonations on the very land itself. And by the flashes of lightning and the reddish glow from below, the mountains far beyond the hillock glistered, as if they were clad in thick sheaths of ice, for the world was untouched by daylight and frigid beyond endurance.

"What has happened here?" said Riatha, clutching her cloak about.

"I know not," said Bair. He bent down and picked up a handful of dust mingled with hard ice crystals and let it sift through his fingers. He cupped his hands about his mouth and exhaled to warm them again. "No wonder it took awhile to cross over: this side is not well matched to the other."

Peering through the blackness, Urus rumbled his agreement but then said, "What is that yon?" He pointed outward, and by lightning flash and reflected ruddy glow they could see jutting up from the ground just beyond the foot of the hill a dark looming shape standing, a faint glimmer low on its side.

"It looks like a menhir," said Riatha, starting off downslope, Urus with her.

"Menhir?" asked Bair, following.

"A tall stone erected by those who have gone on," replied Riatha. "On Mithgar 'twas an ancient Folk who left such megaliths behind. We know not who they were."

"Ah, as in Kolaré an e Ramna?" asked Bair, referring to the ancient ruins—the Hollow of the Vanished—just west of Arden Vale.

"Aye, though in Kolaré an e Ramna they raised no megaliths," said Riatha.

They reached the base of the hill and started eastward, and they finally came to a huge, rough, dark stone partly buried, all ice-clad and unmarked but for a single arcane rune scribed in the stone on the side facing the hill. The rune itself glowed.

"What does it say, *Ythir?*" asked Bair.

"I have not seen its like before. Were Aravan or Silverleaf here, mayhap one or the other could cipher its message."

Urus walked to the opposite side of the dark rock. "No runes over here," he said, gazing up and down its aboveground, ten-foot height. Then he added, "I have seen stones such as this nigh firemountains. Belched up from the heart of the world, they say."

Bair said, "Mayhap that is the cause of the red glow we see against the darkness above, and the explosions we hear: firemountains in fury."

"But so many?" asked Riatha, looking up at the sky with its uncounted crimson blooms against the lightning-streaked, churning pall.

As Urus rejoined them, the roar of another blast resounded, and one of the ruddy glows brightened.

"Oh, Bair, I do think thou hast the right of it. Yet how can that be?"

"I know not, *Ythir,*" said Bair, placing his arm about her, only to discover she was shivering in the bone-dry, glacial air. Bair whipped off his cloak and draped it over her shoulders.

"But thou wilt freeze," protested Riatha, struggling against him to remove the garment.

"Nay, *Ythir,* I'll not," said Bair, forcing the cloak back upon her, "but you need to keep this, for you cannot return ere mid of night and I would not have you die of the cold while waiting."

"But what wilt thou do without thy cloak, *Arran?*" said Riatha.

"Just this," said Bair, grinning, and then a darkness grew about him and swelled, and Hunter stood where he had been. Likewise did Urus clothe Riatha with his cloak, and then a Bear stood with the Silver Wolf.

Of a sudden, the Bear snuffled at the ground and, following its nose, moved away toward the side of a nearby slope and began clawing up ice-clad dirt. Amid dark, glassy blobs, he turned over a small object, and then backed away and looked over his shoulder at Riatha and emitted a soft *"Whuff."*

Riatha came to see what the Bear had found. She knelt, and then burst into tears.

It was a tiny skull. That of a Pysk or a Tomté.

The Bear dug up more ice and dirt, as did the Silver Wolf, and they uncovered the frozen remains—some tiny, some large, some in between—of more victims of an unknown catastrophe, some fire-scarred, others not.

"No more," said Riatha. "Please, no more."

And both the Bear and the Draega stopped, as if they had understood her plea.

Wiping away her tears, Riatha stepped back to the dark volcanic rock. She again peered the rune. Oddly, it was not covered with glaze, almost as if . . .

Riatha reached out and touched the symbol, and she gasped in shock and jerked away. But she reached out once more and tentatively touched the rune again, and then pressed her full hand to it and stood unmoving, her head cocked as if hearing, her gaze unfocused as if seeing something within. . . .

In the night, Pyska and Tomté and Ände and Sprygt and Woodwers and Shamblers and Phael, and Fey and Peri of other kinds stood looking up at the sky.

"What are they?" asked one.

"I don't know," answered another, "but aren't they beautiful?"

In the spangle above and across the vault, a long file of sparkling objects with glowing tails flowing out behind stood in the night like glittering diamonds on a string.

"The Elders name them hairy stars," said a third one, "because of the tails that stream out."

"I see one, two, three . . ."

The count reached forty-seven.

They had appeared a moon before, sweeping more or less at an angle across the sky, and every night they had changed positions, tracking across the stars, shifting slowly, the ends gradually moving closer to shorten the string, or so it appeared, though some claimed that they were not growing closer to one another, but instead were little by little altering their line of flight, the trailing ones to swing behind the one in the lead; how those who made such claim knew this, they did not say. Regardless of whether they were closing up the gaps or simply falling into line, their number still could be counted.

Days passed, and they continued to shift and grow brighter, and finally they were no longer countable, so close to one another they had come or had fallen behind one another in a long line. And a halo had formed about them, and grew larger and brighter still.

The night was glorious when the first huge fireball came screaming down, the air shrieking in agony at its passage, a cluster of smaller fireballs leading and trailing the plunge.

WHMP!

The world shuddered, as if struck a mighty blow, and faults in the bedrock shivered.

Huge gouts of earth spewed up into the sky, and a vast crater was left in its wake.

Forests were flattened, and burst into flame.

Then the sky began raining fiery, dark glassy droplets for hundreds upon hundreds of miles, as of molten stone flung wide.

And there was a thunderous blast so loud it circled the world again and again . . . a hundredfold times or more.

Air began rushing toward the thousand-mile fire, howling on its inward journey.

Firemountains awoke, some born anew, and molten stone and lethal gasses flowed down their sides, and fire and great rocks were blasted into the air to land on the slopes and beyond, some miles away.

Fey screamed and died—Tomté, Pyska, Phael, Shamblers, Liv Vols, Vred Tres, Spryght, and the like—some in an instant, others more slowly in fires and suffocating smoke and dust and falling rock.

The revolving world slowly turned as the dreadful day progressed. . . .

. . . and then the second massive strike came.

Again the whole world shuddered, faults breaking open, molten stone welling up, forests burning, ebon droplets raining from the sky, thunderous booms whelming the land, firemountains belching death.

And more Fey perished in agony.

And a great dark roiling swept across the sky, as the smoke and the dirt and the pulverized rock now filling the air churned past.

Still the world turned on.

WHMP!

The third massive blow struck Feyer. . . .

And then the fourth . . .

And another and another . . .

Until forty-seven altogether had slammed into the world, girdling Feyer entire.

Some hammered the land, others slammed into the oceans, steam blasting outward, great tidal waves rising up, and more bedrock flying wide, vast rifts yawning open, molten stone bursting forth from the deep melt far below the seabeds.

Fey and Peri fled to the surviving in-betweens—those not obliterated—but even there the crossings were difficult, for the world had changed, the in-betweens no longer well matched, and a pitiful measure of all those who had survived could make it across in the times allotted—the dusk for those going to Adonar, mid of night for those passing into Neddra, the dawn for those striving for Mithgar. And at the in-betweens many died waiting.

The sky on Feyer turned black—from upflung rock dust and dirt and the smoke of fires, as well as the belchings of thousands of firemountains. The seas turned into lifeless grey sludge, and the sun could no longer break through the darkness to warm the world. It became progressively colder in this lightless place, and ice began forming from the vapor in the air.

And at one of the crossings into Neddra, a Shambler waited with others for the marks of midnight. And on one of the great rocks hurled out from the gut of the world to smash down nigh, he scribed a Telling Rune, a <wild magic> message for anyone who would touch it, the story of the death of his world.

And as he waited with the others, a lethal gas streamed out from a nearby firemountain to finally flow in stealthy silence along the bottom of the vale.

Riatha gasped, and awoke from her entrancement, tears flowing down her cheeks. She fell to her knees, her face in her hands, and great sobs racked her frame.

Hunter came to her and whined and licked at her fingers, and the Bear sat beside her and moaned. Riatha flung her embrace about the neck of the Bear, and cried into his fur.

It was long ere she recovered.

As the marks of mid of night approached, Riatha called to Urus and then Bair, and their forms shifted back, and she had each of them touch the rune and know the tale of the destruction of Feyer.

Then, drawn and haggard and exhausted by grief, they clambered to the top of the hillock, and made the difficult crossing back into Neddra, where Arandor and his Elven escort awaited.

In the candlelight of the Red Slipper, Bair concluded the tale, for again he was weeping, as were they all, Aylissa once more cloaked in shadow, with Vex wrapped about her and whimpering.

After long moments, Bair stood and went to the bar, Jaith at his side. Wooly somberly went to the others 'round the arc and poured dark Vanchan into goblets.

Finally Pipper said, "Did any escape that dreadful fate?"

Binkton didn't say ought in reply, though with Aylissa in their company, and Hidden Ones throughout various Mithgarian woodlands and remote places afar, it was obvious that many had.

Riatha rallied and said, "When we got back to the Black Fortress, Verai the Seeress said that she had cast a past vision and had watched in horror in her <seeing> as Hidden Ones came through the in-between, fleeing from she knew not what, with Shamblers, Liv Vols, Phael, Tomté, Woodwers, Pyska, and other Fey and Peri all weeping or aiding injured comrades or limping on their own.

"We told her the tale, and so for the first time it was known among those who were not Hidden Ones just what had happened to their world.

"And then did Verai apologize, for she had said we would return unscathed, but clearly we did not, for our hearts are weeping still."

Bair and Jaith returned to the arc of friends, and Bair said, "We crossed over to see what was there and found horror."

As others nodded in agreement, Urus said, "But we also found courage as well."

"How so?" said Tarly.

Urus took a sip of the Vornholt and then said, "At this one in-between, and I ween at crossings elsewhere, there was no panic, no scramble to be the one to get through at the expense of others. Even though the world was dying—by fire and ash and molten stone and smoke and darkness and cold and the onset of ice—still they aided one another and waited their turns and sent some across in their places. All this did the Telling Rune reveal."

Urus then raised his drink in silent salute . . . as did they all, no words needed.

10

The Purging

call up their legion and to assemble the ships to take them to Rian, and by the time they got there, the boy King and his forces were fighting for their lives far south on the grassy plains in the abandoned Land of Ellor.

"The Jordians made a magnificent ride down from Rian through Harth and Gûnar to come to Ellor in the nick of time to save the King's forces and defeat the minions of the Usurper."

"And this Usurper?" said Wooly.

"Oh, him," said Fat Jim. "He was a near cousin, who died by his own hand there on the stolen throne when the boy King himself confronted him and told him his army was defeated and all of his commanders were in shackles.

"The rightful King then awarded the land of Ellor to the Jordians, and they renamed it Valon. I think that the king of Jord gave the land to his younger brother, and he led a great number of Jordians down to Valon. That's why there are two sets of Harlingar, two sets of Vanadurin—one in Jord, the other in Valon—horse people all."

Jaith said, "There is a rather stirring song telling of that war and the ride of the Vanadurin, but it is very long. One day I will sing it, but not tonight."

"Oh, poo," said Aylissa. "I would like to hear it."

"Some day," said Jaith, smiling at the Pysk. "I promise."

After a moment, Binkton said, "Getting back to the crossings from Plane to Plane, I suppose that Durgan's fabled steed *could* have gone through an in-between, seeing as how it was really flesh and blood . . . and not a waggon or something else as outlandish."

Pipper sighed, but then said, "Captain Aravan, d'you think you could sail the *Eroean* through an in-between, one out there on the seas somewhere?"

"An in-between on the ocean?" said Binkton. "Could there even be such a thing?"

"In the sea, I deem there are such," said Aravan, "for 'tis said Kraken cross from Kelgor to Mithgar at the Great Maelstrom. Too, the Children of the Sea are said to have come from elsewhere, mayhap Feyer, for they are Hidden Ones as well."

"Yes, but what about *on* the ocean?" said Binkton. "Are there in-betweens on the surface?"

"Mayhap," said Aravan. "For there are places where ships vanish, and other places where they appear."

"Why couldn't someone drive a wain of supplies across an in-between?" asked Pipper.

"Because, Pip," said Bair, "whatever goes through an in-between has to be captured in the <aura> of the one who is crossing."

"<Aura>?" said Fat Jim.

"The <fire> that surrounds all things," said Bair.

"Oh, magic," said Fat Jim, with a dismissive shrug.

"Not quite," said Bair, "yet I'll leave it at that."

"But horses go across?" said Pipper.

Bair nodded. "Aye. They have their own <fire>, and somehow they are guided by the rider to step the intricate steps required, and in doing so, they get caught up in the crossing dream, the trance, the state of mind required."

"And a wain is too big to be caught in the <aura>, eh?" said Pipper.

"Oh, Pip," said Binkton, "a wain can't do the steps."

"I know that, but if a sword or spear can go across, then why not a waggon?" said Pipper.

"Because a sword can be captured in the <aura> of the one who crosses," said Binkton. Then he turned to Bair. "Right?"

"Ordinary swords are caught in the <aura>, but not tokens of power," said Bair. "Their <fire> remains outside the <aura> of the bearer. Even so, they are borne across. It is a peculiarity of such tokens."

"Like Lady Riatha's sword?" asked Pipper.

"Aye," replied Bair. "Dúnamis, Bane, Bale, mayhap Grayling's bow, my ring, Aravan's Falcon Crystal and his stone of warding and Krystallopŷr—when he yet had it—and other such potent artifacts."

"Well, then," said Pipper, "all you need is to find a waggon that is a token of power." He turned to Binkton and smiled wickedly, as if to say, *So there.*

Aylis broke into delighted laughter. "Mayhap one of the gods will hear Pip's suggestion and possess a wainwright and comply." Again she broke into laughter, its infectious quality causing others to join her, though Binkton merely smiled.

When things calmed down, Wooly said, "You spoke of Grayling's bow, Lord Bair. Just what was it? —Oh, a bow, I understand, but what was it about Grayling's bow that made it so special?"

Bair shrugged, but Riatha said, "As I understand it, Grayling was a Lian Guardian, and he had a bow that seemed to lend unexcelled prowess to the user: incredible distances could it fly an arrow, with accuracy beyond compare."

"Hmm . . ." mused Wooly. Then he said, "Where is Grayling now, and does he yet have the bow?"

"None knows," replied Aravan. "Once when I compared Silverleaf's white-bone bow to that of Grayling's, Silverleaf told me he had trained under Grayling and his bow was a wonder, indeed. Silverleaf went on to say that Grayling vanished sometime ere the First Era began, and it seems he took the bow with him." Aravan turned to Aylis and said, "Mayhap someday a Seer will uncover the answer as to whence he went."

"Had I something of his to guide me, or could I stand somewhere we know he had been," said Aylis, "I would <look>. Yet without an object, 'twould be like seeking a particular grain of sand in all the seashores of the world."

"He was on Atala and on Rwn as well, long ere those isles vanished beneath the waves," said Aravan, "or so Silverleaf did say."

Binkton said, "Were Silverleaf here, mayhap he could tell of a place extant Grayling had been."

Aylis nodded and said, "Perhaps someday I will seek Vanidar Silverleaf out, and then we will go searching."

They fell silent a moment, and then Wooly said, "Still, speaking

of the in-betweens and waggons and such things not a
and blood, and since horses can go through, I wonder
iron horse could cross over."

"Durgan's iron horse?" said Aylissa.

Wooly said, "Durgan's *fabled* iron horse: a legendary
to be made of iron. Swift beyond reckoning, it was, and
ing."

Fat Jim held out a hand of dismissal. "It wasn't made
Wooly. That's just a fable. Durgan did have a magnificent ho
right, dark grey it was, and because of its color he called it
and that's where the legend started."

"How do you know this?" asked Wooly.

"It's a factual story that I learned as a child in Pellar," replied Jim.

"Oh, do tell it," said Aylissa.

"Well, there's not much of a tale to speak of," said Fat Jim.
mean, it was just a small note in the chronicles of Pellar. However,
I would think in the histories of Valon and Jord it's quite a saga."

"Well, tell us whatever it is you know," said Wooly.

Jim took a sip of his dark Vanchan, then said, "It was back in the time of the War of the Usurper, when the throne was stolen from the rightful High King's heir; Reyer was his name, just a wee babe at the time. Reyer's followers took him into hiding, and there he remained, not really knowing just who he was. But when he turned fifteen, Reyer's loyal band told him he was the true High King, and they raised an army to contest the Usurper. One of those Men, Durgan of Jord, was sent to gain aid from the Jordians.

"Durgan set out on Steel on a two-hundred-sixty-mile journey from Challerain Keep to the port of Ander on the Boreal Sea. Practically flying across the land, he and Steel made that leg of the journey in just under three days. There Durgan and the horse boarded a ship and sailed to Hafen in Jord. He offloaded Steel and then rode some six hundred miles from there to Jordkeep, and this he did in but seven days, and that's when the legend began: Steel, the horse made of iron." Fat Jim shrugged and said, "That's it. That's all I know about Durgan's fabled steed."

"But that's not the end of the story, surely," said Aylissa. "What happened to King Reyer and the Usurper?"

"Oh, that," said Fat Jim. "Well, the Jordians took some time to

"Appear, Captain?" said Tarly.

Aravan nodded. "Aye. Appear. Once a Fjordlander ship I helped crew encountered strange roiling waters in the night, and out from the churn under full sail came a craft. We hailed the vessel, but there was no answer, and so we overtook and boarded her. The crew was nowhere to be found, though hot coals were in the galley stove, and in the captain's cabin food was yet warm and partly eaten. It was as if all aboard had gone elsewhere, or the ship had somehow left them behind."

"I thought such stories were nought but old salts' tales," said Wooly.

Aravan shrugged. "I thought so, too, Wooly, right up until the moment that ship appeared in the night."

Bair frowned and glanced at Pipper, then turned to Aravan and said. "Could it be that the craft itself went in-between, but because the crew wasn't in the crossing dream they found themselves swimming for their lives in whatever waters they had been sailing?"

"You might have the right of it, Bair," said Aylis. "For the crew to have come with the ship, everyone aboard would have to be caught up in the rite, else they'd be left behind. Even so, something strange would have to occur, for I deem a ship too large to be caught up in anyone's <aura>."

"Or whoever's <aura> it was caught up in would have to be enormous," said Pipper. "A whale, a Kraken, a Sea Serpent or such, something really big."

Aylis looked at the buccan in astonishment and said, "Mayhap a Child of the Sea, or a creature guided by one. Oh, Aravan, do you think it might be so? When next we encounter a Child, I will ask."

"Lor, Captain," said Wooly. "Child of the Sea or no, I hope you don't go sailing no strange jigging courses, lest we find ourselves dumped in the brine, the *Eroean* nowhere about."

"Should I ever attempt such a thing," said Aravan, smiling, "thou canst be certain that all aboard will be well schooled in the crossing dream."

Pipper leaned over to Binkton and whispered, "If a ship can cross, then mayhap a waggon can do so as well, perhaps on the back of a Dragon."

Now it was Binkton who sighed, yet he said nought as a quietness fell over them all. But then he said, "How do the places of the crossings come about? Can they be just anywhere?"

All eyes turned to Bair, the Rider of the Planes, and he said, "Not just anywhere, Bink. First, I think there has to be one or more aethyric linkages between any two worlds, though unlike the aethyr I and others can see, these linkages remain unseen.

"Second, I—"

"Wait a moment," blurted Pipper. "If links are hidden, then mayhap Dragons can see them."

Again Aylis looked at Pipper in astonishment. Then she turned to Aravan. "Oh, *chier,* can we offer something to a Drake's desire, as did Arin and Egil One-Eye, then mayhap we can induce one to find an alternate in-between to Vadaria, an in-between not on Neddra."

Aravan cocked an eyebrow at Aylis. "Dost thou truly want a Dragon to know the way unto the Mage world?"

"Oh," said Aylis, chapfallen. She sighed and turned to Bair and said, "Please go on."

Bair looked at Pipper, and that buccan shrugged but remained silent.

"Second," said Bair, "even if there are one or more aethyric links connecting any two worlds, still at any given link there must be a match ere a crossing can be made, and the more perfect the match, the easier the crossing."

Again a quietness settled among them, all digesting Bair's words, but then Tarly said, "Well, something else I'd like to hear has to do with crossing in-between, and it's this: as you just said, Bair, a close match is needed, and Lady Riatha mentioned that there was a close match in Dhruousdarda, a crossing that went between Neddra and Mithgar, but she and others destroyed it. What I'd like to know are three things: what is Dhruousdarda; what was this crossing like; and how did you destroy the matching?"

Riatha looked at Aravan. "Wouldst thou tell the tale, or shall I?"

Aravan turned up a hand and said, "Say on, Dara, for I would as well hear thy account of those dire events."

Riatha took a deep breath, then said, "I'll not forget the year—'twas 4E1948 by the High Kings' count—for that not only was the year of the Purging of Drearwood, it was the year of the death of my *jarin*—my brother—Talar. . . .

* * *

The first blush of the oncoming summer was upon the land, and Riatha and the other Lian Guardians were readying for combat, and the Dara's mind was occupied with stratagems and plans. Yet as she reached for her sword, she noted that within the open chest lay Talar's scroll, his most recent missive to her, though it had come three years agone. She took up his letter and unbound it and read the short message again:

Riatha,

There is a monster somewhere within the Grimwall, and he preys upon the innocent and unprotected. I do not speak here of the Draedan in Drimmen-deeve, but instead of a butchering fiend. Jaian of mine, should ought happen to me, seek out Baron Stoke, for he is the evil I hunt.

Talar

Again Riatha felt a cold hand grip her heart, and unto her came a vision of her brother's face, a steely glint in his grey eyes. Twelve seasons in all had passed since she had last read this dispatch, and no word had come to her from Talar since. Where he was, what he did, was unknown.

Once more a dread premonition skittered across her mind, but she told herself that it was merely concern for his welfare, as well as concern about the upcoming strife. She rebound the scroll and placed it back in the chest and took up her sword instead, for the Elves of Arden, in alliance with the Men of the Wilderland, were setting forth this day to purge Dhruousdarda of the Foul Folk and dire creatures who laid waste to caravans and bands of travellers passing through the dread forest also known as Drearwood. Peopled as Dhruousdarda was with Rucha, Loka, Ghûlka, Trolls, and other such *Rûpt*—and mayhap things unknown—it was expected the campaign would take many weeks if the opposition was fierce, less should it be meager.

Yet paltry it might not be, for rumor had it that among the *Spaunen* in Drearwood dwelled one of the last Gargoni; deadly Fearcasters they were, the Draedan of Drimmen-deeve one. And for this cleansing of Drearwood, the Lian had no Wizards among them to deal with such.

Even so, the Ban lay across the land, and that was an advantage the allies had, for the first marks of June had come, the days lengthening, pushing the darkness away. And Foul Folk and others suffered the withering death and would crumble to dust should daylight fall upon them.

Riatha was just buckling Dúnamis in a shoulder harness across her back when Aravan, bearing his crystal spear, stepped into the door of her thatched hut.

"Ready?" he asked.

She nodded, and they went forth into the sunlight, where stood their steeds.

Wending past were mounted Lian Guardians armed and armored, many with glittering shields, all making their way ahorse across the vale and up the face of the western bluff, where they entered the carven tunnel to pass through. And into this grim procession merged Riatha and Aravan.

Up the narrow pathway and into the passageway beyond they rode, where the sound of shod hooves rang and reverberated in the arched granite cavern, a quarter of a mile long through stone. They emerged from a hidden cleft in the rock and then passed through close-set pines, and a dozen miles away down a long slope and across a wide grassy gap Riatha saw the northeastern reach of the deadly forest, the drear tangle of Dhruousdarda.

Her heart pounded louder at the sight of this dread wood, for long had this dark-forested hill country been a region most dire. Many were the stories of lone travellers and small bands who had followed the road through this dismal woodland never to be seen again. And stories came of large caravans and groups of armed warriors who had beaten off grim monsters half seen in the night, and many had lost their lives to these grisly creatures. This land had been shunned by all except those who had no choice but to cross it, or by those adventurers who sought fame, most of whom did not live to grasp their glory. Yet a main trade route—the Crossland Road—lay through this dread realm, and so traders and travellers massed together, and armed escorts hired out their axes and swords and bows and arrows and other such weaponry to see them safely through. Even so, casualties were high, though the larger the caravan, the less likely a full attack from the cowardly *Spaunen*.

Some two years agone, the Men of the Wilderland had proposed an alliance with the Elves of Arden Vale, the purpose of which was to purge these woods of Foul Folk and other creatures dire. It had taken this long for the campaign to be set, with plans and counterplans proffered and examined, some to be found wanting and rejected, others found suitable and accepted.

All events they could think of had been put forward, and tactics were designed to deal with them.

But as Riatha rode down the slope toward the distant dark tangle, she knew that those plans would survive right up to the very first moment of combat, and then would give way to independent groups fighting merely to survive; any victory would come as a bonus. Even so, all knew the strategy, all knew the tactics, and they would regroup as needed and consider what had gone well and what had failed and change their campaign accordingly. Or, if they had had to flee from something o'erwhelming—a Draedan, or some such—when they were far enough away to be safe, then they could plan how to deal with whatever it was they had encountered.

Far in the lead, Alor Talarin, his golden hair gathering sunlight, kicked up the pace, and they rode at a canter toward the rendezvous with the Men of the Wilderland, who would come from the west across Drear Ford toward the northern grasslands, where they would meet and set camp and review the plans for the following day.

And so, swiftly they rode as the sun edged up the sky, Talarin now and again changing the gait to spare the steeds, or pausing to let the horses drink and take grain.

Ere the noontide came, the cavalcade stopped, for it had reached the rendezvous point some forty-two miles west of Arden Vale.

The Elves had rubbed down their mounts and had well settled in when Vanidor Silverbranch—Talarin's youngest *arran* by less than a candlemark to Gildor Goldbranch his twin—called out, "*Athir*, the Men come."

Riatha turned and looked to the west, and she saw a horse-borne force of Wilderlanders nearing, the number of Men triple that of the Lian.

As they rode into camp, the one in the lead, a tall, broad, red-headed Man, raised his hand palm out in greeting to Talarin.

"Hoga," said Talarin with a slight bow as the Man leapt from his horse.

"On the morrow, my lord," Hoga boomed, grinning and gesturing south toward the distant forest, "on the morrow we begin the sweep of that foul place. May none of the Spawn survive." Then he burst out in roaring laughter and said, "Now, have you any of that fine Elven wine?"

As dawn graced the eastern sky, once again Talarin and Hoga spread out the maps. In attendance were Hoga's four sons—Rohr, Mogon, Pell, and Krath—each with reddish hair like their sire, and tall, as was he. At the meeting as well were Gildor and Vanidor, golden-haired as was Talarin, their heights matching his at five foot nine or so. Also attending were Aravan and Riatha and black-haired Flandrena, that Alor an inch or so shorter than either twin.

Talarin pointed to the southeast with his left hand and to the southwest with his right, and then he curved his arms as if in an embrace, the tips of his fingers not touching. And he said, "Two arms of Dhruousdarda—the Drearwood—reach out to hold a great clearing, though there remains a wide gap where the ends do not meet. Should darkness fall and we run afoul of a creature we cannot defeat, then some of us can make for the clearing and race to the gap and out, while others run to the outer border and away." Talarin let his hands fall to his sides.

Hoga growled and shook his head. "I like not this plan to flee. Even so, should we still be there when night falls and come across a Gargon or such, we have no choice but to get beyond its reach and wait for the day to come." Hoga glanced at the eastern sky. "Ban take them all."

"And the Vulgs?" asked Rohr, running his hand along the reddish stubble growing on his chin.

"We have gwynthyme," said Riatha, "though not an unlimited supply. May all of our archers fly their shafts true."

"Would that we had some of those Wee Folk with us," said Pell, his auburn locks peeking out from his leather helm. "I hear they are a wondrous bow-and-arrow Folk."

"Thou art correct, Lord Pell, for I have known several who

were," said Aravan, hearking back to the Waerlinga archers at Caer Lindor during the Great War.

Talarin nodded then traced routes on the map. "I will take a third of our combined force, Hoga, and sweep down the eastern arm; thou wilt take the other two-thirds and range the wider western arm."

Hoga grunted and said, "Rohr and Mogon will lead the Men who accompany you, Lord Talarin. Who do you send to lead the Elves I go with?"

"Vanidor and Flandrena," replied Talarin. "Gildor and Aravan will command under me."

Hoga looked at Riatha. "My lady, would it not be better for you to return to—"

Riatha pushed out a hand of negation to stop Hoga's words. "My Lord, there are many Darai among the Lian force. We are all well skilled in battle."

Vanidor smiled and said, "Fully half the Lian archers who will ride with us are Darai, Lord Hoga. I deem them easily the equal of the Waerlinga Lord Pell did mention."

Hoga sighed and shook his head but said nought.

Talarin said, "Let us hope that our strategy is correct, and that most of the Foul Folk are holed up in the hill country nigh the Crossland Road."

Redheaded Mogan grinned and clenched his fist and said, "I like this plan, for we use Adon's own light as an unbeatable ally."

"Look," said Hoga, gesturing to the east, where the sun now edged over the rim of the world, "we've gone over this plan a thousand times, and everyone knows their part. I say we get on with it."

Talarin smiled and nodded and said, "Indeed."

And so they set out to purge Drearwood of Foul Folk and creatures dire—some four hundred twenty Lian and twelve hundred Men of the Wilderland. Two-thirds of the Elves went with Hoga, along with two-thirds of the Men, and to the west they rode. The remaining one-third of the combined force rode east, following after Talarin.

Into the grim tangle they fared, and the light of day seemed hard-pressed to penetrate the dark woodland. All about them clustered a dim, enshadowed gnarl, blackness mustering in ebon pools among misshapen, close-set boles. Stunted undergrowth clutched desperately at the soil, and distorted trees twisted upward from the gloom-cast ground to grasp at the sky, and jagged branches seemed ready to seize whatever came within reach.

Within the eastern arm the line of Men and Lian spread wide, Aravan to Riatha's right, Mogon to her left, and beyond to either side rode others, and beyond those others still, the force spread across the span of the woods. They were looking for the cracks and splits in the land where Foul Folk sought refuge from Adon's light of day, for should the *Rûpt* do otherwise they would suffer the withering death. And so, down through the dismal woodland rode the Lian and Men, stretched out in a long line, and whenever any came upon an outcropping or a ravine the nearby flankers would draw inward, and they would search most thoroughly. Yet little did they find in the way of *Spaunen* refuge, for they were not yet in the hill country where such places were more likely.

And the sun rode up and across the sky and then sank downward again, but it was June, and the short night was long in coming. And ere the time befell for the force to withdraw, they had finished searching out the eastern arm and had come to the main wood. At a signal from Talarin, Aravan and Rohr turned half of the line to the west and rode to the embraced clearing, while Gildor and Mogon turned the other half to the east, and rode beyond that border of the woods.

As they fared north across the open land, at Aravan's side Riatha said, "Nought whatsoever this day. Mayhap we are right in thinking that the hill country is where most *Spaunen* abide."

"Let us hope so," said Aravan, "else should nightfall spread wide as we are, 'twould go ill for those of us encountering a force of *Rûpt*."

" 'Tis good the days grow longer, then," said Riatha, grinning. "It gives us more time to search and then flee."

Even as Aravan and Rohr and that half of the force reached the campground, so, too, did Gildor and Talarin and Mogon and the other half arrive, well ere the setting of the sun. It was as twilight descended upon the open wold that Hoga and the other two-thirds of the command reached the encampment, for that arm of the woodland was fully ten miles longer as well as being wider.

"Ought?" asked Flandrena when he saw Riatha.

"Nought," replied the Dara. "And thou?"
"Nought," said Flandrena, shaking his head.

In the Red Slipper, Riatha paused in her telling and took a drink from Urus's tankard. As she did so, none said a word, and only the shadows cast by the candle flames seemed to move, wavering as they did in the gloom.

Riatha gave the tankard back to Urus and said, "The next day and the next and the ones after—for a fortnight, all told—we continued our sweep through the woodland, both north and south of the Crossland Road, saving the hill country for last. And in those fourteen days we found a few crevices and cracks and caves, and, using our shields, we entered in daylight, but we found no Foul Folk therein. Of those rifts and holes in the ground, we destroyed those which we could, and those we couldn't we blocked.

"And every eve we fled that dark woodland to the safety of the open wold beyond the reach of the *Spaunen* in the short nights of summer; at times we ran south into Rhone, or east into Lianion, now called Rell, or we fled west into the Wilderland beyond the River Caire.

"But at last came the days when only the hill country of Dhruousdarda was left in our purging, and again our force was divided, this time into three legions, each a third of our total strength: one legion to deal with that part of Dhruousdarda south of the Crossland Road, where a single range of hills do sit; a second legion to take on the rise of tors in the central part of the northern portion of the woodland; the remaining legion to ride to the eastern half of the northern portion, where a final extent does lie."

Riatha looked about the arc of listeners. "Aravan and I were part of the second legion: our objective was to clear out the tors in the central northern section. And in keeping with our strategy and as planned in the winter past, it was in the marks ere the break of dawn on Year's Long Day when our force of Wilderlanders and Lian set out from the Wilderness Hills. We crossed the Stone-arches Bridge over the River Caire to come to the western fringe of Dhruousdarda, for we knew that any Foul Folk yet abroad would be scrambling for refuge from the yet-to-arrive light of day. Likewise, the first and third legions were moving out from their encampments in Lianion and toward their respective goals.

"We had ridden some twenty-five miles eastward along the Crossland Road and had turned into the drear forest when the first blush of the oncoming dawn graced the sky. Another ten miles of riding through the dark woodland brought us in sight of the western end of the tors. And with day now on the land, our search for the bolt-holes of the Foul Folk began. . . ."

"Shield!" called Aravan.

Relor came riding, his shield gleaming in the morning sun; at his side rode Frake, one of the Wilderlanders, axe in hand. They dismounted and stepped to where Aravan and Riatha stood at a crevice in a rock-faced bluff. Blocking the crevice from the light of day was a well-anchored flap made of thick hide. In spite of the covering, a fetor seeped out to foul the air.

Relor angled the glistening shield so that sunlight reflected full on the flap. "Ready," he said.

Frake hefted his war axe in a two-handed grip, and Aravan held Krystallopŷr likewise. They nodded to Riatha, and with her sword Dúnamis, made of dark starsilver and keen beyond reckoning, she sliced the hide up and across and down, the great flap to fall inward.

And sunlight cast by Relor's shield shone full into the cleft.

There came a bellow, chopped short in mid roar, as whatever was within died by Adon's Ban.

Holding her breath against the sickening reek, Riatha peered into the crevice. "Some five paces inward I see a turn."

Relor gave a sharp, piercing whistle, and moments later, Dellana came riding, two of the Wilderlanders at her side.

And while Relor kept the reflected light shining full into the crevice, Dellana moved inside, her own glistering shield in hand, Aravan with the Dara, the two Lian breathing through their mouths against the appalling stench.

Paying no heed to the scatter of bones on the floor, by reflected light Dellana angled her own shield to shine the day down the notch beyond the bend.

"Nought but a dead end," called Aravan. "Come, Dellana, let us leave this cesspit."

On the way out they again passed the massive bones of the victim lying in the dust of its demise; 'twas the remains of a Troll, for only Troll bones and Dragonhide could stand up to Adon's Ban.

"A Troll," said Aravan, upon emerging.

"By the smell of its den I thought so," said Riatha.

They mounted up and rode onward, Dellana and the two Wilderlanders resuming their positions on the line, Relor and Frake likewise, and Aravan and Riatha as well.

On eastward through the tors went the legion, seeking out cracks, crevices, holes, tunnels, and the like, anywhere Foul Folk laired. Many they found, some with flaps—like the Troll hole behind—others with crudely made doors, and these the Men and Elves broke down or chopped through; still others were shielded by boulders rolled across the way, and here they used horses to move the rocks aside and let daylight within. Some crevices were shallow, others quite deep, and many required several of the highly polished shields to angle the daylight down all branches and into all corners. One slot was too small for ought but Rucha, and after the allies had reflected sunlight as far into the hole as they could, they used horses to drag great rocks to bury the entrance under tons of stone, consigning whatever within might yet be alive unto a lingering death.

And as they went from notch to gap to cleft to tunnel, Rucha were slain along with Lokha, Ghûlka, Hèlsteeds, Trolls, Vulgs, and things which none could name: huge, hulking things, larger than Trolls; monstrous long things like snakes, but no snakes these; large multi-legged things, spiderlike; and other things they did not see but only heard their squalls and clickings and mewls and thin hisses as they died. That these latter things were slain by Adon's Ban came as a surprise, for as far as anyone knew, they had not taken part in the Great War of the Ban.

"Mayhap they are of Neddra," said Riatha, "some of Gyphon's get."

Aravan nodded, for her speculation seemed the only answer.

And so as the day progressed, eastward fared the legion through the central tors, opening clefts and crevices and letting daylight shine within, or casting it into the depths using highly polished shields.

Yet the farther east they went, the more uneasy the Men and Elves grew; it was as if they came closer to something quite deadly, something fearsomely dire.

When the sun lay some three fists above the western horizon in the afternoon sky, "Mayhap a Draedan?" asked Riatha.

"Mayhap," said Aravan, glancing to the east where the rocky hills came to an end. "We are nigh the last of the tors—two furlongs or three, no more—and there are yet some candlemarks left in the day, enough time to complete the task, though I take a warband away. Let us speak to Vanidor."

They found Vanidor Silverbranch at another cleft, where Wilderlanders chopped on a door. Vanidor turned when Aravan and Riatha rode nigh, a look of surprise in his eye.

Without dismounting, Aravan said, "Silverbranch, this unease we feel, mayhap 'tis a Gargon, and I ween we need to send a force to see whence the dread emanates and destroy it ere the sun sets."

"If thou dost go, who will command thy regiment?" said Vanidor.

Aravan turned to Riatha, but she shook her head. "I ride with thee, Aravan."

"Then the Wilderlander Pell," said Aravan.

"Leave a Lian at his side," said Vanidor.

"Dellana, I think," said Aravan.

"Well and good," said Vanidor.

In that moment the door to the cleft collapsed, and shrieks cut short sounded from within.

With a handpicked group of Men and Elves, Aravan and Riatha rode easterly, fear growing with every stride. Five shield-bearers were in the group, along with ten Wilderlanders, all armed with sledges and axes, should a door need breaking. As they rode, Aravan and Riatha ranged back and forth, seeking a better fix on the source of the emanations of dread, and they changed their course, angling somewhat east-southeastward. A furlong they went, and then part of another, and the horses skitted and shied, and became reluctant to press forward. Harker, in command of the Wilderlanders, said, "They have more sense than we."

Still they went on, not quite a furlong, and as they came to the end of the tors, Riatha said, "There!" and pointed.

Within a tangle of gnarled trees deep in the black heart of the woods stood what appeared to be an ancient dark temple, and from this place did numbing waves of dread come.

Hearts pounding in alarm, they dismounted, for the horses would go no nearer.

Trembling, their limbs nearly beyond control, they crept toward the dark shrine, its ebon dome sucking all light from the sky, or so it seemed. Aravan glanced at the low-hanging sun and gritted his teeth and pushed on, Riatha, her face pale with fear, at his side. Wilderlanders and Lian followed, some with tears running down their faces, though they knew it not.

Around the great stone edifice they went, the very air seeming darker, as if shadows mustered nigh. And there were no windows in the stone walls, nor any doors, it seemed. Finally, they came to the front of the black sanctum, where a portico loomed above a broad landing, and great double doors stood shut.

With their hearts hammering in dread, their mouths dry, sweat running, the warband looked to Aravan.

He took a shaky deep breath in the pulsing terror, and then signalled the shield-bearers to take up positions to concentrate Adon's light upon the door. And the Elves moved to where the low sun yet shone through the trees and positioned their shields to catch the light and cast it upon the entry.

When all was ready, up three steps went Aravan, Riatha on his right, the Wilderlanders following. Aravan signalled the others to stand wide of the reflected light. Then he tested the door.

It was latched.

He put an eye to the overlapped seam, and then pulled on one panel while pushing on the other. Though the doors shifted but slightly, now he could see part of the latch mechanism through a slot. He drew his long-knife from the scabbard affixed to his thigh. He pressed the point through the crack; it went in a bit and then stopped; the blade was too thick. He pulled, then frowned, for the long-knife had jammed, but at last he tugged it free. He then motioned Riatha forward. With her blood pounding in her ears, as Aravan stepped aside she moved to where he had been and pressed her eye to the crevice, and then inserted the tip of Dúnamis in behind the overlap.

In that moment, Harker came forward with his war axe and whispered, "Lord Aravan, mayhap I can break it down."

But then—

click . . .

. . . came a soft snick, and Riatha looked at Aravan and nodded, just as—

Great numbing waves of dread slammed into them, and Men fell groveling and mewling to the stone of the landing. Beyond the portico shield-bearers collapsed, the reflected sunlight falling away. Riatha dropped to her knees, Dúnamis lost to her grip, and she shrieked and shrieked and shrieked. Aravan was frozen in terror, his voice joining hers. But Harker howled in berserker dread, his fear turned to rage, as some Men are wont to do when terror becomes unendurable, and he slammed the flat of his axe against the door. And the full force of dread from the Gargon whelmed him. Yet screaming, Riatha struggled to her feet and grabbed the door handle and hauled backward, falling hindward as she did so.

The door swung partway open, yet stopped against her collapsed form.

Even so, daylight seeped into the temple, and a great howling roar sounded, and unbearable waves of dread momentarily blasted outward, and Men and Elves even back among the tors sucked air in through clenched teeth, while those at the temple thought their hearts would burst. But then the unendurable terror utterly ceased as the Draedan, the Gargon, the Fearcaster fell to ashes.

Riatha, weeping, took up Dúnamis and shakily got to her feet, and Aravan and the others managed to stand as well . . . all but Harker, for he lay dead, slain by horror beyond what he could bear, for the Gargon had focused the full of his dread upon the Wilderlander, and in that fleeting instant Riatha had been free to haul open the door.

Aravan stepped to the entry and heaved wide first one side and then the other. A reeking oozed outward, an overpowering stench as of a vast nest of vipers. And Aravan's mind hearkened back to the Great War of the Ban, when he had come across where Draedani had been.

At a signal from Aravan, shield-bearers again moved to where the low-angle sun yet shone through the trees, and they cast daylight into the shadowed interior.

Aravan motioned three of the bearers forward, and into the temple he went. Two freestanding colonnades, one to either side, marched away into the dimness. On inward went Aravan and three Lian with shields, Riatha and the Men trailing after.

The building inside was all one great chamber, no other rooms within, and no stairs up or down. Overhead and supported by interior buttresses, the ebon dome arched up into shadow. Centered under the dome and on a pedestal stood a twenty-foot-high statue of a standing nude female—mayhap Human, mayhap Elven, mayhap something else altogether—and her viperous eyes peered down at a point on the floor some four or five paces to the fore. On the pedestal was carved runes that none could read, not even Aravan, who was skilled in many tongues.

"Perhaps a name," said Riatha.

"Most likely," replied Aravan.

By reflected light they examined all the corners and walls, and no other entries nor exits did they find, though a heap of ashes lay nigh the door, the remains of the Fearcaster who had suffered the withering death when Adon's light had shone in.

Riatha looked about. "Hmm . . . a single heap. The Draedan was alone."

Aravan nodded and said, "I deem even the Foul Folk cannot endure the nearness of one of Draedan Kind."

He and the others then stepped from the temple and joined the Lian outside, and Aravan said, "Come, let us leave this place." One of the Wilderlanders hove Harker's body over his shoulders and all headed toward where the horses had been, only to discover that the steeds had bolted. Yet even as Aravan's band turned toward the eastern end of the tors, the full of the legion came riding their way.

They had finished searching out the splits in the land.

Their part of the purging of Drearwood was done.

In the Red Slipper again Riatha took a swallow of Urus's ale.

"Oh, my," said Pipper, "a Gargon must be a dreadful thing. I hope I don't dream of any."

Aravan nodded but said nought.

"A splendid tale, my lady," said Fat Jim. "Well done."

A rumble of agreement arose, but Riatha said, "It is not finished, Jim."

"There's more?"

"Aye."

A quiet fell in the room, and Riatha said, "Out before the dark temple where he had died, we set a funeral pyre for Harker, for had it not been for him, none of us would have survived, I deem, but would all have died of fear.

"Lord Pell said a few words over his slain liegeman, and as twilight fell upon the land he set the bier ablaze. We stood while Wilderlanders sang praises to Harker, for they believe such songs speed the soul to the afterworld.

"And when they were done, I sang a paean unto him. . . ."

Riatha's song came to an end, her clear voice falling silent, and many Wilderlanders wept, for surely Harker's spirit had been sped on its way by the exquisite Elven gift. And the fire crackled and burned and sent sparks flying into the sky, and mayhap Harker's soul was among them.

Then Pell raised his arms as did all the Wilderlanders, and he led them in a long chant, a final rite of soul-sending. And when it was done and silence fell . . .

Ssss . . . thock!

A black-shafted arrow sped through the firelit night and took Pell full in the back, and he pitched forward into the flames.

And with howls and yawls and snarls, out from the dark temple came pouring Rucha and Lokha and Ghûlka on Hèlsteeds and a hurtling pack of Vulgs. And they crashed into the unprepared legion, cudgels bashing, scimitars and tulwars slashing, fangs tearing, and cruel, barbed spears punching through flesh and bone.

And Men and Elves snatched up axe and hammer, bow and arrow, sword and shield, as more Foul Folk poured forth from the temple doorway.

And amid snarls and howls and war cries and screams of death, "Krystallopŷr," whispered Aravan, Truenaming his spear. Then he shouted, "Riatha, to me! The Vulgs! We must stop the Vulgs!"

"Then the Ghûlka," cried Riatha, even as she came running, Dúnamis in hand, the dark silveron blade glittering as if full of stars.

Among whirling swords and bashing shields and hacking axes and slashing tulwars and green-fletched arrows flying opposite those with black shafts, Riatha and Aravan crossed through the mêlée to come unto the first Vulg, the pony-sized black Wolflike creature atop a Man and tearing at his throat. And just as it raised its blood-dripping muzzle, Aravan's Truenamed spear stabbed through its rib cage. The creature howled in agony, and fell in a heap, and the smell of charring bone and cartilage and tissue filled the air as the crystal blade sucked the <fire> from the beast; its flesh sagged and seemed to draw in upon itself, and black fur fell out by the handful, the skin underneath turned mottled and withered; its eyes clouded and grew dim and its legs trembled and its paws scrabbled at the ground; its lips shrank back from its deadly teeth to turn into a horrid grin, and nought was left of the dire creature but a desiccated corpse.

But opposite Aravan and leaping out from the mêlée—

—"Aravan! Behind!" shrieked Riatha, and Aravan jerked his crystal-bladed spear from the Vulg and turned in time to meet a second Vulg in midspring.

Thuck! the spear slammed full into the chest of the hurtling beast, and Aravan was hammered backwards, as the creature crashed down atop him. Once again the howl of a Vulg rang out even as the beast died. And a Ghûlk turned his head and spurred his Hèlsteed toward the cry.

And as he charged through the mêlée, swords rived his flesh and arrows slammed into his body, yet he paid them no heed, for he was one of the corpse-foe, and only beheading or dismemberment or fire or wood through the heart or a special blade could harm him. And he sneered at these pathetic attempts to bring him down.

Now he came nigh the slain beast, even then nought but a dry husk of what it had been, and Aravan, stunned, feebly struggled to get out from under, while before him and athwart the way stood one of the cursed Dolh—an Elf—a female, with a dark sword in hand.

Thock! Another arrow struck the Ghûlk, punching into his abdomen. Scoffing, he wrenched it out and threw it aside. Then he charged, his barbed spear leveled at the female's head. He would take her through the eye.

But she ducked under his point, and as the Hèlsteed thundered past, her dark blade slashed through the air, and, bitter beyond all reckoning, it clove through the Ghûlk's arm above the elbow, severing it from his body, the limb and spear to crash to the ground. And the Ghûlk howled in pain, and black ichor gushed from him, for the starsilver blade was special, even though it had not been Truenamed; it had delivered a wound from which the Ghûlk would not recover, his unnatural life spewing out through the remaining stump of his arm.

Her sword in hand, Riatha spun in time to see the corpse-foe tumble from the saddle and the Hèlsteed gallop on. Aravan managed to gain his feet, and as he drew his spear from the slain Vulg he said, "Nicely done, Riatha. Now let's go after the rest."

Back and forth raged the battle, Riatha and Aravan concentrating on killing Vulgs, the two of them taking on other foe when confronted. And amid slaughter and maiming and cries of the dying, they sought out and slew four more Vulgs, the remainder of the pack.

Now they turned their attention to the Ghûlka, and with crystal spear and starsilver blade they slew corpse-foe and Hèlsteed alike.

Even so, the Rucha and Lokha were many, and the outcome of the battle hung in the balance, but then the cries of silver clarions sounded in the east, and the Foul Folk looked up in alarm, and with horns blowing wildly, charging into the conflict came Flandrena and Rohr and their legion: a hundred and forty Lian and four hundred Wilderlanders. Swords riving, arrows flying, axes cleaving, hammers crushing, they crashed into the Foul Folk, and in but instants more than two-thirds of the Spawn fell.

Shrieking in fear, the *Rûpt* ran for the temple doors, many of them slain even as they fled.

"Quick," called Riatha to Aravan. "We must see where their secret chamber lies. None must escape our blades."

Rallying Men and Elves, up the steps they charged, riving as they went, hewing into the mob of *Rûpt* trying to get through the doors.

And as they fought their way to the entry, over the heads of milling Rucha and by the light from the still-burning pyre, Riatha in the fore of the press of sword-bearing, axe-wielding allies saw a hooded figure in a dark robe toward the rear of the great chamber stepping arcane steps and chanting arcane chants, Foul Folk stepping at his side. And they were fading, fading.

With a shrill cry and heedless of the foe, she charged forward, bashing *Spaunen* aside, Dúnamis ready, and she managed to reach the place of the rite, where she swung at the disappearing form. But her starsilver blade whistled through empty air where the robed figure had been, for he was gone in-between.

Now Riatha had to fight her way free of the clustering Spawn.

Her blade licked out again and again, fatal with every thrust. She took a cut across her chest, and a stab in the back, yet those about her drew hindward, for she was deadly.

And then Aravan and a host of others, Flandrena among them, won to her side, and the Foul Folk threw down their weapons and tried to flee, yet no quarter was given whatsoever, and they were slaughtered to the last Ruch.

With wounds bound and Vulg bites treated with gwynthyme—Vanidor among those bitten—dawn came unto Drearwood. And in the pale light the survivors collected the dead and laid pyres. As to the foe, no pyres were needed, for daylight had turned them to dust. Concerning the few Rucha and such who might have fled the battle and escaped to the tors, Aravan, Flandrena, Vanidor, and Rohr deemed they were too minor a group to pursue. After all, the doors into the hillsides had been destroyed, entrances collapsed, boulders drawn over the openings of other clefts and holes; hence most of those who had scattered were likely to have died with the first touch of dawn.

Grief laid a dolorous mood o'er the legions, for a great number had died in combat, and many an Elven Death Rede had ridden on the aethyr to loved ones afar.

The pyres were set aflame, and the chants and elegiac praises of the Wilderlanders were augmented by the songs of the Lian as souls were sung into the sky that early morn.

Yet even as the fires burned and funeral laments were sung, Riatha, her own wounds bound, drew Aravan and Flandrena and Vanidor and Rohr into the temple. There she described what she had seen, pointing to the place on the floor upon which the viperous gaze of the statue was fixed, for that was where the robed being had faded and vanished. And when she had told of his disappearance, she said, "There is no secret chamber within, but rather this temple is an in-between to Neddra, or so it is I deem."

"If that is true, then how did they cross unto here ere the noontide?" asked Vanidor.

"And then back over ere the marks of mid of night?" added Flandrena.

"I deem the hooded one I saw was a Black Mage, though who I cannot say," replied Riatha. "Somehow he used his art to ease the way. Either that or this rune-scribed statue is a token of power that does the same."

Aravan nodded and gestured about and said, "Too, this place might be a perfect match, for otherwise the crossing to one or the other side out of the traditional marks would be too difficult. Still, in the past some have crossed over at odd times. Yet I deem Riatha is right: a token of power or a casting seems needed to do what was done."

"How can we keep this from happening again?" asked Rohr, the tracks of tears yet streaking his face, for Pell, the youngest of his three brothers, had been slain.

"Destroy the match," replied Flandrena, Vanidor nodding in agreement.

"How?" asked Rohr.

Aravan looked at the statue and the rows of pillars and then overhead. "Thy Men have mauls and hammers, Lord Rohr. Have them fell these freestanding columns and break the statue and pedestal to shards, then bring the dome crashing down o'er all. We'll fill this place with great heaps of stone, and the crossing will be no more."

And thus did Men and Elves bring horses forward and tie ropes on the huge likeness of a viper-eyed female, and with calls to the steeds, their shod hooves slipping on the stone floor, Men and Elves pulling as well, the great statue slowly tilted from its rune-marked base, at last to crash headlong to the dark granite and shatter into shards.

With sledges, they broke the plinth into pieces, smashing the block with its arcane symbols to rubble.

Then they roped the steeds to the freestanding columns and toppled them as well, some to crash into others and fell several at a time.

Then Lian and the Wilderlanders clambered to the roof and stepped to the perimeter of the large black dome centered thereon, and with mauls and war hammers they began smashing away at the base of the vault, on all sides Men and Elves breaking through the encircling stone blocks. And of a sudden, the entire dome gave way, and with a thunderous *Whoom . . . !* it crashed to the floor, smashing into the wreckage below and bursting apart, grit and shards to explode upward through a boiling churn of stone dust and then fall back once more. And as the cloud was shredded by the wind, and the dust cleared, the Men and Elves could see the temple below was filled with thousands of tons of rubble.

The Lian and Wilderlanders clambered back to the ground, and when all were down Rohr asked, "What about the walls? Shall we destroy them as well?"

"Nay, my friend, it is enough," said Vanidor, Aravan and Flandrena nodding in agreement.

In the Red Slipper, Riatha looked about and said, "And thus did Rohr and the Men of the Wilderland with help from the Lian of Arden Vale destroy the match in the heart of Dhruousdarda, and no more did Foul Folk come to Mithgar that way. . . .

"And so was the Purging of Drearwood done, though at a fearful cost."

Riatha fell silent, and for a while, no comment was made.

But then Fat Jim said, "How came Flandrena and Rohr and their legion to the rescue? I mean, I thought they were combing another set of hills."

"They were, Jim," said Riatha. "But while our legion swept our range from east to west, theirs swept opposite—west to east. And the western end of our range of hills was but a league or so from the eastern end of theirs. They heard the sounds of combat and came riding in haste."

Pipper and Binkton were frowning and trying to riddle out what Riatha had said about the western end and the eastern end and sweeping opposite and such, but finally Pipper said, "They heard the fighting, Bink. That's good enough for me."

"Regardless," said Bink, "the purging of Drearwood was done and the temple destroyed, and that's good enough for me."

Again a silence descended upon them all, but then Bair said, "When I was six my *ythir* and *athir* took me along on a glorious hunt in Drearwood. We jumped up a stag, and, in spite of *Athir's* protests, ere I knew it, I had transformed into Hunter, and he pursued that buck through the woods of Dhruousdarda. I remember Hunter passing the shell of that dark temple in the midst of the woodland. It was just beyond that dismal sanctum Hunter took down the stag."

"Thou wert a willful six-year-old," said Riatha, smiling in remembrance.

Urus snorted. "He is yet willful, my love."

"Like sire, like son," said Bair, grinning.

Aravan smiled, remembering that day as well, for on the eve following the chase, as the hunting party of Elves took rest and the stag roasted o'er a fire pit, it was then that six-year-old Bair had pledged to Aravan that he would help run down the yellow-eyed Man as well as aid in the recovery of the Silver Sword. And some nine years later a willful fifteen-year-old Bair, a new-made Guardian, had run away from home to catch up to Aravan and honor his pledge. And in the days after, Aravan had come to realize that he alone could not succeed without the Dawn Rider's aid.

Aravan's thoughts were interrupted as Fat Jim raised his drink and said, "Here's to the Lian and the Men of the Wilderland and the purging of Drearwood."

As Aravan hoisted his own glass he looked at Bair and silently added, *And to those whose word is their bond.*

11

Armor

"Y'know," said Pipper, "I'm glad Drearwood was purged of Foul Folk and others of that ilk, else Danby and Kip and Cousin Triss would've had to sneak by when they went up to the Iron Tower."

"Modru's Iron Tower?" blurted Fat Jim, his eyes wide in amaze.

As Pipper nodded, Wooly said, "Just who were these fools, and why ever did they go?"

Binkton huffed and said, "Just who do you think you are calling fools, Mister Wooly? It was our cousin and two of her friends, and they're no fools."

Wooly held out a hand in apology. "I-I'm sorry to have said that, Bink, one of them being a kinfolk of yours, but it's just that the Iron Tower . . . well, it's a dreadful place in every tale I've ever heard. And I always thought that anyone who would go into Gron without an army about them, much less to the Tower itself, well they would just have to be, um, er"—Wooly scratched his head, trying to think of a polite way to put it, finally settling upon—"let's just say they would be 'lacking in judgement' . . . or at least if I went there alone, that's what folks would say about me."

"Well, you didn't go, Wooly," said Fat Jim, "but I think you are lacking in judgement anyway." He broke into roaring laughter, and others smiled at Wooly's expense.

Finally, Aylissa said, "Though Wooly put it badly, still what he asked has merit: who went to the Iron Tower, and why would they take it in their heads to do such a thing?"

Binkton, not mollified in the least, settled back and refused to answer, but Pipper said, "It was Danby Candlewood, Kipley Larkspur, and our cousin, Trissa Buckthorn. And they didn't just 'take it in their heads' to go to the Iron Tower; instead, they were summoned."

"Summoned?" asked Aravan.

"By whom?" said Bair. "The only one I can think of who might inhabit the Tower would be the ghost of Modru."

"No," said Pipper, "it wasn't the ghost of Modru, but rather that of Aurion Redeye."

"Aurion Redeye's ghost dwells in the Iron Tower?" said Aylissa.

"No, no," said Pipper. "They had to go to the Iron Tower because that's where the black armor was."

"It wasn't *in* the Iron Tower, Pip," said Binkton, pulled from his snit by the course of the conversation, "but out across the bridge and a bit to the west. That's where the tomb is."

"Ah, then," said Riatha, enlightened, " 'twas Lady Buckthorn and her two lieutenants."

"Lady Buckthorn?" said Bair.

"Yes, *Arran,*" said Riatha. "During the Dragonstone War, whilst thou and Aravan were out gallivanting across the Sindhu Sea—"

Bair looked at Aravan and silently mouthed *Gallivanting?* Aravan merely smiled.

Riatha ignored their side-play. "—on your way to the isle in the middle of the Great Swirl, others of us were assembling in the South Reach of Valon to do battle with the Mighty Dragon, or so he did style himself. Among the Free Folk rallying unto the side of the High King was a company of Waerlinga archers, led by Lady Buckthorn and her two lieutenants." Riatha turned to Pipper. "Am I not right?"

Pipper nodded, and Riatha said, "Yet Aurion Redeye is long dead; even so, thou didst say, Pip, that his spirit summoned a trio of Waerlinga unto the Iron Tower."

"Well, not exactly to the Iron Tower itself," said Pipper, "but to the middle tomb of the three out front."

Riatha nodded and said, "I have heard part of this tale from Lady Buckthorn herself, but not all, and I ween others here have heard none of it. Pip, Bink, ye twain have the full of the tale for the telling, and we would hear such."

Pipper looked at Binkton and shrugged, and Bink said, "You start it, Pip, and I'll chime in when needed."

"This will be long in the telling," said Pip, "and we'll need something to wet our throats."

Wooly leapt up and moments later he was back with two foaming tankards of the Vornholt.

Using two hands, Pipper took a sip and set his tankard aside. He looked about and after a deep breath he said, "Well, there were really *three* chain shirts involved, three that Aurion recalled. You see, it all began back just before the onset of the Winter War. It was Yule Eve and Princess Laurelin's birthday, and Tuck, Danner, and Patrel were—"

Binkton interrupted to say, "That's Tuckerby Underbank, Danner Bramblethorn, and Patrel Rushlock, three buccen of the Company of the King. Those three buccen were from the Bosky, and—"

"Who's telling this part," burst in Pipper, "you or me?"

"Why, you are, Pip," said Binkton.

"Then button your lip," said Pipper.

"I was just helping out," said Bink, "and—"

"Button!" snapped Pipper, glaring.

Binkton sighed and put his fingers to his mouth and made a buttoning motion.

"As I was saying," Pipper resumed, "Princess Laurelin"—he shot Binkton a glare—"of Riamon, was having a birthday party on Yule Eve; on the morrow, First Yule, Year's Long Night, she would be nineteen. She was betrothed to Prince Galen, Aurion Redeye's eldest son, but he was away in the Dimmendark, leading one hundred warriors to see what was afoot therein. Anguished by his absence, the princess was in Challerain Keep awaiting her beloved's return, and there she made fast friends with Tuck, and he cheered her greatly. So, to keep the sadness from her heart, she invited Tuck and Danner and Patrel to her party. But Tuck said they hadn't anything to wear, and she said that she could take care of that. . . ."

Smiling secretively unto herself, the princess led the three Warrows into the castle, to the old living quarters of the royal family, to a long-unused room. Inside was a waiting servant, there to assist the three young buccen, much to their surprise.

"I shall return in a trice," said Laurelin, mischievously. They heard the sound of a distant gong, and the princess added, "Hasten, for the guests now gather and we would not be late to the feast." She slipped out the door and left them with the attendant.

In an adjoining room three hot baths had been prepared in great copper tubs, and the Warrows wallowed and sloshed in the soapy suds but were soon herded out by the servant who bade them to hurry and dry themselves for betimes the princess would return. The servant laid out for them soft silken garments, both under- and over-: stockings and shoes, beribboned trews, blue for Tuck, scarlet and pale green respectively for Danner and Patrel, with jerkins to match—and they fit as if sewn for them by the royal tailors. But as fine as these clothes were, the three young buccen had a greater surprise in store, and they were astounded: the attendant presented them with three mail corselets of light chain: silveron for Tuck, with amber gems inset among the links, and a bejeweled belt, beryl and jade, to be clasped about the waist; Danner's ring-linked armor was black, plain but for the silver and jet girt at his middle; and Patrel was given golden mail with a gilded belt: gold on gold. Helms they wore, simple iron and leather for Tuck and Patrel, a studded black one for Danner. And at the last they were given cloaks, Elven-made, the same elusive grey-green color as was worn by Lord Gildor.

They gaped at each other in astonishment. "Why," said Danner, "we look like three warrior princelings!"

"Just so," came a tinkling laugh. Laurelin had returned, now dressed in a simple yet elegant gown of light blue falling straight to the floor from a white bodice, and blue slippered feet peeked from under the hem. Her wheaten hair was garlanded with intertwining blue and white ribbons, matching those crisscrossing the bodice. A small silver tiara crowned her head.

"You *do* look like princelings," she said, a smile in her dove-grey eyes, "but that is befitting mine escorts, warriors three."

"But how . . . where?" stammered Tuck, holding out his arms and pirouetting, indicating the raiment and armor upon Danner and Patrel and himself. "Tell me the answer to this mystery before I burst!"

"Oh, *la!*" laughed Laurelin, "we can't have you bursting on my birthday eve. As to the mystery, it is simple: once apast, my Lord Galen showed me where first he and then Igon quartered as children. Here I knew were closets of clothing worn by the seed of Aurion. And I thought surely some would fit you three, and I was not wrong. But happiest of all, here, too, was the armor of the warrior princelings of the Royal House of Aurion: the silver you wear, Sir Tuck, is from Aurion's own childhood, handed down to him from his forefathers; silveron it is, and precious, said to be Drimmendeeve work of old. And, too, Sir Tuck, I chose the silver armor for you because you wear your *dammia*'s silver locket." Laurelin smiled as Tuck blushed before the other young buccen.

The princess then turned to Danner. "The black, Sir Danner, comes from Prince Igon's childhood, made just for him by the Dwarves of Mineholt North who dwell under the Rimmen Mountains in my Land, Riamon. It is told that the jet comes from a mountain of fire in the great ocean to the west."

Laurelin spoke to Patrel. "Your golden armor, Captain Patrel, is Dwarf-made, too, and came from the Red Caves in Valon. It was my beloved, Prince Galen, who wore it as a youth, and I hold it to be special because of that."

Princess Laurelin turned again to Tuck. "There, you see, the riddle is now solved, though simple it was, and hence you must not burst after all. You are, indeed, wearing clothing and armor fit for princelings, yet they never graced a more fitting trio." The princess smiled, her white teeth showing, and the young buccen beamed in response.

Pipper paused to lift the great tankard of ale and take a drink, and Binkton unbuttoned his lip and said, "It was nigh the stroke of midnight, when a wounded warrior—one of Prince Galen's one hundred—came and said that the Dimmendark was moving toward Challerain Keep and that the war with Modru had begun.

"King Aurion ordered the last of the women and children and oldsters to leave the Keep and follow the others who had gone before down the Post Road to safety. Princess Laurelin was one of these who had to go.

"And so the next day, Tuck and Danner and Patrel went to bid her farewell, and they took the clothes they had worn to her birthday feast, and they bore with them the mail corselets as well. They found the princess in her chambers, taking one last look before departing, and when they tried to return the armor. . . ."

"Oh, pother!" she declared. "If ever you needed armor now is the time, for war comes afoot."

"But my lady," protested Patrel, "these hauberks are precious: heirlooms of the House of Aurion. We could not take them. They must be returned."

"Nay!" came the voice of the King as he stepped into Laurelin's parlor behind them. "The princess speaks true. Armor is needed for my Kingsguards. Even now the leather-plate armor made for your company these past days is ready in my armories for your squads to don. But though I did not think of the Dwarf-made chain of my youth or that of my sons, Lady Laurelin remembered it. Now, too, she is right, yet not only because armor is needed, but also because you are the captain and lieutenants of the Wee Folk Company, and my Men will find it easier to single out a Waerling in gold, silver, or black to relay my orders to. And so you will keep the mail corselets." King Aurion raised his hands to forestall their contentions. "If you take issue with the gift, surely you cannot oppose me if we call it a loan. Keep the Dwarf-made armor, and, aye, the clothes, too, until I personally recall it; and if I never do so, then it is to remain in your hands, or in the possession of those you would trust. Gainsay me not in this, for it is my command." The Warrows bowed to the will of the King.

"And so, the Warrows came into possession of the armor," said Binkton, "and they wore it throughout the Winter War. And when the war was finished, and all made ready for a final leave-taking . . ."

Ere they parted, sad farewells were said as damman and buccan embraced Man and Woman, and they kissed one another, and then it was time to go. Yet Laurelin whispered into Galen's ear, and the High King turned to Tuck and Patrel.

"I am told that Aurion, my sire, commanded that until he personally recalled it, the Dwarf-made armor you now wear was to remain in your hands or in the possession of those you would trust."

Galen's eyes turned to the west and north toward distant Rian where lay Challerain Keep and his slain father. And he raised his voice so that all could hear: "Hearken unto me as I reaffirm the command of my sire: unless the shade of King Aurion recalls it, the armor is yours—silveron for Tuck, gilt for Patrel, and in the northern Wastes of Gron, black for Danner Bramblethorn."

Now Binkton paused to sip from his tankard, and Pipper said, "And a thousand years passed—"

"A thousand and nine," said Binkton.

"Button!" said Pipper, and so Binkton did.

"And a thousand years passed," said Pipper, "but in September in the High King's year of 5E1009, in the depth of the darktide . . ."

In a small cote on a small farm nigh the Boskydell village of Midwood in Eastdell, in the mid marks of night Trissa Buckthorn jerked awake. *What had . . . ?* Of a sudden the young damman gasped and scrambled hindward to fetch up against the headboard, for in the moonlight at the foot of her bed stood a tall figure armed and armored as if for battle, yet he wore a king's crown and his left eye was covered by a scarlet patch. And the light of stars and the just-risen moon seemed to pass straight through the being.

Forty-five miles as the raven flies to the north and west, in the village of Willowdell in another bedchamber, there at a glassmaker's stead, Kipley Larkspur also gasped awake, for there as well at the foot of the young buccan's cot stood the kingly phantom in the night.

And some twelve miles farther on, in the study of The Root where he had fallen asleep, another young buccan, Ravenbook Scholar Danby Candlewood, awoke with a start at his desk to see in the starlight the very same apparition.

And to all three the ghostly night visitor spoke the very same message, though his lips moved not and his one good eye seemed focused elsewhere: *Patrel, Danner, Tuckerby, I now call ye and the Dwarven armor into service again, for a great storm is coming from the east, leaving nought but devastation in its wake. As ye did on Yule Eve, and must needs this Yule Eve as well, don the chain, take up thy bows, and gather the Company of the King, for that's when the coin will come, and these will be needed at the ferry in Valon a sevenday ere the Trine.*

The specter vanished, and Trissa, Kipley, and Danby slept on, two in their beds, one at his desk, for they had not wakened at all.

Trissa seemed distracted as she served breakfast hotcakes to Alver, granther to the young damman.

"Is something wrong this morning, Triss?" he asked.

Trissa sighed and sat down. "I think I was awakened last night." She poured syrup over her hotcakes. "Either that or it was a very vivid dream."

"Hmm . . ." said Alver, reaching for the butter. "Do you remember it?"

"Oh, yes," Trissa said. "The specter of a King dressed for battle came in the night, and he stood at the foot of my bed and he spoke to three heroes of the Winter War—Patrel and Danner and Tuckerby—and he told them that he was recalling some armor, or at least I think it was some ar—"

Trissa gasped and her words jerked to a halt, for her granther had dropped his knife with a clatter and had gone deathly pale.

"What is it, Granther?" said Trissa, alarmed.

The eld buccan shakily took up his cup of tea and managed a sip. Then he said, "Y've always known that Patrel Rushlock was an ancestor of yours, that there's a direct line back to him."

"Yes, Granther, but what does that have to do with my drea—?"

Alver held up a hand to stop her question. "Did the specter have a red eye-patch?"

Trissa nodded.

"Then it was Aurion Redeye who came in the night, and he's calling in a pledge made long past."

"A pledge?"

"Aye. Aurion gifted the armor to those three—gold for Patrel, black for Danner, and silver for Tuckerby. And when they said it was too kingly a grant, he said that it was to remain with them, or with those they would trust, until he personally recalled it. Patrel, along with Danner and Tuckerby, bowed to the King's will, and by doing so, they pledged that they, *or those in whom they had faith,* would wear the armor and fight for the King. It's all right there in *The Ravenbook*."

"What does this have to do with the apparition coming to me in the night?" asked Trissa, frowning in puzzlement.

Alver sighed, then reached across the table and took her hand. "Oh, child, don't you see? Who better to trust than one directly in your own line?"

Now it was Trissa who paled. "Oh, Granther, surely it was just a dream. I cannot believe that a king would come fetching after me to answer a pledge made long past. I am no buccan, no Thornwalker. I am a damman, and there must be a thousand folk more skilled at warfare than me."

"Perhaps, child, yet Merrilee Holt was a damman, and a Thornwalker as well. She was a natural at strategy and tactics, because she had a good head on her shoulders, as do you. And she was skilled with a bow, in which you have a fair hand as well. Hear me, because Aurion came to you, you must hearken back to a couplet that Patrel, your great-granther many times removed, wrote in a song that's sung still, a song penned a thousand years ago when he told of Aurion's gift:

Yours is the armor to wear,
Yours is the burden to bear.

"I would not have this be, Triss, yet I think Captain Patrel's words were meant to echo down through the years unto this very day. I had thought this call would come betimes, but not now, not now. That it came for you was unexpected, yet it has to be, for your sire is dead and I am too old and you are the last of the line."

Looking about, as if seeking an answer, Trissa said, "Oh, Granther, what am I to do?"

His green eyes looked into hers of green, and he said, "Desperate times call for desperate measures, Triss, and it might be that those times have come upon you. If the King did call for you, I have every confidence that you will rise to the occasion. After all, you have the blood of a hero in your veins."

"Well, I don't know about that, Granther, rising to the occasion, I mean. Even so, again I ask, what am I to do?"

The eld buccan pondered a moment and finally said, "You must go to Woody Hollow, to The Root."

"Why Woody Hollow?"

"Because, child, that is where Patrel's armor rests, there at The Root, and you have been called."

"But Granther, it is quite far, and you would be all alone."

Alver shrugged. "Twenty leagues—sixty miles—that's all. Two days and some by pony at a leisurely pace; less if you press. And as for me being alone"—Alver grinned—"*pshaw,* I've the geese for company, and their hissing and honking is company enough."

"But what if the apparition was only a dream?"

Trissa's granther sat for a moment pondering, but finally he said, "If the King truly called, then there will be two others who come: one to answer for Danner, the other for Tuckerby. If they do not show up, then mayhap it was only a dream."

Trissa sighed. "Well, I suppose it won't hurt to go to Woody Hollow, to The Root." She stood and looked out the window and toward the meadow, where a great white flock of geese foraged in the tall and still-green grass. "Isn't that where the curator of the Ravenbook Scholars resides?"

At her granther's nod, Trissa said, "Again I say, I suppose it can't hurt, making the journey. After all, I'll probably be back here in no time—a sevenday, at most. Besides, I've always wanted to see *The Ravenbook.*"

"Aye, *The Ravenbook:* I've seen it myself, once long past, right there in Woody Hollow. In fact that was where I first read the part containing the pledge. Go there, Triss, and read at least that part of the book; see for yourself what the King said as well as Patrel and Danner and Tuckerby's response."

The next morning, Trissa saddled her pony and tied on her bedroll and filled her saddlebags with provender for a few days on the road. Then she took up the ancient bow and quiver said to have been Patrel's very own, and after a tearful farewell to Granther Alver, during which he slipped three silver pennies into her pocket, she mounted up and rode away, geese honking and hissing at her passage and lowering their heads as if to charge. She headed north and west, and soon was skirting the dawn-side border of the forest known as Eastwood.

Early September was on the land, and but a few leaves had begun to turn, for autumn was yet to come. Even so, there was a nip in the air, and Trissa's hunting leathers stood her in good stead. At times she walked and often she stopped to give the little steed a rest and to take grain and water, and occasionally to take food and water herself and to care for other needs. Trissa fared north all that day as the sun journeyed up the sky and across and down, and that night after having cared for her pony, and while stars wheeled overhead, she slept under the eaves of the Eastwood, her small fire burning low, and then turning to embers, and then going out altogether.

The next day was much like the first, and most of the following day as well, but then she came to a small two-track byway that led to the Crossland Road, there where Byroad Lane started or ended, depending on which way one fared. Up the lane she went and through Budgens, where at the north end of that hamlet stood a monument on a knoll. Nineteen names were scribed thereon, names of the Warrows who had fallen during the Battle of Budgens during the Winter War. Scribed thereon as well were the words: LET IT BE SAID NOW AND FOR ALL THE DAYS HEREAFTER THAT ON THIS DAY THE STRUGGLE BEGAN, AND EVIL MET ITS MATCH.

Past this knoll rode Trissa, and through a ford, where she paused to let her pony take water. Then on she went, the road rising and falling, but she could see on the slopes on the far side of a swift-running rill the village of Woody Hollow.

She rode over a bridge above the stream and past a mill and into the streets of the town. Ahead she could see, at the edge of the lane, hanging by hook and eye from a post arm, a painted signboard swinging slightly in the breeze and proclaiming the establishment to be the One-Eyed Crow. On the placard, a black bird with cocked head and gimlet eye stared out at passersby, as if examining them for shiny objects that birds such as these are said to covet.

On the stoop before this small clapboard sided, thatch roofed inn sat a pair of granther buccen, mugs of ale in hand, the two enjoying the sun in the September air.

"Could you tell me the way to The Root?" called Trissa.

"Just keep going, young dammsel," replied one of the oldsters, his voice a bit thin and reedy. "Stay on this street till it comes to a long curve sweeping left, and when it sweeps right take the first lane on the left."

"Thank you," called Trissa, and up the long road she went to finally come to the lane, and then to the burrow known as The Root.

Dismounting, she tied her pony to a hitching post, and then went up the rock-lined pathway to the door and knocked, in spite of the sign that said CLOSED.

Moments later, a black-haired, blue-eyed buccan answered. He looked at her and then at the sign, and, frowning, he said, "I'm afraid The Root's not open. You'll have to come back on the morrow, and even then we might still be closed."

"Oh, but I've come such a long way," said Trissa, as a chestnut-haired buccan came and looked over the other one's shoulder. "And I'm not here to take the historical tour."

"You're not?" said the first buccan. "Then why . . . ?"

"Well, you see, I had this dream, or perhaps saw an apparition or specter or some such, of a king, the moonlight went straight through, and there is this armor, and I'm the last of Patrel's line, and, oh, I'm not making any sense at all, am I?"

"You are making perfectly good sense," said the black-haired buccan, pulling her inside. "We've been expecting you, Captain."

Pipper stopped to take a drink of ale, and he motioned for Binkton to carry on.

"Well," said Binkton, "as you might imagine, Cousin Triss was startled at anyone calling her 'Captain.' But as soon as they got her inside, they took her jacket and introduced themselves and went to the dining room and explained it all. . . ."

"Lieutenant Danby Candlewood of The Root, at your service, Captain," said the dark-haired buccan, hanging Trissa's leather jacket on a peg by the door. "And this is Lieutenant Kipley Larkspur of Willowdell."

Kipley bowed and said, "At your service as well."

Trissa saw before her two young buccen, both in their middle twenties, Danby standing some three foot six, amber-eyed Kipley three foot seven. They in turn saw a fair-haired, green-eyed young damman, perhaps just barely twenty, who stood no more than three foot one, if even that.

In spite of her confusion at being called "Captain," Trissa said, "Trissa Buckthorn of Midwood. —Or just outside it, rather."

"Come, come," said Danby. "Let us sit. We were just about to have afternoon tea. We can speak of High King Aurion—or his ghost, that is—and what we have to do, for Aurion Redeye came to us as well . . . let me see, what was it, four nights past?"

As they walked along a walnut-wood-panelled hallway, with day shining down through several small skylights along its length, both Kipley and Trissa affirmed, indeed, that it had been four nights past, and Danby said, "Ah, well, with your answer, Captain, I see he got to all three of us in the very same darktide."

"Mayhap in the very same candlemark," said Kipley. He glanced at Trissa and said, "I take it your bedroom is on the east side of your dwelling?"

"Y-yes," said Trissa, "but how did you know that?"

"Well, you said the moonlight went straight through," said Kipley.

Trissa frowned. "And . . . ?"

Kipley grinned. "You see, my bedroom is on the east side of my cote, too, and the half-moon had just risen and its light was shining right across and through King Redeye, and for it to do that, well, it had to be right at the marks of midnight, for that's when a waning half-moon rises. And since a waning half-moon is directly overhead at dawn, well, your room simply couldn't have been on the west side, for the sun would be up before any moonlight reached those windows."

"In my case," said Danby, "it was only the stars beaming down through the overhead glass that shone through the specter, for I fell asleep in the study, and its main window faces the west. The moon was on the wrong side for me, and the skylight hadn't yet admitted any of its beams, and so I am uncertain as to the time of night King Redeye appeared, though I think Kipley's right—he came in the mid marks of night."

As Danby turned into the dining room, which had a skylight in its ceiling as well, Trissa said, "You're talking as if seeing a ghost is the most common thing in the world, and what seems to interest both of you is whether or not the moon was up or down."

Kipley laughed. "I came three days ago, and Danby and I have been at this since then, and it's nearly all we've left to talk about."

Trissa shook her head and said, "Well, if that's your interest—moonlight and such—why couldn't my bedchamber be on the south or north?"

Kipley grinned. "Well, you said 'straight through,' and I took that to mean straight on, and if your room faced the south the angle would be a glancing one rather than straight on."

"And the north?" said Trissa.

Kipley barked a laugh and said, "On the north you wouldn't get any direct moonlight at all."

"Oh. Right," said Trissa, feeling a bit foolish.

"It's a puzzle, though," mused Danby, pulling out a chair for Trissa. "I mean, how could an apparition appear to the three of us simultaneously?" He looked at Kipley, but that buccan merely shrugged.

As Trissa took the proffered seat, a damman bearing a tea service entered the chamber. She paused and looked at Trissa and said, "And just who might this be?"

"Mother," said Danby, "this is Captain Patrel"—he slapped his forehead with the palm of a hand—"er, rather, Captain Trissa Buckthorn. She's the last of Patrel's line and has been summoned, too. Captain Buckthorn, my mother, Iris Candlewood."

"Oh, my dear," said Iris, setting the tea service to the table and then looking sympathetically at Trissa, "did you see the ghost of the King as well?"

As Trissa nodded, Iris said, "Well then, there's nothing for it, but that you must answer the call."

"But I am so ignorant," said Trissa. "I'm just a simple crofter on my granther's farm just north of Midwood, and I don't know much of what this is all about, nor even what questions to ask. I especially don't know why these two persist in calling me 'Captain.' "

"Well, my Danby is a Ravenbook Scholar, and he will sort all things out for you," said Iris. Beaming, she turned to her bucco. "I'm off to the market, Danny. I'll be back in a trice. In the meanwhile, tell this pretty damman what she needs to know. And for Adon's sake, tell her why she is the captain."

With that, Iris swept from the chamber, leaving Trissa and Danby and Kipley in her wake.

Trissa watched her go, then turned to Danby and said, "Well . . . ?"

"Kip, would you serve," said the blue-eyed buccan. "I'll be right back."

As Danby rushed from the room, Kipley took up the teapot and filled three cups. "Milk? Honey?"

Looking in the direction Danby had gone, Trissa said, "Milk, please." She turned back to Kipley. "Everyone seems to have rushed off but you and me."

Kipley smiled and passed her a cup and saucer, and a small plate for the biscuits. "Oh, I expect Danby'll be right back. I think he—"

Danby came hurrying in, a rather large and thick, grey, leather-bound tome under one arm. "I've brought my copy of *The Ravenbook,* Captain," he said, plopping the voluminous work down next to Trissa, "so that you can read some of the relevant passages for yourself."

He took his own cup of honey-sweetened tea from Kipley, along with one of the small plates.

Kipley passed the biscuits around, and when all had been served, Danby asked, "Now, for your questions, Captain."

Trissa looked first at one buccan and then the other and said, "Why do you insist on calling me 'Captain' and yourselves 'Lieutenant'?"

"Well, it's right here," said Danby, opening the book and thumbing through pages until he came to the place he sought. "It was right after a buccan named Tarpy was accidentally killed as he tried to defend the King's messenger from a Vulg sent by Modru to stop him from rallying the Boskydells."

He turned the book about for her to read. . . .

Captain Darby called the Thornwalker Fourth together at Spindle Ford, and a service was said for Tarpy, and for the unnamed herald. And through it all, Tuck's eyes remained dry, although many others wept. And then Captain Darby spoke to all the company:

"Buccen, though we have lost a comrade, life goes on. The High King has called a muster at Challerain Keep, and some from the Bosky are duty-bound to answer. I will send couriers to start the word spreading, and others then will respond to the call. Yet some must go forth now and be foremost to answer. It has fallen our lot to be the first to choose, and these are the choices: to remain and ward the Bosky, or to answer the King's summons. I call upon each now to consider well and carefully, and then give your answer. What will it be? Will you Walk the Thorns of the Seven Dells, or will you instead stride the ramparts of Challerain Keep?"

Silence descended upon the Thornwalkers as each contemplated his answer—silence, that is, except for one who had already made up his mind: Tuck stepped forward five paces until he stood on the ice alone. "Captain Darby," he called, and all heard him, "I will go to the High King, for Evil Modru has a great wrong to answer for. —Nay! two wrongs: one lies atop the Rooks' Roost, the other sleeps 'neath this frozen river."

Danner strode forward to stand beside Tuck, and so, too, did Patrel. Arbin, Dilby, Delber, and Argo joined them, and so did all of Patrel's squad. Then came others, until a second squad had formed. More began to step forward, but Captain Darby cried, "Hold! No more now! We cannot leave the ford unguarded. Yet, heed: when others come to join our company, then again will I give you the same choice. Until that time, though, these two squads will be first, and the High King could not ask for better.

"Hearken unto me, for this shall be the way of it: Patrel Rushlock, you are named captain of this Company of the King, and your squad leaders are to be Danner Bramblethorn of the first squad and Tuckerby Underbank of the second. Captain Patrel, as more squads are formed, they shall be dispatched to your command. And this is the last order I shall give you: lead well. And to the Company of the King, I say this: walk in honor."

The next morning, forty-three grim-faced Boskydell Warrows rode forth from the Great Spindlethorn Barrier and into the land of Rian. They came out along the road across Spindle Ford, each armed with bow and arrows and cloaked in Thornwalker grey. Their destination was Challerain Keep, for they had been summoned.

Trissa looked up from her reading. "And what has this to do with you calling me 'Captain'?"

"Don't you see," said Danby, "Patrel was named captain, and Danner and Tuckerby were named his lieutenants. You are the last of Patrel Rushlock's line, and Kip and I are in the line of Danner and Tuckerby. So, you are the captain and we are—"

"Oh, no," said Trissa. "I am no captain."

"Well, you just have to be," said Danby. "For I am entirely too harebrained and Kipley is too, um, how did you put it, Kip?"

"Too much of a woolgatherer," said Kipley. "We need a leader, not a dreamer nor a scatterbrain."

"B-but—" sputtered Trissa.

Danby interrupted: "Have you any common sense, Captain?"

"My granther says I do," said Trissa.

"Well, there you are," said Danby. "We haven't a shred of it, you see."

Trissa looked from one to the other. "And we are to form a Company of the King and go to the plains of Valon? A fledgling, a scatterbrain, and a dreamer?"

At Danby and Kipley's vigorous nods, Trissa said, "Adon, help us."

"He'll have to," said Danby. "You see, before we can go to Valon, we'll first have to go to Gron—or at least Kip has to go—to Gron, to Claw Moor, to the very doorstone of the Iron Tower itself and rob a tomb."

"What?" exclaimed Trissa, looking at Kipley. "Whatever for?"

"Well, you see," said Kipley, "that's where the black armor is."

In the Red Slipper Binkton stopped and took a long pull on his tankard, and Pipper said, "Those three spent the rest of the day talking of their ancestors and such, and making plans for the days ahead, Cousin Triss doing most of the thinking, for it seems Danby was right: neither he nor Kipley appeared to have a lick of common sense. . . ."

After Trissa took care of her pony and washed up from her travels, Iris called them all to dinner, and they spoke of how The Root had come to be a repository of artifacts from the Winter War, and they talked of the Ravenbook Scholars.

Iris said, "The Candlewoods, Greylocks, Fairhills, Underbanks and other such have always been Ravenbook Scholars." She turned to her bucco and beamed at him.

"Not always, Mother," said Danby, "not always. There were none before the Winter War." He turned to Trissa. "You see, Captain, it all started when Raven Underbank, Tuckerby and Merrilee's only child, their dammsel, helped Tuck complete the history of that conflict at the behest of the High King, as recorded in *Sir Tuckerbank's Unfinished Diary and His Accounting of the Winter War.* That's it's *official* name, and quite a mouthful it is. But Tuck himself saved us from that jawbreaker, for he called the final work *The Ravenbook*, after his dammsel Raven, for she oversaw the scholars who came to help with the work, and she did much of the scribing herself and was a great help in the research. Tuck was blind, you see, and he needed her aid. Anyway, she married Willen Greylock and had a daughter, Robin, and she married a Fairhill, and had her own children, and so on and so forth through many begettings, until my own sire was born—Bromley Candlewood—and he and my mum had me. And so that's how Tuckerby's blood came to flow in my veins."

At the mention of Bromley's name, Trissa noted that tears sprang into Iris's eyes, and so Trissa did not ask where Danby's sire was. Instead she said, "And what about you, Kipley? How are you linked to Danner?"

"Oh, me, ah, well, hurm . . ." Kipley took a drink of tea. "It's not clear at all how Danner's blood came to me. Y'see, there's some that say he never took a mate. It's for certain that he never married, else that would have been recorded in Tuck's diary, and therefore in *The Ravenbook.* Family rumor has it that when Danner was in the Dinglewood, he and a damman went off in the forest, and, well, you know. Then again it might have been in the Eastwood, back when they getting ready to free Brackenboro from the Ghûls. And there's some who say that he didn't have a child whatsoever, but that his sire and dam—Hanlo and Glory Bramblethorn—birthed another babe, now that Danner was gone.

"Regardless, whether it was through Danner and some unknown damman, or through Danner's own sire and dam, down through the ages Danner's blood came to me, or so King Redeye's visit at my cote in the night would seem to say."

"Then again, maybe it was someone Danner trusted," said Danby. "After all, *The Ravenbook* says that the armor could be, as King Aurion said, 'in the possession of those you would trust.' "

"But Danner's armor is not in the possession of anyone, except perhaps Danner's ghost," said Kipley. "But you're right, Danby; maybe I don't have any of Danner's blood whatsoever. Perhaps it's the blood of someone he would trust."

Trissa said, "My granther told me 'who better to trust than one directly in your own line?' and so, Kipley, I think you must be directly linked to Danner, mysterious damman or no."

"What about you, Captain?" asked Danby. "How did Patrel's blood come to you?"

"In a rather straight line," said Trissa. "Family history has it that after the Winter War, Patrel gave up being a Thornwalker altogether and became a bard instead. In a quiet ceremony with no fanfare whatsoever, he married another bard—Gayla, I think, was her name—and they had children. And the firstborns married and had buccoes and dammsels of their own. And so it went down through many firstborns, though somewhere along the way, at least one firstborn was a dammsel, perhaps more firstborns were dammsels, too. Regardless, one of these firstborn dammsels married a Buckthorn. Finally, Patrel's blood came to my sire, and he and my dam had me. I didn't know my parents at all well; I have only a handful of vague memories of them. You see, they were killed by a falling tree in the Eastwood during a storm."

"Oh, I'm sorry," said Danby. "My own sire is dead, too, of the fever, four years back."

Iris got up from the table and went through the door to the kitchen.

Trissa watched her go. "I was but a youngling of three when my parents were killed, and even though Da had two sisters, I was raised by Granther Buckthorn. Even so, as I say, I am told I descended from Patrel in a rather straight line." Trissa looked at Danby and Kipley and sighed and shook her head. "Ah, three heroes of the Winter War a thousand years agone, and it all came down to the three of us, in whose very own veins flows the anointed blood of Tuck, Danner, and Patrel."

A silence fell over the trio, but then Kipley said, "Just our luck, eh?"

"Right," said Trissa, as Danby nodded, for they both knew what Kipley meant.

Iris returned from the kitchen, bearing a peach cobbler for dessert. Trissa saw that her eyes were yet bright with tears, but she said nought.

After dessert, Trissa insisted on helping with the dishes, and she and Iris stood in the kitchen, Trissa scraping and washing, Iris drying and putting away.

"Danby's all I have left," said Iris. "I'm afraid for him."

"Me, too, I'm afraid," said Trissa.

"Even so, dear," said Iris, "you and he and Kipley have to answer to the High King's call."

Of a sudden Iris broke into tears, and Trissa embraced her, and Iris whispered, "Take care of my bucco, please."

"I will," murmured Trissa in response, though she didn't know how she could.

Finally, the dishes were done, and Iris poured three cups of tea and put milk in one for Trissa and honey in another for Danby and both in the cup for Kipley, and then she sent Trissa out the side door and down the hall with the tray to join Danby and Kipley in the study. It was a rather large room, walnut-panelled with a window opening onto the west and a skylight overhead. There were several comfortable chairs therein, some sized to fit Men, as were the heavily beamed ceilings throughout The Root. Bookcases lined the walls, and scrolls and tomes and pamphlets were jammed rather helter-skelter upon the shelves. A large and quite ornate walnut desk sat out from one of the walls, a writing table out from another. Small end tables sat at hand by the chairs, with small, lit lanterns thereon, for evening drew down on the land.

After Trissa served each with a cup of tea and sat down, she said, "About this call of the King, what do you have in mind?"

"Um, er, Captain, we were hoping you would know what to do," said Danby, Kipley nodding in agreement.

"Hmm . . ." Trissa set her tea aside and stood and stepped to the open window. A cool September breeze wafted through, and the *chirrup*ing of crickets sounded in the dusk. "Well, I would like to see the armor that brought me here, but first—"

"Oh," said Danby, leaping to his feet, "let me take you to it. We can—"

"No, no, Danby," said Trissa. "Not yet. As I was about to say—"

"But, Captain, it will only take a momen—"

"Lieutenant, be seated," snapped Trissa.

"Um, uh, well, right, yes sir, er, ma'am," said Danby, and he eased back onto the edge of his chair, ready to spring into action if so ordered.

"Does this mean you'll be our captain, Captain?" asked Kipley.

"Have I any choice?" said Trissa.

Kipley and Danby looked at one another and grinned, and then at Trissa and shook their heads.

Trissa shook her own head and then put her hands behind her back and began pacing. "It seems we need to do the following things:

"First, get someone to begin rounding up forty Thornwalkers to form the Company of the King. And to do that, I need to know who is in charge of the Thornwalkers in these parts." She stopped in her tracks and looked at Danby and Kipley, and they both stared back at her blankly.

Trissa sighed and began pacing again. "Regardless, we can find out on the morrow. From what Redeye said, we'll need them assembled and ready by Yule Eve, though what a coin has to do with it, I haven't a clue."

"Oh, that," said Danby. "It just means the High King will send a Gjeenian penny to the Bosky calling for aid."

Trissa stopped in her pacing. "A Gjeenian penny?"

"Yes," said Danby. "It hearkens back to the time of the Great War of the Ban, when a Gjeenian penny was used by the High King to summon King Agron and his army to aid in a war. The penny was borne by Tipperton Thistledown and Beau Darby from the Wilderland to—"

Trissa pushed out a hand to stop Danby's flow of words. "Danby, it is enough that it is a symbol for summons. You can tell me the entire tale on our journey to Gron.

"And speaking of that journey"—Trissa took up her pacing again—"the second thing we'll need is a map to see just how far we have to go to fetch the black armor." Again she paused and looked at Danby. "Have we such a map that will show the way? —No, no, don't get up, Lieutenant, just answer the question."

At Danby's nod, again Trissa began pacing. "Third, we'll need to think of what will be required to make the journey to the Iron Tower and back, including how many and what type of weapons we need." Again she paused and looked at the two of them. "Does either of you wield a bow or sling or long-knife?"

Kipley nodded. "Even though I'm a simple apprentice—my sire's a glassblower; we make bottles and mugs and vases and such—I have a fair hand at loosing an arrow. And I've been known to hurl a sling bullet with accuracy, as well as have some skill with a long-knife."

Trissa smiled. "Good." She turned to Danby, and he shook his head.

"You have no weapon skills whatsoever?" asked Trissa.

"I'm a scholar, Captain, not a warrior," replied Danby.

Trissa took a deep breath and slowly let it out and again stepped to the window and looked at the distant sky all lavender and indigo in the fading twilight. "Well, there's nothing for it but that we'll simply have to teach Danby while we are on the way to and from the Iron Tower. Kip, you'll be our weaponsmaster."

"Yes ma'am," said Kipley, grinning.

Trissa turned from the window and said, "I'll need lessons in slinging and blade work. Danby, you'll take lessons in bow and blade.

"Now, as to strategy and tactics—"

"Oh. Oh," said Danby, holding up his hand as if he were in a classroom.

"Yes, Lieutenant," said Trissa.

"Well, Captain, I have read of all the battles and ambushes and skirmishes of the Great War of the Ban, and of the Winter War, and of the Battle of Kraggen-cor. I have also pored over the notes of the Ravenbook Scholars on these things. Studying the strategy and tactics of all the encounters you might say is a hobby of mine."

"Have you any practical experience in these things?" asked Trissa.

"No, Captain. None whatsoever."

Again Trissa sighed. "It's academic knowledge, then, eh?"

"Well, Captain," said Danby, a slight edge to his voice, "it's not as if we've had any wars to fight in the last seven hundred and eighty years."

"You're right, Danby, and I apologize. But, list, you will have to teach Kipley and me what you know of these things on the way to and from the Iron Tower as well."

"And on the trip to Valon," said Kipley.

"Oh, yes," said Trissa. "On the way to Valon, too."

Danby grinned and settled back in his chair, and Trissa said, "All right, here's what we'll do. First I want to see the armor." Trissa pushed out a hand to stop Danby from leaping up. "Then we'll look at the map and plan our journey to Gron as well as to the ferry in Valon, wherever that is."

"I think that has to be the Argon Ferry, Captain," said Danby.

"Have you a map showing that as well?" said Trissa.

Danby nodded. "Well and good," said Trissa. Then she said, "On the morrow we have several things to do: Danby, you will find out who the leader of the Thornwalkers is 'round these parts; Kipley, you will arrange for whatever supplies we think we need for the journey; and I will arrange for the pack ponies we will need to bear those supplies. —Oh, my. We'll need funds. I have but three silver pennies, and—"

"As a Ravenbook Scholar, I get an annual stipend from High King Garon," said Danby, "though I don't know if I have enough put away for our needs."

"If not, Danby, then we'll have to go begging," said Trissa.

Kipley cleared his throat and said, "Don't you think, Captain, since this is the High King's business, merchants and hostlers and the Thornwalkers will gladly pay the way, knowing that the High King will reimburse them?"

"Especially if you go, um, 'begging' properly accoutered," added Danby, "in the golden armor and all, a sword at your side, a bow at your back, a quiver at your hip and such."

"What, me? Wear the armor?" said Trissa.

"Did you think that you were simply going to sling it over the back of your pony, Captain?" said Kipley. "Especially when we ride into Gron, or Valon, or anywhere along the—"

"All right, all right, Lieutenant," said Trissa. "I get your drift. I'll wear the armor and other such." She looked at Danby. "Speaking of the armor, perhaps we need to see if it even fits."

Danby, hesitant, asked, "You mean right now, Captain?"

"Yes, Lieutenant, right now."

Danby shot out of his seat like a sling bullet loosed. He snatched up a lamp and, calling out, "Follow me," through the doorway and down the hallway he bolted. By the time Trissa and Kipley reached the corridor, Danby had vanished. Trissa turned to Kipley, a question in her eyes, but before she could speak, Danby poked his head out from an archway and said, "Well, come on, you two slow coaches, the candlemarks are melting away, and— Oh, um, er, I'm sorry, Captain. I shouldn't have called you a—"

Trissa waved a hand of dismissal as she stepped into another one of the large, high-ceilinged, walnut-panelled rooms. It held an impressive array of arms and armor as well as cloaks and boots and uniforms, some of them Warrow-sized, others obviously meant for Men. Flags and shields and spears adorned the walls, as well as paintings and portraits and sketches and maps and such, their shadows cast upward by the lamplight. Glass cases held daggers and horns and slings and other small items, including coins and diaries and small mementos.

"Here's where we bring visitors, Captain," said Danby, rushing about the chamber and lighting lanterns in wall sconces, "those who've come to see things from the Winter War, and the War of Kraggen-cor, and even some such items hearking all the way back to the Great War of the Ban."

"Oh, my," said Trissa, her eyes wide with the wonder of it all, for she had never seen such ere now. "It's quite an array."

"Yes, it got to be too much for the study, so we dug out this chamber and bricked and timbered and finally panelled it and moved everything in here, including the mementos we had in storage."

With the room now well lit, Danby stepped to a stand where gilded armor was racked, along with a simple iron and leather helm and a man's long-knife—just the right length to be a sword for a Warrow. "Here we are, Captain. This was Patrel's."

"Let's see if it fits," said Kipley.

"Oh, my," said Trissa, "but I am rather small for a buccan's armor."

Danby laughed. "Did you know that Patrel was only three feet tall? And you are, what, three feet as well?"

"I'm three foot and a quarter inch," huffed Trissa, straightening up to her full height.

Kipley grinned. "And a quarter inch, eh?"

"Indeed," said Trissa, then she returned Kipley's grin. "Oh, well, let me try it on."

As they fitted her into the chain, Danby said, "Um, er, it might be a bit tight about the, uh, hem, ah—"

"Bosom?" suggested Trissa.

Danby reddened, but said, "Ah, hurm, yes, bosom."

The chain shirt fit splendidly.

"I say," said Danby, "while I slip into Tuck's old mail, Kip, fit her out with helm and blade."

As Danby took up the silver chain, Kipley handed Trissa the leather-and-iron helm, and after she donned it, he asked, "Are you left-handed or right-?"

"Right," she said, and Kipley then clipped a long-knife in its sheath to the scabbard-rings on the left side of the belt.

"I said I was right-handed," said Trissa.

"Yes," replied Kipley, "and you put a sword on the left side to make it easier to draw by reaching across and pulling it."

Trissa withdrew the long-knife from its scabbard. "Ah, yes." Then she added, "Oh, my," upon seeing the golden runes along the glittering steel.

To one side, Danby said, "That long-knife is known as the Atalar Blade, for it was forged in Duellin, and it came from the tomb of Othran the Seer. It was borne for a time by High King Galen during the Winter War. Galen gave it over to Patrel to take with him when he went with the Raiders to fell the bridge at the Iron Tower."

"These runes," said Trissa, "what do they say?"

"I think none knows," answered Danby. "I think they must be in the language of the gods."

Trissa sighed and looked at Kipley. He shrugged, for he knew not what the runes meant either. Trissa then tried to resheathe the blade, but ran into difficulty.

"Steady the scabbard with your left and angle it for the return," said Kipley.

She did so, and it went in without a hitch.

"Here," said Danby, now accoutered in the silveron mail and helm, with a long-knife at his own belt. Over Trissa's shoulder he draped a green-and-white baldric, a small argent horn thereon. "It's the Horn of the Reach," he said, when she looked at him questioningly. "You'll use it to signal or rally the Company of the King."

"The Horn of the Reach," breathed Trissa, holding the horn reverently. Then she looked at Danby. "The Horn of Narok?"

Danby nodded. "It won the War of Kraggen-cor."

"Oh, my," said Trissa. "But I don't know how to sound a horn. You'd better keep it, Danby."

Danby shook his head. "No, no. It belongs to the captain of the Company of the King. I'll teach you how to blow it on the way to the Iron Tower."

Kipley laughed. "It seems we'll all be learning from one another as we go—strategy and tactics, plying weapons, and sounding horns . . . and if you can, Captain, you'll have to teach us common sense, and that might be harder than you think."

As Trissa laughed, Danby said, "Now all we need do is get the black mail for Kip, and then we'll make a fine trio, don't you think?"

In that moment Iris came into the room, and when she saw Trissa and Danby armed and armored for war, she burst into tears and fled.

In the Red Slipper, all sat quiet while Pipper took a long sip of the Vornholt, and when he set the large tankard aside and gestured at Binkton, that buccan took up the next part of the tale:

"Cousin Triss and Danby and Kipley then looked at the map hanging high on one of the walls, and they picked out the route they would travel to get to Danner's tomb, there at the Iron Tower. . . ."

"Just where are we and where is this tower?" asked Trissa as she looked at the cloth map hanging on the wall, the canvas patched here and there and stained with age, its lower edge burnt as if it had been rescued from a fire.

Danby took a long tapered stick and raised it up to not quite touch the old fabric. "Here is Woody Hollow, and way up here"—he raised the pointer—"is Gron, and just over here is the Iron Tower."

"My goodness," said Trissa. "It seems as if from here to there might be quite a long way. What is the scale of this map? And, oh, have you one on vellum, one that we can lay out flat and not put our necks in cricks looking up as we are?"

"Oh, certainly," said Danby. He set aside the stick and stepped to a cabinet and retrieved a roll. "Here, let's take this to the dining room where we can spread it out on the table."

Moments later the map was lying flat on the board, its corners held down by saltcellars and pepper mills.

"Let me see. . . ." said Trissa. Using the scale and the span of her hand and following the route indicated by Danby, she measured off the distance from Woody Hollow to the Iron Tower. "Oh, my. That's some seven hundred miles altogether." She frowned. "Just to get there that's two fortnights and a sevenday by pony, if we don't run into trouble."

"Mayhap a bit more," said Danby. "Grûwen Pass is quite rugged, they say."

Trissa nodded. "All right, three fortnights going, and a like amount to get back. Six fortnights altogether. If we leave within a day or so, then it will be early December when we return."

"Well, then," said Kipley, "that's before Year's Long Night—First Yule. That ought to make Redeye happy, since that was the day he said we needed to be ready."

Danby shook his head. "Actually, what he said is that First Yule is when the coin will come . . . the summons from High King Garon."

"Regardless," said Kipley, "if we get back in early December, then we'll meet Redeye's date."

"Only if the Company of the King is ready as well," said Trissa, "and for that we need the aid of the Thornwalker captain of Woody Hollow. But we'll take care of that on the morrow. For now, we have a journey to plan." Again she looked at the map. "What towns are along the way?"

"In the Bosky or out?" asked Danby.

"Beyond the Thornwall," said Trissa.

"Why, Stonehill," said Danby, pointing. "Then there's a small village of Greenslope along the Crossland Road right at the edge of the Wilderness Hills in the Wilderland. But farther on, I don't know of a thing. Oh, some isolated farms and such are out there, but I know of no towns in Drearwood or past, except maybe Arden Vale; but there's a rumor that after the Winter War the Elvenholt was abandoned. I don't know if that's true or false, but we can't count on help from them."

"Well, then," said Trissa, "I assume that in Stonehill and Greenslope we can replace what we have used, but I don't think we can count on the crofters along the way to have what we might need. If we assume we'll need provender for ourselves and the ponies for at least eighty or so days altogether, I'd say we each need a pony to ride as well as two pack-ponies apiece simply to carry our food. That's three horselings each, nine altogether."

"You rode in here on one, Captain," said Kipley, "and I have mine. What about you, Danby?"

"I don't have a pony," said the scholar.

"You don't?" said Kipley. "Then how do you get around?"

"I walk," said Danby. "If it's a long journey, I take the Red Coach."

"Back to the task at hand," said Trissa. "Where can I arrange for seven more ponies altogether?"

"There's a stable down at the Pony Field," said Danby. "Mr. Peacher runs it."

"What about the journey to the Argon Ferry?" said Kipley. "Don't we need to plan that as well?"

"Where is the ferry?" asked Trissa.

Danby pointed and again Trissa used the span of her hand to gauge the distance. "Goodness, that's right at a thousand miles . . . fifty days of travel or so. Should we leave when the coin comes, then that will put us there in late February or early March."

"If Ralo Pass is not snowed in," said Kipley, pointing at the col through the Grimwall between Rell and Gûnar.

"Perhaps we ought to go through Gûnar Slot," said Danby, pointing at a notch well east of the pass.

"Hmm . . ." mused Trissa. "That adds mayhap a hundred miles—five days—to the overall journey."

"But it's safer," said Danby.

"We'll cross that bridge when we come to it," said Trissa. She looked at Danby. "What I want to know is, King Redeye spoke of the Trine. Just what is the Trine?"

Danby shrugged. "I don't know, but perhaps some of the Ravenbook Scholars might."

"And where are these scholars?"

"Oh, most of them are at the Cliffs, over in Westdell," said Danby.

"Well, we have to be at the ferry ere whenever the Trine falls, and so I think you need to send word and find out just what the Trine is."

Danby nodded. "I think my dam wants to go by the Red Coach to see some old friends there at the Cliffs. The west-running coach comes through two days from now. I'll ask her to see what they can tell us. After all, by the time we get back from Gron, she might have an answer."

Trissa nodded. "All right, then. It seems we have gathered all we can for now." She looked at each of them and said, "Here are our assignments for the morrow: Danby, you find out who the Thornwalker captain is hereabout, and bring him to The Root. I'll want to talk to him first thing. Kipley, as soon as we know who he is and convince him of our mission, you and he will arrange for eighty-four days of food for us to take on our journey to Gron; grain for the ponies and field rations for us, please, and not anything fancy; it has to be compact and able to last for six fortnights without spoilage: crue will do, and mayhap some bacon. Also get a small supply of cooking gear, just in case we down a bit of game. We'll need a lantern or two, as well as rope and—"

Kipley pushed out a hand to stop her flow of words. "Captain, I've spent many a night out on the hunt. I think I can supply us quite well."

Trissa nodded and then said, "It'll be cold in Gron, and winter ere we return, and winter when we ride to Valon. We'll need quilted down clothing to—"

"Oh, my," said Danby. "I have some of the cold-weather gear in storage worn by Warrows during the Winter War. If it's yet good then it might do."

"Very well," said Trissa. She frowned in thought and then said, "After you arrange for the supplies, Kipley, then I'll go with the Thornwalker captain and arrange for the ponies and their grain as well.

"Danby, we'll need good maps to guide us. —Oh, and I think we all need to make copies of King Redeye's words, as many as we can before we have to leave. Have your dam help us in that task. I think the Thornwalker captain will need them."

She paused a moment in thought, and finally shrugged and said, "Does either of you have any suggestions or questions? No? Well then, what say we get some sleep? After all, we've a busy day coming."

"Yes ma'am," said Danby, taking up one of the lamps. "Your quarters are this way, Captain."

Danby showed her to a bedchamber, and as he and Kipley walked away Trissa overheard Danby remarking to Kipley, "I say, did you see how easily she planned and all? It seems she does have common sense, eh?"

"Right," said Kipley, "and it's a good thing, too, for neither you nor I have a lick of it, and that's for certain. I mean, here we've been for three days now, and in less than three candlemarks she's come up with what we need to do just to get started, and . . ."

Kipley's voice faded away as the two of them turned a hallway corner. Behind, Trissa softly closed the door to her chamber. "Oh, lor, if they're depending on me they truly must be desperate."

But as she was drifting off to sleep, she seemed to hear her granther's voice: *Yours is the armor to wear. Yours is the burden to bear. Desperate times call for desperate measures, and you have the blood of a hero in your veins.*

"Yes, Granther," Trissa murmured, "and it's that very same blood that has thrust the desperate times upon me."

"Captain Banderel, this is Captain Buckthorn of the King's Company," said Danby. "Captain Buckthorn, Captain Banderel."

Trissa stood and stepped 'round the desk and shook hands with Norv Banderel, that buccan looking from Danby to Trissa and back, his eyes wide with wonder at these armor-clad, weapon-bearing Warrows.

"The Company of the King, you say?" asked Norv.

"Indeed, Captain," said Trissa as she resumed her seat behind the desk. Silver-clad Danby took a stance back and to her right, while leather-clad Kipley stood to her left.

They were in the study at The Root, a place where Norv had never been. Oh, once apast he had toured the memento room, but never had he been elsewhere in this burrow. And the sight of a damman in golden armor, along with the buccan in silver and another in leather, and with the flags of the Bosky and of Pellar on staffs behind and to either side of her, well, it looked so very *official.*

Even so, Norv said, "What can I do for you, Captain?"

Trissa took a deep breath and said, "High King Aurion tells me, rather, told the three of us, that there is a great storm coming from the east, and that Warrows are wanted. I would have you send out word to the Thornwalkers that forty are needed to serve—the number of the original Company of the King during the Winter War."

"Forty, eh?"

"Forty who are good with bow and arrow, and whatever other weapons skills they might have," said Trissa.

"And when—? Hoy, now, wait a moment, did you say High King Aurion? Aurion Redeye?" asked Norv.

Trissa stood and stepped 'round the desk again and gestured to one of the comfortable chairs. "Have a seat, Captain Banderel, for I have a tale to unfold."

In that moment, Iris swept in bearing a silver service, and then all sat down and took midmorning tea as Trissa told of Aurion's visitation. As Trissa concluded the tale she said, "Had Aurion Redeye simply come to one of us, perhaps it would merely have been a dream. To two of us, and mayhap it would simply have been a coincidence. But with him having come to all three, then it is a bodeful warning, and we need to take heed."

Norv scratched his chin and nodded. "Well, it's like those folks down to Budgens say, 'Whenever them Kings get into troubles they allus find they got to call on a Warrow or two to settle them troubles, whatever they might be.' " He looked at Trissa and said, "What would you have me do, Captain?"

"First, here are copies of what the specter of Aurion Redeye said, as we three collectively remember it." Trissa handed Norv a small bundle of handwritten notes she and Danby and Kipley and Iris had prepared that morning. Norv silently read the one on top:

The Visitation of High King Aurion Redeye

Patrel, Danner, Tuckerby, I now call ye and the Dwarven armor into service again, for a great storm is coming from the east, leaving nought but devastation in its wake. As ye did on Yule Eve, and must needs this Yule Eve as well, don the chain, take up thy bows, and gather the Company of the King, for that's when the coin will come, and these will be needed at the ferry in Valon a sevenday ere the Trine.

As Norv finished and looked up, Trissa said, "Captain Banderel, we know not what the apparition meant when he spoke of 'a great storm coming from the east,' yet I think he means war, hence I ask that you send riders with copies of this message to each of the Seven Dells and alert the Thornwalkers and the citizenry, for I would they all know the exact words. Have the mayors make copies and post them in every town square."

"Just a moment, Captain Buckthorn," said Norv, and from his coat pocket he pulled out a small case and opened it. Inside were a notebook and a capped bottle and a quill. He uncapped the inkwell and set it on the table at hand, and put the case on his knee and began jotting notes. After a moment, he looked up. "Anything else?"

"Just in case the threat reaches this far, as was done in the Winter War, I suggest you assemble companies of Thornwalkers to barricade and ward each of the five entries through the Thornwall."

Norv frowned. "Five?"

Trissa nodded. "As I am reminded by Danby, the fifth one is the abandoned Northwood tunnel, whence the Horde came through during the Winter War."

"Ah, yes," said Norv, again writing in his book. "I had forgotten that bit of history." He looked up at Danby and grinned, and Danby shyly ducked his head.

Trissa said, "Next, as Redeye requested, assemble a Company of the King, forty Thornwalkers; all must be well skilled with the bow; whatever other weaponry they might have in their bag of tricks will come as a bonus. Outfit them with boiled-leather breastplates, for Danby tells me that is what the original company wore. Have them gather at the village of Stickle along the Tineway down by Tine Ford and be ready by First Yule—Year's Long Night—to travel to the Argon Ferry in Valon—ponies, supplies, and all. If Danby and Kipley and I are not back from Gron by then"—Iris gasped, but held her tongue—"appoint new captains and send them onward. It will be winter by then, so make certain that all are outfitted in cold-weather gear."

Trissa paused, and a moment later Norv looked up. "Right. Anything else?"

Trissa nodded. "I would also have you go to the market with Kipley and arrange for supplies for Kipley and Danby and me to travel to Gron and back: some six fortnights worth of food altogether; crue will do."

"Hmm . . ." said Norv, jotting again. "They'll be baking all night."

"We'll need even more to travel down to Valon," said Kipley. "It's nearly a thousand miles to the ferry."

"Right," said Norv, dashing another note. He looked up and grinned. "Worry not, for I will have the Company of the King well supplied if we have to strip the entire Bosky of field rations."

"Well and good," said Trissa. "After you and Kipley arrange for our trip to Gron and back, I would have you return here and go with me to the Pony Field, for though I have my own riding mount, as does Kipley, we will need one more for Danby to ride and six pack animals to bear our supplies, as well as carry rations of grain to sustain the steeds."

Norv grunted an assent.

"In the meanwhile," said Trissa, "those of us who are free will remain at The Root and make more copies of King Redeye's words."

Trissa turned to Iris and handed her a copy of Aurion's message. "Madam, I would have you catch the Red Coach and fare to the Cliffs in Westdell, and there set the Ravenbook Scholars to researching. We need to know just what this 'Trine' is and how it might bear on our mission, for we must be at the Argon Ferry at least a sevenday ere then. Whatever you and the Scholars discover, send word to us, or to Captain Banderel, and he will see it gets to us."

Iris took the note, and a look of relief mingled with determination passed across her face; after all, her bucco was going into peril, and whatever aid she could give, she would.

In the Red Slipper, Binkton paused for a gulp of the Vornholt, and Pipper took up the tale.

"It seems that Cousin Triss had a good head on her shoulders after all, and in a trice they had supplies and ponies, and messengers were riding pell-mell across the Bosky to each of the Seven Dells, bearing copies of Aurion Redeye's bodeful words.

"On the tenth of September Iris Candlewood boarded the Red Coach at its stop in Budgens and set out for the Cliffs, where the Ravenbook Scholars and their libraries were housed.

"On the tenth as well, Cousin Triss and Danby and Kipley, riding ponies and towing packponies bearing supplies and winter gear, set out for Gron, for Claw Moor, for the tomb before the gates of the Iron Tower, for that's where the black armor lay. . . ."

After a tearful farewell to Iris in Budgens, Trissa and Danby and Kipley set out for Gron, their destination some seven hundred miles away by the route they planned. They had not two, but three packponies each, for Mr. Peacher knew that more feed was needed for the ponies than either Trissa or Norv had calculated. And he advised them to replenish the grain at every town and farm along the way.

East along the Crossland Road they went, pausing in Willowdell for Kipley to fetch his bow and quiver and long-knife and a few other odds and ends, and to get a pry bar, for it had occurred to him that if they were going to break into his ancestor's tomb, such a tool might be needed. Then he told his sire and dam just where he was off to. They had already known of Redeye's visitation, and so it did not arrive as unexpected news. Even so, that Kipley was actually going into Gron came as a blow, and a second tearful farewell ensued.

They rode onward, and at every hamlet and town along the way, folks paused in their doings as the golden- and silveron- and leather-armored trio passed by. For Aurion Redeye's notice had been posted in the town squares, and every community was abuzz with the words.

They stopped in Raffin that eve, and the people came to the inn to see for themselves these descendants of heroes. Some were impressed, others not, yet all wished them a safe journey.

Trissa was somewhat embarrassed by all the attention, for she had done nought to deserve it, but Kipley seemed to revel in it, and shy Danby simply held back and spoke only when spoken to.

On they pressed the next day and passed into the miles-long tunnel through the Great Thornwall Barrier leading to The Bridge and continuing on beyond, the span itself along the Crossland Road over the Spindle River.

As they crossed the wooden-beamed bridge itself, Trissa paused to look at this marvel called the Spindlethorn Barrier:

Dense it was; even birds found it difficult to live deep within its embrace. Befanged it was, atangle with great spiked thorns, long and sharp and iron-hard, living stilettoes. High it was, rearing up thirty, forty, and in some places fifty feet above the river valleys from which it sprang. Wide it was, reaching across broad river vales, no less than a mile anywhere, and in places greater than ten. And long it was, stretching completely around the Boskydells, from the Northwood down the Spindle, and from the Updunes down the Wenden, until the two rivers joined one another; but after their merging, no farther south did the 'Thorn grow. It was said that only the soil of the Bosky in these two river valleys would nourish the Barrier. Yet the Warrows had managed to cultivate a long stretch of it, reaching from the Northwood to the Updunes, completing and closing the 'Ring. And so, why it did not grow across the rest of the land and push all else aside remained a mystery; though the grandams said, *It's Adon's will,* while the granthers said, *It's the soil,* and neither knew the which of it for certain.

Here at The Bridge, as well as at the other crossings—fords all—far in the past Warrows had worked long and hard to make ways through the Barrier, ways large enough for commerce: for waggons and horses and ponies and travellers. Oh, not to say that one couldn't penetrate the Barrier without travelling one of these Warrow-made ways, for one could push through the wild Spindlethorn; it just took patience and determination and skill to make it from side to side, for one had to be maze-wise to find a way, usually taking days to wriggle and slip and crawl through the random-fanged labyrinth from one marge to the other; and never did one penetrate without taking a share of wounds. No, even though Warrows seemed skilled at it, and legend said that Dwarves were even better, still ways through the Barrier must needs be made for travel and commerce.

But the work was arduous, for the Spindlethorn itself was hard, so hard that at times tools were made of it, and arrow-points and poniards from the thorns; and it burned only with great difficulty and would not sustain a blaze. Yet again and again, over many years, Warrows cut and sawed and chopped and dug, finally forming ways through the Barrier. And as if the Spindlethorn itself somehow could sense the commerce, the ways stayed open on the well-used routes; but on those where travel was infrequent, the 'Thorn grew slowly to refill the Warrow-made gap. Some had, in fact, been allowed to grow shut: the one at Northwood was one, though that took a great, long time, and had not yet completely closed on the far side of the river, and so it was "plugged" instead. But here at The Bridge and at Wenden Ford and Spindle Ford and Tine Ford, the ways had remained open, looking to all like dark, thorn-walled tunnels, for the Great Barrier was thickly interlaced overhead.

But as Trissa sat astride her pony on the wooden span above the Spindle River, a splash of blue sky slashed overhead.

"It's a wonder, isn't it?" said Kipley.

"Indeed," replied Trissa, then rode on into the tunnel beyond, all unwarded at this time, for peace lay upon the land, though that might soon change.

They camped that night and the next under the eaves of the Eastwood, that aged forest showing scarlets and golds and russets in the quickening autumn.

The next days they rode on and on, stopping in Stonehill overnight, and replenishing their supplies the next morn, and then pressing on.

Along the hills bordering the Weiunwood they fared, that shaggy forest to the north, the Bogland Bottoms to the south. And still on the Crossland Road they fared, the route heading easterly. The way curved between Beacontor and Northtor, the last two crests of the Signal Mountains, an ancient chain worn down by weather and wind to nought but craggy prominences upon which balefires were set to call Men to arms in the event of war.

And the days grew shorter, the nights longer, as eastward the trio went, and at dawn and dusk of each of these days, Kipley and Trissa trained Danby in bow and arrow. During the stops to feed and water the ponies, Trissa and Danby took lessons from Kipley in swordplay. As they rode, however, Danby taught Trissa how to sound the Horn of the Reach, her notes at first rather feeble, but gaining in strength as the journey progressed. When she could sound it well, he then began teaching her the various calls—assemble, retreat, ride at a trot, at a canter, a gallop, halt, the brisk morning call, the forlorn notes of "day is done," and other such needed horn cries. By day as well, Danby spoke of strategy and tactics and warfare, and of ambuscades and how to place members of a squad such that the arrows and other missiles loosed at the foe came at them from crossing angles and how that was a tactical advantage. Around their campfires at night, Danby drew in the soil and used pebbles to illustrate his points. And by the very questions Trissa asked and the single-mindedness she applied to a tactical problem at hand, and by the plans growing therefrom, though she was but a fledgling, mayhap by her example she did indeed begin to teach common sense to a scatterbrain and a dreamer. As she said, "It is a matter of priority and focus and bringing your knowledge to bear, as well as anticipating those things that might go wrong, and understanding consequences should they do so, and trying to find a way to avoid such calamities. When that becomes second nature, then common sense you will have."

Beyond Beacontor they came into the Wilderland, and there travel was swift, and some days they rode as much as thirty or so miles, while yet preserving their steeds.

In the main the weather favored them, for it was fall and the skies were usually clear, yet a time or two it drizzled upon them, and they and the ponies were miserable and chill.

Across this wold they went, staying in crofters' or hunters' dwellings or byres, replenishing whatever supplies they could at each stop. Finally, in the midst of a pouring rain, they came to Greenslope, and here they stayed in a warm, cozy inn, and had baths, and drank ale, and ate good hot fare, and slept in actual beds.

"Lor," said Danby, "but I didn't know how comfortable my life was until we came upon this rugged way."

Kipley burst out in laughter. "You think this is rugged? Wait until we get into Gron."

"As if you would know, Lieutenant," said Trissa.

"Well, Captain," said Kipley, "I can imagine."

The next morning it was raining still, and so they stayed another day, but that night the rain stopped, and in the morn they left the comfort of the inn. Here, too, they left the easy travel of the Crossland Road, and they struck out northeasterly through a long gap in the Wilderness Hills and headed for Drear Ford across the River Caire.

In midafternoon three days later they splashed through the chill waters and entered the land of Rhone, and angled east-northeast. To the south stood the Drearwood, and along its northern border rode the trio. They looked upon that dark tangle with apprehension, for though it was said that long years past the Men of the Wilderland and the Elves of Arden Vale had purged that dreadful snarl of Foul Folk and other creatures dire, still it was a place to be avoided, or so the three of them thought.

Four days later in the evening they came to a twenty-mile notch leading to Grûwen Pass, a thirty-five-mile rift through the join where the chain of the Rigga Mountains butted into that of the Grimwalls.

Kipley looked at the broad gap and said, "Beyond that slot lies Grûwen Pass, and beyond it lies Gron."

Danby said nought in response, but Trissa said, "We will start through on the morrow, but for now, I'll deal with the ponies, while you, Danby, get out your bow; Kipley will watch you shoot. Then after a bit of swordplay and our meal, I'd like to go over the strategy and tactics of ambuscades again."

And so, as they had routinely done, they fell into the ways of the camp, though ever since they had come unto Drearwood, they would take turns at watch through the night. And on watch with each of them was Danby's Elvenblade Bane, for it had a blade-jewel that was said to glow with a blue werelight should creatures of ill intent come nigh—Foul Folk in particular.

It took four days altogether to fare through the twenty-mile gap and the thirty-five miles of Grûwen Pass and the twenty-mile gap beyond, and each of these days Danby would relate to them details of the battle that had taken place there during the Winter War, when Vidron's Legion and the Lian of Arden Vale, dreadfully outnumbered, had withstood the onslaught of a full *Spaunen* Horde day after day after day.

"You see, the way is narrow at places," said Danby on the first day in the Pass, gesturing up at the stone rising about, "and the Horde couldn't bring their full force to bear on the scant number of Allies."

"A lesson well worth knowing," said Trissa, as onward they rode.

Each of two nights in the pass itself, spatterings of sleet were driven upon them as a frigid wind blew down from the towering crests above—or mayhap from the far-off Boreal Sea—and not only did the trio huddle in their winter gear and their blankets for warmth, but also they blanketed the steeds, for the ponies grew chill as well.

At last they cleared the narrow walls of the pass and the length of Grûwen Vale beyond, the stone of the valley dropping down toward the plains of Gron below, and that somber land seemed all rock and desolation and frost.

Onward they rode, day after day, the Grimwall Mountains to their right, the desolation of Gron to their left.

Along a narrow strip of land they fared and past the vast swamp known as the Gwasp, that dreadful mire looming leftward, steam rising from its decaying heart. Three nights in all they spent along its marge, and on those nights they heard splashings and ploppings and slitherings, and the calls of creatures they knew not, and on the second of those nights they heard a sobbing, as of a woman in distress. Yet Danby said that the sobbing was to be ignored, for it was not a person, but a creature dire instead. At night as well they saw bobbing lights, as of lanterns being borne. "Will-o'-the-wisps," said Danby, "ghost candles, some would say."

And upon two of those three nights did the blade-jewel of Bane faintly flicker, though nought of ill intent came unto the camp. After consultation with Danby, Trissa concluded that whatever caused the muted glow was too distant to be of concern.

Through silt-laden icy streams they splashed to finally come to a gape between a spur of the Grimwall and the Mountains themselves, and up onto Claw Moor they rode, the Iron Tower itself yet some fifty miles ahead.

Two days later, as the nighttide swept toward the west, they topped a rise, and in the fading light of a cloud-laden day they saw a dark fortress standing before them: massive it was, and formidable, and beringed by a deep crevasse plummeting into ebon depths below. A great iron drawbridge spanned the chasm, and just beyond the gulf, sheer walls of black stone blocks rose up to towering battlements. In the center of this ringed fortification stood a high tower, its dark walls ruddy in the dying light of day. And Trissa and Danby and Kipley each took a deep breath, and their eyes swept the ramparts for some sign of foe, some deadly enemy who now held the place, for they had come at last to the dreaded Iron Tower and would not be caught unaware.

"Well," said Kipley, "there's nothing for it but to go on. I mean, we've come too far to turn back now."

"It never entered my mind to turn back," said Trissa. "At least not until we get what we came after."

"Remember, Captain," said Danby, "retreat is always an option."

"But not one I would yet take," replied Trissa. "Danby, draw Bane and keep watch on that blade-gem."

"Oh, right," said Danby, and he drew the Elven long-knife from its scabbard and held it across his lap. Its jewel emitted no light.

Trissa glanced at him and then ahead and took another deep breath and said, "Come on," and kicked her heels into her pony's flanks and rode forward and downslope.

And as they fared onward, night engulfed the land, and the clouds blew southward and thickened; only now and again did a rift in the dark pall above allow the light of the half-moon high in the sky to gleam through. And then even that was gone when they arrived at their destination.

In the black of night before a cold Iron Tower on a moor in faraway Gron, Trissa and Danby and Kipley stood at the door of a tomb. Heavy was the stone and dark, all Dwarven-made, perhaps. By the lantern they bore, the Warrows could see three names deeply carved in the rock. Two of the names were HARVEN CULP and ROLLO BREED, and under the third name another phrase was added, such that the whole of it said: DANNER BRAMBLETHORN, KING OF THE RILLROCK.

Kipley hefted the pry bar and said, "Ready?"

Trissa said, "No time like the present."

Kipley placed the thin tip of the bar in the faint seam along one edge of the jamb, and together the three managed to pry the metal-bound door open just enough to permit them to enter, yet, hesitating, they looked at one another, their jewellike eyes wide with apprehension.

"I like not this robbing of graves," said Danby.

"Nevertheless we must do so," replied Trissa. "I mean, Aurion Redeye recalled the black, too." She shuddered in memory. "And I think none of us would defy him and chance another visitation. Besides, time is short, and the way to Valon is long, and the others will be waiting."

Gritting his teeth and gripping a dagger in his right hand, Kipley grabbed up the lantern and held it high and edged into the blackness beyond, the others following after, all of their hearts in their throats.

Inside they paused and peered around as if seeking ghosts, but all they saw was a sarcophagus, the stone with carven figures 'round the perimeter depicting a battle above a gate along a castellated wall. "It shows the Raiders as they fought to drop the bridge," said Danby, "perhaps the most critical fight of the Winter War, and one in which Danner played a key role."

Trissa stood shivering, but not from the cold. "Come on," she said, gritting her teeth and stepping forward, "let's get the armor and leave."

Again Kipley used the crowbar to pry, and they managed to slide the stone lid crossways on the coffin. Inside and laden with a film of dust was the desiccated corpse of a Warrow, of a buccan, of Danner Bramblethorn, and collapsed eyes stared up from a parchment-skinned skull into the trio's own. The remains were clad in a black mail shirt, and clothing clung to the skeleton as well—silken it was, as if made for a prince. A black studded helm cupped the head, and a plain but empty long-knife scabbard was girt on a silver and jet belt at the waist. The parchment-fleshed arms were folded across the chest, as if in repose, but clutched in skeletal fingers were two weapons, one in each hand: a Man's long-knife, gleaming and sharp though entombed ages agone, a single rune inlaid along the unblemished steel blade.

"That's Reachmarshal Ubrik's long-knife," breathed Danby. "He gave it to Danner to use during the raid."

Grasped in the bony fingers of the other hand was a bow, and a quiver of arrows was hooked to the belt at the hip of the remains.

"Though we've come for the armor," said Trissa, "I think the blade should be taken as well, Kipley, but not the bow, for it has not been maintained throughout the centuries and the wood is likely to crack."

Kipley turned away from the sarcophagus and said, "I can't do this."

"You must, Lieutenant," snapped Trissa. Then her voice softened. "Kip, we'll bring it back and restore everything when all this is over. Consider it merely a loan."

"Are you going to return the gilded mail?" said Kipley. "The silveron mail, too?"

"Oh, yes," said Danby. "And the black comes back here. I wouldn't have it any other way."

Kipley took a deep breath and turned and said, "Then I'd better get started, eh?"

He stood long moments in silence, looking down upon Danner's remains, and he whispered something, though too faintly for the others to hear. Then, taking the greatest of care, Kipley slowly and cautiously took the helm from the head. He set it atop the crosswise sarcophagus lid. Then he undid the belt and scabbard and slipped it from the waist, and set it on the lid as well. Carefully he took the long-knife from the fingers of the remains, and slipped it into the scabbard. Lastly, with help from Trissa, he removed the chain shirt.

He then lay his own long-knife into the coffin with the remains and said, "Should you need a weapon, Danner, use mine as I'll use yours."

Then once more he stood long moments in an attitude of prayer, and finally he looked up and said, "All right, let's close the lid and seal the tomb again."

Later that night after they had made camp, Kipley tried on the armor and belt and helm. They fit him as if custom-made.

In that moment the waxing half-moon shone through a rift in the clouds and shed light down on the Iron Tower and on the three Dwarven-made crypts, as well as down on three armed and armored Warrows—in gold, in silver, in black.

In the night, Bane's blade-jewel glowed, somewhat stronger than back at the Gwasp, but the gleam did not strengthen, and the darktide otherwise passed uneventfully.

The next morning under leaden skies it began to snow. Trissa cast her hood over her head and said, "Let us be gone from this dismal place, for I would our journey unwind."

And so, exactly three fortnights from the moment their trek to Gron had begun, they decamped and started southward in whiteness falling all 'round. They were headed for the Boskydells, and to Valon beyond, not knowing what lay in the future, knowing only that they had been called.

In the Red Slipper, Pipper said, "Well, they did unwind that journey, going back in the opposite direction along the same route they had taken to the tower and tombs. And the way home was just as uneventful as the trek there, though the weather turned foul, and they took some six days just to get through Grûwen Pass, for it had iced over, and all the footways and rocks and such were clad with several layers of frozen rain, and the three of them had to go slowly for fear one of the ponies would break a leg.

"Regardless, they got back to the Boskydells on the eighth of December, and when they came to the Great Barrier, they found it well warded by a large force of Thornwalkers. The captain at the entry along the Crossland Road told them that all the tunnels in and out were now closed and guarded, and that more Thornwalkers were being trained throughout the Seven Dells.

Two days later the trio reached Willowdell, where they stopped for an overnight stay with Kipley's parents, who were overjoyed to see their bucco safely returned from "that dreadful old Gron." There they also took a good hot meal, and soaked for candlemarks in warm soapy water.

"In the noontide of the next day the trio arrived at Woody Hollow, some six fortnights and a nineday after setting out."

Pipper reached for his tankard, and signalled for Binkton to take up the tale.

Binkton nodded and said, "The first thing they did was go to see Captain Banderel, and he told them that some of the King's Company were already in the village of Stickle awaiting the arrival of the three of them. He also said that no word had come from the Cliffs, nor had Iris returned, and perhaps the Ravenbook Scholars had no knowledge whatsoever as to just what the Trine might be.

"Regardless, the trio took all the ponies to Mr. Peacher's stables, and asked him to groom and feed them well and give them a long rest, for they had served admirably. Then, because those steeds had been on the road for three months, Trissa arranged for twelve fresh ponies—three riding and nine packponies—for the journey to Valon.

"Then the three went up to The Root, where they lit the hearths and heated water and fixed tea and then a good hot meal, after which they soaked once more in warm baths to ease their travel-weary bones.

"The very next day, they arranged for another six fortnights of supplies, and the day after, they set out for the village of Stickle along the Tineway down by Tine Ford. . . ."

It was snowing as they left Woody Hollow, and down through Budgens and beyond the Crossland Road they went, where they came upon the trace along the western eaves of the Eastwood. They followed this the rest of the day, and the snow quit just as they stopped that night. The next day they continued along the trace, and the woodland on their left came to an end, and five miles later they intercepted the Tineway some twenty miles east of Thimble, and they followed the road as it fared a bit south of easterly and headed for the village of Stickle this side of Tine Ford, some ninety miles away.

Over the next three evenings they camped twice and stopped once at one of the small hamlets along the road, and at every village the citizenry turned out to see the two armed and armored lieutenants and their armed and armored damman captain.

In late afternoon of the eighteenth of December, Trissa and Danby and Kipley arrived at Stickle, and they were directed to the Tineway Inn, where they met with Captain Willoby of the Southdell Thornwalkers, and they found awaiting them forty Thornwalkers in leather.

At last the Company of the King was assembled.

That evening, Trissa called them all together in the common room. Splendid in gold, a helm on her head, a blade at her side, a bow across her back, a quiver of fletched arrows at her hip, she stood on a table where all could see just who she was.

She turned 'round and looked at each and every one, and finally she said, "I am Captain Trissa Buckthorn, and yon in silveron is Lieutenant Danby Candlewood, and there in black is Lieutenant Kipley Larkspur. I know none of you, yet over the next weeks I promise I will come to know each and every one.

"Fate has brought us all together, for a dark storm comes from the east, leaving devastation in its wake, or so King Redeye says. What this storm might be, I cannot say, yet just as we have in wars long past, once again the Boskydells must answer the call. Ever have we Warrows come to the High King's aid, and so will we once more. A long trek lies ahead of us, for we are summoned to Valon, and there we will find just what destiny awaits. Yet no matter the challenge, we will persevere, for after all we are Warrows and the Company of the King."

A great cheer broke out, and Trissa stepped down from the table. Danby and Kipley came to her side, great smiles on their faces, and she said, "Let us hope we yet cheer when all of this is done."

The next morning, Trissa and Danby and Kipley met with Captain Willoby.

"I'm only here to help see you off," he said. "And to tell you what I've arranged for in the way of supplies. Not only will your Company of the King have packponies in tow, but I have additionally sent several waggonloads ahead to Valon, but you will no doubt catch up with them when you go. Here is a list of what is on each waggon—food, additional arrows, extra bows, medicines, and such, along with some spare clothing. I also stand ready if you need my help in other things."

"I do, Captain," said Trissa. "You see, we will need to divide the forty buccen into two squads, and I could use your help in assessing the strengths and experiences and skills of each one."

Captain Willoby nodded. "When would you start?"

"Right now," said Trissa.

Over the next two days Trissa and Danby and Kipley and Willoby spoke with every one of the forty, placing each with the first squad under Kipley or with the second under Danby.

On First Yule, in early morning, dressed in their winter garb, the company made ready to depart—ponies and packponies laden with arms and armor and other gear. At last all was ready, yet Captain Buckthorn had not yet given the signal. It was as if she were waiting for something, a sign, an omen, or such.

And at the long tunnel through the Spindlethorn Barrier, on the far side of the ford, there where one of the thorn barricades was erected, a sentry called, "Oi! A light!" and those on ward peered beyond the barricade to see a torch, its light growing swiftly. Now they could hear the pounding of hooves, horses rather than ponies. Onward it came, growing louder, until a black steed ridden by a grim-faced Man with a remount trailing thundered to a halt out before the barrier.

"In the name of the High King, open up, for I am his herald, and war is afoot!" cried the Man, holding his torch aloft in the shadows of the tunnel so that all could see that indeed he was garbed in a tabard of red and gold, the colors of the High King.

"Your mission?" called down the sentry.

"Ai! A darkness comes from the east," cried the messenger, his horse curvetting, "and I am sent to muster this land, for all must answer to the call if the Realm is to brave the coming storm. And here at your Thornwall I am told to show you this"—he held up a leather thong laced through a hole in a coin—"though I know not what it means."

The eyes of all the Warrows on the barricade focused on the small disk of grey metal, for it was a Gjeenian penny, the cheapest coin in the realm, a symbol hearking back to the Warrows Tipperton Thistledown and Beau Darby and the Great War of the Ban. There was a coin just like it in the Centerdell town of Rood, to be sent to the King should the Bosky be in desperate straits. And though none on the barrier had ever wished to see such a dreadful sign, still they had known this one was coming, for the specter of Aurion Redeye had said it would.

"Open the barricade," ordered the sentry, and four set aside their bows to move the barrier.

"We were expecting you," said the sentry to the horseman.

"Expecting me?" said the Man.

"Aye," replied the sentry. "Just beyond the far side of the Thornwall is the village of Stickle, and there the Warrow Company of the King even now prepares to answer your call."

"How came you to know I would come?"

"It seems a ghostly visitation appeared to three Boskydellers," replied the sentry, "three who are each separately related by blood to three heroes of the Winter War: a damman, Captain Buckthorn, and two buccen, Lieutenants Candlewood and Larkspur. The apparition called upon them to don the royal armor loaned long past and join in the fight to come. And so the entire Bosky is on alert, and our Company of the King is ready to march, now that you have arrived."

The barrier at last was open and the Realmsman rode through, but at the sight of the yawning black maw of the thorn tunnel on the far side of the ford he paused and sighed. "Ah, wee ones," he said to the warders, "riding through your Great Thornwall is like passing through the yawning black maw of Hèl."

"Would you have a hot cup of tea before going into that yawning maw?" asked one of the Warrows afoot, looking up, marveling at how huge both horses and Men seemed to be.

The Man smiled down at the buccan. "Would that I could, but I must away."

At a light touch of spurs to flank, the black steed trotted forward out of the mouth of the Thornwall and into the ford not yet frozen, the horse gingerly stepping toward the far bank, the remount trailing behind. The Warrows signalled the Beyonder Guard at the aft-gate to let the Man pass, then they turned and closed their own gate, while at the distant shore the barrier was removed. Taking a deep breath, the Realmsman rode into the darkness beyond, his torch held high, dimly illuminating the way.

As the Realmsman faded from view in the shadowy passage beyond, the buccen behind looked at one another and grimly smiled. Redeye had called forth the Warrows, and they had answered true.

Nearly two more miles in all did the Realmsman ride within the Spindlethorn, but at last he reached the far extent, and he quenched his torch and placed it with the others nigh the barrel of pine oil for travellers to use going the other way.

A mile more and he came to the village of Stickle, and there assembled was what he saw as a ragtag bunch ready to ride to Valon. He showed them the Gjeenian penny, and a tiny damman in golden armor reached out and took it. As the Realmsman paused a moment to gulp down a cup of tea, the Warrows of the so-called Company of the King mounted up and, at the sound of a silver clarion call blown by their diminutive captain, they rode away to the cheering of the populace in the direction whence he had just come, bearing the coin with them.

The Realmsman switched his saddle to the remount and leapt astride, and took one last look at the retreating Warrows. Then he shook his head and spurred onward for the Crossland Road and Wenden and Trellinath beyond, realms where *real* warriors could be found. After all, and in spite of the legends concerning them, these were a small Folk, quite insignificant; what matter that they joined in the battle, eh?

In high spirits, the Company of the King set out for Valon. Through the Spindlethorn they went, and along the Tineway, aiming for the small town of Junction, more of a stage stop than a village, there where the Tineway ended at the Post Road. It was perhaps the closest Human habitation to the Boskydells.

Just ere the noontide those in the rear of the column heard a call from behind, and galloping after came a buccan on a steed, three remount ponies trailing. As word came along the line, Trissa sounded a halt and waited for the Warrow to come pounding up, his ponies in a lather.

"Where is Danby?" the buccan called as he rode in among the

company. "Danby Candlewood, the Ravenbook Scholar, are you among the company?"

Danby pressed his mount forward. "Here I am," he answered, even as others pointed his way.

The buccan urged his pony toward Danby and called out, "Findle Preece, at your service. I have a message from the Cliffs, from Lady Candlewood."

"From my dam? Is everything all right? Is she well?"

"Aye," said Findle, haling his mount up short next to Danby's. He reached into a message pouch at his side and hauled out a wax-sealed parchment and gave it over to Danby.

Danby's hands shook as he broke open the seal. Two pages were attached. Quickly he scanned the first page, then handed it to Trissa as he read the second page.

Trissa read:

My dear Danny:

I do not know just what this means, but it was found long past by a Ravenbook Scholar in the basement archives among the ruins of the old library at Challerain Keep nearly a century after the Winter War. He made a copy of the scrap he found it on. It seemed to have nought to do with the Winter War or the Ravenbook, but he was curious and thought it strange and brought it back with him to the Cliffs. It is the only thing the Scholars could discover here among our own archives that mentions the Trine. In their opinion it is part of a longer poem, but this fragment is all that was recovered.

I do wish you well, my bucco, and wish your companions well, too. Be safe.

With all my love,
Mum

Danby handed the second page to her, even as she handed the first page on to Kipley. The second page read:

The years do flow to and fro,
And much happens by chance.
Yet some rare things do repeat
In time's recurring dance.
When shifting stars come to balance,
And the Sun rides the midline,
Boundaries tremble in equilibrium,
And all the Planes align,
In the time of the Trine, the Trine,
In the time of the Trine.

Danby looked at Findle and said, "Know you the contents of this missive?"

"Aye," said Findle. "I was there when the fragment was found."

Danby nodded. "Does any have a guess as to what it means?"

"We are not at all certain of anything except for one line in the whole of it," said Findle. "As best as we can determine, the phrase 'the sun rides the midline' has to refer to either Springday or Autumnday, for that is when the sun rides the midline and day and night are in balance. Even so, that this day might be called the Trine has never been known to us."

Trissa ordered the company to dismount and treat the steeds to a bit of grain, and for a scout to find a stream nearby for them to take water. "We might as well have a meal ourselves, cold rations only. Danby, Kipley, Findle, to me."

When they had gathered, Trissa said, "I deem 'tis Springday we are wanted in Valon, or rather, a sevenday ere then. Else King Redeye would not have come when he did.

"Even so, what think you it means 'Boundaries tremble in equilibrium and all the Planes align'?"

"I take it these lines refer to the High, Middle, and Low Planes," said Danby.

He looked at Kipley, and that buccan merely shrugged, but Findle said, "That's our best guess as well, though what that has to do with ought, I cannot say."

Danby studied the parchment again, and then said, "The poem seems to suggest that the boundaries only tremble in the Time of the Trine, as if it doesn't happen every Springday . . . or Autumnday, for that matter."

Trissa frowned, and finally said, "Look, we have some weeks ahead to see what we can deduce. I suggest we take care of our steeds, have a bite to eat, and then get on the road to Valon."

"I want to write my dam a response," said Danby. He looked at Findle. "Could you take a letter back with you?"

"Oh, indeed," said Findle. "But I'll tell you this: my ride back will be a deal more leisurely than my ride here."

Just as evening drew nigh, the Warrow company came unto Junction, and Men and Women paused in their doings to watch the Warrows ride into town.

They spent the night bedded down in the hayloft of the stables of the Red Coach of the Post Road, for the only hostelry of that hamlet was not big enough to house forty guests.

Onward went the Company of the King, riding by day and camping by night. When they arrived at the village of Luren, they were told that a small waggon train of supplies had headed for Ralo Pass, yet that some days after that group of Warrows had passed through the town the way across the Grimwalls had become snowed in, though perchance the pony-drawn wains had made it through ere then. With the pass blocked Trissa had no choice but to go toward Valon by a different route, and so the next morning they forded the Isleborne River to come into the land of Rell, where they fared east along the Old Way. They were headed for Gûnar Slot, that great cleft through the Grimwall where the mountains changed course: running away westerly on one side of the Slot, curving to the north on the other.

A sevenday later they turned south along the Gap Road, and toward the long notch they fared, and snow fell down upon them.

The next day they rode into the vast cleft, which ranged in breadth from seven miles at its narrowest to seventeen at its widest. And the walls of the mountains to either side rose sheer, as if cloven by a great axe. Trees in winter dress, their stark limbs laden with snow, lined the floor for many miles, and beyond the trees long barren stretches of vertical stone frowned down at the riders from one side or the other. The Gap Road ran for nearly seventy-five miles through Gûnar Slot, and so the company planned on camping in the great notch no more than three nights in all. Yet fate took a hand, and they were trapped for five days altogether by a raging blizzard, and it was all they could do to keep themselves and their steeds alive during this time.

Yet at last the blizzard let up, and Trissa got the company moving again, but the snow was deep, and progress slow, and it took another sixday just to win free of the treacherous notch.

Now across the rolling plains of Gûnar they rode, that land ringed 'round by mountains, and only the Alnawood some three hundred miles to the west was occupied, for there lay the Barony of Allworth with its Foxwood Manor, a manor built long past by Baron Fallon, a Man whom legend would have be a thief or a bard or a trickster named Fallon the Fox, son of Delon and Ferai.

Yet the Warrows knew not of this distant mansion, nor of Fallon, for the time of the Fox was long in the past, nigh the end of the First Era.

And so on south they rode, the days growing slightly warmer as they went, not only because winter had passed through its depths, but also because they rode toward a warmer clime, and the farther south they went, the less the snow.

A fortnight later they came to Gûnarring Gap, there where the Gap and the Ralo and the Reach and the Pendwyr Roads all came together, and lo! here it was that they caught up with the waggons of supplies that Captain Willoby had sent ahead, for they, too, had run into trouble, there at the exit of Ralo Pass, where they had been caught in one of the Grimwall blizzards as well.

Twelve Warrows there were, managing six waggons, each wain pulled by four ponies, and the drivers said that they were to join the Company of the King as soon as they reached their destination: the Argon Ferry.

The mounted company entire replenished what it had used, lading all their saddlebags and packponies with crue and bacon, and salt and spices, and grain for the steeds; then on the Warrows pressed, for they yet had some four hundred miles to go, and February was already upon them, and Trissa would have the Company of the King arrive no later than the early onset of March.

It was two days later when a company of Elves overtook the Warrows. These Lian were from Arden Vale—'twas Riatha and

Urus and Inarion and dark-haired Ellisan and a host of Lian Guardians. They had been delayed by the blizzard as well, though travelling on horses as they did, the pace of the Elves was somewhat swifter than that of the Company of the King.

Dara Ellisan rode alongside Trissa, and upon a horse in tow rode a damman, a silver lock through her raven-black hair, her amber eyes smiling, her chest crisscrossed with bandoliers filled with daggers: 'twas Faeril Twiggens Fenn, and she and Trissa exchanged greetings and information. Trissa told of King Redeye's visitation, to the wonder of the Elves, and though Faeril called out unto the Lian, none among that company knew of the Trine nor what it might portend. "Even so," said Ellisan, turning 'round in her saddle to speak, "if King Garon has Magekind among his company, then mayhap they will know, for it seems an esoteric thing they might recognize." Then the Lian rode onward, Faeril saying that she would bear word to High King Garon that the Warrows were on the way.

Southeasterly along Pendwyr Road went the company of the Wee Folk, and within days they came alongside the Red Hills on the right, and they knew that the ferry was ten or so days away.

On the twenty-seventh of February, the Company of the King at last rode in amongst a great muster of allies, two hundred and fifty thousand altogether. It was more folk gathered in one spot than any buccan or damman or Elf or Mage or Dwarf or Human or ought else had ever seen.

At last Captain Buckthorn and Lieutenants Candlewood and Larkspur made their way to the High King's side, and the damman in golden armor gave the King back his coin. And Garon, along with his sixteen-year-old son Ryon, welcomed them heartily into his camp. Garon, a small Man and a bit rotund, and his somewhat taller, brown-haired, brown-eyed son gathered the three Warrows 'round the campaign table and using maps showed them where the foe had entered the High King's realm, and he told them what the Legions would face.

That was when the Warrows learned that the enemy from the East commanded a Dragon.

Ebonskaith was his name.

In the Red Slipper Binkton sighed and shook his head, "That really came as a blow to Cousin Triss, for well she knew that a single Dragon alone could devastate an entire army. I mean, she knew all about what happened when Black Kalgalath came during the war at Kachar."

Pipper shook his head. "Actually, it was Danby who had read of that terrible time. He was the one who told her."

Binkton took a long pull from his tankard and then said, "Danby, Triss, or even Kipley, it doesn't matter which one knew about that war; what mattered was that the foe had a Dragon at its beck."

"No, what really mattered," said Pipper, setting his own tankard aside, "is that even though there was a Dragon among the ranks of the enemy, still the Company of the King stood fast at the side of High King Garon."

Binkton blinked owlishly and waved a negligent hand and reached once more for his tankard and said, "Regardless, Pip, my throat is still dry, so you take up the tale."

Pipper took a quick swig of ale and then turned to the others and said, "Well, Dragon or no, Cousin Triss told King Garon of the visit of King Redeye, and of the mysterious words having to do with the Trine, and then she showed him the note from Iris.

"King Garon then called for one of the Mages to— Oh, did I tell you that there were Mages among the gathered host? No? Well, there were. A thousand one hundred and twenty some-odd had come because of a millennia-old dreadful vision of a great slaughter, and they put their powers at the behest of the High King.

"Anyway, three of the Mages came to the King's campaign tent, where again Cousin Triss told her tale, and . . ."

"Hmm . . ." Arilla frowned, the Mage small of stature and brown of hair and eyes and wearing a yellow robe. "That the shade of Aurion would refer to it is no mystery, for we have long believed the Trine to be the time a terrible slaughter will occur, one involving Dragonkind."

"What is the Trine?" asked Trissa.

Standing to Arilla's right, Alorn, a ginger-haired Mage in a brown robe, said, "Once every ten millennia or so, the Planes are in congruency, and the barriers to the ways between are weakened, hence it is much easier to cross the in-between."

"And . . . ?" said Garon.

"Nothing," replied black-haired Belgon, that red-robed Mage standing to Arilla's left. "It is simply a weakening of the barriers."

"Ah," said Trissa. "That's what the entire fragment of the poem Iris sent meant when it said:

The years do flow to and fro,
And much happens by chance.
Yet some rare things do repeat
In time's recurring dance.
When shifting stars come to balance,
And the Sun rides the midline,
Boundaries tremble in equilibrium,
And all the Planes align,
In the time of the Trine, the Trine,
In the time of the Trine.

"I take it the 'boundaries' referred to are the boundaries between the Planes. And when they 'tremble in equilibrium,' they are weakened, and I assume that the 'time of the Trine' refers to the coming Springday. Hence, I suspect that this Golden Horde from the East will arrive on Springday . . . either that or we will be engaged in a critical battle on that day."

Trissa looked up at Arilla, and that Mage smiled and nodded and said, "You are correct, Lady Buckthorn. It is true that the Trine will come on Springday, and when the sun has risen up a quarter of the morning sky—six candlemarks after sunrise—it will ride exactly at the midline." Arilla then turned to Garon. "And as we have said, my lord, there is a terrible vision of death and destruction and slaughter on the plains of Valon, we think at the time of the Trine."

Garon nodded but said, "I plan to stop them here at the Argon, rather than on those plains."

"If your vision is true," said young Prince Ryon, "then since Springday arrives on the twenty-first of the oncoming month, we have many days to prepare for the arrival of the Eastern Horde. And can we stop them here, then we shall wholly prevent this bodeful fate you and your Kind have foreseen."

Two days later, a combined contingent of Avenians and Garians and Elvenkind came from the east, bearing their wounded across the Argon. And in spite of Ryon's words of having many days to prepare, in the distance behind appeared the first elements of the Golden Horde.

Some days later the full of the foe arrived, and they massed on the far shore of the Argon, some two miles away.

"Oh, lor," breathed Danby, "they look to be numberless."

"It's not the Horde that concerns me," said Kipley, "but that great black Dragon yon."

"Ebonskaith," said Ellisan, standing at their side. "'Tis Ebonskaith the Mighty, most puissant of all Drakes, now that Daagor and Black Kalgalath are gone."

Some distance away stood High King Garon and Prince Ryon and all the King's war commanders and advisors, Trissa among them. And they, too, looked at the vast Horde and the great dark Dragon as well.

Garon turned to Mage Arilla. "Do you know how to defeat the Drake?"

"Debate now rages among my kind," replied the Sage. "Yet whether we can influence him through subtle means or whether we must take direct action—"

"Subtle means? Direct action?" asked the wee damman in golden armor.

"Indeed, Lady Buckthorn," replied Arilla. "Can we simply maze his mind, we may win that way—through guile. Some, though—Belgon among them—say that lightning or cold will win the day, while others advise fire, for Drakes fight Drakes with tooth and claw and fire, or with acid and poison gas if they be Cold-drakes instead."

"But is there any other way to battle the Drake?" asked the damman. "Something we who wield not the astral <fire> can use instead? A weapon or mayhap a lure?"

Arilla glanced about and, seeing no Dwarves standing nigh, in a quiet voice said, "The Dwarves of Blackstone advised we use heavy shafts tipped with the deadliest of poison and hurled by ballistas, saying that the *smüt* of the Hidden Ones—the Fox Riders, in particular—should do the deed. When asked, they said they attempted to try it once, yet the Drake was upon them ere they were ready to cast the bolt. We then asked where they got the Pysk poison; they would only say it was left over from a successful campaign against a band of Trolls at the end of the First Era. They would answer no more, for it seems their pride was pricked by this failure of arms against the Drake. Too, that we would even question them about this loss stung their Dwarven dignity, and they stormed off in high dudgeon."

"Just like a Dwarf," said Inarion. "Even so, their plan may have merit."

"Well, although we have ballistas here," said Garon, "we have no Fox Rider poison."

Ryon looked at his father. "Then, as Lady Buckthorn has suggested, can we not offer the Drake something which will win him to our cause? Neither cunning nor guile nor force nor poison, but something Dragons desire?"

Garon frowned and looked to his advisor, Fenerin. The Elf smiled at Ryon. "Art thou thinking of the prize Arin Flameseer and her band offered Raudhrskal long past?"

"Something of the sort," replied Ryon.

Fenerin turned up a hand. "Ah, Prince Ryon, we have no Krakens here, and I cannot think of ought else that would turn a Drake's head."

"Except mayhap the lost Dragonstone," said Arilla.

"Again, Sage Arilla, you name a thing we do not have," said Garon, as he gazed across the river at the massing foe. "Even so, if you can find a way to deal with the Dragon, then we hold an advantage. Though we are outnumbered, still I believe the River Argon is a formidable ally, and we will win, slaying them as they try to cross against the Fjordlander ships and those of the Jutes as well as those of my fleet." Garon looked at the bow of Lady Buckthorn. "And many will fall to the slings and arrows of the Warrows, as well as our other missileers, and we will kill them with our swords and axes and spears and maces and morning stars and other fell weaponry as they try to step ashore; for on the river and when debarking then they will be most vulnerable." Garon paused and sighed and looked at Arilla. "On the other hand, if you of Magekind cannot stop the Drake, then I am afraid we are fordone."

A hard glint came into Ryon's eye. "But we will fight regardless, eh, sire?"

Garon nodded. "Aye, Son, that we will, for by fighting we purchase time for the young and old, for the halt and the lame, and for our loved ones to mayhap find safety in the west."

"My Lord King," said Trissa, "I would ask where do you think to station my two squads?"

"In the forefront, Lady Buckthorn."

"My lord, I would have my two squads stand apart from one another, for then our arrows will fly in a crosswise manner. I mean, my lord, if such a tactic is good in an ambush, it should be just as good against a foe coming head-on, for should we miss one, we will surely strike another. I deem more foe will be felled this way.

"Of course, we will need those with sword and spear and other such weaponry to protect our own flanks."

The King's eyes widened. "Well thought, Lady Buckthorn." He looked at the other commanders standing nigh, but it was Commander Rori who said, "There is much merit to what Lady Buckthorn says, my lord. Let the archers loose shafts thwartwise until they must retreat behind the front ranks when the enemy host is upon us, should any win across the Argon to step upon this shore."

"Let it be so," said Garon. "All archer companies are to spread along the line and fly arrows in an angled pattern. As Lady Buckthorn points out, we will fell more foe by loosing slantwise across the enemy files than down the length of them."

And so they made plans for the full of the force to meet the enemy as they tried to cross the mighty Argon and land on the near shore, but as the mid-March days came, those plans fell to ruin, for then it was that an ancient foe, the Fists of Rakka—Hyrinians, Chabbains, and the Kistanians—came in a mighty fleet of some two thousand ships and landed southward along the nearside shore, and their numbers fully matched that of the Allies, and counting the Golden Horde across the river wide, the High King's host was outnumbered fully three to one, and his ships were outnumbered even more.

Pipper paused to take a drink of ale, then said, "Well, you all know what happened at the Battle of the Argon, and so I won't bother you with that tale, for it is a story told often and is quite well known. Needless to say, the Allies suffered great losses and were defeated there by the west river bank, and they left behind their burning encampment and withdrew along Pendwyr Road to make a stand at the Red Hills, and the Golden Horde and the Southerlings caught up with them there, and all the Dragons came. . . ."

* * *

Dawn found the survivors of the two forces facing one another: the remainder of the King's legions—now but one hundred and fifty thousand warriors in all—in the vale looking out; the Golden Horde and the Fists of Rakka—their combined numbers now nearly four times greater—looking in.

But then from the morning horizons all 'round there came the heavy beat of vast leathery pinions, as hundreds upon hundreds of Dragons winged through the sky, all to settle on the crags and tors of the Red Hills above the High King's host and bellow their rage in unbridled fury.

And as horses reared and screamed in terror and the Allies blenched in dread, and as the Golden Horde and Fists of Rakka gasped in fear, from his golden tent upon the Plains of Valon came the victorious laughter of the one who commanded the Drakes. . . .

And even as the High King's host quailed, a silver call split the air, the clarion sounded by a wee damman, the horn a signal to stand fast. And the milling Men and the riders of the legions looked upon a company of Warrows standing resolute, three of whom were accoutered in chain shirts—a damman in gold and two buccen, one in silver, the other in black. And all the Warrows bore bows nocked with arrows, and they looked grimly across the space where the massed forces of the foe stood. Steadfast was this small company, three in chain, with leather-clad Warrows spread to either side, Prince Ryon not far away. And it was said that these Wee Folk, stalwart and grim, and their company of deadly archers, had slain foe beyond number; even so, the foe that remained was yet beyond number still. Once more the clarion cry split the air, and all the Men were heartened, and by the example of the Wee Folk, they stopped their milling and gained control of their steeds and resumed their ranks.

And when all seemed settled, the damman in golden armor glanced up at the hills behind, then looked at the teeming enemy before them and gritted, "I believe a Dragon now blocks the back way out. If so, we are truly trapped. And so, Danby, on this day, retreat is not an option."

"It matters little, I think," said the buccan in black beside her, eyeing the Fire-drakes above.

"Oh, lor," said the buccan in silver, "I hope we get a chance to give as good as we get." He then glanced at the rising sun and said, "By the bye, this is the day Redeye spoke of: this is the day of the Trine. And if the Mages are right, here in this place the cusp will come in the early marks of midmorn."

Somewhere nearby, among the Lian, someone began singing a Death Song, as Elves are wont to do when all hope is lost.

Pipper took another gulp of ale. "Of course, that was the day the Mages had foreseen, and indeed there was a great slaughter on the plains of Valon, but not a slaughter that anyone expected. Again, I won't bother you with that tale, for it is a story told often and is quite well known.

"Yet let me say this, that when the Dragons came, it was the Warrows who stood fast amid all the chaos and quailing.

"Regardless, after the carnage, the surviving Allies returned to the Argon, and the dead who had perished on that field were mourned and great pyres were raised and their spirits sent into the sky. Among those so honored were fully a third of the Warrow Company of the King. Still, the Warrows had slain uncounted foe for every one of theirs felled, and the then–High King paid great tribute to them even as he wept. Even so, even though the slain were honored and the living as well, Cousin Triss said that she thought her heart would bleed forever.

"After the funerals, the great army disbanded, and the survivors set out for their homes, the Warrows riding northwesterly in the company of the Elves of Arden Vale. . . ."

Up along Pendwyr Road they went and through Gûnarring Gap, and just on the other side of that opening Trissa put Henly Cress of Eastpoint in charge of the company, and in spite of their protests—for they would stay with their captain—she sent them onward along the road to Ralo Pass, for it was now mid-April, and that way should be open again. And, along with the Elves, she and Danby and Kipley turned north along the Gap Road, for they would fare to Gron and return the black armor and helm and sword unto Danner in his tomb.

Many advised that they simply keep the chain and set it in a place of honor there in The Root. After all, if Aurion Redeye called upon them again, there would be no need to make the trek to the tomb in Gron were the armor already at hand. But, no, Kipley would have it no other way: Danner must rest in honor, his arms and armor restored.

And so, up the Gap Road they went, and along the Old Way beyond.

They spent some days in Ardenholt, there in the Hidden Stand. But just ere Summerday, they bade good-bye to Faeril and Urus and Riatha and Ellisan and the others, and onward they went, out the secret way there at the north end of the vale. And they refused an escort of Elvenkind, who would go with them into that drear land, saying that this was something they needed to do alone.

Up through Grûwen Pass and down into the wastes of Gron beyond they went, travelling this part of their journey back along the way they had taken but some six months past. And as they rode the eastern flank of the Gwasp, the mosquitoes and biting flies swarmed all 'round, for summer was now upon the mire, and the bloodsucking creatures did teem. Yet Trissa did find some gyllsweed, and she crushed the plants and smeared the odious juice upon them all, including the ponies and packponies.

"Gaah!" said Kipley as Trissa swabbed his exposed skin, "I think I'd rather the bloodsuckers than this wretched smell."

"In a moment or two you'll get used to it," said Trissa.

"Ha!" replied Kipley. "I think that's just wishful thinking."

As Trissa stepped to Danby, a handful of the wet pulp in her grip, a dreadful scream came from the dark environs of the Gwasp, and then a sobbing, as of a Woman in distress.

"Pay it no mind," said Danby. "You heard it when we rode this way before."

"Are you certain?" said Trissa. "I mean it—"

"Believe me, I've read of these things, Triss," said Danby. "It's a lure to draw unwary into a trap. They say it's some kind of animal or plant or a mixture of the two, unable to move about, but one that draws creatures into its grasp; as they say some plants snare insects in their embrace, so, too, does this thing trap large animals in its clutch. And I'd rather that none of us fall victim."

And so, Trissa smeared them all with the gyllsweed, and over the next three days they passed unmolested along the swamp and beyond.

Up through Claw Gap and onto the moor they went, to finally

come to the Iron Tower, and once again they arrived in the dusk, though this time the sky was clear and a waxing half moon rode high overhead, shedding its silver light down.

As night fell, once more they stood before the three tombs, Trissa and Kipley eyeing the door of the central crypt, Danby on watch behind.

"Well, there's nothing for it," said Kipley. "It's time to—"

"Hsst!" shushed Danby.

"What is it?" whispered Trissa, wrenching 'round, Kipley likewise turning to see what had caused the warning.

"Look there," said Danby, pointing.

"Where?" hissed Kipley.

"There atop the wall above the gate."

"I don't see anythi— Oh. Movement. Something scuttles. But what—?"

All three dropped into a crouch.

Trissa made her way to the ponies, where she retrieved her bow and Kipley's, as well as two quivers of arrows and a small lantern.

After she and Kipley were armed, Trissa said, "Danby, what is it?"

"I-I don't know," he replied. "But it's gone."

"Pull Bane and see if it glows," said Kipley.

"Oh, right," said Danby, slinging his bow across his shoulder and drawing the blade.

The gemstone glittered with a blue light.

"I think we need to see whether or no this thing is a threat," said Trissa.

"What do you mean?" said Kipley.

"I mean for us to go to the Iron Tower and see if it is full of Foul Folk. If it is, then we need to get the Elves and others and come and clean this den of Spawn."

Danby sucked air in through his clenched teeth and then said, "You're right, Captain." He turned to Kipley. "Trissa's right."

They tethered the packponies to standing stones, and then they mounted their riding steeds and rode toward the downed drawbridge.

As they crossed the iron span, Danby, his blue-glowing sword in hand, said, "This isn't right."

"What?" said Trissa.

Danby pointed at the battlement above. "Modru's iron mask, it isn't there."

"Modru's mask?" asked Trissa.

"His iron-beaked helm was nailed above the gate as a mute warning to all who would follow evil's path."

"Oh, my," said Trissa, but she rode on.

They came under the walls and into a courtyard. To the left were stables, where once Hèlsteeds had been housed. Here they tethered the ponies, and went forward on foot: Trissa and Kipley with arrows nocked, Bane aglow in Danby's hand.

Ramshackle buildings were scattered here and there—barracks, storehouses, smitheries, privies, and such—and all had the air of long abandonment: the boards grainy and weathered and a-rot, gaps where some planks had fallen; stones cracked by freeze and thaw, mortar crumbling; roofs fallen in; tiles shattered alongside collapsed walls.

"Keep your eye on the blade-gem, Danby," said Trissa. "See if it gets brighter. That way we'll know if we are nearing the source of peril. Kipley, stand ready with your bow."

Back and forth they swung, this way and that, trying to determine the direction in which Bane's glow grew more intense. And slowly they came to believe that the source of peril emanated from the great building midmost in the fortress, the one with the tower rising out of the center.

This way they went, the glow of the blade-gem growing brighter, and they finally came to steps leading up and within. With shaking hands Danby lit their lantern, and took it up in his left, Bane in his right, its blade-gem shrieking of peril. And with their hearts pounding in dread, past a nearly disintegrated iron-banded door tilted outward and hanging on its bottom hinge they crept, to come into the black halls beyond, the lamplight nearly swallowed by the gloom within.

"This is Modru's Iron Tower," whispered Danby, his voice quavering. "I mean, the fortress is known as the Iron Tower, but so is this very building as well as the tower in the center. Here were his prisons in the dungeons below; here was his evil sanctum in the tower above; and up there it was that the Myrkenstone rested." Danby glanced at Bane's bright blade-jewel. "And here it is that the evil emanates."

By lantern light, they glanced into rooms along the enshadowed hallways—living quarters, storerooms, a great dining hall, a kitchen, an audience hall, and other chambers they could not name, all dust-laden and unoccupied.

Up a flight of stairs they went, to the dark second floor above, and then to the third, the light in the gemstone growing brighter with every step. It was on the third floor they found an entry into the central tower, and they came into a great dark open space, and moonlight shone in through window slits along a spiral stairway twisting widdershins upward past unlit torches into clutching shadows above.

"His evil sanctum is there," said Danby, pointing toward the high darkness with Bane.

"Modru's?" asked Kipley.

Danby nodded, and Trissa said, "But Modru is dead, and whatever or whoever it is that causes Bane to glow is likely above." She took a deep breath and said, "Danby, keep Bane in hand. Kipley, stand ready with your bow, as I will stand ready with mine."

Again she took a deep breath, and slowly expelled it, then said, "Let's go."

Up the steps they wound, past landing after landing, the hollow core of the tower falling into the depths below, an enshadowed vault above.

At last they came to a gaping hole where an iron-banded door once had been, splinters yet clinging to the twisted straps and shattered wood lying ascatter upon the landing.

And Bane's light now flowed along the keen edges of the bitter blade.

"Make ready," hissed Trissa, and with her bow drawn to the full, she said, "Let's go."

Danby held the light on high and inward they stepped.

Nothing came charging at them.

Bows ready, sword in hand, the trio moved into the chamber. In the midst of the floor sat a large stone pedestal, scored and burned as if a great fire had once blazed thereon. To one side stood a stone sacrificial altar, with iron clamps to hold down a victim, the altar's surface tilted to let blood flow freely down the channels to the waiting stone basin below.

Around the walls were shelves, bearing astrolabes and other arcane instruments and charred and burnt tomes sitting amid ashes and broken glassware strewn. Up above these, a raised stone catwalk encircled the room.

As the trio crept deeper into the chamber, Kipley nodded his head toward a glassblower's oven, a hod of *kōk* at its side, and murmured, "Modru must have fashioned his own."

"His own what?" whispered Trissa.

"His own glass instruments for his vile alchemistry."

Toward the back of the chamber were instruments of torture: a rack, a cage, tongs and pliers, a brazier, shackles on chains affixed to a wall, an iron post in the mid of the floor, with chains and shackles for holding a prisoner there as well, a chair with wrist and leg manacles affixed and a ratcheted band for slowly crushing a victim's chest and another one to fit his skull.

Trissa turned away from these things and said, "How could anyone do such terri—"

A shrill *Eeeeee* . . . squealed throughout the chamber, and something or someone huge sprang from the shadows and fled through the doorway and beyond.

Startled nearly out of their wits, the Warrows stood frozen for a heartbeat, but then Kipley shouted, "After it!" and he bolted for the portal.

"Kipley, wait!" cried Trissa, and she sprinted after, Danby running behind.

Kipley had momentarily paused on the landing, and as Trissa and Danby came through the doorway, he started down the long spiral stairway, Trissa and Danby following.

Somewhere ahead in the shadows below they could hear their quarry hurtling down the steps, blotting out the moonlight as it passed by the window slits.

Kipley came to a landing and stopped and drew his bow to the full, and as the thing passed the next window slit, Kipley let fly, but his arrow shattered against the stone wall just behind as onward the unknown entity fled.

Once again Kipley took up the pursuit, now following Trissa and Danby, for they had passed behind him even as he loosed at the thing.

And down the twisting stairs into the darkness below they sped, chasing after a creature or being. What it was, they knew not, yet they were determined to pursue, for Bane glowed with blue fire, and that meant evil was afoot.

Finally they reached the great open stone floor below, darkness thick all 'round, a darkness but barely pressed back by the small lantern Danby bore. And in that moment the flame guttered and sputtered and went out.

Only wan moonlight through the narrow slits above now lighted the chamber . . . that and Bane's gem-glow.

Danby knelt and laid Bane aside and tried to bring the lantern back to life, the striker futilely casting sparks 'gainst a dry wick.

It was then that with a mewling cry something huge loomed out of the darkness, a thing with hideous features like those of a gargoyle glared at them, and grasped in one hand it held a stone dagger on high as it rushed forward.

"Look out!" cried Trissa, even as she loosed an arrow at the thing, Kipley's shaft flying after.

Ss-sss . . . th-thock!

Both arrows struck the thing in the chest, and it fell forward and crashed down atop Danby even as he snatched Bane up from the floor. And that bitter blade pierced the creature through and through even as Danby was smashed under.

The monster let out a piteous whine, and the air left its lungs, never to fill them again. Its bladder loosed, as did its bowels, and a terrible stench filled the chamber.

"Quick," gasped Trissa. "We've got to get Danby out from under."

She and Kipley laid aside their bows and struggled to roll the thing from atop the buccan, and only with great effort did they manage to turn it partway over and pull Danby free.

He did not move.

"We need light," said Trissa. "Get one of the torches from the stairwell."

As Kipley ran toward the steps, Trissa put her ear to Danby's chest, but through the silveron armor she heard nought. But she found a pulse in his neck, and listened to his shallow breathing. And even as Kipley returned with the torch, and used the lantern striker to light the wrappings, Danby moaned and feebly moved, and then opened his eyes, and groaned, "I feel like the tower fell on me."

Trissa wiped away the tears from her cheeks and then gestured toward the monster. "I think it almost did."

With a gasp, Danby sat bolt upright. "The thing, the thing, is it—?"

"It's dead," said Trissa. "Two arrows and Bane did it in. —But you, Danby, any bones broken? Ribs?"

Carefully the buccan probed his chest. "Just bruises, I think," he said through clenched teeth. "Unh, help me up."

Trissa helped Danby to his feet, and with Kipley holding the torch, they examined the creature.

Perhaps ten feet tall and gaunt it was, its ribs and hip bones protruding, its bonelike limbs nigh fleshless, though its stomach was round and protruding. Its thin arms were so long as to have its hands reach well past the knees, its skeletal fingers lengthy.

"Well, it's as tall as a Troll, but I don't think it is one," said Danby, "what with these great long arms and skinny frame. Besides, your arrows pierced it, and they wouldn't have punched through an Ogru's stonelike hide, were it of that ilk."

"Speaking of its arms," said Kipley, "I would guess even when it walked, its hands would nearly touch the floor. Huah! Its span must be a full sixteen feet from fingertip to -tip, and its reach from shoulder to knuckle some seven feet in all."

"But look at its horrid face," said Trissa.

"That's not its face," said Danby, moaning softly and holding his rib cage as he bent over. Then he pulled free the vizard and straightened and turned to Trissa and held it up. "It's Modru's iron-snouted helm."

"Oh, Adon," said Kipley, staring down at the creature, "I think the monstrous mask is better than what I see."

The shape of the creature's skull was appalling, for it sloped up from a wide jaw and narrowed as it went past close-set eyes to a small, rounded top, with sprigs of hair jutting out from its nearly bald and tiny pate.

"I believe Humans call this a pinhead," said Danby, "not a very nice name." Danby frowned, as if trying to catch an elusive thought, and then his eyes flew wide in revelation and he said, "Oh, my, this must be the creature of the dark."

"Creature of the dark?" said Trissa.

"When Laurelin was trapped in the dungeons below, she sensed a *thing* with long arms was reaching through the bars of her cell and trying to grasp her. Fortunately she stayed against the back wall and eluded its long reach and clutch."

"A creature of the dark, eh?" said Kipley. "Mayhap that's why it fled."

Danby frowned. "Your meaning is . . . ?"

"Perhaps it was afraid of our light," said Kipley. "I mean, it didn't attack until the lantern went out."

"I wonder if it actually attacked," said Trissa, "or was simply trying to flee."

"It had a knife," said Kipley, looking about, then stepping away.

Danby said, "I think it was attacking, Triss, for Bane senses creatures of evil intent and its blade-gem glows blue. —And speaking of Bane . . ." He stepped to the creature and grasped Bane's hilt.

"See. Here it is," called Kipley, stooping down and taking up the stone knife, even as Danby pulled Bane free of the chest of the slain monster. The sharp edges yet flamed blue.

"Hsst!" hissed Danby. "Get your bows."

Trissa snatched up her weapon and set an arrow to string.

"There's another creature about," said Danby, eyeing the darkness 'round. "The monster is dead, but the gemstone yet speaks of—"

In that moment Kipley stepped closer, stone knife in hand, and the gemstone flared brightly.

Danby's eyes widened and he shook his head. "That can't be. I mean, Bane only senses creatures of evil intent, or so I've always believed." He looked at the knife in Kipley's grip. "Unless . . ."

"Unless what?" said Trissa.

"Oh, my, I think this must be the stone knife that went missing," said Danby.

"Stone knife?" Kipley frowned and looked down at the knapped blade.

"A sacrificial knife Modru made from a fragment of the Myrkenstone," said Danby. "He was going to use it to slaughter Laurelin up there on the altar above, but Tuck stopped all of that. Anyway, afterward, the stone knife went missing. They thought it had been burnt up, but here it is. We need to destroy this thing, for it is a token of evil."

"How can you destroy a token of evil?" asked Trissa.

"Well, in Tuck's case," said Danby, "he used the—"

"Burn it!" interjected Kipley.

"How can you burn stone?" said Trissa.

"Well, melt it is what I really mean," said Kipley.

"How can we do that?" said Danby.

"Don't you see, there's a glassblower's furnace above, and a scuttle of *kōk* at hand. We'll simply melt this stone knife."

"A glassmaker's furnace can melt stone?" said Trissa, a dubious look in her eye.

"Indeed," said Kipley, "and what better way to destroy this thing?"

Danby frowned. "You said a funny word: was it *kōk*?"

"Yes. *Kōk* is a glassblower's fuel. The Dwarves make it from a black rock that burns. It's better by far than charcoal, for it burns much hotter and cleaner."

"And you think it'll destroy this piece of Myrkenstone?"

"Come on," said Kipley. "I'll show you." He started for the spiral stairway again, and up the steps they went, and Trissa snatched another torch and then one more from the wall in case the one Kipley carried went out.

"Pump those bellows," said Kipley.

"Lor, but these are huge," said Danby, as he and Trissa hauled down on the handle and forced air from the great flexible chamber and into a pipe and through the blazing *kōk*, and radiant heat reflected off the glazed interior walls of the oven and raised the temperature even more.

"Probably Modru had a Troll do the pumping," gasped Trissa.

"I'm going to throw it in now," said Kipley, and, wrapping his cloak 'round his left hand for protection, he opened the oven door and pitched the stone knife in. Then he slammed the door to and dogged it shut and stepped to the bellows to help with the pumping.

Ungh! . . . Ungh! . . . they grunted, raising the great handle and then hauling it down again, and with every great *whoosh!* the temperature inside the oven rose and rose as the refractory surfaces within cast the heat back upon itself.

Ungh! . . . Ungh! . . .

"This is like being in a slave galley rowing across the sea," said Trissa, her voice straining just to get out. "All we need is a drum!"

Ungh! . . . Ungh! . . . Ungh! . . .

"I say, Kip, is the oven supposed to be glowing on the outside, too?" said Danby.

The whole of the oven glowed cherry red.

Kipley looked and said, "Uh, oh," as the red turned to orange.

"What?" said Trissa.

"It's not supposed to do that."

"Well then, stop it," said Trissa, even though she and the two buccen yet pumped, the walls now turning yellow.

"I can't," said Kipley, and he stopped pumping, the other two stopping as well.

"What'll we do, Kip?" asked Danby, as the outer walls of the oven shifted to white, the heat stifling, the incandescence blinding.

"I say we run!" cried Kipley.

Out from the chamber they bolted, and down the steps. They needed no torch to guide them, for an intense glare streamed out the door and lighted the entire stairwell. And the trio twisted downward, fleeing from a runaway furnace, fleeing from . . . from . . . they knew not what.

Even as they reached the bottom of the steps and ran for the doorway beyond, Danby skidded to a halt and darted back inward.

"Danby, you fool!" cried Kipley, stopping, Trissa sliding to a halt as well. "What by Hèl are you doing?"

Danby came racing back outward, Modru's iron mask in hand. He passed them by, and they darted after, heading down staircases and running for the doorway out of the hallways beyond the central tower. Even as they fled from the building, and down the steps beyond, blinding light streamed from the top of the tower, illuminating the entire fortress.

Across the courtyard and among the warehouses and barracks and outer buildings they ran, the luminance growing brighter still. At last they came to the stables, and they untied the ponies and leapt astride, and raced for the gateway, and as they galloped across the downed drawbridge, iron-shod hooves ringing on iron, with a great flash of light and a terrible blast something behind detonated, and a blinding flare lit up the fortress and the moor beyond as the entire top of the tower blew apart, while onward the Warrows raced and fiery debris rained down all 'round.

As the last of the hot, smoke-trailing fragments rattled and spattered to the ground, Danby and Kipley and Trissa haled their little steeds to a stop before the distant tombs. And Kipley said, "Huh. Mayhap melting the knife wasn't such a good idea after all."

Trissa nearly fell off her pony, laughing as hard as she did. But at last she pointed through the moonlight at the smoldering remains of the tower and managed to gasp out, "Look at it this way, Kipper, destroy it you certainly did." And she burst into laughter again, Kipley and Danby guffawing as well.

But finally they got control of themselves, and rode back to the fortress, where Danby again hung Modru's iron mask above the gate.

Then they broke into Danner's tomb once more, and dressed his remains in the black armor and the studded helm, and returned Marshal Ubrik's long-knife to Danner's side, Kipley taking up his own long-knife in exchange. "Thank you, my friend," Kipley whispered. And then they exited and sealed the door once more.

And the next day they rode away, heading for the Boskydells and home.

And behind them Modru's hideous iron-beaked helm glared down from the gate above, once again serving as a warning to all who would hew to evil's ways.

In the Red Slipper, Pipper said, "They made it back to a heroes' welcome, did Cousin Triss and Danby and Kipley. And then did the captain and her two lieutenants go to Northdune and Downyville and Greenfields and Eastpoint and Rood and all the other towns and places in between, and they visited each and every buccan who had fought there on the banks of the Argon, as well as seeing the families of those nineteen buccen who had given their all in the battle. Much did they weep as they spoke of the bravery of those who had been slain, and, using the Horn of the Reach, for each family who had lost a loved one Cousin Triss sounded the lorn notes of the "day is done" call, and they all wept some more. And these visits seemed to ease the hearts of the kindred, though as Cousin Triss says, her own heart bleeds still."

Pipper fell silent, and for long moments, none said ought. But then Riatha softly said, "Well told, Pipper. Well told, Binkton."

"Hear, hear," agreed Fat Jim.

"I say," said Wooley, "what did those three do after the war?"

"Well," said Pipper, "Danby went back to The Root as a Ravenbook Scholar, and I believe is there still. Kipley has started his own glassware business, down in Midwood, for it seems that he and Triss hit it off afterward and got married."

"I might point out," said Binkton, "should Cousin Triss and Kipley have any little buccoes and dammsels then the lines of Patrel and Danner will have merged . . . and if the armor is ever called up again, well, who knows how that will go?"

As Binkton blinked owlishly and drank the last of his Vornholt, Pipper said, "Cousin Triss and Kipley are living on Granther Buckthorn's farm, and she and Alver went back to raising geese. Not only do they produce the best Yule-geese in all of the Bosky, they produce the best goose-down in the Bosky as well—for pillows and comforters and winter gear and other such. They also provide the very best watch-geese for those who live in the Bosky, especially along the main routes through the Dells—the Crossland Road, the Upland Way, Two Fords Road, and the Tineway—anywhere that Beyonders travel, for at times unsavory sorts fare along those ways, and geese are the best watchers of all."

"Huah!" barked Fat Jim. "So your cousin is a goosegirl, eh?"

"Goosedamman, I'll have you know," said Binkton.

Fat Jim laughed and said, "Ah, me, I stand corrected."

Pipper yawned hugely and said, "Time for bed," and drained the last of his tankard. He stood up from his chair, and lurched forward a step or two, then plopped bottom-down to the floor. "Whoo," he said, and then laid back to stare at the ceiling, "I'm quite dotty, it seems."

"Well, that doesn't surprise me at all," said Binkton, looking into his own empty tankard, and starting to rise, "what with all that Vornholt you've swigged. And—"

Binkton took but a single step, then fell flat on his face.

And as grey dawn paled outside the Red Slipper, Urus and Bair each took a Warrow up and started for the stairs. And Bair was heard to say, "Oh, how I pity them when they awaken, for I've been there myself, and once was quite enough for me to find my limits."

Behind, Aravan gave a soft chuckle, then he and the others rose and stepped out the door to watch the coming of day.

12

Leave-Takings

"Cap'n! Cap'n!"

Aravan looked up from his breakfast to see Noddy running into the common room.

Breathless, the young Man slid to a stop at the table. "Cap'n, there's a great pack o' Wolves comin' adown th' street. Big as ponies they are."

Bair leapt up from his chair. "Black ones? Slavering fangs?"

All at the table were now on their feet—Aravan, Aylis, Urus, Riatha, Jaith, Pipper, and Binkton—grasping at slings and morning stars and blades of various kinds. All about the room, Dwarves likewise gripped the helves of weapons and started across the chamber to come to Aravan's side, while Fat Jim on the stage set down his squeeze-box and took up a belaying pin, as did his chorus and cloggers.

Noddy shook his head. "No, not black Wolves, but white or grey or silvery or some such. Monstrous big whitish Wolves."

Bair looked at Urus and Riatha. "Could it be that—?"

A piercing scream shattered the air, and Yellow Nell ran by and up the stairs.

And a Mage and a huge white 'Wolf walked into the common room—the Mage some six foot tall or so, his hair long and white, his piercing eyes grey and with the hint of a tilt, and his ears tipped, but less than those of an Elf. He was dressed in soft grey leathers, a black belt with a silver buckle at his waist. His feet were shod with black boots of soft and supple leather. The 'Wolf, the Draega, the Silver Wolf on the other hand stood some four foot high at the shoulder, and his fur was a dazzling, almost transparent white that cast a silvery sheen. And his dark tongue lolled over grinning white fangs.

"Dalavar!" called Bair. "Greylight!" and he rushed forward to embrace the Wolfmage as Aravan called out, "Stand down! These are friends!"

Weapons were lowered, some went back into sheathes, and the Dwarves returned to their tables and once more took up their eating and gambling and drinking and other endeavors, while the skirl of Fat Jim's squeeze-box again rode on the air, the sailors behind resuming their chantey and the ones to the fore their clogging. Burly Jack set his bung mallet under the bar once more and returned to polishing mugs and glasses and serving his customers.

Jaiṭh stepped forward and threw her arms about Greylight's neck and buried her face in his soft, white, clean-smelling fur. "It's good to see you again, old friend," she murmured. Greylight suffered her embrace in silence.

Holding the Mage at arm's length, "Where is the rest of the pack?" asked Bair.

"I left them warding the door, for I would not have us disturbed." Dalavar grinned and gestured about. "Little did I know the entire crew of the *Eroean* would be inside."

Bair barked a laugh and then said, "Did Shimmer come as well?"

"She is outside with Trace, Beam, and Longshank."

"I must see her and the others," said Bair. "But ere then, tell me what brings you here, Great-Uncle?"

Pipper looked at Binkton and mouthed, *Great-Uncle?*

Bink turned up his hands and shrugged.

"Two things," replied Dalavar. "First, Bair, I have come to take you to Vadaria . . . to the College of Mages for training."

"Training?" said Bair, motioning for Dalavar to take a seat at the table.

As they sat down, Jaith released Greylight and resumed her place as well, the Draega to settle to the floor.

Bair said, "Dalavar, I am no Mage. I can only see the aethyr, not manipulate it."

Dalavar smiled and shook his head. "This from the one who

took Adon to task. Listen, my lad, with your heritage, your blood, you'll be surprised at what you can do."

Bair frowned and looked at Jaith. *"Chier?"*

A glorious smile lit her face, and she said, "I've not been to Vadaria, and I would see that world."

Bair grinned and said, "All right, Mage Dalavar, on condition Jaith goes with me then will I follow you there."

"I would not have it any other way," the Wolfmage replied. "We can leave at dawn."

Bair shook his head. "Nay, Dalavar, for first *Athir, Ythir,* Jaith, and I must report to the High King on our mission in Hyree."

At these words, Dalavar cocked a questioning eyebrow. "I'll tell you on the way," added Bair.

"Arran," said Riatha, "thine *athir* and I can report to King Ryon if Mage Dalavar desires to leave on the morrow."

They looked at the Wolfmage, and he said, "I am not comfortable in the cities, overcrowded with Mankind as they are. Too, I ween that Greylight and the pack would take ill to such. Yet if it is needed for Bair and Jaith to go to King Ryon—"

"No," said Bair, "for as *Ythir* says, she and *Athir* can see the King and tell him of our deeds." Bair broke out laughing and added, "And mayhap present him with four separate rings of ruby and sapphire and emerald and diamond, eh, Da?"

As the two of them laughed and were joined by the others, Dalavar said, "There is a tale here for the telling."

Jaith grinned and nodded and said, "The way to Vadaria is long, with much time for talking 'round campfires."

After the moment had passed, Pipper cleared his throat. "Mage Dalavar, you said there were two things that brought you here. What is the second? I mean, there *is* a second thing, isn't there? Something perhaps having to do with Bair going to Vadaria? It's all connected, you know."

Dalavar laughed. "Would you mayhap have a long-ago ancestor named Beau Darby?"

"As a matter of fact, yes," said Pipper, his eyes widening in surprise. "Both Bink and I do."

"I thought so," said Dalavar. "He often told me the same."

"The same?" said Binkton.

"That it's all connected."

"Oh, that," said Binkton. "It is, you know."

"Even so," said Pipper, "returning to my question, the second thing is . . . ?"

Dalavar laughed, then looked about to make certain that no Men were within hearing. "Many days back I did a casting and <saw> the *Eroean* 'rounding the Cape of Storms. I deemed you were on your return, and would moor in Arbalin Bay." Dalavar again looked about, then reached into his cloak and withdrew a scroll and gave it over to Aravan. "I brought you this. It comes from one of my . . . 'charges' in Darda Vrka."

"Darda Vrka?" said Binkton.

Dalavar nodded. "Some would call it the Wolfwood."

"Ah," said Binkton. "I have heard of it."

Aravan untied the ribbon and carefully unrolled the ancient, yellowed vellum.

It was a map.

Aravan looked long, then said, "Is this what I think it is?"

"I am not certain," said Dalavar, "but if it is and you go in-between, you'll have to teach your Drimma warband and these two Waerlinga the crossing rite."

"What is it?" asked Binkton.

"The crossing rite?" said Pipper. "It's the way to go in-between. You knew that, Bink."

"No, Pip, I meant, what is on the scroll?"

They both looked at Aravan.

"The way to a long-lost, untamed world, my friends," replied Aravan. He handed the scroll to Aylis.

"Oh, my," she said after a moment. "Can this truly be the Gate to Elorim?"

Both Aylis and Aravan looked at Dalavar, but he merely shrugged and said, "I do hope so, for many of those I have shepherded throughout the ages have gone seeking this place, fleeing the encroachment of Man."

"What place?" asked Binkton.

"Elsewhere," said Dalavar. Again he looked about, then added, "Speak not to anyone of it, not any beyond this circle."

"Not even to Aylissa?" asked Pipper.

"Aylissa?"

"She's a Pysk," said Binkton.

"A Fox Rider," added Pipper.

"Ah," said Dalavar. "She can be included in the circle."

"The Drimma as well," said Aravan.

Dalavar nodded. "Anyone but Mankind. —And Foul Folk, of course. We would not have them know of this haven."

"My crew will know," said Aravan, "for even though it is my custom to leave Long Tom and the sailors in charge of the *Eroean* when we reach an uncharted shore, still we speak of what we find. Too, as we did in the Lost City of Jade, we take Men ashore to help in the lading of any cargo. Even so, the Men we choose are honorable, as thou dost know, Mage Dalavar, for thou didst choose many of this crew ten years apast, during the Dragonstone War. And as did thee then, Aylis looks into the hearts and minds of new recruits to <see> their sense of honor and integrity, to verify that they will hold to a pledge, regardless of circumstance. And know this as well, all will take a vow of secrecy. Hence, when Aylis and I and the scouts and the warband go exploring inland, should we find the Gate to Elorim, then none of Mankind beyond the sailors will know, and even they will know little."

Dalavar nodded and said, "Then speak to none of this map nor gate until all are pledged."

"Not even to Long Tom and Nikolai?" asked Pipper.

Aravan sighed and said, "Not even them."

Urus looked at Riatha and cocked an eyebrow. She smiled and nodded. Urus turned to Aravan and said, "Even though I have Human blood in my veins, I am a Baeran and other things as well. Riatha and I would go with you to this mysterious refuge, that is if you will have me, and if you've room on your craft."

Aravan looked up from the map. "I would welcome ye both."

Bair sighed but said, "It sounds like a venture Jaith and I would embrace, yet I would learn what Magekind can teach me as well. Hence, it's to Vadaria I go."

"Fear not, Bair," said Dalavar, "If it is what I believe it to be, you will go to Elorim one day."

The next morn, Bair and Jaith, Urus and Riatha, and Aravan, Aylis, Binkton and Pipper, and a small shadowy form all strolled down to the docks, where Dalavar and a pack of Draega waited. They exchanged embraces and kisses and farewells, and as she held

Bair, Riatha murmured, "Care for Jaith and stay safe, my child," and he responded, "You and Da as well be safe." Then Jaith and Bair in the company of Dalavar and the pack of Draega boarded the ferry for Merchants Crossing, the town on the shores of Jugo. And as they trod up the gangway and onto the boat, passengers already aboard shied away from the great 'Wolves: they all clustered at one end of the craft, while the Mage and his company stood at the other.

And after the ferry pulled away, with Bair and Jaith waving goodbye, then did Riatha and Urus board the two-masted dhow. They cast off and pushed out from the slip, then raised sail and set out for Caer Pendwyr, where they would report to High King Ryon and bestow him with four bejewelled rings.

With Bair and Jaith and Dalavar and the Draega gone, and Urus and Riatha away, the remainder of that small circle returned to the Red Slipper, and over the next days they talked of the journey ahead, while the crew of the *Eroean* relaxed and fought and gambled and sang and drank and dallied with the ladies of the Red Slipper.

As for the arc of friends at the hearth, they continued to gather each eve, and they spent a moon and a sevenday telling tales in the wavering candlecast shadows. Toward the mid of this time, Urus and Riatha returned from Caer Pendwyr and rejoined the hearthtale group.

During the daytimes, though, Aravan and Aylis and Long Tom spent the afternoons meeting with the glut of Men who wanted to sign aboard the *Eroean* and fill any of the five positions now open on the sailing crew. One by one they came into a small room, where Long Tom and Aravan asked each of them questions as to his experience and skills. Aylis sat apart and jotted notes in a journal as she peered intently at every one of the applicants, and each of them felt as if she were seeing to the depths of his very soul.

In the latter days of the interviews, a ferry from Merchants Crossing arrived, and with it came Brekk and eight Dwarves, enough to bring the *Eroean*'s Châkka warband to full strength.

Finally, in concert with Long Tom, and relying heavily on Aylis, Aravan chose the Men to fill out the remainder of the crew.

The dreadful events in the Lost City of Jade had taken their toll, yet once again the Elvenship was up to her full complement.

Aravan settled the bill with Burly Jack, and a hefty sum it was, and he left a generous bonus for each member of the staff of the infamous inn—cooks, maids, and bottle-washers all, including the Red Slipper ladies.

Then the crew entire—warriors and sailors and scouts—spent the next few days aboard ship.

Upon arrival at the *Eroean,* Long Tom assembled all hands on deck, and with Aylis looking on and Aravan leading, the Men and Dwarves took an oath to reveal no secrets of the Elvenship: the old hands renewing their pledge; the new hands vowing for the first time. Then all pledged a second time to never divulge to anyone the fact that they would sail with a Pysk, for she was one of the Hidden Ones, and preferred to keep it that way. Finally, the Dwarves and Men took an oath to reveal nought of this voyage whatsoever to anyone not of the crew. And when the pledging was done, Aravan looked to Aylis, and she nodded in satisfaction.

Under the tutelage of Nikolai and Brekk, the new crew members spent days familiarizing themselves with the ship and their duties, while the old hands spent time setting things shipshape, some removing the scars the hull had taken in combat with the Rovers of Kistan and laying on new paint where needed.

And as they readied the craft, Aylis, sitting in the sunshine atop the aft cabin, paused from recording in her journal the tales they had told one another in the nights before the hearth. She relaxed and watched as members of the Châkka warband refitted ballistas, or laded fireballs and huge arrows aboard, or sharpened axes or polished war hammers or oiled crossbows and such. And while Aylis did so, she reflected on the Châkia—the mates of the Châkka—and her knowledge of the Châkia's long-held secret, a privity she had inadvertently discovered during her stay in Kraggen-cor. She looked down at her journal filled with many a tale, and she knew that the story of the veiled Châkia was one she would neither scribe nor reveal, for some secrets are meant to be kept, and theirs was one of those.

Within a sevenday, all was ready, and Aravan had rowers in dinghies hale the ship to a pier, and there he tied up; and with the docks and ship abustle and cargo nets on booms swinging up and across decks and below, they laded on kegs and crates and barrels and bales of food and water and other such goods for the long voyage ahead. When the last of the provisions was lashed down in the holds, Aravan granted the crew one last day of shore leave, for they would sail morrow's eve and it would be many a moon ere they saw these shores again.

To the Red Slipper the sailors and warriors went, while Aravan and Aylis and Urus and Riatha stayed aboard, along with Pipper and Binkton and Aylissa and Vex.

Late the next afternoon the crew returned, a few carrying others over their shoulders. The ladies of the Red Slipper, some weeping, came down to the docks as well, for they would see the crew off. Long Tom and his family were there, Little Tom with his eyes agog at the magnificence of the ship. Long Tom gave Little Tom a hug and a kiss, then he scooped up his tiny wife Larissa in his arms and kissed her long and deeply. He set her afoot and turned and boarded the *Eroean,* the last of all of the crew.

As the sun set and dusk drew down and the tide began to flow outward, "Get us underway, Tom," said Aravan, when the big Man reported in.

"Aye, aye, Captain," replied Tom.

He turned to Noddy and Nikolai. "Cast off fore, cast off aft, hale in the gangway, and rowers row."

These two called out orders, and ship's crewmen waiting on the pier cast the hawsers from the pilings and, while others drew the large mooring lines up and in and coiled them on the deck, the ones adock quickly reboarded and pulled up the gangway and stowed it in its place below. Rowers in the dinghies haled the ship away from the quay and turned her bow toward the mouth of Arbalin Bay.

Even as the dinghies were lifted up to the davits, Noddy piped the crew to raise the staysails, and on these alone did the craft get underway; and in the deepening twilight, folk on the piers called out farewells and blew heartfelt kisses, some on the *Eroean* returning the sentiments in kind.

As the Elvenship cleared the mouth of the harbor and rode out on the ocean prime, "Where to, Captain?" said Fat Jim, steersman again, his arm no longer in a sling. "What be our heading? Where be we bound?"

Aravan looked out across the broad Avagon Sea, the cool night air filling the silks above. Then he stepped up behind Aylis at the aft starboard rail and pulled her close and she leaned back into him.

With Men standing adeck and looking up at the captain embracing his lady, he reached 'round and cupped her right hand in his and pointed her finger and raised her arm and aimed at a bright gleam in the western sky. "Set our course on the evening star yon, all sails full, for we go to the rim of the world and beyond."

The bosun then looked at Long Tom, and at the big Man's nod he piped the orders, and Men scrambled to the ratlines and up to the yardarms, where they unfurled silks, the great sails spilling down in wide cascades of cerulean, while others of the crew stood ready at the halyards and sheets; and as this was done, Noddy strode along the deck and called out, "Look smart, Men. You heard th' cap'n. Set those sails brisk, f'r surely we're bound on a venture grand th' loiks o' which th' w'rld has ne'er seen."

And with all silks flying in a following wind and filled to the full—mains and studs, jibs and spanker, staysails, topsails, gallants and royals, skysails and moonrakers and starscrapers—and with a luminous white wake churning aft in the night-dark Avagon Sea, her waters all aglimmer with the spangle of light from the stars above, westerly she ran, the Elvenship *Eroean,* the fastest ship in all the seas.

She was bound for the rim of the world and beyond. . . .

. . . the rim of the world . . .

. . . and beyond. . . .

To the rim of the world and beyond

Afterword

And thus did the *Eroean* sail to the rim of the world and beyond, and so, too, do I think that my travels across Mithgar have done the same. It has been a terrific voyage, yet I believe beyond the rim of that wondrous place lie new vistas, new destinations.

I do want to thank all of you who have journeyed at my side across those realms, and I hope you will continue to trek with me through whatever new lands I explore. I think there be tygers and wyrms and other dread dangers and splendid marvels where I go, and I could use a bit of company.

~ Dennis L. McKiernan
May 2004

About the Author

Born April 4, 1932, I have spent a great deal of my life looking through twilights and dawns seeking—what? ah yes, I remember—seeking signs of wonder, searching for pixies and fairies and other such, looking in tree hollows and under snow-laden bushes and behind waterfalls and across wooded, moonlit dells. I did not outgrow that curiosity, that search for the edge of Faery when I outgrew childhood—not when I was in the U.S. Air Force during the Korean War, nor in college, nor in graduate school, nor in the thirty-one years I spent in Research and Development at Bell Telephone Laboratories as an engineer and manager on ballistic-missile-defense systems and then telephone systems and in think-tank activities. In fact I am still at it, still searching for glimmers and glimpses of wonder in the twilights and the dawns. I am abetted in this curious behavior by Martha Lee, my helpmate, lover, and, as of this publication, my cherished wife of forty-seven years.